PENGUIN CLASSICS

THE BLAZING WORLD AND OTHER WRITINGS

MARGARET LUCAS CAVENDISH, Duchess of Newcastle (1623–73), was the youngest and minimally educated child of a wealthy Essex family. In 1643, the year after the outbreak of the English Civil War, she became a Maid of Honour to Queen Henrietta Maria, travelling with her into Parisian exile in 1644. There, in 1645, she married the widowed William Cavendish, Marquis (later Duke) of Newcastle (1593–1676), who had been commander of Charles I's forces in the north, and a well-known patron of arts and letters. The Newcastles lived lavishly on credit in Antwerp from 1648 until the Restoration allowed their return to England in 1660. Between 1653 and 1668 Margaret Cavendish published a dozen substantial books including poetry, moral tales, speculative fiction, romance, scientific treatises, natural philosophy, familiar letters, closet drama, orations, an autobiographical memoir and a biography of her husband. The sheer quantity and variety of Cavendish's published writing was unprecedented amongst earlier English women. These publications, and her cultivation of personal singularity, made her an infamous figure both in her own lifetime and since, subverting patriarchal codes of femininity while championing the legitimacy of monarchy. She appears in theatrical cameos in the writings of contemporaries like Pepys and Dorothy Osborne, and in subsequent accounts of maverick women by such writers as Charles Lamb and Virginia Woolf. Through her generically experimental and diverse writings, Margaret Cavendish emerges as an ironically self-designated spectacle, and as the self-proclaimed producer of hybrid creations and inimitable discourses, which are finally beginning to receive the attention that her life has rarely lacked.

KATE LILLEY (BA Hons., Sydney; Ph.D., London) began work on early modern women's writing as Julia Mann Junior Research Fellow at St Hilda's College, Oxford (1986–9). Her articles on seventeenth-century women's writing appear in *Women, Texts and Histories 1575–1760* (1992) and *Women/Writing/History 1640–1740* (1992). She is now a Lecturer in English at the University of Sydney. Her poetry is represented in *The Penguin Book of Modern Australian Poetry* and *The Penguin Book of Australian Women Poets*.

MARGARET CAVENDISH
DUCHESS OF NEWCASTLE

The Blazing World

and Other Writings

Edited by
KATE LILLEY

PENGUIN BOOKS

PENGUIN BOOKS

Published by the Penguin Group
Penguin Books Ltd, 80 Strand, London WC2R 0RL, England
Penguin Group (USA), Inc., 375 Hudson Street, New York, New York 10014, USA
Penguin Group (Canada), 90 Eglinton Avenue East, Suite 700, Toronto, Ontario, Canada M4P 2Y3
(a division of Pearson Penguin Canada Inc.)
Penguin Ireland, 25 St Stephen's Green, Dublin 2, Ireland (a division of Penguin Books Ltd)
Penguin Group (Australia), 707 Collins Street, Melbourne, Victoria 3008, Australia
(a division of Pearson Australia Group Pty Ltd)
Penguin Books India Pvt Ltd, 11 Community Centre, Panchsheel Park, New Delhi – 110 017, India
Penguin Group (NZ), 67 Apollo Drive, Rosedale, Auckland 0632, New Zealand
(a division of Pearson New Zealand Ltd)
Penguin Books (South Africa) (Pty) Ltd, Block D, Rosebank Office Park,
181 Jan Smuts Avenue, Parktown North, Gauteng 2193, South Africa

Penguin Books Ltd, Registered Offices: 80 Strand, London WC2R 0RL, England

www.penguin.com

First published by Pickering and Chatto 1992
Published in Penguin Classics 1994
Reprinted with a new Chronology and Further Reading 2004

036

Printed and bound in Great Britain by Clays Ltd, Elcograf S.p.A.

ISBN: 978–0–140–43372–2

www.greenpenguin.co.uk

CONTENTS

ACKNOWLEDGEMENTS

I would like to thank staff at Fisher Library, University of Sydney, and the Bodleian Library, Oxford; the Australian Research Council; my editors, Janet Todd and Melanie McGrath; and for various kinds of assistance and support, Tim Armstrong, Rosalind Ballaster, Judith Barbour, Deirdre Coleman, Bruce Gardiner, Margaret Harris, Dorothy Hewett, Jeri Johnson, Merv Lilley, Bill Maidment, Tony Miller, David Norbrook, Simon Petch, Susan Wiseman. Melissa Hardie's help has been unstinting and invaluable.

INTRODUCTION

The range of Margaret Cavendish's literary and scientific ambition, as well as her overt and frequently asserted desire for fame, has long made her an exemplary instance of woman as spectacle. The historical figure she cuts has aroused praise and blame, incredulity and pathos. As Virginia Woolf wrote, 'her poems, her plays, her philosophies, her orations, her discourses – all these folios and quartos in which, she protested, her real life was shrined – moulder in the gloom of public libraries, or are decanted into tiny thimbles which hold six drops of their profusion'.[1]

Margaret Cavendish (née Lucas) was born in Essex in 1623, to a rich family, the youngest of eight children. Her father died when she was two, and it was her mother who provided an early and continuing example of female independence and administrative competence. At the outbreak of the Civil War in 1642, the Lucas family moved to the Royalist stronghold of Oxford, where Margaret became a Maid of Honour to Queen Henrietta Maria. In 1644, she travelled as one of the Queen's party into Parisian exile, where she met and married William Cavendish, the widowed Marquis of Newcastle. Thirty years Margaret's senior, Newcastle had been commander of Charles I's forces in the north, and was well known as a patron of arts and letters, and as a famous horseman. Though her marriage to Newcastle was socially and intellectually advantageous, it also committed Margaret to a life closely governed by the political fortunes of the Royalists.

After the execution of Charles I and the declaration of the Commonwealth in 1649, Newcastle was formally banished and his estates confiscated. He and Margaret lived in exile in

Antwerp until the Restoration allowed them to return home, except for a crucial period in which Margaret returned to England, accompanied by her brother in law, Charles Cavendish, to petition for financial compensation for the loss of her husband's estate. The petition failed but it was during this interregnum in Margaret's married life, between late 1651 and early 1653, that she began to write and publish: a practice which she pursued energetically, copiously and diversely for the rest of her life. The sheer quantity and variety of Cavendish's published work was extremely marked amongst women writers of the seventeenth century, and unprecedented amongst earlier English women writers.[2]

Cavendish launched her career as a writer by publishing two volumes in quick succession in 1653, *Poems, and Fancies* and *Philosophical Fancies* (in prose and verse). They were issued emphatically under her own name, like all the books that she subsequently published. If it was rare for a woman to seek publication, it was still more unusual for a woman to provide an unambiguous authorial signature. Margaret Cavendish's writing career may have been inaugurated by her separation from her husband and return to England, but it was consolidated in range and quantity in exile, where she wrote another four books with her husband's active encouragement and financial support.

In 1655 Cavendish issued another pair of reflections on political, philosophical, scientific and aesthetic topics, written in Antwerp. *The World's Olio* (1655) is an engaging prose miscellany which includes 'The Inventory of Judgement's Commonwealth'. This condensed utopian blueprint looked forward to Cavendish's later experiments in this mode, 'The Animal Parliament' and *The Blazing World*. *Philosophical and Physical Opinions* (1655, reissued 'much altered' in 1668 as *Grounds of Natural Philosophy*) continued her attempt to insert herself into a masculine public sphere, particularly through the discourse of the new science.[3] In *Nature's Pictures*, published in 1656, Cavendish again assembles a collection of short prose pieces and poetry, but it also signals her concerted expansion into other prose genres (or kinds). It is Cavendish's most ambitious and copious generic experiment, including moral fables, romance novella ('Assaulted and Pursued Chastity'), fictionalized treatise ('The She Anchoret'), and the autobiographical memoir, 'A True Relation'.[4] At the same time she gave notice of her intention to publish a collection of closet drama also written in Antwerp, but its publication was delayed until 1662 after the manuscript was lost at sea.[5]

By the time the Newcastles returned to England at the Restoration, Cavendish's reputation and infamy as a woman and as a writer was well established. No longer in the political vanguard, the Newcastles retired almost immediately to their least damaged estate, Welbeck in Nottinghamshire. It was there that Margaret wrote another seven books of orations, letters, scientific speculation, utopian fiction, biography, poetry and closet drama, as well as overseeing a number of reissues and revised editions, before her sudden death in December, 1673, at the age of fifty.[6]

Margaret Cavendish was devoted to personal excess, and the number of substantial, elaborately produced books she wrote and published under her own name and at considerable expense, in a career spanning twenty years, constituted her most radical and deliberate infringement of contemporary proprieties. But Cavendish's writing is not only copious and unusually secular, it is also overtly polemical and formally experimental. Her writings, collectively and individually, demonstrate an abiding fascination with kinds as such, and particularly with impure and unexpected hybrids. An interrogation of systems of knowledge and modes of description, as well as the fluid relations between gender and genre, informs all of Cavendish's writing, and marks it as generically self-conscious and ambitious.

Like most students of genre, her imagination is not primarily focused on normative or pure kinds. It is most engaged by that which troubles or resists categorization, thereby engendering reflection on the nature and function of categorization itself. Both Cavendish herself, and her writings, have similarly challenged categorization. That the spectacle of Cavendish as a writing woman has disturbed commentators is clear. Her writings have suffered a similar resistance, leading generations of commentators to suggest that paraphrase is as much as, or more than, her work requires.[7]

This collection contributes to the overdue project of making Cavendish's writing available and accessible to the modern reader, so that the contents of her books, and not the mere fact of their existence, may begin to receive the attention that her life has (relatively speaking) rarely lacked. It includes three notable experiments in short fiction. The first two, 'The Contract' and 'Assaulted and Pursued Chastity', are romance narratives taken from *Nature's Pictures* (1656); neither has been reissued since the seventeenth century. The third is her utopian fantasy, *The Description of a New World, Called The Blazing World.* Thought to be the only text of its kind by a seventeenth-century woman,[8] it was first published as the fictional companion piece to Cavendish's lengthy scientific treatise, *Observations Upon Experimental Philosophy* (1666). In the context of recent critical interest in utopian writing and the history of women's writing, *The Blazing World* has begun to attract the attention it deserves.[9] Perhaps we are at least one instance of that future audience which Margaret Cavendish so fervently desired, for certainly her work is compelling in terms of the current remapping of literary histories, and the relations of gender and literary genres.

There *is* pathos, and some would say justice, in the historical diminution of so extravagant a textual self-witnessing, but the works represented here demonstrate Cavendish's real interest as a writer of prose fiction, particularly in terms of her experiments with allegory and romance, utopia and the imaginary voyage. Cavendish self-consciously produced herself as a fantastic and singular woman, and that labour of self-representation successfully dominated seventeenth century and later accounts of both her life and writing. Pepys's often-quoted remark, 'The whole story of this Lady is a romance, and all she doth is romantic'[10], was a shrewd reading of a woman who represented herself as figuratively hermaphrodite.[11] Her idiosyncratic dress combined masculine and feminine elements in a parodic masquerade of gender, while her rare and highly theatrical public appearances never failed to draw an audience.[12] But her singularity has also, and perhaps more commonly, been interpreted as monstrous, and her texts similarly characterized as deformed in various ways: chaotic, old-fashioned, uneven, contradictory and insane.[13]

Virginia Woolf, in *A Room of One's Own*, figures Margaret Cavendish as 'a vision of loneliness and riot . . . as if some giant cucumber had spread itself over all the roses and carnations in the garden and choked them to death'.[14] It is a fanciful but hardly innocent conceit, representing Cavendish as producing disproportionate and monstrously masculine texts. Amongst contemporary women, Dorothy Osborne remarked, on the publication of Cavendish's first book, 'there are many soberer people in Bedlam; I'll swear her friends are much to blame to let her go abroad'.[15] Osborne's confusion of Cavendish's book and her person, whether witting or unwitting, is characteristic of the atextual way in which Cavendish's work – and indeed life – has tended to be read: as a vehicle for or byproduct of personality, and a receptacle for ideas.

At first Cavendish's extremely unfeminine works were thought to be not her own work. The 'Epistle' which introduces Cavendish's autobiographical memoir refutes the gossip 'that my writings are none of my own' (p. 363) in a complex way. She uses it as the ground of a more sophisticated questioning of the continuity between text and self, as well as the relations between thinking, writing and speaking, 'for I have not spoke so much as I have writ, nor writ so much as I have thought' (p. 367). The closing paragraph of the 'Epistle' is characteristic of Cavendish's ironic self-defence, and of her rhetorical dexterity:

> But if they will not believe my books are my own, let them search the author or authoress: but I am very confident that they will do like Drake, who went so far about, until he came to the place he first set out at. But for the sake of after-ages, which I hope will be more just to me than the present, I will write the true relation of my birth, breeding, and to this part of my life,

> not regarding carping tongues, or malicious censurers, for I despise them.
>
> Margaret Newcastle

As she maintains, the life cannot bear witness to the truth of authorship. Instead she supplies the text *of* her life in lieu of any incontrovertible proof, and as a further instance of the endlessly asymmetrical but productive relations of experience and writing. Cavendish's numerous prefaces and addresses to the reader constitute a fragmentary but copious poetics, probably the most extensive theorization we have available to us of an individual seventeenth century woman's relation to the resources of writing and publication, and the gendered construction of knowledge, in a secular context.

Cavendish used the interdicted practices of writing and publishing to challenge the negative consequences for women of patriarchal codes of femininity, delighting in the subversive potential of generic and intellectual hybridization. In her polemical prefaces Cavendish trenchantly defends her own right to publish, and to participate in current debates, but she also insists on the rational and sensitive capacities of all women, and the educational handicap under which they labour. The egalitarian potential of her sexual critique is, however, seriously curtailed by an equally powerful commitment to the prerogatives of absolute monarchy and hierarchical privilege so thoroughly undermined in the 1640s and '50s. In part this allegiance might be traced to the fact that Cavendish's marriage to the Marquis, later Duke of Newcastle, was extremely socially advantageous. As Mendelson argues, 'Margaret displayed the exaggerated respect of an *arriviste* for a title' (Mendelson, 22). But Newcastle was also in exile, and Margaret was courted by him when she herself was in the service of the exiled Queen Henrietta Maria.

Cavendish adopted an entirely defensive position with respect to radical political theory, but her political conservatism does not vitiate the power of her sexual critique, and need not surprise us any more than the familiar alliance of 'radical' politics and 'conservative' sexual politics. Catherine Gallagher has argued that it is a commitment to absolutism which contradictorily enabled Margaret Cavendish's critique of women's effective exclusion from political subjecthood and citizenship. I would suggest that Cavendish's simultaneous insistence on the (unrecognized) justice of her social privilege, shaped by her experiences in the years of political exile, and her call for the development of women's (unrecognized) potential, stems from her extraordinarily ambivalent position with respect to the discourses of power. She was the socially inferior wife of a defeated and later displaced Royalist leader; the minimally educated maid-in-waiting of a deposed queen; the youngest of a large family, financially straitened and physically decimated in the course of the Civil Wars. For nearly twenty years Cavendish lived as a purely English-speaking resident of France and the Netherlands, the opulence of her married life sustained by her husband's perpetual, and remarkably successful, negotiations with creditors. Though she dined with Descartes, and infamously visited the all-male enclave of the Royal Society in London,[16] she could not appropriate for herself the (masculine) position of dilettante in its honorific sense. In terms of politics, gender and discourse, Cavendish could never achieve the full membership she craved, though she tried to turn her maverick status to her own advantage.

This ambivalence is crucial to Cavendish's most explicitly autobiographical writings, 'A True Relation' and her biography of the Duke of Newcastle. In these texts she offers idealized representations of her family, her husband and her marriage in the context of a tragic narrative of the suffering imposed on them (and her) by political events. She offers a catalogue of losses which not even the Restoration could restore. In her writings, Margaret Cavendish campaigned for the restoration of what had been taken from her and hers, as Royalists, and for the supply of what, as a woman, had never been available to her. These variously enabling and disabling factors pivoted around Cavendish's mutually supportive marriage – a partnership which she continually figured as the generative utopian space of her own productivity – but her writing raises the question of the relation of women to restoration in general, and the Restoration in particular.

Cavendish's response to the narrow territory with which women were supposed to concern themselves was a desire for encyclopaedic coverage. This will to inclusiveness has often been used as proof of her unsound scholarship and unbecoming lack of modesty. Her scientific speculations have been routinely ridiculed, but Lisa Sarasohn has shown that Cavendish's secular atomism and, later, extreme materialism were not implausible or disreputable in their historical context. Sarasohn argues that the combination, in Cavendish's avowedly speculative writing, of skepticism and gender critique 'shows how the radical implications of one area of thought can reinforce and strengthen the subversive tendencies of another, quite different attack on authority' (Sarasohn, p. 290).

Both 'The Contract' and 'Assaulted and Pursued Chastity' first appeared in *Nature's Pictures drawn by Fancy's Pencil to the Life* (1656). This is Cavendish's most ambitious attempt to combine modes and genres, as the title page indicates: 'In this volume there are several feigned stories of natural descriptions, as comical, tragical, tragi-comical, poetical, romancical, philosophical, and historical, both in prose and verse, some all verse, some all prose, some mixed, partly prose, and partly verse. Also, there are some morals, and some dialogues; but they are as the advantage loaves of bread to a baker's dozen; and a true story at the latter end, wherein there is no feignings.' The whole volume runs to almost 400 closely printed pages, beginning with six prefatory addresses to the reader. The closing epistle, 'A Complaint and Request', specifically addresses the reader acquainted not only with this book but Cavendish's publications to date. In this, her fifth book issued in three years, she assumes a continuing audience for her work: those implied readers whose existence confirms her career as a writer in a public sense.

Both stories from *Nature's Pictures* included here concern the eventual marriage of a young and wealthy heroine to a younger brother whose fortune is made by the death of the first heir. Both men, initially married to wealthy, older widows, are offered as desirable and sexually libertine. The narrative denouement requires the removal of the present wife, respectively through annulment and death, and the reform of the rakish husband by the virtuous, beautiful and brilliantly accomplished heroine. William Cavendish was just such a dissolute and successful younger brother, whom Margaret Cavendish married after the death of his first wife, a rich widow. Clearly Margaret Cavendish was rewriting the narrative of her own history as romance, focusing her main attention and admiration on the advantageous production of woman as spectacle. In particular she charts the difficult progress of the exceptional, and exceptionally chaste, woman to her just reward: a brilliant marriage and her own title.

Cavendish was pointedly censorious about the deleterious effects of romance on the minds and conduct of female readers. The heroine's guardian in 'The Contract' 'never suffered her to read in Romancies, nor such light books' (p. 185), while Miseria, the heroine of 'Assaulted and Pursued Chastity', refuses to read romances, choosing mathematical treatises instead. Cavendish herself claimed never to have read romances, but did not scruple to write what she called 'romancical' books. Her own experiments with the feminized romance mode dramatize women's sexualized access to power through marriage and eroticized friendship.[17] Similarly, they play out the empowering possibilities of disguise or masking, allowing women the opportunity to excel in literally masculine or masculinized roles (Empress, Viceregent, General, legal advocate, 'son').

Cavendish repeatedly feminizes the aristocratic and chivalric trope (or figure) of the fair unknown. In her stories, the woman as stranger effortlessly and instantaneously seduces all who encounter her, and is able to profit by the recognition of her own status as fetish. These narratives centre on the strangeness of woman, both inherent and circumstantial, and her ability to solicit and shape 'the gaze of wonder'.[18] Though her plots lead to, or hinge on, advantageous marriage, each of these stories also privileges relations between women as asymmetrical doubles. An adversarial contest between current and future wives forms the climax of 'The Contract', while eroticized platonic love and female patronage are crucial to 'Assaulted and Pursued Chastity' and *The Blazing World.*

In 'The Contract', an orphaned infant heiress is brought up by her father's brother, whose own children are dead. A marriage contract is mooted between the niece and a Duke's younger son.[19] When the child is almost seven the Duke falls ill and the contract is ratified as his dying wish. The son 'seemed to consent, to please his Father', but after the Duke's death 'did not at all reflect upon his contract'. He goes to war, fortuitously inherits the Dukedom on the unexpected death of his elder brother, and marries a rich widow who 'claimed a promise from him' (p. 185). The spurned niece recognizes the potential unhappiness of such an arrangement, and the value of her own financial independence, for 'who are happier than those that are mistresses of their own fortunes?' (p. 186). It is her uncle who seeks revenge, vowing to take his niece to the city and make her 'a meteor of the time'. There he escorts her to lectures on natural philosophy, physics, chemistry, music, and to courts of law, always 'masked, muffled, and scarfed'. At sixteen she is literally unveiled at court in a series of carefully planned and titillating appearances.

The niece designs her own clothes, and is thus partly the orchestrator of, and commentator on, her own spectacular singularity: 'what doth my uncle mean to set me out to show? sure he means to traffic for a husband; but Heaven forbid those intentions . . .'. On her first appearance she dresses all in black 'like a young widow'. Entering the masque after all the court is seated, 'as if a curtain was drawn from before her', she displaces the performance as the chief wonder. At her second appearance she dresses in white satin embroidered with silver, 'like a Heaven stuck with stars'. Again, she enters late, without veil or jewellery, to be 'more prospectious' (p. 193), and is received as 'some divine object': 'the beams of all eyes were drawn together, as one point placed in her face, and by reflection she sent a burning heat, and fired every heart'. (p. 193) The men wait on her, while the women watch with envy, but it is the two most prominent men in the assembly, the aged Viceroy and the unhappily married Duke, who are singled out as chief admirers. The young woman, unwittingly at first, desires only the man to whom she was betrothed as a child, faithful to the terms of the contract.

Against the wishes of his niece, the uncle verbally accepts the Viceroy's proposal of marriage, while the Duke and the still unnamed young lady exchange letters declaring their love. The Duke confesses his youthful error, and repents his disobedience to his father and to the strictures of contractual and moral obligation, urging her to 'place [her]self' (p. 203) by recourse to law. This boudoir scene in which the Duke asserts a husbandly prerogative is followed by another intimate confrontation, this time between the rival lovers in the Viceroy's private chamber. It is only now that the name of the placeless and anonymous young woman is revealed as the Lady Delitia, by the man who is now prepared and able to say, 'she is my wife, and I have been married to her almost nine years'. Once the obstacle of the Viceroy's pre-contract has been disposed of by a combination of violent intimidation and legal nicety, the uncle agrees to support Deletia in a suit to establish her rightful claim over that of the current Duchess.

In the final movement of the narrative Deletia proves her excellence as a student. Her years as an obscure courtroom observer have prepared her to act confidently and argue eloquently as her own advocate but, in fact, such a demonstration is legally superfluous. Its narrative importance is as another scene of seduction, for, as the judges inform Delitia, 'the justice of your cause judges itself' (p. 213). Similarly, though the mutual desire of the Duke and Delitia may be legally beside the point, it is narratively and generically essential to the satisfactory conclusion of the romance. This is the third 'courtly' spectacle at which Deletia proves to be the chief wonder and, once again, other women are her only opponents, for this contest is really between the current, inauthentic Duchess and her authentic replacement who 'came not from nobility, but . . . the root of merit, from whence gentility doth spring' (p. 211). Deletia fulfils her uncle's plan for revenge by indeed becoming a 'meteor of the age', able to choose any man as her husband; but her revenge is not against the Duke for breach of contract, but rather in deleting the manipulative widow he married. Revenge is sweet, however: the spurned Viceroy proposes to the Duchess and the tale ends by foreshadowing a double wedding. This neat reversal (corresponding in rhetoric to the scheme chiasmus) privileges the force of the initial marriage contract, and the weakness of the second, realigning the couples according to the moral of the desirability of a younger wife.[20]

'The Contract' is a contained and elegantly structured narrative, with powerful set-pieces and confrontations. The other two texts included here are more complex, lengthy and ambitious. They extend Cavendish's ambivalent fascination with the possibilities of romance as the scene of a woman's heroic agency and successful negotiation of the theatres of power; and her commitment to the representation of women as subjects of desire and subjects in discourse.

'Assaulted and Pursued Chastity' is an allegorical romance in which an anonymous heiress is forced from her home and family in the Kingdom of Riches by the dangers of war. Shipwrecked in the Kingdom of Sensuality, she is 'assaulted and pursued' by that kingdom's married Prince, whose behaviour is by turns noble and dissolute. After shooting and wounding the Prince to preserve her honour, the young lady, now known as 'Miseria', is driven to a near-fatal suicide attempt. She cuts her hair and escapes dressed as a page, leaving letters signed 'Affectionata'. Disguised as a boy named 'Travellia' she stows away on a ship which proves to be southward bound on a voyage of discovery. Travellia's presence on the ship is discovered by the Captain, but her disguise remains intact.

The Captain finds in Travellia a 'son', she in him a 'father'. The amorous romance plot is temporarily displaced by a filial romance and this literal ship of fortune then bears the new couple into the generic territory of the imaginary voyage while the main sexual plot is deferred. The heroine's cross-dressing and change of name inaugurates a masculinized adventure and travel narrative, which in turns leads to an interlude in a fantastic kingdom; but the significance of Travellia's female virtue is never forgotten as a motive-force in the construction of the plot, for it is that which rescues the Captain and his adopted 'son' from shipwreck and guides them into a scene of mutual wonder.

In this self-contained episode Cavendish offers an extended catalogue of curiosities which anticipates *The Blazing World*'s intense interest in new hybrids and mixed species, as well as the later text's descriptive and allegorical richness. As Travellia and the Captain travel deeper into the kingdom, and further away from the scene of initial contact, the quality of the materials catalogued becomes more luxurious and the objects themselves more artful and elaborate. Even the appearance of the inhabitants alters to demonstrate a profound physical difference between subjects of different rank: unlike the men with deep purple skin and black teeth by whom they are met, 'all those of the Royal blood, were of a different colour from the rest of the people, they were of a perfect orange colour, their hair coal black, their teeth and nails as white as milk, of a very great height, yet well shaped'. The royals also have skins 'wrought, like the Britons'. These ornamental markings are cultural inscriptions of rank on skin which is already hierarchically colour-coded, but they also signify a primitive and decadent potential in those of greatest power which links them with the spear-carrying natives first described – for we learn that they are all cannibals, who will only accomplish true civility by means of this narrative of providential contact.

In the course of a year's imprisonment, and at the Captain's urging, Travellia proves her intellectual capacity by learning the language of their captors and, in a violent *coup de théâtre*, averts their destiny as sacrifices. Identifying herself and her 'father' as messengers of the gods, she embarks on a series of instructive sermons 'forbidding vain and barbarous customs, and inhumane ceremonies ... by which doctrine they were brought to be a civilized people.'

This fantastic episode establishes Travellia's credentials as an effective 'son', and prepares the way for the more elaborate drama of multiple disguises and partial disclosures which ensues when the Prince re-enters the narrative. In an interim passage on an uninhabited island the Captain tells the suspicious Prince what he knows of Travellia, the Prince penetrates Travellia's disguise, and Travellia unfolds the secret of her closeted gender to the Captain, who promptly rescues the 'son' who proves to be a daughter in distress.

Travellia and the Prince next meet in the service of monarchs of neighbouring countries, Amity and Amour, where they are drawn into a second plot of assaulted and pursued chastity, hinging on the unsuccessful courtship of the Queen of Amity by the King of Amour. The initial impediment is the Queen's desire to maintain absolute sovereignty and independence, but the arrival of Travellia adds another twist to the complexities of unrequited love when the Queen chooses Travellia, the fair unknown, on the merits of beauty and character alone. As Travellia had been abducted by the Prince in the story's beginning, now the Queen is abducted by the King, and Travellia and the Prince, unbeknownst to each other, become leaders of the armies of Amity and Amour.

With the help of the Captain's experience Travellia proves herself an effective military strategist and an inspiring leader, until single combat between the two commanders once again exposes her fraudulent masculinity: the Prince's long-averted sexual assault occurs in a displaced form as a sword-wound sustained in a military assault. The partial recognition scene, in which the Prince literally penetrates Travellia's disguise, takes place on the battlefield over the heroine's unconscious and bleeding body, but the Prince's remorse and chivalry gives the victory to the forces of Amity while he becomes the willing prisoner of love.

Once more a series of disclosures of the truth of Travellia is set in train. The secret faithfully kept by the Captain goes with him to the grave, but Travellia's daughterly grief affectively and grammatically prepares the way for her narrative uncloseting: 'the young general when *he* came into the temple, who was clad all in mourning, only *his* face was seen, which appeared like the sun when it breaks through a dark and spongy cloud: their beams did shine on those watery drops that fell upon *her* cheeks, as banks where roses and lilies grew, there standing on a mounted pillar spake *her* father's funeral speech' (my italics). The Prince subsequently reveals Travellia's secret, forcing her to declare herself first to the monarchs and then to the people of Amity.

The duel between Travellia and the Prince put an end to the assault and pursuit, and, in narrative terms, cleared the ground for the removal of the technical impediment to marriage: news of the death of the Prince's wife arrives just as the loss of her (second) 'father' confirms Travellia's need for another male guardian. It is the independent Queen of Amity who remains the most problematical figure. In despair she prays to Cupid and is granted a displacement of desire on to the King, and a conversion of sexual passion for Travellia into manageable platonic love i.e. Amity. Like 'The Contract', the double plot of 'Assaulted and Pursued Chastity' ends in double marriage. The King and Queen rule in Amour while the Prince and Princess rule in neighbouring Amity, Travellia acting as Viceregent by the Queen's and the people's request. Neither the Kingdom of Riches, nor the Kingdom of Sensuality, is ever mentioned again and Travellia's unstable name is finally resolved in the title of 'Princess'.

Ten years after the publication of 'Assaulted and Pursued Chastity', Cavendish issued *The Blazing World*, a text which similarly combines elements of romance and utopia, and has sometimes been described as science fiction. Once again the genre of the imaginary voyage is linked to a plot of abduction and sexual assault. Instead of cross-dressing or masking, female freedom in this text is granted through various strategies of disembodiment and spectacular self-presentation.

The project of utopian representation announced in the full title, *The Description of a New World Called The Blazing World*, involves Cavendish in a deliberate paradox, for, as she argues in *Nature's Pictures*, 'descriptions are to imitate and fancy to create; for fancy is not an imitation of nature, but a natural creation, which I take to be the true poetry: so that there is as much difference between fancy, and imitation, as between a creature and a creator'. A non-imitative or fantastic description is therefore a hermaphroditic foundation for a text.

The Blazing World is already improbably and hermaphroditically coupled with a serious treatise on natural philosophy, *Observations Upon Experimental Philosophy*, in both its printings of 1666 and 1668. In *Observations* Cavendish asserts that 'Art produces hermaphroditical effects, that is, such as are partly natural, and partly artificial ... [but] art itself is natural, and an effect of nature, and cannot produce anything that is beyond, or not within nature'. It is through a thoroughgoing pursuit of hybridization that Cavendish raises the utopian possibility of a productive or honorific singularity. This singularity exceeds existing categories whilst asking to be read in terms of them, as a model of surpassing. Every invention and description of a fantastical compound authorizes the Duchess's textual and personal singularity as authentically poetic and a new nature.

In the epilogue to *The Blazing World*, Cavendish writes: 'I added this piece of fancy to my philosophical observations, and joined them as two worlds at the ends of their poles; both for my own sake, to divert my studious thoughts ... and to delight the reader with variety.... But lest my fancy should stray too much, I chose such a fiction as would be agreeable to the subject I treated in former parts ...' ('To the Reader'). Promiscuously mixing what she calls romancical, philosophical and fantastical elements, Cavendish composes a new generic mixture in *The Blazing World*, while the description itself thematizes the proliferation of new hybrids as the very principle of natural classification in the Blazing World.

The Blazing World is an extravagant text which revels in the self-consciously fantastic representation of opulence, ornament, novelty and variety as well as the rhetoric of description and amplification, accounting and recounting. But this extravagance does not function simply in the service of commodity fetishism. Consumption is linked to the desire for reparation or restoration of various kinds: aesthetic, economic, sexual, ideological and epistemological. Though the pleasure of the account is figured as its own not inconsiderable reward, for both reader and writer, the text is haunted by the recognition of loss, denial and contingency. The text also attempts a comprehensive survey of the state of knowledge, and a tour of the disciplines, but in doing so repeatedly discovers the precariousness and self-interestedness of all truth-claims.

The Blazing World combines a narrative of the effortless rise of a woman to absolute power, with a narrative of the liberty of the female soul and the emancipatory possibilities of utopian speculation and writing specifically for women. Its first miracle conforms to the romance imperative of virtue rewarded. An anonymous 'young Lady' is abducted by a foreign merchant and, as the ship passes from 'the very end point of the pole of that World, but even to another pole of another world' (p. 3), owner and crew freeze to death and then 'thaw, and corrupt' (p. 4). The merchant's initial crime against rank, property and propriety is appropriately punished by a fatal crossing between worlds, while the 'distressed Lady' is honoured with the highest recognition of her innate merit: 'the Emperor rejoicing, made her his wife, and gave her an absolute power to rule and govern all that world as she pleased'.

The sudden metamorphosis of the anonymous young Lady into the Empress of the Blazing World occasions the text's first extended blazon or catalogue, which is later virtually reproduced at crucial moments in the staging of the Empress's domestic and imperial power. The description proper of the site of the Blazing World is inaugurated by the introduction of the woman as stranger, but it is she who becomes the most wonderful sight in the Blazing World, a reversal marked by her ritual blazoning and re-presentation as Empress, newly attired in the literally blazing costume of power:

> Her accoutrement after she was made Empress, was as followeth: On her head she wore a cap of pearl, and a half-moon of diamonds just before it; on the top of her crown came spreading over a broad carbuncle, cut in the form of the sun; her coat was of pearl, mixt with blue diamonds, and fringed

> with red ones; her buskins and sandals were of green diamonds: in her left hand she held a buckler, to signify the defence of her dominions; which buckler was made of that sort of diamond as has several different colours; and being cut and made in the form of an arch, showed like a rainbow; in her right hand she carried a spear made of white diamond, cut like the tail of a blazing-star, which signified that she was ready to assault those that proved her enemies.(pp. 13–14)

Building on the rhetorical centrality of the aristocratic figure of the blazon in her *Blazing World*, Cavendish's Empress is a kind of hermaphrodized warrior queen, whose representation recalls the cult of Elizabeth I and the masques of Henrietta Maria.[21] In the preface to the *Blazing World*, Cavendish crowns herself 'Margaret the First' – 'though I cannot be Henry the Fifth, or Charles the Second, yet I endeavour to be Margaret the First' – in an ironic trope of the female author's construction of, and control over, a textual empire, and an imperial narrative: 'And although I have neither power, time nor occasion to conquer the world as Alexander and Caesar did; yet rather than not to be mistress of one, since Fortune and the Fates would give me none, I have made a world of my own.' In the course of the narrative the Empress succeeds in putting down rebellion both at home and abroad, through a combination of the seductive manipulation of self-image as allegorical display, and a campaign of terror through burning.

The self-coronation of 'Margaret the First' in the preface, partly authorized by the Duke of Newcastle's commendatory poem which precedes it, is displaced into another more extravagant story of husbandly permission which Cavendish herself calls 'romancical'. The function of the blazon in this narrative subverts its customary role in the patriarchal coding of a figure of woman. Here, the catalogue dwells on the account and itemization of costume, materials, colours and the emblematic accessories of power. It functions iconographically to ratify a seduction which has already occurred within the narrative – the seduction of the Blazing World by the young lady – and which is now extended to the reader. The blazon also serves to externalize and further materalize a blazing virtue which has already literally preserved the heroine from rape and death by exposure.

Though the rise to power of Cavendish's Empress is staged through the authorizing gaze of men, her blazoning by the female narrator is at once a description and demonstration, for the reader, of the Empress's absolute power over her new male subjects. It is a second moment of wonder and the point at which the young lady, now reconstructed as Empress, exceeds masculine ratification. The literal body of female virtue is never made available for representation. Indeed it is through the miraculous abandonment of corporeality that the souls of women are able to commune with each other as platonic lovers, and move freely and invisibly from one world and one body to another.

'Margaret the First' recuperates the blazon in a tableau of female investiture and, in doing so, stages a different power relation: the female author's creation and description of an obscure imperial heroine as unnamed stand-in. Developing the story of reciprocal love and service of Travellia and the Queen of Amity in 'Assaulted and Pursued Chastity', *The Blazing World* turns out to be a utopia compulsively interested in the erotics of female doubling and collaboration. The conventionally labyrinthine geography of the Blazing World is matched by the intricately recursive plotting of its narrative of mutually beneficial platonic love between women in the context of their enabling and prestigious marriages to largely absent husbands.

Embedded within the romance plot of *The Blazing World* is a mirror-narrative of fortunate female:female abduction, of which none other than the 'Duchess of Newcastle' is the beneficiary. Through the introduction of 'Margaret Newcastle' as the Empress's scribe, the Duchess as author-scribe of *The Blazing World* stages a self-confirming dialogue on the production of fictional worlds as an immensely pleasurable compensatory activity for women:

> The Duchess of Newcastle was most earnest and industrious to make her world, because she had none at present (p. 98) . . .

> which world, after it was made, appeared so curious and full of variety; so well ordered and wisely governed, that it cannot possibly be expressed by words, nor the delight and pleasure which the Duchess took in making this world of her own. (pp. 100–101)

Like the body of the Empress, the Duchess's world is not available for description, although its existence and excellence is verified by the Empress's admiration.

The Blazing World offers an heroicized sexual allegory of Cavendish's own life and times: 'abducted' by the course of the Civil War from the royalist kingdom of EFSI (England, Scotland, France and Ireland), she makes a brilliant marriage in exile. As a utopian space of reparation, wish-fulfilment and plenitude triangulated by representations of pre- and post-revolutionary England ('EFSI' and 'E'), the Blazing World offers an imaginary vantage point from which to observe, critique and revise the course of history, the state of knowledge and the forms of power. Insofar as *The Blazing World* provides a space in which the historical Duchess of Newcastle can vindicate and demonstrate her infamous 'singularity', she also distinguishes between the utopian properties of her fictional 'description' and the limited aesthetic compensations provided by the book in which it appears. Like all utopian texts, *The Blazing World* cannot forget its place of origin, its 'true relation'.

Cavendish's final gesture, simultaneously inviting and defensive, seeks to ground the efficacy of her description in reception, in the seduction of readers. She extends to these projected subjects both a promise and a threat:

> if any should like the world I have made, and be willing to be my subjects, they may imagine themselves such, and they are such, I mean in their minds, fancies or imaginations; but if they cannot endure to be subjects, they may create worlds of their own, and govern themselves as they please. But let them have a care not to prove unjust usurpers and to rob me of mine . . . (p. 160)

This uneasy dialectic between insolent self-sufficiency and the desire for 'subjects' whose existence will ratify her independent sovereignty, is characteristic of Cavendish's authorial rhetoric and narrative projections. In such textual strategies it is possible to witness the simultaneously defiant and abject construction of the publishing woman writer and her implied readers, present and future. She emerges as an ironically self-designated hermaphroditic spectacle and as the self-proclaimed producer of hybrid creations and inimitable discourses. Such a claim to complete singularity, so often thematized in Cavendish's writing, should be situated in terms of her experiments with the generic frames of feminized romance and masculinized utopia. The prose fiction included here represents a powerful negotiation of gender and genre, and of sexual ideology, privileging the hermaphroditic as an arena of mobility and supplementarity, particularly enabling to women. More straightforwardly, the proliferation of literal and figurative couples and doubles in these and other texts by Cavendish, and their actual or implicitly contractual basis, dramatizes an heroic figure of woman, who ingeniously turns patriarchalized scenarios of power and seduction to her own benefit.

Cavendish's narratives of female virtue rewarded are supplemented by complex authorial commentaries or meta-narratives. Through them she addresses the reader who, located in the world beyond the text, necessarily escapes her control. It is this extratextual, historically unspecific and mobile relation which constitutes the most important seduction of all, for it is the gaze of the reader which will guarantee the utopian viability of the author's signature, outside the closed system of the library catalogue or publisher's list. My role as editor and introducer adds another level to this recursive process of female collaboration. On behalf of, and in the spirit of, Cavendish's own authorial interventions and ambitions, this collection solicits new readers and new readings.

NOTES

[1] Virginia Woolf, 'The Duchess of Newcastle' [1925], in *Virginia Woolf, Women and Writing*, ed. Michele Barrett, London: The Women's Press, 1979, 79.

[2] See Patricia Crawford's invaluable, 'Women's Published Writings 1600-1700', in *Women in English Society 1500–1800*, ed. Mary Prior, London: Methuen, 1985, 211–82. The only comparable figure is Aphra Behn, whose first play was produced in London in 1670. On sixteenth and early seventeenth century women's writing, see Elaine V. Beilin, *Redeeming Eve: Women Writers of the English Renaissance*, Princeton: Princeton University Press, 1987, and Ann Rosalind Jones, *The Currency of Eros: Women's Love Lyric 1520–1640*, Bloomington: Indiana University Press, 1991.

[3] For Cavendish's relation to the new science see Lisa Sarasohn, 'A Science Turned Upside Down : Feminism and the Natural Philosophy of Margaret Cavendish', *Huntington Library Quarterly* 47 (1984), 289–307, Sylvia Bowerbank, 'The Spider's Delight: Margaret Cavendish and the "Female" Imagination' in *Women in the Renaissance*, eds K. Farrell, E.H. Hageman, A.F. Kinney, Amherst: University of Massachusetts, 187–203, and Gerald D. Meyer, *The Scientific Lady in England, 1650–1760*, Berkeley: University of California Press, 1955, ch.1. For a broader introduction see M. Hunter, *Science and Society in Restoration England*, Cambridge: Cambridge University Press, 1981. For an overview of a number of recent studies of Cavendish's relation to the new science see Eric Lewis, 'The Legacy of Margaret Cavendish', *Perspectives on Science* 9 (2001), 341–64.

[4] 'A True Relation of my Birth, Breeding and Life', in *Nature's Pictures*, London: A. Maxwell, 1656, 368–391. 'A True Relation' was dropped from the second edition of 1671, presumably because its authenticating function was no longer considered necessary. On Cavendish and autobiography see Dolores Paloma, 'Margaret Cavendish: Defining the Female Self', *Women's Studies* 7 (1980), 55–66, and Mary Beth Rose, 'Gender, Genre and History: Seventeenth-Century English Women and the Art of Autobiography', in *Women in the Middle Ages and the Renaissance*, ed. Mary Beth Rose, Syracuse: Syracuse University Press, 1986, 245–78.

[5] On Cavendish's drama see Sophie Tomlinson, '"My Brain the Stage": Margaret Cavendish and the Fantasy of Female Performance', in *Women, Texts and Histories 1575–1760*, eds Clare Brant and Diane

Purkiss, London: Routledge, 1992, and Susan J. Wiseman, 'Gender and Status in Dramatic Discourse: Margaret Cavendish, Duchess of Newcastle', in *Women/Writing/History 1640–1740*, eds Isobel Grundy and Susan J. Wiseman, London: Batsford, 1992.

[6] As well as Sara Heller Mendelson's elegant and condensed biography, *The Mental World of Stuart Women: Three Studies*, Brighton: Harvester, 1987, there are two full-length studies: Douglas Grant's readable and reliable, *Margaret the First*, London: Rupert Hart-Davis, 1957, and Kathleen Jones, *A Glorious Fame: The Life of Margaret Cavendish*, London: Bloomsbury, 1988. Other helpful overviews of Cavendish's life and work are Janet Todd, *The Sign of Angellica. Women, Writing and Fiction, 1660–1800*, London: Virago, 1989, ch.3, and Marilyn L. Williamson, *Raising Their Voices: British Women Writers, 1650–1750*, Detroit: Wayne State University Press, 1990, ch.1.

[7] Some notable exceptions are the sympathetic, generically motivated accounts offered by B.G. MacCarthy, *Women Writers: Their Contribution to the English Novel 1621–1744*, Cork: Cork University Press, 1944, Paul Salzman, *English Prose Fiction 1558–1700*, Oxford: Clarendon Press, 1985, ch.16, and Elaine Hobby, *Virtue of Necessity: English Women's Writing 1649–88*, London: Virago, 1988. Catherine Gallagher, 'Embracing the Absolute: The Politics of the Female Subject in Seventeenth-Century England', *Genders 1* (1988) 24–39, offers a textually sophisticated reading of Cavendish as 'Tory feminist'.

[8] Two specialized check-lists agree on this: R.W. Gibson and J. Max Patrick, 'Utopias and Dystopias 1500–1750', in *St. Thomas More: A Preliminary Bibliography of his Works and of Moreana to the Year 1750*, New Haven: Yale University Press, 1961, and Lyman Tower Sargent, *British and American Utopian Literature 1516–1985: an annotated, chronological bibliography*, New York: Garland, 1988. See also, Kate Lilley, 'Blazing Worlds: Seventeenth Century Women's Utopian Writing', in *Women, Texts and Histories 1575–1760*, eds Clare Brant and Diane Purkiss, London: Routledge, 1992.

[9] See Gallagher, Todd, Salzman and Sarasohn. For an early, relatively favourable discussion of Cavendish as an anti-decadent prose writer see MacCarthy. Salzman includes a fully modernized and repunctuated text of *The Blazing World* in his valuable recent collection, *An Anthology of Seventeenth-Century Fiction*, Oxford: Oxford University Press, 1991.

[10] Samuel Pepys, *Diary*, 11 April 1667, eds Robert Latham and William Matthews, Vol.8, London: Bell and Hyman, 1974, 163.

[11] It is important for Cavendish's writing, and my own discussion, that 'hermaphrodite' can mean, consisting of, or combining the characteristics of, both sexes, and more generally, a person or thing combining any two opposite qualities or attributes.

[12] For an account of Margaret Cavendish's dress, see Mendelson, 46. James Fitzmaurice offers an interesting discussion of the frontispiece portraits of Cavendish as images of the 'solitary genius as melancholic' in 'Fancy and the Family: Self-characterizations of Margaret Cavendish', *Huntington Library Quarterly* 53 (1990), 198–209.

[13] See, respectively, Bowerbank, 197–201; Mendelson, 38; MacCarthy, 131; Frank Manuel and Fritzie Manuel, *Utopian Thought in the Western World*, Cambridge, Mass.: Harvard University Press, 1979, 7.

[14] Virginia Woolf, *A Room of One's Own* [1929], St Albans: Triad/Panther, 1979, 59–60.

[15] Dorothy Osborne, *Letters from Dorothy Osborne to Sir William Temple*, ed. Kingsley Hart, London: Folio Society, 58.

[16] See S.I. Mintz, 'The Duchess of Newcastle's Visit to the Royal Society', *Journal of English and Germanic Philology (1952)*, 168–76.

[17] On romance as 'feminized' see Helen Hackett, '"Yet tell me some such fiction": Lady Mary Wroth's *Urania* and the "femininity" of Romance', in *Women, Texts and Histories 1575–1760*, eds Clare Brant and Diane Purkiss, London: Routledge, 1992, and Rosalind Ballaster, *Seductive Forms*, Oxford: Clarendon, 1992.

[18] For a brilliantly suggestive discussion of 'the gaze of wonder' in relation to the blazon and the prospect see Patricia Parker, *Literary Fat Ladies: Rhetoric, Gender, Property*, London: Methuen, 1987, ch.7.

[19] The average age of first marriage for the upper landed classes in the seventeenth century was mid-twenties, according to Lawrence Stone, *The Family, Sex and Marriage in England 1500–1800*, London: Weidenfeld & Nicholson, 1977. Some aristocratic marriage negotiations involving children are documented in Margaret J.M. Ezell, *The Patriarch's Wife: Literary Evidence and the History of the Family*, Chapel Hill: University of North Carolina Press, 1987, 22–34. She comments that child marriages 'can be assumed to have been extraordinary', 'confined to families with extensive property interests to protect' (28).

[20] Lawrence Stone shows that, although 'odd cases are known from the late sixteenth century', breach of contract suits 'did not become common until about the 1670s', *Road to Divorce: England 1530–1987*, Oxford: Oxford University Press, 1990, 86.

[21] On the cult of Elizabeth, see, for instance, Frances Yates, *Astraea: The Imperial Theme in the Sixteenth Century*, London: Routledge, 1975; Roy Strong, *The Cult of Elizabeth: Elizabethan Portraiture and Pageantry*, London: Thames and Hudson, 1977, and Philippa Berry, *Of Chastity and Power: Elizabethan Literature and the Unmarried Queen*, London: Routledge, 1989. On Henrietta Maria, masques and Margaret Cavendish see Tomlinson, n.5.

NOTE ON THIS EDITION

The copy-text of *The Blazing World* is the Harvard Library copy of the first edition (1666), which has been checked against the second edition (1668). The copy-text for 'The Contract' and 'Assaulted and Pursued Chastity' is the British Library copy of the first edition of *Nature's Pictures* (1656).

Spelling has been modernized, except that some archaic or eccentric hyphenated forms have been retained because Cavendish shows a distinct preference for them. Grammar and punctuation have not been modernized or otherwise altered except where strictly necessary for sense. Any interpolations are enclosed in square brackets.

Cavendish's extremely idiosyncratic punctuation and grammar have usually been seen as simply a function of her lack of formal education, and carelessness in overseeing the preparation and printing of her manuscripts. It seems to me important not to discount the defiance with which Cavendish treated normative writing practices at every level, and the way in which she assimilated that contempt to a gendered and elitist critique of the modish or commonplace.

In the preface to the second book of *The World's Olio* (1655), Cavendish argues specifically for the transgressive potential of grammatical singularity, drawing an implicit comparison between a figure of woman and the equally specularized body of her texts:

> as for the grammar part, I confess I am no scholar, and therefore understand it not, but that little I have heard of it, is enough for me to renounce it....those that are nobly bred have no rules but honour, and honesty, and learn in the school of wisdom to understand sense, and to express themselves sensibly and freely, with a graceful negligence, not to be hidebound with nice and strict words, and set phrases, as if the wit were created in the inkhorn, and not in the brain; besides say some, should one bring up a new way of speaking, then were the former grammar of no effect...everyone may be his own grammarian, if by his natural grammar he can make his hearers understand the

sense; for though there must be rules in a language to make it sociable, yet those rules may be stricter than need to be, and to be too strict makes them too unpleasant and uneasy. But language should be like garments, for though every garment hath a general cut, yet their trimmings may be different, and not go out of the fashion; so wit may place words to its own becoming, delight, and advantage....As for wit, it is wild and fantastical, and therefore must have no set rules; for rules curb, and shackle it, and in that bondage it dies. (*The World's Olio*, 1655, 94)

Clearly, for Cavendish, writing was far from innocent and her 'fantastical' grammar seems integral to that.

CHRONOLOGY

1623 Margaret Lucas born, youngest of eight, St John's nr Colchester, Essex.

1625 Death of Margaret's father, Thomas Lucas, Earl of Colchester.
Accession of Charles I; Charles m. Henrietta Maria.

1637 René Descartes, *Discours sur la Methode*. Ben Jonson dies.

1641 Anna van Schurman's *The Learned Maid* (Leyden; trans. 1659).

1642 Outbreak of Civil War. Theatres closed.
Lucas family move to Royalist base at Oxford.

1643 Margaret becomes Maid of Honour to Henrietta Maria, Oxford.

1644 Henrietta Maria escapes to Paris, Margaret attending.
Battle of Marston Moor: William Cavendish into exile.
John Milton, *Areopagitica*.

1645 Margaret m. William Cavendish, Marquis of Newcastle (b.1593) in Paris.

1646 End of First Civil War.

1647 Margaret's sister Mary Lucas Killigrew and mother, Elizabeth Leighton Lucas, die of natural causes; her brother Sir Charles Lucas executed (with Sir George Lisle) and the family tomb broken open.

1648 Second Civil War. Newcastles move to Antwerp.

1649 *30 January*: Trial and Execution of Charles 1. Commonwealth declared.
14 March: Newcastle banished, estates confiscated.
Gerrard Winstanley, *The True Leveller's Standard*.

1650 Descartes dies. Anne Bradstreet, *The Tenth Muse*.

1651 *November*: Margaret to London with her brother-in-law, Charles Cavendish.

December: Unsuccessful petition to sequestration committee. Thomas Hobbes, *Leviathan*.

1653 Cromwell declared Lord Protector.
Early March: Margaret returns to Antwerp.
Late March: Publishes *Poems and Fancies*.
May: Publishes *Philosophical Fancies*.
Ann Collins, *Divine Songs and Meditations*.

1654 Charles Cavendish dies. Anna Trapnel, *The Cry of a Stone*.

1655 Margaret publishes *The World's Olio* and *Philosophical and Physical Opinions*.

1656 Margaret publishes *Nature's Pictures*. James Harrington, *Oceana*.

1660 Restoration of monarchy and House of Lords.
Newcastles return to England, retire to Welbeck, Nott.
Theatres reopen. Royal Society founded.

1661 Coronation of Charles II. Anne Finch born.

1662 Margaret publishes *Orations of Divers Sorts* and *Plays*.

1663 Revised *Philosophical and Physical Opinions* issued.

1664 Margaret publishes *Sociable Letters* and *Philosophical Letters*.

1665 Newcastle made Duke by Charles II.
Robert Hooke, *Micrographia*. The Great Plague.

1666 *Observations on Experimental Philosophy* with *The Blazing World*.
Margaret Fell, *Womens Speaking Justified*. Great Fire of London.

1667 Margaret publishes *Life of William Cavendish*, visits Royal Society.
Katherine Philips, *Collected Poems* (posth.). Milton, *Paradise Lost*.

1668 Reissues of *Observations* plus *Blazing World*, *Orations of Divers Sorts*, *Grounds of Natural Philosophy*, *Poems or Several Fancies*; first publication, *Plays never Before Printed*.

1670 Behn's first play, *The Forced Marriage* produced.

1671 Reissues of *The World's Olio* and *Nature's Pictures*.

1673 *15 December*: Margaret dies.

1674 7 *January*: Buried in Westminster Abbey. Her sisters, Lady Pye and Anne Lucas chief mourners.

Bathsua Makin, *An Essay to Revive the Ancient Education of Gentlewomen*.

1675 *Life of William Cavendish* reissued. Greenwich Observatory opened.

1676 Newcastle dies, interred beside Margaret.

Letters and Poems in Honour of the incomparable Princess Margaret, Duchess of Newcastle, ed. William Cavendish.

WORKS BY MARGARET CAVENDISH

Poems, and Fancies, 1653. 2nd edn, 1664. 3rd edn, *Poems, or Several Fancies in Verse: with the Animal Parliament, in Prose*, 1668.

Philosophical Fancies, 1653.

The World's Olio, 1655. 2nd edn, 1671.

Philosophical and Physical Opinions, 1655. 2nd edn, 1663. Reissued as *Grounds of Natural Philosophy*, 1668.

Nature's Pictures, 1656 (including 'A True Relation of my Birth, Breeding and Life'). 2nd edn, 1671.

Plays, 1662.

Orations of Divers Sorts, 1662. 2nd edn, 1668.

CCXI Sociable Letters, 1664.

Philosophical Letters, 1664.

Observations upon Experimental Philosophy. To which is added, The Description of a New World Called the Blazing World, 1666. 2nd edn, 1668.

The Life of . . . William Cavendish, 1667. 2nd edn, 1675. Latin translation by Walter Charleton, 1668.

Plays, never before Printed, 1668.

SELECTED MODERN EDITIONS

Bowerbank, Sylvia and Sara Mendelson, eds *Paper Bodies: A Margaret Cavendish Reader*, Calgary: Broadview Press, 1999.

Fitzmaurice, James, ed. *Margaret Cavendish: Sociable Letters*, New York: Garland Publishing, 1997.

James, Susan, ed. *Margaret Cavendish: Political Writings*, Cambridge: Cambridge University Press, 2003.

O'Neill, Eileen, ed. *Margaret Cavendish: Observations upon Experi-*

mental Philosophy, Cambridge: Cambridge University Press, 2001.

Partington, Leigh Tillman, ed. *The Atomic Poems of Margaret (Lucas) Cavendish*, Women Writers Resource Project, Emory University; Website: http://chaucer.library.emory.edu/wrrp/index.html.

Shaver, Anne, ed. *Margaret Cavendish: The Convent of Pleasure and Other Plays*, Baltimore: Johns Hopkins University Press, 1999.

Women Writers Online, the Brown University Women Writers Project, www.wwp.brown.edu.

FURTHER READING

Ballaster, Ros, 'Restoring the Renaissance: Margaret Cavendish and Katherine Philips', in *Renaissance Configurations: Voices, Bodies, Spaces 1580–1690*, ed. Gordon McMullan, London: Palgrave, 2001.

Battigelli, Anna, *Margaret Cavendish and the Exiles of the Mind*, Lexington: Kentucky University Press, 1998.

Boesky, Amy, *Founding Fictions: Utopias in Early Modern England*, Athens: University of Georgia Press, 1996.

Burgess, Irene, 'Recent Studies in Margaret Cavendish, Duchess of Newcastle (1623–1674); William Cavendish, Duke of Newcastle (1593–1676); and Jane Cavendish Cheyne (1622–1669)', *English Literary Rennaissance* 32: 452–73, 2002.

Campbell, Mary Baine, *Wonder and Science: Imagining Worlds in Early Modern Europe*, Ithaca, NY: Cornell University Press, 1999.

Clucas, Stephen, ed. *A Princely Brave Woman: Essays on Margaret Cavendish, Duchess of Newcastle*, London: Ashgate, 2003.

Cottegnies, Line and Nancy Weitz, eds *Authorial Conquests: Essays on Genre in the Writings of Margaret Cavendish*, Fairleigh Dickinson University Press, 2003.

Holmesland, Oddvar, 'Margaret Cavendish's *Blazing World:* Natural Art and the Body Politic', *Studies in Philology* 96: 457–79, 1999.

Ingram, Randall, 'First Words and Second Thoughts: Margaret Cavendish, Humphrey Moseley, and "the Book"', *Journal of Medieval and Early Modern Studies* 30: 101–24, 2000.

Iyengar, Sujata, 'Royalist, Romancer, Racialist: Rank, Race and Gender in the Science and Fiction of Margaret Cavendish, *English Literary History* 69(3): 649–72, 2002.

Kahn, Victoria, 'Margaret Cavendish and the Romance of Contract', *Renaissance Quarterly* 50: 526–66, 1997.

Kegl, Rosemary, '"The World I Have Made": Margaret Cavendish, Feminism and *The Blazing World*', in *Feminist Readings of Early Modern Culture*, eds Valerie Traub, Lindsay M. Kaplan and Dympna Callaghan, Cambridge: Cambridge University Press, 1996.

Keller, Eve, 'Producing Petty Gods: Margaret Cavendish's Critique of Experimental Science', *English Literary History* 64: 447–71, 1997.

Khanna, Lee Cullen, 'The Subject of Utopia; Margaret Cavendish and Her Blazing World', in *Utopian and Science Fiction by Women*, eds Jane L. Donawerth and Carol A. Kolmerten, New York: Syracuse University Press, 1994.

Lawrence, Karen R., *Penelope Voyages: Women and Travel in the British Literary Tradition*, Ithaca, NY: Cornell University Press, 1994.

Leslie, Marina, 'Evading Rape and Embracing Empire in Margaret Cavendish's Assaulted and Pursued Chastity', in *Representing Virginity in the Middle Ages and the Renaissance*, eds Marina Leslie and Kathleen Coyne Kelly, University of Delaware Press, 1999.

Leslie, Marina, *Renaissance Utopias and the Problem of History*, Ithaca, NY: Cornell University Press, 1998.

Masten, Jeffrey, *Textual Intercourse: Collaboration, Authorship and Sexualities in Renaissance Drama*, Cambridge: Cambridge University Press, 1997.

Mendelson, Sara Heller, *The Mental World of Stuart Women: Three Studies*, Brighton: Harvester, 1987.

Pacheco, Anita, ed. *A Companion to Early Modern Women's Writing*, Oxford: Blackwell, 2002.

Rees, Emma, ed. Cavendish Issue, *Women's Writing* 4(3), 1997.

Rogers, John, *The Matter of Revolution: Science, Poetry and Politics in the Age of Milton*, 1996.

Rosenthal, Laura J., *Playwrights and Plagiarists in Early Modern England: Gender, Authorship, Literary Property*, Ithaca, NY: Cornell University Press, 1996.

Schwarz, Kathryn, 'Chastity, Militant and Married: Cavendish's Romance, Milton's Masque', PMLA 118: 270–85, 2003.

Spiller, Elizabeth, 'Reading through Galileo's Telescope: Margaret Cavendish and the Experience of Reading', *Renaissance Quarterly* 53: 192–221, 2000.

Taneja, Gulshan, ed. Cavendish Issue, *In-Between* 9(1–2), 2000.

Whitaker, Katie, *Mad Madge*, New York: Basic Books, 2002.

Wilcox, Helen, ed. *Women and Literature in Britain 1500–1700*, Cambridge: Cambridge University Press, 1996.

Wiseman, Susan, 'Margaret Cavendish among the Prophets: Performance Ideologies and Gender in and after the English Civil War', *Women's Writing* 6: 95–111, 1999.

For James Fitzmaurice's regularly updated online Cavendish bibliography visit http://jan.ucc.nau.edu/~jbf/CavBiblio.html.

THE CONTRACT

A noble gentleman that had been married many years, but his wife being barren, did bear him no children; at last she died, and his friends did advise him to marry again, because his brother's children were dead, and his wife was likely to have no more: so he took to wife a virtuous young Lady, and after one year she conceived with child, and great joy there was of all sides: but in her child-bed she died, leaving only one daughter to her sorrowful husband, who in a short time, oppressed with melancholy, died, and left his young daughter, who was not a year old, to the care and breeding of his brother, and withal left her a great estate, for he was very rich. After the ceremonies of the funeral, his brother carried the child home, which was nursed up very carefully by his wife; and being all that was likely to succeed in their family, the uncle grew extreme fond and tender of his niece, insomuch that she grew all the comfort and delight of his life.

A great Duke which commanded that province, would often come and eat a breakfast with this gentleman as he rid a-hunting; and so often they met after this manner, that there grew a great friendship; for this gentleman was well bred, knowing the world by his travels in his younger days; and though he had served in the wars, and had fought in many battles, yet was not ignorant of courtly entertainment. Besides, he was very conversible, for he had a voluble tongue, and a ready understanding, and in his retired life was a great student, whereby he became an excellent scholar; so that the Duke took great delight in his company. Besides, the Duke had a desire to match the niece of this gentleman, his friend, to his younger son, having only two sons, and knowing this child had a great estate left by her father, and was likely to have her uncle's estate joined thereto, was earnest upon it: but her uncle was unwilling to marry her to a younger brother, although he was of a great family; but with much persuasion, he agreed, and gave his consent, when she was old enough to marry, for she was then not seven years old. But the Duke fell very sick; and when the physicians told him, he could not live, he sent for the gentleman and his niece, to take his last farewell; and when they came, the Duke desired his friend that he would agree to join his niece and his son in marriage; he answered, that he was very willing, if she were of years to consent.

Said the Duke, I desire we may do our parts, which is, to join them as fast as we can; for youth is wild, various, and inconstant; and when I am dead, I know not how my son may dispose of himself when he is left to his own choice; for he privately found his son very unwilling thereto, he being a man grown, and she a child. The gentleman seeing him so desirous, agreed thereto.

Then the Duke called his son privately to him, and told him his intentions were to see him bestowed in marriage before he died.

His son desired him, not to marry him against his affections, in marrying him to a child.

His father told him, she had a great estate, and it was like to be greater, by reason all the revenue was laid up to increase it; and besides, she was likely to be heir to her uncle, who loved her as his own child; and her riches may draw so many suitors when she is a woman, said he, that you may be refused.

He told his father, her riches could not make him happy, if he could not affect her. Whereupon the Duke grew so angry, that he said, that his disobedience would disturb his death, leaving the world with an unsatisfied mind.

Whereupon he seemed to consent, to please his father. Then were they as firmly contracted as the priest could make them, and two or three witnesses to avow it.

But after his father was dead, he being discontented, went to the wars; but in short time he was called from thence, by reason his elder brother died, and so the Dukedom and all the estate came to him, being then the only heir: but he never came near the young Lady, nor so much as sent to her, for he was at that time extremely in love with a great lady, who was young and handsome, being wife to a grandee [who] was very rich, but was very old, whose age made her more facile to young lovers, especially to this young Duke, who returned him equal affections; he being a man that was favoured by nature, fortune, and breeding, for he was very handsome, and of a ready wit, active, valiant, full of generosity, affable, well fashioned; and had he not been sullied with some debaucheries, he had been the completest man in that age.

But the old gentleman, perceiving his neglect towards his niece, and hearing of his affections to that lady, strove by all the care and industry he could to give her such breeding as might win his love; not that he was negligent before she was contracted to him; for from the time of four years old, she was taught all that her age was capable of, as to sing, and to dance; for he would have this artificial motion become as natural, and to grow in perfection, as she grew in years. When she was seven years of age, he chose her such books to read in as might make her wise, not amorous, for he never suffered her to read in romancies, nor such light books; but moral philosophy was the first of her studies, to lay a ground and foundation of virtue, and to teach her to moderate her passions, and to rule her affections. The next, her study was in history, to learn her experience by the second hand, reading the good fortunes and misfortunes of former times, the errors that were committed, the advantages that were lost, the humour and dispositions of men, the laws and customs of nations, their rise, and their fallings, of their wars and agreements, and the like.

The next study was in the best of poets, to delight in their fancies, and to recreate in their wit; and this she did not only read, but repeat what she had read every evening before she went to bed. Besides, he taught her to understand what she read, by explaining that which was hard and obscure. Thus she was always busily employed, for she had little time allowed her for childish recreations.

Thus did he make her breeding his only business and employment; for he lived obscurely and privately, keeping but a little family, and having little or no acquaintance, but lived a kind of a monastical life.

But when the niece was about thirteen years of age, he heard the Duke was married to the Lady with whom he was enamoured; for her husband dying, leaving her a widow, and rich, [she] claimed a promise from him that he made her whilst her husband was living, that when he died, being an old man, and not likely to live long, to marry her, although he was loath; for men that love the pleasures of the world, care not to be encumbered and obstructed with a wife, but [he] did not at all reflect upon his contract; for after his father died, he resolved not to take her to wife; for she being so young, he thought the contract of no validity: but [the lady] seeming more coy when she was a widow, than in her husband's time, seeking thereby to draw him to marry her, and being overcome by several ways of subtlety, [he] married her. Whereupon the uncle was mightily troubled, and was very melancholy; which his niece perceived, and desired [of] him to know the cause.

Whereupon he told her. Is this the only reason, said she? Yes, said he; and doth it not trouble you, said he? No, said she, unless I had been forsaken for some sinful crime I had committed against Heaven, or had infringed the laws of honour, or had broken the rules of modesty, or some misdemeanour against him, or some defect in nature, then I should have lamented, but not for the loss of the man, but for the cause of the loss, for then all the world might have justly defamed me with a dishonourable reproach:[1] but now I can look the world in the face with a confident brow, as innocence can arm it. Besides, it was likely I might have been unhappy in a man that could not affect me; wherefore, good Uncle, be not melancholy, but think that fortune hath befriended me, or that destiny had decreed it so to be; if so, we are to thank the one, and it was impossible to avoid the other; and if the fates spin a long thread of your life, I shall never murmur for that loss, but give thanks to the gods for that blessing.

O, but Child, said he, the Duke was the greatest and richest match, since his brother died, in the kingdom; and I would not have thy virtue, beauty, youth, wealth, and breeding, stoop to a low fortune, when thou mayst be a match fit for the Emperor of the whole world in a few years, if you grow up, and go on as you have begun.

O, Uncle, said she, let not your natural affection make you an impartial judge, to give the sentence of more desert than I can own; if I have virtue, it is a reward sufficient in itself; if I have beauty, it is but one of nature's fading favourers; and those that loved me for it, may hate me when it is gone; and if I be rich, as you say I am like to be, who are happier than those that are mistresses of their own fortunes? And if you have bred me well, I shall be happy in what condition soever I am in, being content, for that is the end and felicity of the mind.

But if thou hadst been in love with him, said her uncle, where had been your content then? for no education can keep out that passion.

I hope, said she, the gods will be more merciful than to suffer such passions I cannot rule. What manner of man is he, said she? for I was too young to remember him.

His person, said he, is handsome enough.

That is his outside, said she; but what is his inside? What is his nature and disposition?

Debauched, said he, and loves his luxuries.

Said she, heavens have blessed me from him.

Well, said her uncle, since I am crossed in thy marriage, I will strive to make thee a meteor of the time, wherefore I will carry thee to the metropolitan city for thy better education; for here thou art bred obscurely, and canst learn little, because thou hearest nor seest little; but you shall not appear to the world this two or three years: but go always veiled, for the sight of thy face will divulge thee; neither will we have acquaintance or commerce with any, but observe, hear, and see so much as we can, not to be known.

Sir, said she, I shall be ruled by your direction, for I know my small bark will swim the better and safer for your steerage;

wherefore I shall not fear to launch it into the deepest or [most] dangerous places of the world, which I suppose are the great and populous cities. So making but small preparations, only what was for mere necessity, they took their journey speedily, carrying no other servants but those that knew and used to obey their master's will; and when they came to the city, they took private lodging; where after they had rested some few days, he carried her every day, once or twice a day, after her exercise of dancing and music was done; for he was careful she should not only keep what she had learned, but learn what she knew not: but after those hours, he carried her to lectures, according as he heard where any were read, as lectures of natural philosophy, for this she had studied least: but taking much delight therein, she had various speculations thereof; also lectures of physic, and lectures of chemistry, and lectures of music, and so divers others, on such days as they were read. Also, he carried her to places of judicature to hear great causes decided; and to the several courts, to hear the several pleadings, or rather wranglings of several lawyers: but never to courts, masques, plays, nor balls; and she always went to these places masked, muffled, and scarfed; and her uncle would make such means to get a private corner to sit in, where they might hear well; and when he came home, he would instruct her of all that was read, and tell her where they differed from the old authors; and then would give his opinion, and take her opinion of their several doctrines; and thus they continued for two years.

In the meantime, her beauty increased according to her breeding, but was not made known to any as yet: but now being come to the age of sixteen years, her uncle did resolve to present her to the world, for he knew, youth was admired in itself; but when beauty and virtue were joined to it, it was the greater miracle. So he began to examine her; for he was jealous she might be catched with vain gallants, although he had observed her humour to be serious, and not apt to be catched with every toy; yet he knew youth to be so various, that there was no trusting it to itself.

So he asked her, how was she taken with the riches and

gallantry of the city, for she could not choose but see lords and ladies riding in their brave gilt coaches, and themselves dressed in rich apparel, and the young gallants riding on prancing horses upon embroidered footcloths as she passed along the streets.

She answered, they pleased her eyes for a time, and that their dressings were like bridal houses, garnished and hung by some ingenious wit, and their beauties were like fine flowers drawn by the pencil of nature; but being not gathered by acquaintance, said she, I know not whether they are virtuously sweet, or no; but as I pass by, I please my eye, yet no other ways than as senseless objects; they entice me not to stay, and a short view satisfies the appetite of the senses, unless the rational and understanding part should be absent; but to me they seem but moving statues.

Well, said he, I hear there is to be a masque at court, and I am resolved you shall go, if we can get in, to see it; for though I am old, and not fit to go, since my dancing days are done, yet I must get into some corner to see how you behave yourself.

Pray, said she, what is a masque?

Said he, it is painted scenes to represent the poet's heavens and hells, their gods and devils, and clouds, sun, moon, and stars; besides, they represent cities, castles, seas, fishes, rocks, mountains, beasts, birds, and what pleaseth the poet, painter, and surveyor. Then there are actors, and speeches spoke, and music; and then lords or ladies come down in a scene, as from the clouds; and after that, they begin to dance, and everyone takes out according as they fancy. If a man takes out a woman, if she cannot dance, or will not dance, then she makes a curchy[2] to the King, or Queen, or chief grandee, if there be anyone, if not, to the upper end of the room, then turn to the man, and make another to him; then he leaves, or leads her to them she will take out; and she doth the like to him, and then goeth to her place again. And so the men do the same, if they will not dance; and if they do dance, they do just so[.] When the dance is ended, and all the chief of the youth of the city come to see it, or to show themselves, or all those that have youthful minds, and love sights, and fine clothes; then the room is made as light with candles, as if the sun shined, and their glittering bravery makes as glorious a show as his gilded beams.

Sir, said she, if there be such an assembly of nobles, beauty, and bravery, I shall appear so dull, that I shall be only fit to sit in the corner with you; besides, I shall be so out of countenance, that I shall not know how to behave myself; for private breeding looks mean and ridiculous, I suppose, in public assemblies of that nature, where none but the glories of the kingdom meet.

Ashamed, said he, for what? You have stolen nobody's goods, nor good names, nor have you committed adultery, for on my conscience you guess not what adultery is; nor have you murdered any, nor have you betrayed any trust, or concealed a treason; and then why should you be ashamed?

Sir, said she, although I have committed none of those horrid sins, yet I may commit errors through my ignorance, and so I may be taken notice of only for my follies.

Come, come, said he, all the errors you may commit, although I hope you will commit none, will be laid upon your youth; but arm yourself with confidence, for go you shall, and I will have you have some fine clothes, and send for dressers to put you in the best fashion.

Sir, said she, I have observed how ladies are dressed when I pass the streets; and if you please to give me leave, I will dress myself according to my judgement; and if you intend I shall go more than once, let me not be extraordinary brave, lest liking me at first, and seeing me again, they should condemn their former judgement, and I shall lose what was gained, so shall I be like those that made a good assault, and a bad retreat.

But Sir, said she, if you are pleased I shall show myself to the most view, let me be ordered so, that I may gain more and more upon their good opinions.

Well, said her uncle, order yourself as you please, for I am unskilled in that matter; besides, thou needst no adornments, for nature hath adorned thee with a splendrous beauty. Another thing is, said he, we must remove our lodgings, for these are too mean to be known in; wherefore my steward shall go take a large house, and furnish it nobly, and I will make you a fine coach, and take more servants, and women to wait upon you; for since you have a good estate, you shall live and take pleasure; but I will have no men visitors but what are brought by myself: wherefore entertain no masculine acquaintance, nor give them the least encouragement.

Sir, said she, my duty shall observe all your commands.

When her uncle was gone, Lord, said she, what doth my uncle mean to set me out to show? Sure he means to traffic for a husband; but Heaven forbid those intentions, for I have no mind to marry: but my uncle is wise, and kind, and studies for my good, wherefore I submit, and could now chide myself for these questioning thoughts. Now, said she, I am to consider how I shall be dressed; my uncle saith, I am handsome, I will now try whether others think so as well as he, for I fear my uncle is partial on my side; wherefore I will dress me all in black, and have no colours about me; for if I be gay, I may be taken notice of for my clothes, and so be deceived, thinking it was for my person; and I would gladly know the truth, whether I am handsome or no, for I have no skill in physiognomy; so that I must judge of myself by the approbation of others' eyes, and not by my own. But if I be, said she, thought handsome, what then? Why then, answered she herself, I shall be cried up to be a beauty; and what then? Then I shall have all eyes stare upon me; and what am I the better, unless their eyes could infuse in my brain, wit and understanding? Their eyes cannot enrich me with knowledge, nor give me the light of truth; for I cannot see with their eyes, nor hear with their ears, no more than their meat can nourish me which they do eat, or rest when they do sleep. Besides, I neither desire to make nor catch lovers, for I have an enmity against mankind, and hold them as my enemies; which if it be a sin, Heaven forgive, that I should for one man's neglect and perjury, condemn all that sex.

But I find I have a little emulation,[3] which breeds a desire to appear more beautiful than the Duke's wife, who is reported to be very handsome; for I would not have the world say, he had an advantage by the change: thus I do not envy her, nor covet what she enjoys, for I wish her all happiness, yet I would not have her happiness raised by my misfortunes; for charity should begin at home; for those that are unjust, or cruel to themselves, will never be merciful and just to others. But, O my contemplations, whither do you run? I fear, not in an even path; for though emulation is not envy, yet the bias leans to that side.

But, said she, to this masque I must go, my uncle hath pressed me to the wars of vanity, where Cupid is general, and leads up the train: but I doubt I shall hang down my head, through shamefastness,[4] like a young soldier, when he hears the bullets fly about his ears: but, O Confidence, thou god of good behaviour, assist me. Well, said she, I will practice against the day, and be in a ready posture. So after two or three days, was the masque; and when she was ready to go, her uncle comes to her, and sees her dressed all in black.

Said he, why have you put yourself all in black?

Sir, said she, I mourn like a young widow, for I have lost my husband.

Now by my troth, said he, and it becomes thee, for you appear like the sun when he breaks through a dark cloud. Says he, I would have you go veiled, for I would have you appear to sight only when you come into the masquing room; and after the masque is done, all the company will rise as it were together, and join into a crowd: then throw your hood over your face, and pass through them as soon as you can, and as obscure, for I will not have you known until we are in a more courtly equipage. So away they went, only he and she, without any attendance; and when they came to enter through the door to the masquing room, there was such a crowd, and such a noise, the officers beating the people back, the women squeaking, and the men cursing, the officers threatening, and the enterers praying; which confusion made her afraid.

Lord, Uncle, said she, what a horrid noise is here? Pray let us go back, and let us not put ourselves unto this unnecessary trouble.

O Child, said he, camps and courts are never silent; besides, where great persons are, there should be a thundering noise to strike their inferiors with a kind of terror and amazement; for poets say, fear and wonder makes gods.

Certainly, said she, there must be great felicity in the sight of this masque, or else they would never take so much pains, and endure so great affronts to obtain it: but, pray Uncle, said she, stay while they are all passed in.

Why then, said he, we must stay until the masque is done, for there will be striving to get in until such time as those within are coming out.

But when they came near the door, her uncle spoke to the officer thereof; pray Sir, said he, let this young Lady in to see the masque.

There is no room, said he, there are more young ladies already than the Viceroy and all his courtiers can tell what to do with.

This is a dogged fellow, said her uncle; whereupon he told her, she must put up her scarf, and speak [her]self; for everyone domineers in their office, though it doth not last two hours; and are proud of their authority, though it be but to crack a louse; wherefore you must speak.

Pray Sir, said she to the door-keeper, if it be no injury to your authority, you will be so civil as to let us pass by.

Now by my troth, said he, thou hast such a pleasing face, none can deny thee: but now I look upon you better, you shall not go in.

Why Sir? said she.

Why, said he, you will make the painter and the poet lose their design, for one expects to enter in at the ears of the assembly, the other at their eyes, and your beauty will blind the one, and stop the other; besides, said he, all the ladies will curse me.

Heaven forbid, said she, I should be the cause of curses; and to prevent that, I will return back again.

Nay Lady, said he, I have not the power to let you go back, wherefore pray pass.

Sir, said she, I must have this gentleman along with me.

Even who you please, said he, I can deny you nothing, angels must be obeyed.

When they came into the masquing room, the house was full;

now, said her uncle, I leave you to shift for yourself: then he went and crowded himself into a corner at the lower end.

When the company was called to sit down, that the masque might be represented, everyone was placed by their friends, or else they placed themselves. But she, being unaccustomed to those meetings, knew not how to dispose of herself, observing there was much jostling and thrusting one another to get to places[.] When she considered she had not strength to scamble[5] amongst them, she stood still. When they were all set, it was as if a curtain was drawn from before her, and she appeared like a glorious light; whereat all were struck with such amaze, that they forgot a great while the civility in offering her a place. At last, all the men, which at such times sit opposite to the women to view them the better, rose up, striving every one to serve her: but the Viceroy bid them all sit down again, and called for a chair for her. But few looked on the masque for looking on her, especially the Viceroy and the Duke, whose eyes were riveted to her face.

When the masquers were come down to dance, who were all women, the chief of them being the daughter of the Viceroy, who was a widower, and she was his only child, they took out the men such as their fancy pleased, and then they sat down; and then one of the chief of the men chose out a lady, and so began to dance in single couples[.] The Duke being the chief that did dance, chose out this beauty, not knowing who she was, nor she him: but when she danced, it was so becoming; for she having naturally a majestical presence, although her behaviour was easy and free, and a severe countenance, yet modest and pleasing, and great skill in the art, keeping her measures just to the notes of music, moving smoothly, evenly, easily, made her astonish all the company.

The Viceroy sent to enquire who she was, and what she was, and from whence she came, and where she lived, but the enquirer could learn nothing. But as soon as the masque was done, she was sought about for, and enquired after, but she was gone not to be heard of: whereupon many did think she was a vision, or some angel which appeared, and then vanished away;

for she had done as her uncle had commanded her, which was, to convey herself as soon away as she could, covering herself close. So home they went, and her uncle was very much pleased to see the sparks of her beauty had set their tinder hearts on fire. But as they went home, she enquired of her uncle[,] of the company; pray Sir, said she, was the Duke or Duchess there?

I cannot tell, said he, for my eyes were [so] wholly taken up in observing your behaviour, that I never considered nor took notice who was there.

Who was he that first took me out to dance? said she.

I cannot tell that neither, said he, for I only took the length of your measure; and what through a fear you should be out, and dance wrong, and with joy to see you dance well, I never considered whether the man you danced with moved or no, nor what he was: but now I am so confident of you, that the next assembly I will look about, and inform you as much as I can: so home they went. But her beauty had left such stings behind it, especially in the breast[s] of the Viceroy and the Duke, that they could not rest. Neither was she free, for she had received a wound, but knew not of it; her sleeps were unsound, for they indeed were slumbers rather than sleeps; her dreams were many, and various: but her lovers, that could neither slumber nor sleep, began to search, and to make an enquiry; but none could bring tidings where she dwelt, nor who she was. But the Viceroy cast about to attain the sight of her once again; so he made a great ball, and provided a great banquet, to draw an assembly of all young ladies to his court. Whereupon her uncle understanding, told his niece she must prepare to show herself once again; for I will, said he, the next day after this ball, remove to our new house.

Sir, said she, I must have another new gown.

As many as thou wilt, said he, and as rich; besides, I will buy you jewels.

No Sir, said she, pray spare that cost, for they are only to be worn at such times of assemblies which I shall not visit often for fear I tire the courtly spectators, which delight in new faces, as they do new scenes. So her uncle left her to order herself; who dressed herself this time all in white satin, all embroidered with silver.

When her uncle saw her so dressed, now by my troth thou lookest like a Heaven stuck with stars, but thy beauty takes off the gloss of thy bravery; now, said he, you shall not go veiled, for thy beauty shall make thy way; besides, we will not go too soon, nor while they are in disorder, but when they are all placed, you will be the more prospectious.[6]

But the cavaliers, especially the Duke and the Viceroy, began to be melancholy for fear she should not come; their eyes were always placed at the doors like sentinels, to watch her entrance; and when they came to the court, all the crowds of people, as in a fright, started back, as if they were surprised with some divine object, making a lane, in which she passed through; and the keepers of the doors were struck mute, there was no resistance, all was open and free to enter. But when she came in into the presence of the lords and ladies, all the men rose up, and bowed themselves to her, as if they had given her divine worship; [excepting] only the Duke, who trembled so much, occasioned by the passion of love, that he could not stir: but the Viceroy went to her.

Lady, said he, will you give me leave to place you?

Your Highness, said she, will do me too much honour.

So he called for a chair, and placed her next himself; and when she was set, she produced the same effects as a burning glass;[7] for the beams of all eyes were drawn together, as one point placed in her face, and by reflection she sent a burning heat, and fired every heart. But he could not keep her; for as soon as they began to dance, she was taken out, but not by the Duke, for he had not recovered as yet [from] love's shaking fit. But the young gallants chose her so often to dance, for every one took it for a disgrace, as not to have the honour to dance with her, insomuch that few of the other ladies danced at all, as being creatures not worthy to be regarded whilst she was there.

But the Viceroy, for fear they should tire her, and she not daring to deny them, by reason it would be thought an affront, and rude, or want of breeding, made the Viceroy call sooner for the banquet than otherwise he would have done. Besides, he perceived the rest of the ladies begin to be angry, expressing it by their frowns; and knowing nothing will so soon pacify that bitter humour in ladies as sweetmeats, he had them brought in. But when the banquet came in, he presented her the first with some of those sweetmeats, and still filling her ears with compliments, or rather chosen words, for no compliment could pass on her beauty, it was beyond all expressions.

At last, he asked her where her lodging was, and whether she would give him leave to wait upon her.

She answered him, it would be a great grace and favour to receive a visit from him; but, said she, I am not at my own disposing, wherefore I can neither give nor receive without leave.

Pray, said he, may I know who is this happy person you so humbly obey.

Said she, it is my uncle, with whom I live.

Where doth he live? said he.

Truly, said she, I cannot tell the name of the street.

He is not here, Lady? said he.

Yes, said she, and pointed to him. And though he was loath, yet he was forced to leave her so long, as to speak with her uncle: but the whilst he was from her, all the young gallants, which were gathered round about her, presented her with sweetmeats, as offerings to a goddess; and she making them curtsies, as returning them thanks for that she was not able to receive, as being too great a burden; for she was offered more sweetmeats than one of the Viceroy's guard could carry.

But all the while the Duke stood as a statue, only his eyes were fixed upon her, nor had he power to speak; and she perceiving where he was, for her eye had secretly hunted him out, would as often look upon him as her modesty would give her leave, and desired much to know who he was, but was ashamed to ask.

At last, the Duke being a little encouraged by her eye, came to her.

Lady, said he, I am afraid to speak, lest I should seem rude by my harsh discourse; for there is not in the alphabet, words gentle nor smooth enough for your soft ears, but what your tongue doth polish: yet I hope you will do as the rest of the gods and goddesses, descend to mortals, since they cannot reach to you.

Sir, said she, but that I know it is the courtly custom for men to express their civilities to our sex in the highest words, otherwise I should take it as an affront and scorn; to be called by those names I understand not, and to be likened to that which cannot be comprehended.

Said the Duke, you cannot be comprehended; nor do your lovers know what destiny you have decreed them.

But the Viceroy came back with her uncle, who desired to have his niece home, the banquet being ended.

But when the Duke saw her uncle, he then apprehending who she was, was so struck, that what with guilt of conscience, and with repenting sorrow, he was ready to fall down dead.

Her uncle, seeing him talking to her, thus spoke to the Duke.

Sir, said he, you may spare your words, for you cannot justify your unworthy deeds.

Whereat she turned as pale as death, her spirits being gathered to guard the heart, being in distress, as overwhelmed with passion. But the bustle of the crowd helped to obscure her change, as well it did smother her uncle's words, which pierced none but the Duke's ears, and hers.

The Viceroy taking her by the hand, led her to the coach, and all the gallants attended; whereat the ladies, that were left behind in the room, were so angry, shooting forth words like bullets with the fire of anger, wounding every man with reproach: but at the Viceroy they sent out whole volleys, which battered his reputation: but as for the young Lady, they did appoint a place of purpose to dissect her, reading satirical lectures upon every part with the hard terms of dispraises. So all being dispersed, the Viceroy longed for that seasonable hour to visit her.

But the Duke wished there were neither time nor life: I cannot hope, said he, for mercy, my fault is too great, nor can I live or die in quiet without it; but the miseries and torments of despairing lovers will be my punishment.

But the old gentleman was so pleased to see his niece admired, that as he went home, he did nothing but sing after a humming way; and was so frolic, as if he were returned to twenty years of age; and after he came home, he began to examine his niece.

Said he, how do you like the Duke? for that was he who was speaking to you when I came.

She answered, that she saw nothing to be disliked in his person.

And how, said he, do you like the Viceroy?

As well, said she, as I can like a thing that time hath worn out of fashion.

So, said he, I perceive you despise age: but let me tell you, that what beauty and favour Time takes from the body, he gives double proportions of knowledge and understanding to the mind; and you use to preach to me, the outside is not to be regarded; and I hope you will not preach that doctrine to others you will not follow yourself.

Sir, said she, I shall be ruled by your doctrine, and not by my own.

Then, said he, I take my text out of virtue, which is divided into four parts, prudence, fortitude, temperance, and justice. Prudence is to forsee the worst, and provide the best we can for ourselves, by shunning the dangerous ways, and choosing the best; and my application is, that you must shun the dangerous ways of beauty, and choose riches and honour, as the best for yourself.

Fortitude is to arm ourselves against misfortunes, and to strengthen our forts with patience, and to fight with industry. My application of this part is, you must barricade your ears, and not suffer, by listening after the enticing persuasions of rhetoric to enter; for if it once get into the brain, it will easily make a passage to the heart, or blow up the tower of reason with the fire of foolish love.

Temperance is to moderate the appetites, and qualify the

unruly passions. My third application is, you must marry a discreet and sober man, a wise and understanding man, a rich and honourable man, a grave and aged man, and not, led by your appetites, marry a vain fantastical man, a proud conceited man, a wild debauched man, a foolish prodigal, a poor shark, or a young inconstant man.

And fourthly and lastly, is justice, which is to be divided according to right and truth, to reward and punish according to desert, to deal with others as we would be dealt unto.

My last application is, that you should take such counsel, and follow such advice from your friends, as you would honestly give to a faithful friend as the best for him, without any ends to yourself; and so goodnight, for you cannot choose but be very sleepy.

When he was gone, Lord, said she, this doctrine, although it was full of morality, yet in this melancholy humour I am in, it sounds like a funeral sermon to me: I am sure it is a preamble to some design he hath, pray God it is not to marry me to the Viceroy; of all the men I ever saw, I could not affect him, I should more willingly wed death than him, he is an antipathy to my nature; good Jupiter, said she, deliver me from him. So she went to bed, not to sleep, for she could take little rest, for her thoughts worked as fast as a feverish pulse.

But the Viceroy came the next day, and treated with her uncle, desiring her for his wife.

Her uncle told him, it would be a great fortune for his niece, but he could not force her affection; but, said he, you shall have all the assistance, as the power and authority of an uncle, and the persuasions as a friend can give, to get her consent to marry you.

Pray, said the Viceroy, let me see her, and discourse with her.

He desired to excuse him, if he suffered him not to visit her; for, said he, young women that are disposed by their friends, must wed without wooing. But he was very loath to go without a sight of her: yet pacifying himself with the hopes of having her to his wife, presented his service to her, and took his leave.

Then her uncle sat in council with his thoughts how he

should work her affection, and draw her consent to marry this Viceroy, for he found she had no stomach towards him; at last, he thought it best to let her alone for a week, or such a time, that the smooth faces of the young gallants, that she saw at the masque and ball, might be worn out of her mind. In the meantime, she grew melancholy, her countenance was sad, her spirits seemed dejected, her colour faded, for she could eat no meat, nor take no rest; neither could she study nor practise her exercises, as dancing, etc. Her music was laid by: neither could she raise her voice to any note, but walked from one end of the room to the other, with her eyes fixed upon the ground, would sigh and weep, and knew not for what; at last, [she] spoke thus to herself[.] Surely an evil fate hangs over me, for I am so dull, as if I were a piece of earth, without sense; yet I am not sick, I do not find my body distempered, then surely it is in my mind, and what should disturb that: my uncle loves me, and is as fond of me as ever he was; I live in plenty, I have as much pleasure and delight as my mind can desire. O but the Viceroy affrights it, there is the cause; and yet methinks that cannot be, because I do verily believe my uncle will not force me to marry against my affections; besides, the remembrance of him seldom comes into my mind; for my mind is so full of thoughts of the Duke, that there is no other room left for any other; my fancy orders places, and dresses him a thousand several ways: thus have I a thousand several figures of him in my head[.] Heaven grant I be not in love; I dare not ask anyone that hath been in love, what humours that passion hath: but why should I be in love with him? I have seen as handsome men as he, that I would not take the pains to look on twice: but now I call him better to mind, he is the handsomest I ever saw: but what is a handsome body, unless he hath a noble soul? He is perjured and inconstant; alas, it was the fault of his father to force him to swear against his affections. But whilst she was thus reasoning to herself, in came her uncle; he told her, he had provided her with a good husband.

Sir, said she, are you weary of me? Or am I become a burden, you so desire to part with me, in giving me a husband?

Nay, said he, I will never part, for I will end the few remainder of my days with thee.

Said she, you give your power, authority, and commands, with my obedience, away; for if my husband and your commands are contrary, I can obey but one, which must be my husband.

Good reason, said he, and for thy sake I will be commanded to; but in the meantime, I hope you will be ruled by me; and here is a great match propounded to me for you, the like I could not have hoped for, which is the Viceroy, he is rich.

Yet, said she, he may be a fool.

O, he is wise and discreet, said he.

Said she, I have heard he is ill natured, and froward.[8]

Answered her uncle, he is in great power and authority.

He may be, said she, never the honester for that.

He is, said he, in great favour with the King.

Sir, said she, princes and monarchs do not always favour the most deserving, nor do they always advance men for merit, but most commonly otherwise, the unworthiest are advanced highest; besides, bribery, partiality, and flattery, rule princes and states.

Said her uncle, let me advise you not to use rhetoric against yourself, and overthrow a good fortune, in refusing such a husband as shall advance your place above that false Duke's Duchess; and his estate, with yours joined to it, it will be a greater than his, with which you shall be served nobly, attended numerously, live plentifully, adorned richly, have all the delights and pleasures your soul can desire; and he being in years, will dote on you; besides, he having had experience of vain debaucheries, is become staid and sage.

Sir, said she, his age will be the means to bar me of all these braveries, pleasures and delights you propound; for he being old, and I young, he will become so jealous, that I shall be in restraint like a prisoner; nay, he will be jealous of the light, and my own thoughts, and will enclose me in darkness, and disturb the peace of my mind with his discontents; for jealousy, I have heard, is never at quiet with itself, nor to those that live near it.

Come, come, said he, you talk I know not what; I perceive you would marry some young, fantastical, prodigal fellow, who will give you only diseases, and spend your estate, and his own too, amongst his whores, bawds, and sycophants; whilst you sit mourning at home, he will be revelling abroad, and then disturb your rest, coming home at unseasonable times; and if you must suffer, you had better suffer by those that love, than those that care not for you, for jealousy is only an overflow of love; wherefore be ruled, and let not all my pains, care, and cost, and the comfort of my labour, be lost through your disobedience.

Sir, said she, I am bound in gratitude and duty to obey your will, were it to sacrifice my life, or the tranquility of my mind, on the altar of your commands.

In the meantime, the Duke was so discontented and melancholy, that he excluded himself from all company, suffering neither his Duchess, nor any friend to visit him, nor come near him, only one old servant to wait upon him; all former delights, pleasures and recreations were hateful to him, even in the remembrance, as if his soul and body had taken a surfeit thereof. At last, he resolved she should know what torment he suffered for her sake; and since he could not see nor speak to her, he would send her a letter: then he called out for pen, ink, and paper, and wrote after this manner.

Madam,

The wrath of the gods is not only pacified, and pardons the greatest sins that can be committed against them, taking to mercy the contrite heart, but gives blessings for repentant tears; and I hope you will not be more severe than they: let not your justice be too rigid, lest you become cruel. I confess, the sins committed against you were great, and deserve great punishment: but if all your mercies did fly from me, yet if you did but know the torments I suffer, you could not choose but pity me; and my sorrows are of that weight, that they will press out my life, unless your favours take off the heavy burden: but howsoever, pray let your charity give me a line or two of your own writing, though they strangle me with death: then will my soul lie quiet in the grave, because I died by your hand; and when I am dead, let not the worst of my actions live in your memory, but cast them into oblivion, where I wish they may forever remain. The gods protect you.

Sealing the letter, he gave it to his man to carry with all the secrecy he could, bidding him to enquire which of her women was most in her favour, praying her to deliver it to her mistress when she was all alone, and to tell the maid he would be in the street to wait her command. The man found such access as he could wish, the letter being delivered to the Lady; which, when she had read, and found from whom it came, her passions were so mixed, that she knew not whether to joy or grieve; she joyed to live in his thoughts, yet grieved to live without him, having no hopes to make him lawfully hers, nor so much as to see or speak to him, her uncle was so averse against him; and the greatest grief was, to think she must be forced to become another's, when she had rather be his, though forsaken, than by another to be beloved with constancy. Then musing with herself for some time, considering whether it was fit to answer his letter, or no; if my uncle should come to know, said she, I write to him without his leave (which leave I am sure he will never give) I shall utterly lose his affection, and I had rather lose life than lose his love; and if I do not write, I shall seem as if I were of a malicious nature, which will beget an evil construction of my disposition, in that mind I desire to live [in] with a good opinion. And if I believe, as charity and love persuades me, that he speaks truth, I shall endanger his life; and I would be loath to murder him with nice scruples, when I am neither forbade by honour nor modesty, religion nor laws[.] Well, I will adventure, and ask my uncle pardon when I have done; my uncle is not of a tiger's nature, he is gentle and will forgive, and a pardon may be gotten: but life, when once it is gone, will return no more. Then taking pen, ink, and paper, [she] writ to him after this manner.

Sir,

I am obedient, as being once tied to you, until you did cut me off, and throw me away as a worthless piece, only fit to be trodden under the feet of disgrace, and certainly had perished with shame; had not my uncle owned me, I had been left destitute. And though you are pleased to cast some thoughts back upon me, yet it is difficult for me to believe, you, that did once scorn me, should humbly come to sue to me: but I rather fear you do this for sport, angling with the bait of deceit to catch my innocent youth. But I am not the first of my sex, nor I fear shall not be the last, that has been, and will be deceived by men, who glory in their treacherous spoils; and if you beset me with stratagems, kill me outright, and [do] not lead me prisoner, to set out your triumph: but if you have wars with your conscience, or fancy, or both, interrupting the peace of your mind, as your letter expresses, I should willingly return to your side, and be an arbitrator; yet the fates have destined it otherwise. But what unhappy fortune soever befalls me, I wish yours may be good. Heavens keep you.

Here, said she, give the man, that brought me the letter, this. The man returning to his lord so soon, made him believe he had not delivered her that letter.

Well, said the Duke, you have not delivered my letter.

Yet, but I have, said he, and brought you an answer.

Why, said the Duke, it is impossible, you stayed so short a time.

Then, said he, I have wrought a miracle; but, said he, you did lengthen my journey in your conceits, with the foul ways of difficulties.

I hope, said the Duke, thou art so blessed as to make as prosperous a journey, as a quick despatch; leave me awhile, said he while[9] I call you. But when he went to open the letter, time brings not more weakness, said he, than fear doth to me, for my hands shake as if I had the palsy; and my eyes are so dim, that spectacles will hardly enlarge my sight. But when he had read the letter, joy gave him a new life: here, said he, she plainly tells me, she would be mine; she saith, she would return to my side, if the fates had not destined against it, by which she means, her uncle is against me; well, if I can but once get access, I shall be happy forever. So after he had blessed himself in reading the letter many times over, I will, said he, strengthen myself to enable myself to go abroad, for as yet I am but weak; and calling to his man, he bid him get him something to eat.

Did your Grace, said the man, talk of eating?

Yes, answered the Duke, for I am hungry.

By my troth, said the man, I had thought your hands, mouth, appetite and stomach had made a bargain; the one, that it never would desire meat nor drink; the other that it would digest none; the third, that it would receive none; and the fourth, that it would offer none; for on my conscience you have not eat[en] the quantity of a pestle of a lark this week;[10] and you are become so weak, that if a boy should wrestle with you, he would have the better.

You are deceived, said the Duke, I am so strong, and my spirits so active, that I would beat two or three such old fellows as thou art; and to prove it, I will beat thee with one hand.

No pray, said he, I will believe your Grace's report, and leave your active Grace for a time, to fetch you some food.

When his man came in with the meat, he found the Duke a-dancing.

I believe, said he, you carry your body very light, having no heavy burdens of meat in your stomach.

I am so airy, said the Duke, as I will caper over thy head.

By my troth, said he, then I shall let fall your meat out of my hands, for fear of your heels.

Whilst the Duke was at his meat, he talked to his man; why hast thou lived an old bachelor, and never married?

O Sir, said he, wives are too chargeable.

Why, said the Duke, are you so poor?

No Sir, answered he, women are so vain, besides they do not only spend their husband's estates, but makes his estate a bawd to procure Love servants, so as his wealth serves only to buy him a pair of horns.

Pray thee, let me persuade thee to marry, and I will direct thee to whom thou shalt go a-wooing.

Troth Sir, I would venture, if there had been any example to encourage me.

Why, what do you think of my marriage, do not I live happily?

Yes, said he, when your Duchess and you are asunder, but

when you meet, it is like Jupiter and Juno, you make such a thundering noise, as it frights your mortal servants, thinking you will dissolve our world, your family, consuming our hospitality by the fire of your wrath; rolling up the clouds of smoky vapour from boiled beef, as a sheet of parchment[.] When you were a bachelor we lived in the golden age, but now it is the iron age, and Doomsday draws near.

I hope, saith the Duke, thou art a prophet, but when Doomsday is past, you shall live in Paradise.

In my conscience, Sir, said he, fortune hath mismatched you; for surely nature did never intend to join you as man and wife; you are of such different humours.

Well, said the Duke, for all your railing against women, you shall go a-wooing, if not for yourself, yet for me.

Sir, said he, I shall refuse no office, that your Grace employs me in.

Go your ways, said the Duke, to the Lady's maid you gave the letter to, and present her with a hundred pounds, and tell her, if she can help me to the speech of her Lady; you will bring her a hundred pounds more, and if you find her nice, and that she says she dare not, offer her five hundred pounds or more, or so much, until you have out-bribed her cautious fears.

Sir, said the man, if you send her many of these presents, I will woo for myself, as well as for your Grace, wherefore by your Grace's leave, I will spruce up myself before I go, and trim my beard, and wash my face, and who knows but I may speed, for I perceive it is a fortunate year for old men to win young maids' affections, for they say, the Viceroy is to be married to the sweetest young beautifullest lady in the world, and he is very old, and in my opinion, not so handsome as I am: with that the Duke turned pale.

Nay, said the man, your Grace hath no cause to be troubled, for 'tis a lady you have refused, wherefore he hath but your leavings.

With that the Duke up with his hand, and gave him a box on the ear: thou liest, said he, he must not marry her.

Nay, said the man, that is as your Grace can order the

business; but your Grace is a just performer of your word, for you have tried your strength, and hath beaten me with one hand.

The Duke walked about the room, and after he had pacified himself, at last spoke to his man; well, said he, if you be prosperous, and can win the maid to direct me the way to speak to her Lady, I will cure the blow with crowns.

Sir, said he, I will turn my other cheek to box that, if you please.

Go away, said the Duke, and return as soon as you can.

Sir, said he, I will return as soon as my business is done, or else I shall lose both pains and gains; good fortune be my guide, said he, and then I am sure of the world's favour, for they that are prosperous shall never want friends, although he were a coward, a knave, or a fool, the world shall say, nay, think him valiant, honest and wise.

Sir, said he to the Duke, pray flatter Fortune, and offer some prayers to her deity in my behalf, though it be but for your own sake; for he that hath not a feeling interest in the business, can never pray with a strong devotion for a good success, but their prayers will be so sickly and weak, as they can never travel up far, but fall back as it were in a swoon, without sense[.] In the meantime the Viceroy and the uncle had drawn up articles, and had concluded of the match without the young Lady's consent; but the uncle told her afterwards, she must prepare herself to be the Viceroy's bride: and, said he, if you consent not, never come near me more, for I will disclaim all the interest of an uncle, and become your enemy[.] His words were like so many daggers, that were struck to her heart: for her grief was too great for tears: but her maid, who had ventured her Lady's anger, for gold had conveyed the Duke into such a place, as to go into her chamber, when he pleased, and seeing her stand as it were, without life or sense, but as a statue carved in stone, went to her, which object brought her out of a muse, but struck her with such amaze, as she fixed her eyes upon him, as on some wonder, and standing both silent for a time, at last she spake.

Sir, said she, this is not civilly done, to come without my

leave, or my uncle's knowledge: nor honourably done, to come like a thief in the night to surprise me.

Madam, said he, Love, that is in danger to lose what he most adores, will never consider persons, time, place, nor difficulty, but runs to strengthen and secure his side, fights and assaults all that doth oppose him, and I hear you are to be married to the Viceroy: but if you do marry him, I will strive to make you a widow the first hour, cutting your vows asunder: and your husband, instead of his bride, shall embrace death, and his grave shall become his wedding bed, or I will lie there myself shrouded in my winding sheet from the hated sight of seeing or knowing you to be another's: but if knowledge lives in the grave, think not yourself secure when I am dead; for if ghosts as some imagines, they can rise from the earth, mine shall visit you and fright you from delights, and never leave you until you become a subject in death's kingdom; but if you are cruel and take delight to have your bridal health drunk in blood, marry him, where perchance we may be both dead drunk with that warm red liquor.

Sir, answered she, it is an unheard of malice to me, or an impudent and vainglorious pride in you, neither to own me yourself, nor let another, but would have me wander out of my single life, that the world may take notice and say, this is your forsaken maid; and I live to be scorned and become friendless, for my uncle will never own me, which will prove as a proclamation to proclaim me a traitor to gratitude, and natural affection, by committing the treason of disobedience.

Said the Duke, you cannot want an owner whilst I live, for I had, nor have no more power to resign the interest I have in you, than Kings to resign their crown that comes by succession, for the right lies in the crown, not in the man, and though I have played the tyrant, and deserved to be uncrowned, yet none ought to take it off my head, but death, nor have I power to throw it from myself, death only must make way for a successor.

Then said she, I must die, that your Duchess may have right, and a free possession.

Nay, said he, you must claim your own just interest and place yourself.

What is that, said she, go to law for you[?]

Yes, said he.

Where if I be cast, said she, it will be a double shame.

You cannot plead, and be condemned, said he, if Justice hears your cause: and though most of the actions of my life have been irregular, yet they were not so much corrupted or misruled by nature, as for want of good education, and through the ignorance of my youth, which time since hath made me see my errors; and though your beauty is very excellent, and is able to enamour the most dullest sense, yet it is not that alone that disturbs the peace of my mind, but the conscientiousness[11] of my fault, which unless you pardon and restore me to your favour, I shall never be at rest.

I wish there were no greater obstacle, said she, than my pardon to your rest: for I should absolve you soon, and sleep should not be more gentle, and soft on your eyes, than the peace to your mind, if I could give it, but my uncle's dislike may prove as fearful dreams to disturb it: but indeed if his anger were like dreams, it would vanish away, but I doubt it is of too thick a body for a vision.

Says the Duke, we will both kneel to your uncle, and plead at the bar of either ear, I will confess my fault at one ear, whilst you ask pardon for me at the other; and though his heart were steel, your words will dissolve it into compassion, whilst my tears mix the ingredients.

My uncle, said she, hath agreed with the Viceroy: and his word hath sealed that bond, which he never will break.

Says the Duke, I will make the Viceroy to break the bargain himself, and then your uncle is set free: besides, you are mine and not your uncle's; unless you prove my enemy to deny me, and I will plead for my right: Heaven direct you for the best, said she, it is late, goodnight.

You will give me leave, he said, to kiss your hands.

I cannot deny my hand, said she, to him that hath my heart.

The next day the Duke went to the Viceroy's, and desired to have a private hearing, about a business that concerned him; and when he had him alone, he shut the door, and drew his sword; which when the Viceroy saw, he began to call for help.

Call not, nor make a noise, if you do, Hell take me, said the Duke, I'll run you through.

What mean you, said the Viceroy, to give me such a dreadful visit?

I come, said the Duke, to ask you a question, to forbid you an act, and to have you grant me my demand.

Said the Viceroy, that question must be resolvable, the act just, the demands possible.

They are so, said the Duke[.] My question is, whether you resolve to be married to the Lady Deletia[?]

Yes, answered he.

The act forbidden is, you must not marry her.

Why, said the Viceroy?

Because, said he, she is my wife, and I have been married to her almost nine years.

Why, said he, you cannot have two wives?

No, said he, I will have but one, and that shall be she.

And what is your demand?

My demand is, that you will never marry her.

How, says the Viceroy? Put the case you should die, you will then give me leave to marry her?

No, said the Duke, I love her too well, to leave a possibility of her marrying you: I will sooner die, than set my hand to this, said the Viceroy.

If you do not, you shall die a violent death, by Heaven, answered he, and more than that, you shall set your hand never to complain against me to the King[.] Will you do it, or will you not? for I am desperate, said the Duke.

Said the Viceroy, you strike the King in striking me.

No disputing, says he, set your hand presently, or I will kill you.

Do you say, you are desperate?

Yes, answered he.

Then I must do a desperate act to set my hand to a bond I mean to break.

Use your own discretion, to that[.]

Come, said he, I will set my hand before I read it; for whatsoever it is, it must be done; after he set his hand he read[:]

Here I do vow to Heaven, never to woo the Lady Deletia, nor to take her to wife, whereunto I set my hand. To this paper too, said the Duke.

Here I do vow to Heaven, never to take revenge, nor to complain of the Duke to my King and master, whereunto I set my hand.

Saith the Duke, I take my leave, rest you in peace, Sir.

And the Devil torment you, said the Viceroy! O Fortune, I could curse thee with thy companions, the Fates, not only in cutting off my happiness, in the enjoying of so rare a beauty, but in stopping the passage to a sweet revenge: and though I were sure, there were both gods and devils, yet I would break my vow, for the one is pacified by prayers, and praises, and the other terrified with threats; but, O the disgrace from our fellow creatures, mankind, sits closer to the life, than the skin to the flesh. For if the skin be flayed off, a new one will grow again, making the body appear younger than before; but if a man be flayed once of his reputation, he shall never regain it, and his life will be always bare and raw, and malice and envy will torment it, with the stings of ill tongues; which to avoid, I must close with the Duke in a seeming friendship, and not defy him as an open enemy, lest he should divulge my base acts done by my cowardly fear[.] But they are fools that would not venture their reputations, to save their life, rather than to die an honourable death, as they call it; which is to die, to gain a good opinion, and what shall they gain by it? A few praises, as to say, he was a valiant man; and what doth the valiant get, is he ever the better? No, he is tumbled into the grave, and his body rots, and turns to dust[.] All the clear distinguishing senses, the bright flaming appetites are quenched out; but if they were not, there is no fuel in the grave to feed their fire; for death is cold, and the grave barren; besides, there is no remembrance in the grave, all is forgotten, they cannot rejoice at their past gallant actions, or remember their glorious triumphs, but the only happiness is, that though there is no pleasure in the grave, so there is no pain; but to give up life before nature requires it, is to pay a subsidy before we are taxed, or to yield up our liberties before we are prisoners. And who are wise that shall do so[?] No, let fools run headlong to death; I will live as long as I can, and not only live, but live easily, freely, and as pleasant as I can; wherefore to avoid this man's mischief, which lies to entrap my life, I will agree with him; and I had rather lose the pleasures of one woman, than all other pleasures with my life; but to do him a secret mischief he shall not escape, if I can prevail; but I perceive this Duke, since he can have but one wife, intends to set up a seraglio[12] of young wenches, and by my troth, he begins with a fair one, and whilst he courts his mistress, I mean to woo his wife, for he hath not sworn me from that. So that my revenge shall be to make him a cuckold, so the Viceroy went to the Duchess; and after he had made his complimental addresses, they began to talk more serious[ly].

Madam, said he, how do you like the rare beauty which your husband doth admire so much, that he is jealous of all that look on her, and would extinguish the sight of all men's eyes but his own, and challenges all that make love to her, threatens ruin and murder to those that pretend to marry her.

Answered she, if he be so enamoured, I shall not wonder that my beauty is thought dead, my embraces cold, my discourse dull, my company troublesome to him, since his delight is abroad: but, said she, I am well served, I was weary of my old husband, and wished him dead, that I might marry a young one; I abhorred his old age, that was wise and experienced; despised his grey hairs, that should be reverenced with respect[.] O the happiness I rejected that I might have enjoyed! For he admired my beauty, praised my wit, gave me my will, observed my humour, sought me pleasures, took care of my health, desired my love, [was] proud of my favours, my mirth was his music, my smiles were his Heaven, my frowns were his Hell; when this man thinks me a chain that enslaves him, a shipwreck wherein all his happiness is drowned, a famine to his hopes, a plague to his desires, a Hell to his designs, a devil to damn his fruitions.

Nay certainly, said he, that woman is the happiest that marries an ancient man; for he adores her virtue more than her beauty, and his love continues; though her beauty is gone[,] he sets a price of worth upon the honour and reputation of his wife, uses her civilly, and gives her respect, as gallant men ought to do to a tender sex, which makes others to do the like; when a young man thinks it a gallantry, and a manly action, to use his wife rudely, and worse than his lackey, to command imperiously, to neglect despisingly, making her the drudge in his family, flinging words of disgrace upon her, making her with scorn the mirth and pastime in his idle and foolish discourse amongst his vain and base companions; when an ancient man makes his wife the queen of his family, his mistress in his courtship, his goddess in his discourse, giving her praise, applauding her actions, magnifying her nature; her safety is the god of his courage, her honour the world to his ambition, her pleasure his only industry, her maintenance the mark for his prudence, her delights are the compass by which he sails, her love is his voyage, her advice his oracle; and doing this, he doth honour to himself, by setting a considerable value upon what is his own; when youth regards not the temper of her disposition, slights her noble nature, grows weary of her person, condemns her counsels, and is afraid his neighbours should think his wife wiser than himself, which is the mark of a fool, and a disease most men have (being married young). But a man in years is solid in his counsels, sober in his actions, graceful in his behaviour, wise in his discourse, temperate in his life, and seems as nature hath made him, masculine. When a young man is rash in his counsels, desperate in his actions, wild in his behaviour, vain in his discourses, debauched in his life, and appears not like his sex, but effeminate.

A fair forehead, and a smooth skin, a rosy cheek, and a ruby lip, wanton eyes, a flattering tongue are unmanly, appearing like women or boys, let them never be so valiant; and that appears, as if they would sooner suffer the whip, than handle the sword.

Where an ancient man, every wrinkle is a trench made by time, wherein lies experience to secure the life from errors; and their eyes are like active soldiers, who bow and sink down by the over-heavy burdens of their spoils, which are several objects that the sight carries into the brain, and delivers to the understanding, as trophies, to hang up in the magazine of the memory. His white hairs are the flags of peace, that time hangs out on the walls of wisdom, that advice and counsel may come from and to safely. Nay, the very infirmities of age seem manly; his feeble legs look as if they had been over-tired with long marches, in seeking out his foes; and his palsy hands, or head, the one seems as if they had been so often used in beating of their enemies, and the other in watching them, as they knew not what rest meant.

Sir, said the Duchess, you commend aged husbands, and dispraise young ones, with such rhetoric, as I wish the one, and hate the other; and in pursuit of my hate, I will cross my husband's amours as much as I can.

In the meantime, the Duke was gone to the old gentleman, the young Lady's uncle.

Which when the old man saw him enter, he started, as if he had seen an evil he desired to shun.

Sir, said he, what unlucky occasion brought you into my house?

First, repentance, answered the Duke, and then love; and lastly, my respect which I owe as a duty. My repentance begs a forgiveness, my love offers you my advice and good counsel, my respect forewarns you of dangers and troubles that may come by the marriage of your niece to the Viceroy.

Why? What danger, said he, can come in marrying my niece to a wise, honourable, rich, and powerful man, and a man that loves and admires her, that honours and respects me?

But, said the Duke, put the case he be a covetous, jealous, froward, ill natured, and base cowardly man, shall she be happy with him?

But he is not so, said he.

But, answered the Duke, if I can prove him so, will you marry her to him?

Pray, said he, spare your proofs of him, since you cannot prove yourself an honest man.

Sir, said the Duke, love makes me endure a reproach patiently, when it concerns the beloved: but though it endures a reproach, it cannot endure a rival.

Why, said the old gentleman, I hope you do not challenge an interest in my niece.

Yes, said the Duke, but I do, and will maintain that interest with the power of my life, and never will quit it till death; and if my ghost could fight for her, it should.

Heaven bless my niece, said the old gentleman: what is your design against her? Is it not enough to fling a disgrace of neglect on her, but you must ruin all her good fortunes? Is your malice so inveterate against my family, that you strive to pull it up by the roots, to cast it into the ditch of oblivion, or to fling it on the dunghill of scorn?

Said the Duke, my design is to make her happy, if I can, to oppose all those that hinder her felicity, disturbing the content and peace of her mind, for she cannot love this man; besides, he disclaims her, and vows never to marry her.

Sir, said the gentleman, I desire you to depart from my house, for you are a plague to me, and bring an evil infection.

Sir, said the Duke, I will not go out of your house, nor depart from you, until you have granted my request.

Why, said the gentleman, you will not threaten me?

No, said the Duke, I do petition you.

Said the gentleman, if you have any quarrel to me, I shall answer it with my sword in my hand; for though I have lost some strength with my years, yet I have not lost my courage; and when my limbs can fight no longer, the heat of my spirits shall consume you; besides, an honourable death I far prefer before a baffled life.

Sir, said he, I come not to move your anger, but your pity, for the sorrows I am in, for the injuries I have done you; and if you will be pleased to take me into your favour, and assist me, by giving my wife, your niece, leave to claim the laws of marriage and right to me, all my life shall be studious to return gratitude, duty, and service.

Yes, answered he, to divulge her disgrace, declaring your

neglect in an open court, and to make myself a knave to break my promise.

Sir, said the Duke, your disgrace by me is not so much as you apprehend; but it will be a great disgrace when it is known the Viceroy refuses her, as I can show you his hand to it; and if he deserts your niece, you are absolved of your promise made to him; and to let you know this is a truth, I say here is his hand.

The whilst the old gentleman was reading the papers, the Viceroy comes in.

O Sir, said he, you are timely come; is this your hand, says he?

Yes, answered the Viceroy.

And do you think it is honourably done, said the gentleman?

Why, said the Viceroy, would you have me marry another man's wife[?]

Well, said the old gentleman, when your Viceroyship is out, as it is almost, I will give you my answer; till then, fare you well.

But the Duke went to the young Lady, and told her the progress he had had with her uncle, and his anger to the Viceroy.

But after the old gentleman's passion was abated towards the Duke, by his humble submission, and the passion inflamed towards the Viceroy, he hearkened to the lawsuit, being most persuaded by his niece's affection, which he perceived was unalterably placed upon the Duke. And at last, advising all three together, they though it fit, since the parties must plead their own cause, to conceal their agreements, and to cover it by the Duke's seeming dissent, lest he should be convicted as a breaker of the known laws, and so be liable to punishment, either by the hazard of his own life, or the price of a great fine.

But after friends were made of all sides, the lawsuit was declared, which was a business of discourse to all the kingdom, and the place of judicature a meeting for all curious, inquisitive, and busiless people.

When the day of hearing was come, there was a bar set out, where the Duke and the two ladies stood; and after all the judges were set, the young Lady thus spake.

Grave Fathers, and most equal Judges,

I come here to plead for right, undecked with eloquence, but truth needs no rhetoric, so that my cause will justify itself: but if my cause were foul, it were not pencilled words could make it seem so fair, as to delude your understanding eye.

Besides, your Justice is so wise, as to fortify her forts with fortitude, to fill her magazine with temperance, to victual it with patience, to set sentinels of prudence, that falsehood might not surprise it, nor bribery corrupt it, nor fear starve it, nor pity undermine it, nor partiality blow it up; so that all right causes here are safe and secured from the enemies of injury and wrong. Wherefore, most reverend Fathers, if you will but hear my cause, you cannot but grant my suit.

Whereupon the judges bid her declare her cause.

Then thus it is.

I was married to this Prince; 'tis true, I was but young in years when I did knit that wedlock knot; and though a child, yet since my vows were holy, which I made by virtue and religion, I am bound to seal that sacred bond with constancy, now I am come to years of knowing of good from evil.

I am not only bound, most pious Judges, to keep my vow, in being chastely his, as long as he shall live, but to require him by the law, as a right of inheritance belonging to me, and only me, so long as I shall live, without a sharer or co-partner: so that this lady, which lays a claim, and challenges him as being her's, can have no right to him, and therefore no law can plead for her; for should you cast aside your canon law,[13] *most pious Judges, and judge it by the common law,*[14] *my suit must needs be granted, if Justice deals out right, and gives to truth her own; for should an heir, young, before he comes to years, run on the lender's score, though the lender had no law to plead against nonage,*[15] *yet if his nature be so just to seal the bonds he made in nonage, when he comes to full years, he makes his former act good, and fixes the law to a just grant, giving no room for cozenage*[16] *to play a part, nor falsehood to appear. The like is my cause, most grave Fathers, for my friends chose me a husband, made a bond of matrimony, sealed it with the ceremony of the church, only they wanted my years of consent, which I, by an approvement, now set as my handwriting.*

Say the judges, what says the Duke? Then the Duke thus spake.

I confess, I was contracted to this lady by all the sacred and most binding ceremonies of the church, but not with a free consent of mind; but being forced by duty to my father, who did not only command, but threatened me with his curse, he being then upon his deathbed, and I being afraid of a dying father's curses, yielded to those actions which my affections and free will renounced; and after my father was dead, placing my affections upon another lady, married her, thinking myself not liable to the former contract, by reason the former contract was but of six years of age, whose nonage I thought was a warrantable cancel from the engagement.

Most upright Judges,

My nonage of years is not a sufficient bail to set him free, he being then of full age; nor can his fear of offending his parents, or his loving duty towards them, be a casting plea against me; his duty will not discharge his perjury, nor his fear could be no warrant to do a wrong; and if a fool by promise binds his life to inconveniencies, the laws that wise men made, must force him to keep it. And if a knave, by private and self-ends, doth make a promise, just laws must make him keep it.

And if a coward make a promise through distracted fear, laws that carry more terrors, than the broken promise, profit, will make him keep it.

But a wise, just, generous spirit will make no promise, but what he can, and durst, and will perform.

But say a promise should pass through an ignorant zeal, and seeming good, yet a right honourable and noble mind will stick so fast to its engagement, that nothing shall hew them asunder; for a promise must neither be broken upon suspicion, nor false construction, nor enticing persuasions, nor threatening ruins, but it must be maintained with life, and kept by death, unless the promise[s] carry more malignity in the keeping them, than the breaking of them.

I say not this to condemn the Duke, though I cannot applaud his secondary action concerning marriage; I know he is too noble to cancel that bond his conscience sealed before high Heaven, where angels stood as witnesses; nor can he make another contract until he is free from me; so that his vows to this lady were rather complemental, and love's feignings, than really true, or so authentical to last; he built affections on a wrong foundation, or rather castles in the air, as lovers use to do, which vanish soon away; for where right is not, truth cannot be; wherefore she can claim no lawful marriage, unless he were a free man, not bound before; and he cannot be free, unless he hath my consent, which I will never give.

Then the other lady spake.

Noble Judges,

This crafty, flattering, dissembling child lays a claim to my husband, who no way deserves him, she being of a low birth, and of too mean a breeding to be his wife; neither hath she any right to him in the law, she being too young to make a free choice, and to give a free consent. Besides, he doth disavow the act, by confessing the disagreeing thereto in his mind; and if she was to give a lawful consent, and his consent was seeming, not real, as being forced thereunto, it could not be a firm contract; wherefore, I beseech you, cast her suit from the bar, since it is of no validity.

Just Judges, answered she,

What though he secretly disliked of that act he made? Yet humane justice sentences not the thoughts, but acts; wherefore those words that plead his thoughts, ought to be waived as useless, and from the bar of justice cast aside.

And now, most upright Judges, I must entreat your favour and your leave to answer this lady, whose passions have flung disgraces on me, which I, without the breach of incivility, may throw them off with scorn, if you allow me so to do.

Said the Judges, we shall not countenance any disgrace, unless we knew it were a punishment for crimes; wherefore speak freely.

Why then, to answer to this lady, that I am meanly born. 'Tis true, I came not from nobility, but I can draw a line of pedigree five hundred years in length from the root of merit, from whence gentility doth spring. This honour cannot be degraded by the displeasure of princes, it holds not the fee-simple from the crown,[17] *for time is the patron of gentility, and the older it groweth, the more beautiful it appears; and having such a father and mother as merit and time, gentry is a fit and equal match for any, were they the rulers of the whole world.*

And whereas she says, most patient Judges, I am a false dissembling child[:] I answer, as to my childhood, it is true, I am young, and inexperienced, a child in understanding, as in years; but to be young, I hope it is no crime: but if it be, 'twas made by nature, not by me. And for dissembling, I have not had time enough to practice much deceit; my youth will witness for me, it is an art, not an inbred nature, and must be studied with pains, and watched with observation, before any can be master thereof. And I hope this assembly is so just, as not to impute my innocent simplicity to a subtle, crafty, or a deceiving glass, to show the mind's false face, making that fair, which in itself is foul. And whereas she says, I have been meanly bred, 'tis true, honoured Judges, I have been humbly bred, taught to obey superiors, and to reverence old age; to receive reproofs with thanks, to listen to wise instructions, to learn honest principles, to housewife time, making use of every minute; to be thrifty of my words, to be careful of my actions, to be modest in my behaviour, to be chaste in my thoughts, to be pious in my devotions, to be charitable to the distressed, to be courteous to inferiors, to be civil to strangers; for the truth is, I was not bred with splendrous vanities, nor learnt the pomp and pride of courts; I am ignorant of their factions, envies, and back-bitings, I know not the sound of their flattering tongues, I am unacquainted with their smiling faces, I have not wit to perceive their false hearts, my judgement is too young and too weak to fathom their deep and dangerous designs.

Neither have I lived so long in populous cities, as to share of the luxuriousness therein; I never have frequented their private nor public meetings, nor turned the day into night by disorders; I can play at none of their games, nor can I tread their measures: but I was bred a private country life, where the crowing of the cocks served as waights of the town;[18] *and the bleating of the sheep, and lowing of the cows, are the minstrels we dance after; and the singing of the birds are the harmonious notes by which we set our innocent thoughts, playing upon the heart-strings of content, where Nature there presents us a masque with various scenes, of several seasons of the year.*

But neither low birth, nor mean breeding, nor bad qualities, nay, were I as wicked as I am young, yet it will not take away the truth of my cause, nor the justness of my plea; wherefore I desire you to give my suit a patient trial, and not to cast me from the bar, as she desires; for I hope you will not cast out my suit by an unjust partiality, nor mistake the right measure, and so cut the truth of my cause too short: but I beseech you to give it length by your serious considerations, and make it fit by your just favour; for though truth itself goeth naked, yet her servants must be clothed with right, and dressed by propriety, or they will die with the cold of usurpation, and then be flung into the ditch of sorrow, there eaten up with the ravens of scorn, having no burial of respect, nor tomb of tranquility, nor pyramids of felicity, which by your justice may raise them as high as Heaven, when your injustice may cast them as low as Hell. Thus you become to truth, gods or devils.

Madam, said the judges to the young Lady, the justice of your cause judges itself; for the severest judge, or strictest rules in law, would admit of no debate.

And truly, Madam, it is happy for us that sit upon the bench, that your cause is so clear and good, otherwise your beauty and your wit might have proved bribes to our vote: but yet there will be a fine on the Duke for the breach of the laws.

With that the Duke spake.

Most careful, learned, and just Judges, and Fathers of the Commonwealth.

I confess my fault, and yield myself a prisoner to Justice, to whom she may either use punishment or mercy: but had I known the laws of custom, religion or honour then, as well as I do now, I had not run so fast, nor plunged myself so deep in foul erroneous ways: but wild youth, surrounded with ease, and fed with plenty, born up with freedom, and led by self-will, sought pleasure more than virtue: but experience hath learned me stricter rules, and nobler principles, insomuch as the reflection of my former actions, clouds all my future happiness, wounds my conscience, and torments my life: but I shall submit to what your wise judgements shall think fit.

My Lord, answered the judges, your Grace being a great peer of the realm, we are not to condemn you to any fine, it must be the King, only we judge the Lady to be your lawful wife, and forbid you the company of the other.

Said the Duke, *I shall willingly submit.*

With that, the young Lady spake. *Heaven*, said she, *send you just rewards for your upright actions: but I desire this assembly to excuse the faults of the Duke in this, since he was forced by Tyrant Love to run in uncouth ways, and do not wound him with sharp censures.*

For where is he, or she, though ne'er so cold,
But sometimes Love doth take, and fast in Fetters hold.

The Viceroy being by, said to the other lady; Madam, said he, since the law hath given away your husband, I will supply his place, if you think me so worthy, with whom perchance you may be more happy than you were with him.

I accept of your love, said she, and make no question but fortune hath favoured me in the change.

With that, the court rose, and much rejoicings there were of all sides.

Assaulted and Pursued Chastity

ASSAULTED AND PURSUED CHASTITY

In this following tale or discourse, my endeavour was to show young women the danger of travelling without their parents, husbands or particular friends to guard them; for though virtue is a good guard: yet it doth not always protect their persons, without human assistance: for though virtue guards, yet youth and beauty betrays, and the treachery of the one, is more than the safety of the other: for ofttimes young beautiful and virtuous women, if they wander alone, find but rude entertainment from the masculine sex: as witness Jacob's daughter Dinah, which Shechem forced.[1] And others, whose enforcement mentioned in holy Scripture, and in histories of less authority (sans number) which shows, that Heaven doth not always protect the persons of virtuous souls from rude violences: neither doth it always leave virtue destitute, but sometimes lends a human help, yet so as never, but where necessity was the cause of their dangers, and not ignorance, indiscretion, or curiosity: for Heaven never helps but those that could not avoid the danger: besides, if they do avoid the dangers, they seldom avoid a scandal. For the world in many causes judges according to what may be, and not according to what is, for they judge not according to truth, but show; no not the heart, but the countenance, which is the cause that many a chaste woman hath a spotted reputation: but to conclude, I say, those are in particular favoured with Heaven, that are protected from violence and scandal, in a wandering life, or a travelling condition.

Assaulted and Pursued Chastity

In the Kingdom of Riches, after a long and sleepy peace, overgrown with plenty and ease[,] luxury broke out into factious sores, and feverish ambition, into a plaguey rebellion; killing numbers with the sword of unjust war, which made many fly from that pestilent destruction into other countries, and those that stayed, sent their daughters and wives, from the fury of the inhumane multitude, choosing to venture their lives with the hazards of travels, rather than their honours and chastities, by staying at home, amongst rough and rude soldiers; but in ten years wars, the ignorant vulgar, in the schools of experience, being often whipped [with] misery, had learnt the lesson of obedience, and peace that laid all the time in a swound, revived to life, and love, as the vital spirits thereof, restored to their orderly motions, and zeal, the fire of the public heart, flamed anew, concocting the undigested multitudes to a pure good government[.] And all those that fear, or care had banished, were invited and called home, by their natural affections to their country; a Lady amongst the rest enriched by nature with virtue, wit and beauty: in her returning voyage, [she] felt the spite of fortune, being cast by a storm, from the place she steered to, upon the Kingdom of Sensuality, a place and people strange unto her; no sooner landed, but treachery beset her; those she entrusted left her: and her years being but few, had not gathered enough experience, to give her the best direction[.] Thus knowing not how to dispose of herself, wanting means for support: calling her young and tender thoughts to council, at last they did agree, she should seek a service, and going to the chief city, which was not far from the haven town[,] a skipper whom she had entreated to go along with her[,] left her in a poor and mean house, to chance, time and fortune; where her hostess seeing her handsome, was tempted by her poverty and covetousness, to consider her own profit more than her guest's safety, selling her to a bawd, which used to merchandise, and trafficked to the land of youth, for the riches of beauty. This old bawd, having commerce with most nations, could speak many languages; and this Lady's amongst the rest, [so] that what with her languages and her flattering words, she enticed this young Lady to live with her, and this old bawd (her supposed virtuous mistress) used her kindly, fed her daintily, clothed her finely; insomuch as she began to think she was become the darling of fortune, yet [the bawd] keeps her closely from the view of any, until her best customers came to the town, who were at that time in the country.

[In] the meantime her mistress began to read her lectures of Nature, telling her she should use her beauty whilst she had it, and not to waste her youth idly, but to make the best profit of both, to purchase pleasure and delight; besides, said she, Nature hath made nothing vainly, but to some useful end; and nothing merely for itself, but for a common benefit and general good, as earth, water, air and fire, sun, moon, stars, light, heat, cold and the like. So beauty with strength and appetites, either to delight her creatures that are in being; or to the end, or ways to procure more by procreation; for Nature only lives by survivors, and that cannot be without communication and society. Wherefore it is a sin against Nature to be reserved and coy, and take heed, said she, of offending Nature, for she is a great and powerful goddess, transforming all things out of one shape into another, and those that serve her faithfully and according as she commands, she puts them in an easy and delightful form; but those that displease her, she makes them to be a trouble, and torment to themselves; wherefore serve Nature, for she is the only and true goddess[,] and not those that men call upon, as Jupiter, Juno, and a hundred more, that living men vainly offer unto; being only men and women which were deified for invention, and heroic actions: for these dead, though not forgotten gods, and goddesses, as they are called through a superstitious fear, and an idolatrous love to ceremony, and an ignorant zeal to antiquity, men fruitless pray unto; but Nature is the only true goddess and no other, wherefore follow her directions, and you shall never do amiss, for we that are old, said she, are Nature's priests, and being long acquainted with her laws and customs, do teach youth the best manner of ways to serve her in.

The young Lady being of a quick apprehension began to suspect some design and treachery against her; and though her doubts begot great fears[,] yet her confidence of the gods' protection of her virtue gave her courage, and dissembling her discovery as well as she could for the present, gave her thanks for her counsel. But when she was gone, considering in what a dangerous condition she stood in; and that the gods would not hear her, if she lazily called for help and watched for miracles neglecting natural means[;] she thought the best way was secretly to convey herself out of that place, and trust herself again to chance; by reason there could not be more danger than where she was in[.] But those thoughts [were] quickly cut off; by reason she could find no possibility of an escape being strictly kept by the care of the old bawd, for fear she should give away that by enticement, which she meant to sell at a high rate, wherefore she was forced to content herself; and to satisfy her fears, with hopes of finding some means to be delivered from those dangers, praying to the gods for their assistance to guard her from cruel invaders of chastity[.] But after two or three days, a subject Prince of that country, which was a grand monopolizer of young virgins came to the town, which was the metropolitan city of that country, where as soon as he came, he sent for his chief officer the old bawd to know of her how his customers increased, which when she came, she told him she had a rich prize, which she had seized on, and kept only for his use, telling him she was the rarest piece of Nature's works, only saith she, she wants mature confidence; but time and heat of affection would ripen her to the height of boldness: so home she went to prepare for his coming, adorning her house with costly furniture, setting up a rich bed, as an altar to Venus, burning pleasant and sweet perfumes, as incense to her deity, before the sacrifice of chastity, youth and beauty; and instead of garlands, dressed her with costly and rich jewels, but the fair aspect of her beauty, her lovely features, exact proportion, graceful behaviour, with a sweet and modest countenance, was more adorned, thus by Nature's dress than those of arts, but these preparations turned Miseria, for so she was called[,] from doubts to a perfect belief of what she feared before; and not knowing how to avoid the shipwreck, she grew into a great passion, and disputing in controversies with herself, whether she should lose her honour and live, or save her honour and die[.] Dishonour she hated, and death she feared; the one she blushed at, the other she trembled at: but at last with much struggling, she got out of that conflict, resolving to die; for in death, said she, there is no pain; nor in a dishonourable life no content: but though death, says she, is common to all; yet when it comes not in the ordinary ways of Nature, there must be used violence by artificial instruments: and in my condition there must be used expedition; and considering what ways to take, she bethought of a maidservant that used to make clean the rooms, and such kind of works, to whom she had often talked as she was about her employments, and had gotten much of her affections[.] Her she called and told her, that a wise wizard had advised her, that ever on her birthday, she should shoot off a pistol, and in so doing she should be happy, so long as she used the same custom, but if she neglected, she should be unfortunate, for by the shooting thereof, said she, I shall kill a whole year of evil from doing me hurt, but she told her withal, that it must be that day, and it must be a small one for fear of making a great noise, and done privately for fear her mistress should know of it or anybody else, for it will be of no effect, if above one know of it besides myself. The simple wench easily believing what she said, was industrious to supply her wants, and in a short time brought her desires, which when she had got, her dejected spirits rose, with an overflowing joy. And sitting down with a quiet mind, since before she could not stand nor sit still; for her troubled, and rough thoughts drove her from one end of the room to the other, like a ship at sea, that is not anchored nor ballasted, or with storm tossed from point to point, so was she, but now with a constant wind of resolution, she sailed evenly, although she knew not what coast she should be driven to: but after some expectation, in came the old bawd and the Prince, who was so struck with her beauty, as he stood some time to behold her: at last coming near her, earnestly viewing her and asking her some light questions to which she answered briefly and wittily; which took him so much as he had scarce patience to bargain with the old bawd for her; but when they were agreed, the wicked bawd left them to themselves; where he turning to the young Lady, told her that of all the women that ever he met with, his senses were never so much delighted, for they had wedded his soul to admirations.

She answered, that if his senses or her person did betray her to his lust, she wished them all annihilated, or at least buried in dust: but I hope, said she, by your noble and civil usage, you will give me cause to pray for you, and not to wish you evil; for why should you rob me of that which Nature freely gave? And it is an injustice to take the goods from the right owners without their consent; and an injustice is an act that all noble minds hate; and all noble minds usually dwell in honourable persons, such as you seem to be; and none but base or cruel tyrants will lay unreasonable commands, or require wicked demands to the powerless, or virtuous.

Wherefore most noble sir, said she, show yourself a master of passion, a king of clemency, a god of pity and compassion, and prove not yourself a beast to appetite, a tyrant to innocence, a devil to chastity, virtue and piety; and with that tears flowing from her eyes, as humble petitioners to beg her release from his barbarous intention, but he, by those tears, like drink to those that are poisoned, grows more dry, so did his passions more violent, who told her no rhetoric could alter his affections which when she heard and he ready to seize on her, she drew forth the pistol, which she had concealed: bending her brows, with a resolute spirit [she] told him she would stand upon her guard: for[,] said she, it is no sin to defend myself against an obstinate and cruel enemy, and know said she, I am no ways to be found [] by wicked persons but in death; for whilst I live I will live in honour, or when I kill or be killed I will kill or die for security.

He for a time stood in amaze to see her in that posture, and to hear her high defiance, but considering with himself that her words might be more than her intentions, and that it was a shame to be out-dared by a woman, with a smiling countenance, said he, you threaten more evil than you dare perform; besides, in the grave honour will be buried with you, when by your life you may build palaces of pleasure and felicity; with that he went towards her to take away the pistol from her. Stay, stay, said she, I will first build me a temple of fame upon your grave, where all young virgins shall come and offer at my shrine, and in the midst of these words shot him; with that he fell to the ground, and the old bawd, hearing a pistol, came running in, where seeing the Prince lie all smeared in blood, and the young Lady as a marble statue standing by, as if she had been fixed to that place, looking steadfastly upon her own act, she running about the room called out murder, murder, help, help, not knowing what to do; fear had so possessed her, at last [she] drew her knife, thinking to stab her, but the Prince forbid her, saying, he hoped he should live to give her, her due desert, which if the gods grant, said he, I shall ask no more: so desiring to be laid upon the bed, until the chirurgeons[2] came to dress his wounds[,] staunching the blood as well as they could, the meantime[.] But after the chirurgeons had search[ed] his wounds, he asked them whether they were mortal; they told him they were dangerous, and might prove so; but their hopes were not quite cut off with despair of his recovery; but after his wounds were dressed, he gave order[s] for the young Lady to be locked up close, that none might know there was such a creature in the house, nor to disclose how, or by what means he came hurt, then being put in his litter, he was carried into his own house, which was a stately palace in the city[.] The noise of his being wounded, was spread abroad, and everyone enquiring how he came so, making several tales and reports, as they fancied; but none knew the truth thereof[.] After some days his wounds began to mend, but his mind grew more distempered with the love of the fair Lady; yet loath he was to force that from her, she so valiantly had guarded, and kept: and to enjoy her lawfully he could not, because he was a married man, and had been so five years, for at the years of twenty[,] by his parents' persuasion, being a younger brother at that time, although afterwards he was left the first of his family by the death of his eldest brother[,] he married a widow, being noble and rich: but well stricken in years, never bearing child, and thus being wedded more to interest than love, was the cause of seeking those societies which best pleased him[.] But after long conflicts and doubts[,] fears, hopes and jealousies, he resolved to remove her from that house, and to try to win her by gifts, and persuasions; and sending for a reverent lady, his aunt, whom he knew loved him, [] told her the passage of all that had happened, and also his affection, praying her to take [Miseria] privately from that place, and to conceal her secretly until he was well recovered, entreating her also to use her with all civility, and respect that could be, and going from him, she did all that he had desired her, removing [Miseria] to a house of hers a mile from the city, and there kept her[.] The young Lady in the meantime, expect[ed] nothing less than death, and was resolved to suffer as valiantly as she had acted; so casting off all care, only troubled she lived so idly; but the old lady coming to see her, she prayed her to give her something to employ her time on, for said she, my brain hath not a sufficient stock to work upon itself[.] Whereupon the old lady asked her, if she would have some books to read in; she answered, yes, if they were good ones, or else, said she, they are like impertinent persons, that displease more by their vain talk, than they delight with their company. Will you have some romances, said the old lady? She answered no, for they extoll virtue so much as begets an envy, in those that have it not, and know, they cannot attain unto that perfection: and they beat infirmities so cruelly, as it begets pity, and by that a kind of love; besides their impossibilities makes them ridiculous to reason; and in youth they beget wanton desires, and amorous affections. What say you to natural philosophy, said she? She answered, they were mere opinions, and if there be any truths said she, they are so buried under falsehood, as they cannot be found out[.] Will you have moral philosophy? No said she, for they divide the passions so nicely, and command with such severity as it is against nature, to follow them, and impossible to perform them. What think you of logic? said she[.] Answered she, they are nothing but sophistry, making factious disputes, but conclude of nothing. Will you have history? No said she, for they are seldom writ in the time of action, but a long time after, when truth is forgotten; but if they be writ at present, yet partiality or ambition, or fear bears too much sway, (said she) you shall have divine books, no said she, they raise up such controversies, as they cannot be allayed again, tormenting the mind about that they cannot know whilst they live, and frights their consciences so as makes man afraid to die; but said the young Lady, pray give me play-books, or mathematical ones[.] The first, said she[,] discovers and expresses the humours and manners of men, by which I shall know myself and others the better, and in shorter time than experience can teach me, and in the latter, said she, I shall learn to demonstrate truth by reason, and to measure out my life by the rule of good actions, to set ciphers and figures on those persons to whom I ought to be grateful, to number my days by pious devotions, that I may be found weighty, when I am put in the scales of God's justice; besides said she, I learn all arts useful and pleasant for the life of man, as music, architecture, navigation, fortification, water-works, fire-works, all engines, instruments, wheels and many such like, which are useful[.] Besides, I shall learn to measure the earth, to reach the heavens, to number the stars, to know the motions of the planets, to divide time and to compass the whole world, the mathematics is a candle of truth, whereby I may peep into the works of Nature to imitate her in little therein, it comprises all that truth can challenge, all other books disturb the life of man, this only settles it and composes it in sweet delight.

Said the old lady, by your beauty and discourse you seem to be of greater birth, and better breeding, than usually ordinary young maids have, and if it may not be offensive to you, pray give me leave to ask you from whence you came, and what you are, and how you came here[.] She sighing said, I was by an unfortunate war sent out of my country with my mother for safety, I being very young and the only child, my parents had[.] My father being one of the greatest and noblest subjects in the kingdom, and being employed in the chief command in that war, sent my mother, not knowing what the issue would be, to the Kingdom of Security, where he had been formerly sent as an ambassador, so my mother and I, went to remain there, until the trouble were over; but my father being killed in the wars, my mother died for grief, and left me destitute of friends in a strange country, [with] only some few servants; but I hearing a peace was concluded in the kingdom, I was resolved to return to my own native soil, to seek after my estate which my father left me as his only heir, and when I embarked, I only took two servants, a maid and a man, but by an unfortunate storm I was cast upon a shore belonging to this kingdom, where after I was landed, my two servants most treacherously robbed me of all my jewels, and those monies I had, and then most barbarously left me alone, where afterwards my host sold me to an old bawd, and she to one of her customers, who sought to enforce me, where I, to defend myself, shot him, but whether he be dead or alive I know not; afterwards I was brought hither, but by whose directions you I suppose can give a better account to yourself than I; yet I cannot say, but since I came hither I have been civilly used, and courteously entertained by yourself who seems to be a person of worth, which makes my fears less, for I hope you will secure me from injuries, though not from death[.] And since you are pleased to enquire what I am, and from whence I came, I shall entreat the same return, to instruct me in the knowledge of yourself, and why I was brought hither, and by whose order.

The old lady said, she was sister to the Prince's mother, and a tender lover of her nephew; and to comply with his desires, she was brought there to be kept, until he should dispose of her, then she told her what he was, but never mentioned the affection he had for her, but rather spoke as if her life were in danger. So taking her leave she left her, telling her she would send her such books as she desired. And thus passing some weeks, in the meantime the Prince recovered, resolving to visit this young Lady, who had heard by his aunt the relation of what she was, whose birth made him doubt she would not be so easily corrupted, as he hoped before, and she knowing his birth gave her more hopes of honourable usage[.] Yet sitting in a studious posture with a sad countenance and heavy fixed eyes, accompanied with melancholy thoughts contemplating of her misfortunes past, with a serious consideration of the condition she stood in, advising with her judgement for the future, in comes the Prince. She no sooner saw him, but she trembled for fear, remembering her past danger, and the trouble she was like to run through; but he with an humble behaviour and civil respect, craved pardon for his former faults, promising her, that if she would be pleased to allow him her conversation, he would never enforce that from her which she was not willing to grant, for there was nothing in this world he held dearer than her company, and sitting down by her, began to question her of love, as whether she had engaged her affection to any person of her own country, or anywhere else, she told him no; which answer, being jealous before, imagining she might be so valiant as to wound him more for the sake of her lover than out of a love to honour or reputation, received great content and joy, esteeming it the next happiness, that since she loved not him to love no other.

I wonder at your courage, said he, for usually your sex are so tender and fearful, and so far from using instruments of death, as swords, guns, or the like, as they dare not look at them, but turn their head aside.

She answered, that necessity was a great commandress, and thus discoursing some time, at last he took his leave until the next day: but when he was gone, glad she was. O what a torment will this be, said she, to be affrighted every day with this ravenous lion! but said she, I must get a spell against his fury, and not only against him but against all suchlike, which by her industry she got a subtle poison, which she put in a very small bladder, then she put that bladder of poison in a lock, which she fastened to her arm, that when any occasion served, she might have ready to put in her mouth, which in great extremity she would use: for crushing it but betwixt her teeth, it would expel life suddenly.

The next morning the Prince sent her a present of all kinds of rich Persian silks, and tissues, fine linen and laces, and all manner of toys which young ladies use to make them fine and gay. But she returned them with great thanks, bidding the bringer tell the Prince, that she did never receive a present, but what she was able to return with advantage, unless it were from those that had a near relation, as parents and kindred, or the like; but he when he saw them returned, thought it was, because they were not rich enough, and sent her another present of jewels of great value; which when she had viewed, she said, they were very rich, and costly: but returning them back, said she, I dare not trust my youth with the richesse and vanities of the world, lest they may prove bribes to corrupt my free and honest mind; wherefore tell the Prince, said she, I am not to be catched with glorious baits, and so returned them back.

The Prince, when he saw he could fasten no gifts on her, was much troubled, yet hoped that time might work her to his desires; so went to visit her, where when he saw her, he told her he was very unfortunate, that not only himself, but even his presents were hateful; for he could guess at no other reason why she should refuse them, since they were neither unlawful nor dishonourable to receive.

She answered, that the principles that she was taught, were that gifts were both dangerous to give and take, from designing or covetous persons. He said he was unhappy, for by that she would not receive love, nor give love; thus daily he visited her, and hourly courted her, striving to insinuate himself into her favour by his person and services, as powdering, perfuming and rich clothing, although he was so personable and well favoured, with such store of eloquence, as might have persuaded both ears and eyes to have been advocates to a young heart and an inexperienced brain[.] His service was in observing her humour, his courtship was in praising her disposition, admiring her beauty, applauding her wit, approving her judgement, insomuch that at the last she did not dislike his company; and grew to that pass, as to be melancholy when he was gone, blush when he was named, start at his approaching, sigh, weep, grew pale and distempered, yet perceived not, nor knew her disease; besides, she would look often in the glass, curl her hair finely, wash her face cleanly, set her clothes handsomely, mask herself from the sun, not considering why she did so; but he, as all lovers have watchful eyes, observed she regarded herself more than she used to do, which made him more earnest for fear her passion should cool; protesting his love, vowing his fidelity and secrecy, swearing his constancy to death[.] She said, that he might make all that good, but not the lawfulness; can you said she, make it no sin to God, no dishonour to my family, no infamy to my sex, no breach in virtue, no wrong to honesty, no immodesty to myself?

He answered, it was lawful by nature.

Sir, said she, it is as impossible to corrupt me, as to corrupt Heaven; but were you free, I should willingly embrace your love, in lawful marriage[.]

He told her they were both young, and his wife old, almost ripe enough for death, sith a little time more would cut her down; wherefore, said he, let us enjoy ourselves in the meantime, and when she is dead, we will marry.

No, said she, I will not buy a husband at that dear rate, nor am I so evil, as to wish the death of the living for any advantage, unless they were enemies to virtue, innocence, or religion; but he was so importunate, as she seemed displeased, which he perceiving left off persisting, lest he might nip off the young and tender buds of her affection. But it chanced, not long after, there was a meeting of many nobles at that feast where healths to their mistresses were drank round: where the Prince, who thought it a sin to love to neglect that institution, offered with great ceremony and devotion, for his mistress's health, sprinkling the altar of the brain with fume, burning the incense of reason therein[.] After the feast was ended, he went to see his mistress, whose beauty like oil set his spirits in a flame, which made his affection grow to an intemperate heat; whereat she became so afraid, as she puts the poison into her mouth, the antidote of all evil, as she thought, then told him her intention; but he having more passion than doubt, would not believe her; which she perceiving, broke the bladder asunder betwixt her teeth, and immediately fell down as dead; whereat he was so amazed as he had not power to stir for a time, but at last calling for help, the old lady came to them, he telling her what she had done, as well as his fear would give him leave. The lady having skill in physic,[3] as most old ladies have, reading in herbals[4] and such kind of books, gave her something to make her vomit up the poison, whereat she weakly revived to life again; but she was so very sick, as almost cut off of all hopes of keeping that life; whereat he lamented, tearing his hair, beating his breast, cursing himself, praying and imploring his pardon and her forgiveness, promising and protesting never the like again, she returning no answer, but groans and sighs: but he being a diligent servant, and much afflicted, watched by her, until she mended by the lady's care and skill[.] When she was indifferent well recovered, she began to lament her ill condition and the danger she was in, employing her thoughts how she might escape the snares of spiteful fortune, and gain her friendship; where after some short time, finding opportunity to take time by the forelock, the Prince being sent for to court, and the old lady being not well, whereby she had more liberty, searching about the room [she] found a suit of clothes of the old lady's page, which suit she carried into her chamber, and privately hid it, then taking pen and ink, writ two letters, the one to the Prince, the other to the old lady; so sealing the letters up, and writing their direction, left them upon the table; then she straight stripped herself of her own clothes, which she flung in a black place with her hair that she had cut off; and putting the page's clothes on, in this disguise she went towards the chief city, to which came an arm of the sea up, making a large haven for many ships to lie at anchor in[.] But as soon as she came to the seaside, there was a ship just going off, which she seeing, got into it; her fears being so great, as not to consider, nor examine, wither they were bound; and they were so employed, hoisting their sails, and fitting their tacklings, as they took no notice when she came in:

but being gone three or four leagues from the shore, and all quiet, and free from labour, the master walking upon the deck, seeing a handsome youth stand there in page's clothes, asked him who he was, and how he came there. Said she, I do suppose, you are bound for the Kingdom of Riches, where I desire to go; but coming late, seeing everyone busily employed, I had no time to bargain for my passage; but I shall content you what in reason, you can require.

Said the master, we are not bound to that kingdom, but are sent for new discoveries towards the South, neither have we provision for any more than those that are appointed to go; which when she heard, the tears flowed from her eyes, which became her so well, as moved the master to pity and affection[.] Then asking him what he was, she answered him, that she was a gentleman's son, whom by the reason of civil wars, was carried out of his own country very young by his mother, and so related the truth of his being cast into that kingdom, only she fained she was a youth, and had served a lady as her page; but desiring to return into his own country, had mistaken and put himself into a wrong vessel, but said she I perceive the fates are not willing I should see my native country and friends; but I being young, travel, said she, may better my knowledge; and I shall not neglect any service I am able to do, or you are pleased to employ me in, if you will accept thereof[.] At last her graceful and humble demeanour, her modest countenance, and her well favoured face preferred her to this master's service, who was a grave and a discreet man, who told her, as supposing her a boy, that since [he] was there, he would not cast him out, although, said he, it will be hard for me to keep you, yet you shall partake of what I have allowed for myself[.]

She giving him many thanks, said she would strive to deserve it. But after some weeks, the master fell very sick; in which sickness she was so industrious to recover his health by her diligent attendance and care, as begot such affection in the old man, that he adopted him his son, having no children of his own, nor like to have, he being in years. But having sailed five or six months without any tempestuous winds, yet not without danger of rocks and shelves of sand, which they avoided by their skill, and many times refreshed themselves in those harbours they might put into, which made them hope [for] a pleasant and prosperous voyage.

But fortune playing her usual tricks, to set men up on high hopes, and then to cast them down to ruin, irritated the gods against them, for their curiosity in searching too far into their works, which caused them to raise a great storm, making the clouds and seas to meet, showers to beat them, winds to toss them, thunder to affright them, lightning to amaze them, insomuch as they had neither strength to help themselves, nor sight to guide them, nor memory to direct them, nor courage to support them; the anchor was lost, the rudder was broke, the masts were split, the sails all torn, the ship did leak, their hopes were gone;

Nothing was left but black despair,
And grim Death on their face to stare;
For every gust of wind blew Death into their face,
And every billow digged their burial place.

In this time of confusion, Travellia (for so now she called herself) followed close her old new father, who had as many care-full thoughts, and as great a regard for her safety, as she of herself; and giving order to the pilot that had lost his steerage, to cast over the cock-boat,[5] which no sooner done, but a gust of wind drove them on a rock that split the ship; which as soon as he perceived, he took his beloved and supposed boy, and put him in with himself and the pilot into the boat, cutting that cable, and imploring the favour of the gods, committing themselves to the fates, setting up a little sail for the wind to carry them which way it pleased. No sooner put off, but the ship and all therein sunk: but the gods favouring the young Lady for her virtue, tied up the strong winds again into their several corners: after which they sailing six days, at last were thrust through a point into a large river, which for the greatness might be called a large sea; for though it was fresh water, yet it was of that longitude and latitude, that they could not perceive land for four days together; but at the last they espied land, and coming nigh, they perceived a multitude of people, which when they came to the shore affrighted each other, for those on the land never saw any bark or the like swim upon the water, for they had that propriety to swim naturally like fishes[.] Nor they in the boat never saw such complexioned men; for they were not black like Negroes, nor tawny, nor olive, nor ash-coloured, as many are, but of a deep purple, their hair as white as milk, and like wool; their lips thin, their ears long, their noses flat, yet sharp, their teeth and nails as black as jet, and as shining; their stature tall, and their proportion big; their bodies were all naked, only from the waist down to their twist[6] was there brought through their legs up to the waist again, and tied with a knot, a thin kind of stuff, which was made of the barks of trees, yet looked as fine as silk, and as soft; the men carried long darts in their hands, spear-fashion, so hard and smooth, as it seemed like metal, but made of whales' bones. But when they landed, the people came so thick about them, as almost smothered them. But the grave and chief of them, which seemed like their priests, sent them straight to their chief governors of those parts, as their custom was, as it seemed to them afterwards; for all that was strange or rare was usually presented to their chiefs, so that they stayed not so long as to see the ceremony of that sacrifice they were offering, only they perceived it was a sacrifice of fish to some sea-god; and then [they] set them on a creature half fish, half flesh, for it was in shape like a calf, but a tail like a fish, a horn like a unicorn which lives in the river, but yet would lie upon the sands in great herds or shoals, as seals do, so as they might take [them] for their use at any time, without the trouble of keeping them up, for they were tame and gentle of themselves.

But thus riding along the sand two or three leagues to the governor's house, for all along those sands[,] only upon a bank[,] were houses all in a row built with fishbones, which bones were laid with great art, and in fine works, and so close as stone or brick; the tops of these houses were scales of fish laid like tile or flat; these scales glittered so in the sun, as they looked some ways like silver, other ways like rainbows, in all manner of colours.

When the governor had viewed them, he sent them with other messengers, but on the same beasts, to the next governor; and thus [] riding upon the sands for some days, their food [was] broiled fish, but broiled upon the hot sands, for there was no other food but fish and water-fowls, whereof they had great store, but yet of strange kinds to those strangers' view, for there was no pasture, nor anything like green.

At last they came to a place, which seemed like a forest, for there were a number of bodies of trees, but having neither branches nor leaves, and yet the bodies of those trees, if one may call them so, having no branches, were so big as to hold a family of twenty, or more of the governor's house, for so they serve, for their house was as big as four other[s]; and the bark of those trees, or indeed the wood of the tree quite through, were as all manner of flowers both for colour, shape, and scent, painted and set by nature in the wood; as when the wood was cut one way, flowers were all perfect in shape, but cut another way and they seemed like flowers shed from the stalks; and this wood was so sweet as all the forest smelled thereof.

After the governor of this place had viewed them, he set them on other beasts, and sent them by other messengers; where leaving their fleshly fishy beasts which run back again to the place they were taken from: but those they rode after[wards], were like a stag in the body, which was as big as a horse, black as a coal, a tail like a dog, horns like a ram, tipped with green like buds of trees, as swift as a roe: and thus riding until they came to another forest, where all the trees were very high and broad, whose leaves were shadowed with several greens, lighter and darker, as if they were painted, and many birds of strange colours and shapes[.] Some birds had wings like flies, beaks, bodies and legs like other birds; some the bodies like squirrels, but had feathered wings: there was one, a very fine kind of bird in shape, both for beak, head, body and legs, like a parrot, but instead of feathers, it was covered with hair like beasts, which hairs were of the colour of parrot's feathers, and the wings like bat's wings, streaked like a rainbow; the eyes looked as yellow as the sun, and sent forth a kind of a light like to small rays of the sun; in the midst of the forehead it had a small horn, which grew winding and sharp at the end like a needle: this bird did mount like a hawk in circle, and after would fly down at other birds as they do; but instead of talons, that horn struck them dead, for with its horn it would thrust them into their bodies, and so bear their bodies upon their horn, and fly some certain lengths as in triumphs, and then would light and eat it.

Some birds no bigger than the smallest flies there were, yet all feathered; besides, there were many sorts of beasts, for some had beaks like birds, and feathers instead of hair, but no wings, and their bodies like a sheep. There was one kind of beast in the shape of a camel, and the neck as white as a swan, and all the head and face white, only a lock of hair on the top of his crown of all manner of colours; the hair of his body was of a perfect gold yellow, his tail like his fore-top, but it would often turn up like a peacock's tail, and spread it as broad; and the hairs being of all several colours, made a most glorious show, the legs and feet of the colour of the body, but the hooves as black as jet.

At last, they were carried to another governor who lived in a town, whose house was built with spices; the roof and beams as big as any house need to have, made of cinnamon, and the walls were plastered with the flakes of mace, which flakes were a foot square; the planches[7] were cut thick, like bricks, or square marble pieces, out of nutmegs; the long planches out of ginger, for their nutmegs and races of ginger were as great as men could carry; the house was covered on the top, some with pomegranates' rinds, others of oranges and citrons, but the pomegranates last the longer, but the other smelled the sweeter, and looked the more pleasanter to the eye[.] They never have rain there, nor in any part of the kingdom, for the air is always serene and clear; nor no higher winds than what fans the heat; their exercise was hunting, where the women hunted the females, the men the males.

But as they went to the governor, all the people run about to see them, wondering at them, viewing them round: but the governor seemed to admire the youth much, but durst not keep him, being against the custom, but sent them straight towards the chief city where their King was; where after some days riding, [they] came out of the forest into great plains and champains,[8] which were covered with a sea green and willow-coloured grass, and some meadows were covered with perfect shadows of all manner of sorts of greens. But as they drew near the city, there were great quarries of crystal, as we have of stone. But when they came up to the city, all about without the walls were orchards, and root-gardens, where there grew roots as sweet, as if they were preserved, and some all juicy; most of their fruits grew in shells like nuts, but most delicious to the taste; but their shells were like a net or caul, that all the fruit was seen through, and some kind of fruits as big as one's head, but some were no bigger than ours, others very small; there never fell rain, but dews to refresh them, which dews fell upon the earth, every night they fell like flakes of snow; and when they were upon the earth, they melted; and those flakes to the taste were like double-refined sugar.

At last, they entered the city, which city was walled about with crystal, and all their houses thereof, which houses were built both high and large, and before the houses were arched walks set upon great pillars of crystal; through the midst of the street run a stream of golden sands, and cross the stream were little silver bridges to pass and repass over to each side of the street; on each side of this stream grows rows of trees, which trees were about the height of cypress trees, but instead of green leaves, upon every stalk grew a several sweet flower, which smelled so sweet, that when Zephyrus[9] blew, for they never had high winds, they gave so strong a scent, that to those that were not used to them, did almost suffocate their spirits.

The King's palace stood in the midst of the city, higher than all the other houses; the outward wall was crystal, cut all in triangulars, which presented millions of forms from one object; and all the ridge of the wall was all pointed crystals, which points cutting and dividing the beams of the sun so small, as the wall did not only look sparkling, but like a flaming hoop or ring of fire, by reason the wall went round. To this wall were four open passages, arched like gates; from those passages went walks, and on each side of these walks were trees, the barks thereof shadowed with hair colour, and as smooth as glass, the leaves of a perfect grass-green, for that is very rare to have in that country, Nature hath there so intermixed several colours made by light on several grounds or bodies of things; and on those trees birds do so delight therein, that they are always full of birds, every tree having a several choir by itself, which birds do sing such perfect notes, and keep so just a time, that they do make a most ravishing melody; besides, the variety of their tunes are such, that one would think Nature did set them new every day. These walks lead to another court, which was walled about with agates, carved with all imagery, and upon the ridge of the wall were such agates chose[n] out as most resemble the eyes, for in some agates their colours are naturally mixed, and lie in such circles as eyes, these seem as if so many sentinels lay looking and watching round about. From this wall went a walk, where on each side were beasts cut artificially to the life out of several coloured stones, according as those beasts were they were to resemble. This walk leads to another court which was not walled, but rather railed with white and red cornelians; these rails were cut spear-fashion. From the rails went only a plain walk paved with gold, which went straight to the palace; this palace standing on a little mount, whereto went up a pair of stairs; the stairs went round about the house, ascending by degrees on steps, which steps were of amber, leading up to a large and wide door; the frontispiece thereof was Turkey stones curiously carved in so small works, as if it had been engraven; the palace walls were all pure porcelain, and very thick and strong, yet very clear; it was all roofed or covered with jet, and also paved with the same, so that the black jet was set forth by the white porcelain, and the white porcelain seemed whiter by the blackness of the jet; their windows were only arched holes to let in air. Then in the midst of the palace was a large room like a little enclosed meadow, where in the midst of that room ran a spring of clear water, where the King bathed himself therein. Also, there were brave gardens of all sorts of flowers, where in the midst was a rock of amethyst, and artificial nymphs cut out to the life of mother [of] pearl, and little brooks winding and streaming about of golden sands; the wonder was, that although there were many mines in that kingdom, yet it was very fertile.

At last, they were brought to the King's presence, who was laid upon a carpet made of thistledown, with great attendance about him: but he, and all those of the royal blood, were of a different colour from the rest of the people, they were of a perfect orange colour, their hair coal black, their teeth and nails as white as milk, of a very great height, yet well shaped.

But when the King saw them, he wondered at them; first, at the old man's beard, for they have none; the next, at their habit, which were seamen's clothes; but above all, at the youth, who looked handsome in despite of his poor and dirty garments[.] At last, he would have their clothes pulled off: but no sooner did they come to execute their command[,] but Travellia was so affrighted, that he fell down in a swound[.] Those that touched him started back when they saw him dead; but the old man bending him forward, brought him to life again: whereupon they straight thought that their touching him killed him, and that the old man had power to restore life, which made them afraid to touch them anymore; for that disease of swounding[10] was not known to them; then were their priests and wizards called for, to know from whence they came, and what should be done with them, which priests were only known from the rest of the people, by a tuft of hair growing just upon the crown of the head, and all the head else had no hair, where other priests are only bald upon the crown []; the King and they fell into a great dispute.

The King pleaded hard to keep the youth, but at last the priest had the better, as most commonly they have in all religions, and so carried them away, and kept them a twelve month, but never dared touch them, for fear they should die, because Travellia swounded, but they beckoned and pointed to them, they gave them ease, not employing them to any labour, and fed them daintily of what they could eat: for some meats they could not eat, as man's flesh, for they had a custom in that country, to keep great store of slaves, both males and females, to breed on, as we do breed flocks of sheep, and other cattle[.] The children were eaten as we do lambs or veal, for young and tender meat; the elder for beef and mutton, as stronger meats; they kill five males for one female, for fear of destroying the breed, although they were so fruitful: they never bear less than two at a birth[,] and many times three, and they seldom leave child-bearing, until they are threescore years old, for they usually live there until they are eight score, and sometimes two hundred years, but the ordinary age is a hundred, unless plagues come; but not out of sluttery, or evil, or corrupt air, but with too much nourishment, by reason of their delicious diet, which breeds such a superfluity of humours, that it corrupts their blood[.] As for their houses, they are kept very cleanly, by reason they never eat in them, for their custom was to eat all together in common halls, as the Lacedemonians[11] did, only they had better cheer and more liberty; likewise their women were common to everyone's use, unless it were those women of the royal blood, which is a sort by themselves, as was described before, and therefore never mixed with the rest; but if they did, and were known, it was death; these of the royal blood all their skins were wrought, like the Britons. As for their government, it was tyrannical, for all the common people were slaves to the royal.

But to return to the old man, observing how careful and choice they keep him, he told his son what he thought was their intentions, which was to sacrifice them, and said he, there is no way to escape, unless we had their language, and could make them believe we came from the gods; and that the gods would punish them, if they put them to death, and you are young, said he, and apt to learn; but I am old, and my memory decayed; wherefore now study for your life or never.

Well, said he, since my life lies in my learning, I will learn for my life, which he did so well, that he got in that twelve month their language, so perfect as he understood, and could speak most of it, in which time he understood all that I have delivered to the reader, and besides understood that they had many gods, and goddesses.

The sun was their chief god, and the earth the chief goddess; their next god was the sea, and their goddess the moon, and they prayed to the stars, as some do to saints, to speak in their behalf, and to present their prayer to the sun and moon, which they thought to be as man and wife, and the stars their children; to their gods, they offered none but the males, and those offerings were offered by men; and the men prayed only to the gods; and to their goddesses none but the women; nor none but female offerings were offered unto them: at last by their discourse and preparation, they perceived they were to be sacrificed to the sun, as being both males, as they thought, and with great ceremony, as being strangers, and such rarities, yet they did not touch Travellia, as supposing, if they should, he would die before he was brought to the place of sacrifices; yet in all this time he never disclosed that he could speak their language, nor to understand them; but in this time the old man had got some saltpeter, and burnt wood into charcoal, so made gunpowder, for they had the liberty to go where they would about their temples, and after he had made the gunpowder, he made two things like pistols, although not so curious and neat, yet well enough to serve his turn, and directed his son what he should do and say; whereupon against that day he made himself a garment of a grass which was like to green silk, and with the same he had woven it so finely, as it looked like satin, also the calves of his legs like buskins were several coloured flowers, and a garland of flowers on his head, the soles of his sandals were of that green; but the stripes atop were of flowers like his buskins; in each hand he held the two pistols; his hair which was grown in that time, for he never discovered it, keeping it tied up, untied it, and that day let it down, which spread upon his back, but when the priest which came to fetch him forth, saw him thus dressed, never seeing hair before, for they had none but wool, and very short as Nigers have,[12] was amazed at the sight; and not daring to touch him, went by him as guarding him, as the chief sacrifice to the place, where the King and all his tribe, and all his people waiting for their coming, the King being placed at the head of the altar with a dart in his right hand, the spear of the dart being an entire diamond, cut with a sharp point, to signify the piercing beams of the sun, which spear, he usually struck into the heart of the sacrificed; which heart the priest used to cut out, and gave the King to eat raw, whilst the priest sang songs in the praise of the sun, as the father of all things[.] Thus after some expectations the priest came with their sacrifices, which when the King and people saw, they were all amazed, as well they might; for he appeared most beautiful; but at last they all shouted, and cried out, their gods had beautified and adorned their sacrifices, as being well pleased therewith, making great shouts and noises of joy; but when he came to the altar he called to them, in their own language, at which they grew mute with wonder, and being all silent, he thus spake.

The Speech

O King, and you spectators, why do you offend the gods, in destroying their messengers; which come to bring you life, and to make you happy; had I brought you plagues, then you might have sacrificed me unto your god of lights, as coming from death and darkness, his enemies; but for this your false devotion, the great sun, saith he, will destroy you with one of his small thunderbolts, killing first your priests and then the rest. With that shot off his pistol into the breast of the chief priest, wherewith he straight fell down dead; the noise of the pistol, and the flash of the fire, which they never saw before, and the effect of it upon the priest, struck them with such a horror, and did so terrify them, as they all kneeled down imploring mercy, and forgiveness, with trembling limbs, and weeping eyes, whereupon he told them, there was no way to avoid punishment, but first to fast two days from any kind of nourishment;

next, not to open their lips to speak, and then to obey whatsoever he shall teach them, as being sent from the gods; bidding them go home until their time of fasting were out; and then to return to the temple again, commanding none to remain there, but to leave it to the old man, and he. Which temple was most rich and curiously built, having in that country great art and skill, in architecture.

Whereupon, the King and all the people, rising up, bowing their heads down low, as in humble obedience to commands, praying to him as a god to divert the punishments intended to them, and in sorrow, as lamenting their fault went home, each to his house, sealing up their lips for such a time, from receiving meat, or sending forth words; in the meantime the old man and he had leisure to bethink themselves what to do, having at that time the temple as a palace to live in, none to disturb them, nor to hinder their thoughts from working out their advantage, and sitting in council a long time, disputing with each other, what was best to do, at last resolved the old man should go to the King as sent from the gods, to bid him send a command to all his people to eat such herbs, as a salad, drinking their water without mixture just before they came, for else, said the old man, their hunger will make them impatient, or so dull, as it may stop their ears, by the faintness of their spirits, caused by their empty stomachs, and too much said he, makes them furious, sending up malignant vapours to their brains, which may cause our ruins; but after he had been with the King, he returned back to the temple again, and the King obeyed his desire, as a command from the gods, and brought the people all to the temple, where after they were all gathered together, Travellia advanced himself so much higher than the rest, as they might hear him round.

Then thus spake.

Pious friends, for so I may call you, being willing to please the gods; but your ignorance hath led you wrong ways: yet the gods seeing your zeal, though through a false devotion, pitying your ignorance did by their wisdom find means to appease the wrath of their justice, for every attribute of the gods must have a satisfaction; for right is their kingdom, and truth is their sceptre, wherewith they govern all their works; but the gods hath strewn lots among mankind of moveable things which chance gathers up, and chance being blind mistakes both in the gathering and distributing: now the gods made this chance by their providence when they made man, for man hath no more knowledge of the transitory things of the world, than what chance gives them, who is an unjust distributor, for all external gifts come from her hand, which for want of sight, she gives oft times the beggar's lot to the King, the servants' to the masters, the masters' to the servants: and for the internal gifts which the gods have bestowed on men, are different, as the external are transitory; for some are nearer to perfection, some farther off: yet none have perfect knowledge, for the gods mix man's nature with such an aspiring ambition, that if they had a perfect knowledge of the glory of the gods, and a perfect knowledge of the first cause; and the effects produced therefrom, they would have warred with the gods, and have striven to usurp their authority, so busy and vainglorious hath the gods made the minds of men. Wherefore the gods govern the world by ignorance: and though the goodness of the gods is great, yet their goodness is bound in with their justice, which is attended with terrors, to punish the crimes of men. And even to punish the innocent errors that proceed from that ignorance, which they have muzzled man withal; but as their power made the world; their wisdom rules the world; their justice punishes the world: so their mercy keeps the world from destruction, and their love, not only saves man, but prefers man to a glorious happiness. And some of this love the gods have sent to you, although by your ignorance you had almost cast it from you. And since the gods have sent you knowledge by us, take hold of it: and not willingly fall in your suspicious errors, although it is a difficult pain, even for the gods themselves to persuade man, who is of a cross, superstitious, inquisitive, and murmuring nature, accusing the gods for partiality, saying, they prefer or cast out whom they please, not as man deserves; thus they judge of the gods, by their own passions, but the gods by variations are pleased to continue the world, and by contradiction do govern it, by sympathy delight it, for delight lives not altogether in the power of chance; being created in the essence and soul of man, for though chance can present those things which [cause] antipathies, or sympathies, to the senses which present them to the soul, yet it hath not the power to rule it[.] For the soul is a kind of god in itself, to direct and guide those things that are inferior to it; to perceive and descry into those things that are far above it, to create by invention, to delight in contemplations; and though it hath not an absolute power over itself, yet it is a harmonious and absolute thing in itself, and though it is not a god from all eternity, yet it is a kind of deity to all eternity, for it shall never die; and though the body hath a relation to it, yet no otherwise than the mansion of Jove hath unto Jove[.] The body is only the residing place, and the sensitive spirits are as the soul's angels, or messengers and intelligencers; so the souls of men are to the gods as the sensitive spirits to the soul; and will you dislodge the sensitive spirits of the gods, by destroying and unbuilding each other's body by violent deaths, before it be the gods' pleasure to dissolve that body, and so to remove the soul to a new mansion? And though it is not every creature that hath that soul, but only man, for beasts have none, nor every man, for most men are beasts, only the sensitive spirits and the shape maybe, but not the soul; yet none know when the soul is out or in, but the gods; and not only other bodies may not know it, but the same body be ignorant thereof.

For the soul is as invisible to the sensitive spirits, as the gods to men; for though the soul knows and hath intelligence by the sensitive spirits, yet the sensitive [spirits] have none from the soul; for as gods know men, but men know not gods, so the soul knoweth the senses, but the senses know not the soul; wherefore you must seek all the ways to preserve one another, as temples of the gods, not to destroy and pull them down; for whosoever doth so, commits sacrilege against the gods; wherefore none must die, but those that kill, or would kill others[.] Death must be repaid with death, saith Jove, and only death is in the power of man to call when they please, but life is in the power of the gods, and those that displease the gods shall have a miserable life, not only in the bodily part, which is sensible of pain, and may be tormented out of one shape into another, and be perpetually dying or killing with all manner of torments, and yet never die; as in the shape of a man, feels stabs in the sides, or the like; in the shape of a bull, knocks on his head, or the like; in the shape of a hart, arrows in the haunch, or the like; in the shape of a fish, hooks tearing the jaws, besides all manner of diseases and infirmities; thus burning, hanging, drowning, smothering, pressing, freezing, rotting, and thousands of these kinds, nay, more than can be reckoned, may suffer: thus several bodies, though but one mind, may be troubled in every shape.

But those that please the gods, live easy in every shape, and die quietly and peaceably; or when the gods do change their shapes or mansions, 'tis for the better, either for ease or newness.

Thus have the gods sent us to instruct you, and to stay so long amongst you as you can learn and know their commands, then to return unto them.

With that the King and people bowed their faces to the ground, adoring him as a god, and would have built altars, and offered sacrifices unto him; but he forbade them, telling them they must build altars in their hearts of repenting, humbling, and amending thoughts, and offer sacrifices of prayer and thanksgiving to the great and incomprehensible Jove, and not altars built with hands unto men, nor to offer inhumane sacrifices to gods of their own making.

Thus preaching every day for some time, forbidding vain and barbarous customs, and inhumane ceremonies, teaching and persuading them to believe the gods were not to be known nor comprehended, and that all that they have discovered of themselves to their creatures, was only by their works, in which they should praise them: for and by which doctrine they were brought to be a civilized people, and approved of their teacher so well, that they would do nothing concerning religion, or any other affairs of government without them; and being dismissed for that time, departed, leaving them to themselves in the temple. But at certain and set times the King and people repaired thither to hear him preach, who taught them according to his belief; and whensoever they moved out of the temple, all the people flocked about them with acclamations of joy; and whensoever the King sent for them, as he often did for their counsels, all the princes attended, and people waited upon them, and thus they lived with great splendour, love, and admiration amongst them; their persons were thought divine, their words were laws, and their actions examples, which they kept, and the people followed.

Thus for a while we leave them, and return to the old lady and the Prince.

The old lady sen[t] into Affectionata's chamber (as then called) for so she named herself there, to entreat her company, for therein she took great delight, she being witty in her conversation, and pleasing in her humour: but the messenger bringing his errand, missed of the mark, looking about, and calling aloud, could neither hear nor see her; so returning to the old lady, she was not to be found; whereat she grew into a great passion, not only for her loss, which she thought great, since her love to her, and esteem of her, was not small, which she had for her: but that she apprehended the Prince would think that she had neglected that charge he had entrusted her with.

But whilst she was in this passion, the Prince came in, who had been in the young Lady's chamber, but missing her, thought she had been there: but seeing her not, and the old lady weeping, straight asked her for his mistress; but she through tears and sobs could not answer; whereupon some about her answered, she was gone none could tell where: at whose words, the Prince's countenance and complexion expressed his grief, the one being sad, the other pale, standing in a fixed posture, his body seeming like a statue which his soul had left, being gone to seek after her: but at last, as if it had returned in despair, grew frantic with grief, tearing himself, cursing his misfortunes[.] At last, [he] goeth into her chamber, looking in every corner, even where she could not be, as much as where she might be; for lovers leave no place nor means unsought or untried. At last, he espied a letter upon the table directed to the lady, which he opened, considering not the incivility of breaking up the seal without the lady's leave, for jealous lovers break all such ceremonies; and thus read[.]

Madam,

Pray think me not ungrateful after all your noble favours, that I go away without your leave or knowledge; for could I have stayed with security, nothing but your commands could have forced me from you; or could my life have served you, I would have offered it as a sacrifice to obligation: but Madam, it is too dangerous for a lamb to live near a lion; for your nephew is of so hungry an appetite, that I dare not stay, which makes me seek safety in some other place: but when my thoughts forget your honourable memory, let them cease to think. The gods protect your virtue, and send you health. Fare you well.

Affectionata.

When he had read this letter, and went to lay it on the table again, he perceived another letter directed to him, which he opened and read.

Sir,

You cannot condemn me for going away, since my stay might prove my ruin, you having not power over your passions; but had my life been only in danger, I should have ventured it; not that I am so fond of death as to give my life willingly away; but I am so true a votress to Chastity, that I will never forsake her order, but will carry her habit to my grave; nor will I give Virtue an occasion to weep over my follies, nor Truth to revile me with falsehood, but honour as a garland shall crown my hearse, whilst innocency enshrines my corpse, that Fame may build me a monument in noble minds: but had you been master of your passion, or had the temperance of your affections been equal to your other virtues, I should have joyed to live near you, as saints do to gods; and though my hard fortune has driven me into many dangers, and more I am like to run through by the unknown ways you have forced me into, yet the blessing of Jupiter fall upon you, whatsoever chance to me. Farewell.

Affectionata.

When he had read his letter, he sits down musing with himself a long time; then rose, and without speaking any words, departed to his house in the city.

The old lady, his Princess, seeing him so sad, asked him what was the cause.

He answered, he was sick, and went to bed.

The next day, calling his steward, he settled his estate, and ordered everything according to his mind; then bid him provide so much monies; which done, he sent for his wife, telling her she must not take it ill, if he left her for a short time, for he was resolved to travel, for, said he, I have a quarrel to one that is stolen out of the kingdom, and I cannot be at quiet until I have found the party out to be revenged for the injury done me, bidding her conceal the cause.

She with tears entreated his stay; but no persuasions could prevail to alter his intention, or rather resolution; for love is obstinate; and if it finds not a like return, but a neglect, grows spiteful, rather wishing evil to what they love, than another should enjoy what they would have, and hate themselves out of a displeasure in not having what they desire; so did he, and was impatient until he was shipped and gone; who steered his course towards the Kingdom of Riches, as believing she was sailed towards her own country, for resolved he was to find her out, or to end his days in the search, his life being a burden without her company.

Thus love sailing in the ship of imagination, on the ocean of the mind, tossed on the troubled waves of discontented thoughts, whilst his body sailed in the ship on the ocean of the sea, cutting the salt waves, they were set on by pirates, and were taken prisoners, so that he was doubly captivated, his soul before, and now his body; at first, they used him but roughly, according to their barbarous natures; but by degrees, his noble disposition and affable behaviour got different[13] entertainment.

It chanced some time after, in the sharing of those prizes they got with him, and some others they had got before, they fell out, and from rude words they fell to ruder blows. The Prince apprehending the danger that might befall to himself, strove to pacify them, giving them such reasons in elegant words, that it charmed their ears, and softened their hearts, and ended the strife amongst them, and begot from them such love and respect, that they made him their arbitrator, and divider of the spoils; which he performed with that justice and discretion to each one, that they made him their governor and chief ruler over them; which power he used with that clemency and wisdom, that he was esteemed rather as their god than their captain, giving him all ceremonious obedience. And thus reigning in his watery kingdom with his three-forked trident, we leave him for a time, and visit the old man and adopted son, who now began to grow weary of their divine honours, and like wise men that seek a retired and secured life from the pomp of dangerous glories, bethought themselves how they might get away, and return into their own countries again; for an humble and mean cottage is better beloved by the owner, than the bravest and stateliest palace, if it be another's. Thus putting their designs in execution, they invited the King and people to a solemn meeting in the temple, where Travellia, standing in his usual place, thus spake.

The gods, said he, hath caused me to return from whence we came; and to you great King their command is, to love your people and to distribute justice amongst them, guarding the innocent, punishing the offender, and not to use any cruel ceremony to destroy your own kind, but to instruct them in the right, and to lead them into the ways of truth, as being their high priest amongst them; also to make no wars against your neighbouring kingdoms, but as a defence and guard to your own, for in peace, lives happiness, when wars bring ruin and destruction; and in doing this tranquility shall be as a bed of ease for life to sleep on, and length of days as a chariot for life to ride in to Heaven; where your soul shall dwell in the height of bliss: and in this world, fame shall crown your deeds; and your posterity shall glory in your name.

And to you beloved people, the gods command piety in your devotion; obedience to your King; love to your neighbour; mercy to your enemies; constancy to your friends; liberty to your slaves; care and industry to your children; duty to your parents; and in doing this, plenty shall flow in amongst you; mirth shall dance about you; pleasures shall invite you; delight shall entertain you; peace shall keep you safe, till the gods calls you to partake of the glories of Heaven; and my prayer shall always be; that Jove may preserve you all.

Then going off from the place where he stood, they went to the King, to take their leaves, whereat the King and people wept, and wished, the gods had given them leave to dwell amongst them; but since they could not have their desire therein, they travelled to the river-side in attendance on them, offering them great riches to carry with them, but they desired, nor took they anymore with them, than they thought would defray their charges, in a time of necessity; neither did they build a new ship to sail in, but went in the same boat they came, which had been kept as a relic safe; for the old man considered with himself, that a bigger vessel would be more dangerous without men, to serve therein than the small boat, which they could manage themselves[.] And so with great sorrow of either side, the one to lose their angels, as they thought them to be; the others for the dangers they were to run through[14][,] and thus [they] parted, putting forth their boat from the shore, but the old man who was very skilful at sea, observing what angle they came in, returned the same way, where after six days they were upon the main sea[.] The winds being fair, and the waters smooth, the boat went as swift as an arrow out of a Parthian's bow,[15] and as even as if it meant to hit a mark, but if by a fresh gale the waves did chance to rise, the boat would as nimbly skip each ridge, as a young kid over a green hillock, being as light as Mercury's winged heels; whereat joy filled their hearts with hopes, as winds filled their sails; but various fortune causing several changes in the world, did raise such storms of fears, as drowned all their joys; for a ship freighted with pirates, like a great whale seized on them; pirates letting nothing escape which they can get to make advantage on, so ravenous is their covetous appetite[.] But finding not such a prize as they did expect: but such as rather might prove a burden, [they] consulted to put the old man into the boat again, and to keep only the young youth, [who] being very handsome, they might sell him for a slave, and get a sum of money: but when the old man was to depart, Travellia clasped about him so close, as his tears and the tears of the old man mixed and joined, and flowed as waters through a channel swelled with several brooks; but when he was forced to leave his hold down on his knees he fell, begging he might go or keep his father there[:] said he, pity my father's age; cast him not out alone to sail on the wide and dangerous sea; for though my help is weak, yet I am a stay and staff for his decayed life to lean upon, and I hope the gods have destined me to that end, but if no pity can move your hearts for him, O let it try for me:

Cut me not from the root, though old and dry;
For then poor branch I wither, and shall die.

Nay, said he, I will die when I can no longer help him, for death is in my power, though life is not, but the Prince, who was their commander, hearing a noise, came on the deck, who no sooner saw him, but was struck with compassion, raised by a resemblance of his mistress appearing in the face of the youth; and going to him, bid him dry his eyes, and cease his sorrow, for they both should live together, so long as he could keep them.

Heaven bless you, said he, and may you never part from that you most do love, but when Travellia's tears were stopped, and sight got a passage through his eyes again, and looking up to view that man, from whom his obligation came, no sooner saw his face, but terror struck his heart, and trembling seized her limbs, as if she had seen some hideous and prodigious things.[16] The Prince observing her in that agony, asking him, as supposing her a boy, what made him shake and tremble so, in quivering words she answered, fear as before had shrunk his sinews short; so now joy had extended them too far[.] The Prince then stroking his head, promised they should be used both well, and so returned into his cabin. Thus travelling on the sea, as on a great champaign, the ship like a horse went several paces, according as the waves did rise and fall.

But at last this ship became like a horse diseased with spavens,[17] which broke out, or springing a leak, which they stopped as well as they could for the time, but doubting it could not long hold out; [they] grew very sad, some weeping, some praying, some murmuring, some raving, according as their fear[s] and hopes were: but the Prince who was valiant by nature, expected death with as much patience, as they with fear did apprehend, neither was he struck with terror, but yielded to the fates, and was willing to die; but in the midst of their afflictions [they] at last espied an island; at which sight they all shouted for joy.

Thus in the life of man, many several accidents passeth about, and it chances many times, out of the midst of grief and sorrow, rises up objects of comfort; so was it here, and setting up all their sails, made haste to it, but before they could come close to it, although they were not far from it, the leak broke out again, likewise their fears, for the ship grew so sick, it could swim no farther, but like a lingering disease perished, by little and little, which perceiving, they hoist out of their boat, where the Prince gave order that those which were most afraid, should go first. He himself was the last that went therein, though the boat did go and unload, and return many times, insomuch that not only all the passengers were saved, but all their goods, which no sooner were out, but the ship sunk; thus died with an incurable dropsy; but in these dangers the Prince forgot not Travellia; for why, the prince was more fond of him than Travellia was of himself; for her fears of being known gave her no rest[.] But being all safely arrived in the island, they began to consider what to do; the Prince counselled them to choose out some of the company, and to leave them thereabouts to build up huts, to lay their goods in; and also to cut down some trees, there being great store of wood, choosing that which was most proper and fit to build a new ship, whilst the rest of the company went to seek food, and to discover the place.

This being agreed upon, they divided themselves, and those that travelled up into the island, found it very small, as being not above thirty miles long, and twenty broad, unpeopled; but great store of fish and fowl; few beasts, but those that were, were of a gentle kind; fine meadows full of herbs and sweet flowers, refreshing and shady woods, wherein ran clear springs and bubbling brooks[.] Thus though it was little, it was very pleasant, the greatest inconveniences they found there, was want of houses; for they found the ground somewhat damp with dews, which being an island [it] was subject unto, but the air was serene and clear: the climate a little more than temperately hot, but the time that the ship was a-building, the Prince had a little house, or rather like an arbour, built in the midst of the island, to lodge in, and the rest made little huts for themselves, and several recreations they found to pass away the time[.] But being in that solitary place, the Prince, who was melancholy for the loss of his mistress, grew full of thoughts, and having her picture in his mind drawn to the life, comparing it to Travellia's face, which he often looked upon, began to reason with himself why that might not be she, considering her private escape, and the little acquaintance she had in that country, and seeming of a better breeding than a shipmaster's son could have, it did almost confirm his hopes; but discoursing one day with the old man of several accidents, telling their misfortunes and good hap of both sides, and being both of one country, the old man thinking no harm, discovered by his talking, that Travellia was none of his son, begotten from his loins, but adopted through compassion and affection, and then telling the story how he came into his ship unknown, or without his leave, by which circumstance of time, place, and manner found that it was she, wherewith [at] the joy thereof he could scarce conceal his passion, but dissembled his knowledge, as well as he could, for the present, yet after that time sought an occasion to get her alone, where he for his exercises and pastimes did usually go a-birding, and did command Travellia to carry his bags of shot after him, who loved the service, though she feared the lord, and when they were gone some distance from the rest of the company, and being in a shady wood, the Prince fained himself weary, where setting down to rest, and commanding him to do the like, at last discovered to him how he came to know her[.] She finding herself discovered turned as pale as death, and in that passion of fear prayed him to kill her, or otherwise she should find a way to do it herself.

But the Prince told her he would satisfy himself first, unless she would consent to live with him as his wife, in that island, wherein, said he, we may live free, and secure, without a disturbance.

She musing with herself what to do, believing he was not grown the chaster, with living amongst rude and barbarous people, thought it best to dissemble and give a seeming consent. Whereat the Prince's thoughts were more elevated, than if he had been master of the whole world, whereafter returning to the rest of the company, the one with an overjoyed mind, the other sad and full of perplexed thoughts; but when she came to a place where she might be alone, setting down in a melancholy posture, where for a time without uttering words, or shedding tears, for grief and amazement had congealed the one, and stopped the other, yet at last her smothered sorrow broke out into complaint.

You gods, said she, who will offer sacrifice to your deities since you give innocency no protection, nor let chastity live undefiled. Cruel fates to spin my thread of life, to make me up a web of misery; accursed fortune that brake not that thread with an untimely death, and you unjust powers to torment poor virtue, making it a sin to free itself, for had I leave to die I would not live in shame for to dwell here committing acts dishonourable, although I am forced, yet shall I seem a party guilty, and though no outward accusers, yet my conscience will condemn me; but, O you gods of light, since you regard me not, nor will hear me;[18] *you powers of darkness, hearken unto me, and wrap me up in your dark mantles, of perpetual night, that no eye may see me, and cast me into black oblivion, where no remembrance is.*

The old man her father, who was come from the waterside, where he had been for the directing and ordering of the building of a new ship, came to her in the midst of her complaints, and asked her what she lacked, or if she were sick; I would I were, said she, then might I hope death would reprieve me, but I am worse, for I am miserable, having torments like to those of Hell within my mind; my thoughts are vultures, eating on my carrion infamy, or like the restless stone, that cannot get up to the hill of peace, but rolleth back with fear, and sad remembrance; then telling him what she was, which he did never know before, and what had passed since the first of her misfortunes to that present, and how he had ignorantly discovered her: which, when he heard, he cursed his tongue for telling how, and where he found her.

Father, said she, what is past cannot be recalled, wherefore I must strive to help myself in what's to come; and since I have been dutiful, and you so loving and kind as to save me from the jaws of death, help me now to protect my honour, convey me hence, let me not live here to please his appetite, but cast me to some unknown place, where like an anchoret[19] I may live from all the world, and never more to see the face of man, for in that name all horror strikes my senses, and makes my soul like to some furious thing, so affrighted it hath been.

Said her father, Heaven give you quiet, and me aid to help your designs; but you must, said he, dissemble to compass your designs; wherefore rise, and put on a smooth and pleasant face, and let your discourse be compliant, that you may have a free liberty; for if a doubt should cross his thoughts, you may chance to be restrained and kept by force, which will break that assistance I may bring you.

Whilst they were thus discoursing, the Prince came to them, who had not patience to be long from her, for her absence was his Hell, and her presence was his Heaven; and flattering the old man, my father, said he, for so I may call you now, only let me entreat you I may be your son, and she your daughter, since she you thought was a boy, is proved a girl; and since fortune hath brought us so happily to meet, let us not despise her favours, but make the best use of them to our advantage.

Then telling the old man how that island might be made a paradise, and in what felicity they might live therein, if their peevish humours did not overthrow their pleasures, the old man seemed to approve of all the Prince said; whereupon the Prince took him to be his dear friend, and secret counsellor; for the old man did not omit to give him counsel concerning the settling and advancing of his new and small monarchy, because he thought in doing so he might the better work out his own design, by taking away those suspicions that otherwise he thought he might have.

Then the Prince bidding the old man to have a care, and to order his maritime affairs in overseeing his ships and boats built, for, said he, our chief maintenance will be from the sea; the whilst, said he, I will persuade these men I have here to make this place the staple and port of their prizes, and dwelling.

Then taking Travellia along with him, the old man and he parted for that time; and going to the rest of the company, he persuaded so well with his rhetoric, that they resolved to stay, and build them houses there to live, and also warehouses to lay their prizes in, and from thence to traffic with them into safe and free places; whereupon everyone put himself in order thereunto[.] Some cut down wood, others digged up stones, some carried burdens, some placing and building; thus like bees, some gathered the honey and wax, whilst others made and wrought the combs. The meantime the old man made himself busy at the coast side about ships and boats, as being the chief master employed in that work. But ofttimes he would go out a-fishing in a fisher-boat all alone, bringing several draughts of fish; and when he thought he should be least mistrusted, conveyed victuals therein, and then gave Travellia notice to steal to the waterside; where watching his opportunity, when the Prince was busy in surveying and in drawing the plats[20] and forms of the city he would have built, stole away; where as soon as he came, his old father went, as if he meant to go a-fishing, carrying his nets and the like with him to the boat, his supposed son busy in helping him, and so both being put out to sea; where they had not gone very far, but were taken by sympathetical merchants; who trafficking into the Kingdom of Amity, sold them there to other merchants; where carrying them to the chief city, the Queen of that country, who was an absolute Princess in the rule and government thereof, seeing Travellia, who was brought to her as a rarity, took such a liking to him, that she received him into her family, as also to attend near her person; wherein he behaved himself so well, that he became her favourite, where the old man was treated well for his son's sake.

But in the meantime, the Prince was in a sad condition for the loss of his mistress, who searched about all the island for her, but could hear nothing of her, until he sent to the seaside for the old man, to enquire for her; who had answer back, that the old man and the youth went out a-fishing, but were not as yet returned.

Which he no sooner heard, but guessed aright that they were fled away; whereupon he grew so enraged, that he lost all patience, swearing, tearing, stamping, as if he had been distracted.

But when his fury was abated, his melancholy increased, walking solitary, accompanied only with his sad thoughts, casting about which way to leave that hated place, for all places seemed so where his mistress was not: yet he knew not yet very well what to do, because he had persuaded the rest of the company to abide there, and make it their home, which in order thereunto he knew they had taken great pains; besides, he thought they might despise him, as seeming inconstant, yet stay he could not; wherefore calling them together, [he] spake in this manner.

My friends, said he, we have here a pleasant island unhabited, but what is possessed by ourselves; and certainly, we might become a famous people, had we women to build posterity; making a commonwealth: but as we are all men, we can only build us houses, to live and die in, but not children to survive us.

Wherefore my counsel is, that some of us that are least employed, may take the new ship, and go a-piracing for women, making some adventure on the next kingdom, which may be done by a sudden surprisal, which prizes, if we get, will bring us more comfort, pleasure and profit than any other goods; for what contentment can other riches bring us, if we have not posterity to leave it with.

They all applauded so well of his advice, as they were impatient of his stay, striving who should go along with him, and so pleased they were with the imagination of the female sex, as those whose lot was to stay, prayed for the others' good success, that seldom or never prayed before; but the Prince's intention was only to find that female he lost; caring not to seek those he never saw; but most of those, setting out with great hopes and expedition, of a good return, sailed with a fair wind, three or four days, at last saw land, part of the Kingdom of Amour[.] No sooner landed, but they were beset with multitudes of country people, who flocked together, being affrighted with the arrival of strangers; and being more in numbers than they were, overpowered them, taking them as prisoners[.] They were examined, for what they came? They answered for fresh water, but they believed them not, for, said they, it is not likely you would come in a troop so armed for fresh water, so they bound them, and sent them to the King to examine them farther; and being carried to the chief city where the King was, who was advertised of such strangers, sent for them into his presence to view them[.] And being brought unto them, the Prince, who was of a comely and graceful presence, being a handsome man, bowing his head down low, and in a submissive style, thus spake.

Great King, we poor watery pilgrims; travelling through the vast ocean of the sea to search the curiosity of nature, to whom we may offer our prayers of admiration on her altar of new discoveries, but cruel fortune, who strives to persecute, hath forced us to your coast for the relief of fresh water, for we came not here to rob, nor to surprise, but to relieve our feeble strength; that was almost famished with thirst; not that we were afraid to die, but loath to live in pain; nor would we willingly yield up our lives, unless great honour lay at stake, but if the fates decree our death, what way soever it comes, with patience we submit.

But if great King your generosity dare trust our faiths, so far as to employ us in your service, we may prove such by our courage, as our acts may beg a pardon for those necessitated faults we have committed; and if we die in wars, we die like gallant men, but to die shackled prisoners, we die like slaves, which all noble natures shun.

The King, when he had heard him speak, thus answered the Prince as their accustomed manner was in verse:

Your Faith I'll trust and Courages will try,
Then let us see how bravely you dare die.

The Prince poetically answered again, as he perceived it an usual custom to speak:

Our Lives, said he, we'll give before we yield,
We'll win your battles, or die in the field.

For the King at that time was newly entered into a war with the Queen of Amity; the chief cause was for denying him marriage, he being a bachelor, and she a maid; and their kingdoms joining both together, but he nearer by his affection, being much in love with her, but she was averse and deaf to his suit, besides her people were loath, for fear it should be made a subordinate kingdom, wherefore he sought to get her by force[.] And the King liking the Prince's demeanour, demanded who he was, from whence he came; the Prince told him truly who he was, from whence he came, how he was taken by the pirates, and how long he had lived with them; but not the cause of his journey, but by his discourse and behaviour, he insinuated himself so far into the King's favour, and got such affections in his court living therein, as he became very powerful, insomuch as he was chosen the chief commander to lead out the army, believing him (as he was) nobly born, and observing him to be honourably bred; and they a people given to ease, and delighting in effeminate pleasures, shunned the wars, sending out only the most vulgar people who were rather slaves than subjects[.] All this meeting together produced the choosing of the Prince, who ordered and directed their setting out so well and prudently, as gave them great hopes of a good success[.]

In the meanwhile the Queen was not ignorant of their intentions, nor slack in her preparations, sending forth an army to meet them; but the Queen herself had a war in her mind, as great as that in the field, where love as the general led her thoughts, but fear and doubt ofttimes made great disorder, and especially at that time; for Travellia, on whom she doted, was then sick, in which sickness she took more care to recover him, than to guard herself and kingdom; but the army she sent out, was led by one of her chief noblemen, who marched on until he had view of the other army, and being both met, they set their armies in battle array.

When they were ready to fight, the Prince thus spake in the most general language.

Noble friends, you being all strangers to me, makes me ignorant both of your natures and customs, and I being a stranger to you, may cause a mistrust, both of my fidelity and conduct, as for my experience I am not altogether ignorant of the discipline of war, having been a commander in my own country, neither need you doubt of my zeal, and loyalty to your

King's services, by reason I owe my life to him, for it was in his power to have taken it away, neither can I have more honour bestowed on me from any nation than from this, were I never so ambitious, or basely covetous, to bribe out my fidelity; wherefore, if I lose, as I am persuaded I shall win the day, yet it will not be out of my neglect, falsehood or want of skill, but either it must be through fortune's displeasure, or by your distracted fears, which fear I cannot believe will possess any spirit here, being so full of alacrity, cheerfulness and readiness to meet the enemy, and may the thoughts of honour maintain that heat and fire, not only until it hath consumed this army, but all that shall oppose you[.]

After he had spoke thus to them they began the onset, long was the dispute, but at last by the Prince's courage, which animated the rest by his example; and by his wise conduct and diligent care in rectifying the disordered ranks, and supplying their broken files by fresh men, he got the day, and put the enemy to a rout, killing many, and taking store of prisoners[.] The Prince when he saw that fortune was his friend at that time, though at other times she had frowned, yet now he thought to make his advantage whilst she was in a good humour; wherefore he called to the soldiers to follow their pursuit; but they were so busy in the dividing of the spoils, as they were deaf to all commands, or entreaties, giving their enemies leave to rally their scattered forces, and so to march away, and by that means they got so far before them, as they had time to get up their spirits, and strengthen their towns by fortification, to man their forts, and to entrench themselves, which if they had followed their victory, they might have taken a great part of the country, for all places, as towns, forts, and the like, seldom stand out, but yield to a victorious army; yet it must be whilst the terror and fright of their losses hath wholly possessed their minds, leaving no place for hope[.] But when the Prince thought they had lost the opportunity through the covetousness of the soldiers, he sent a messenger to the King of the victory, and with the reasons why he could not follow the same, but if his Majesty would give permission he would march on, and try out his fortune[.] In the meantime, the Queen hearing of the loss of her army was much perplexed, then musing with herself what way she were best to take, she straight went to Travellia who was indifferently well recovered, to him she related the sad news, then asking his counsel what she were best [to] do.

He told her his opinion was, for her to call a council of the gravest and noblest of her subjects, and those whose age had brought experience: for if worldly wisdom dwells anywhere, it is in aged brains, which have been ploughed by various accidents; and sowed with the seed of observation, which time hath ripened to a perfection[;] these are most likely, said he, to produce a plentiful and good crop of advice; but young brains, said he, want both, manuring and maturity, which makes their counsels green, and unwholesome, whereupon they called a council, where after they had disputed long, at last they all agreed in one consent, that the best was for her to go herself in person, to animate her soldiers, and to give a new life to their dejected spirits; whereat she was much troubled, by reason Travellia was not so well as to travel with her, and to leave him, seemed worse to her than death; but after her council was broken up, she returned to him, and told him what her council had decreed.

And this, said she angrily to him, was by your advice? For, had I not called a council, but had sent a general of my own choice, it would not have been put to a vote, for me in person to have gone; but had you had that love for me, as I have for you, I should have had better advice; and with that [she] wept[.] Heaven knows, said she, the greatest blow fortune can give me, is to go and leave you behind me; he seeing her weep thus spake.

Beauty of your sex, and Nature's rarest piece; why should you cast your love so low upon a slave so poor as I, when kings their kingdoms hazard for your sake? and if your people knew, or did suspect your love to me, they would rebel and turn unto your enemy: besides, conquerors are feared and followed, where losing is a way to be despised, and trod into the earth with scorns. Alas, I am a creature mean and poor, not worthy such a queen as you, and 'twere not wise to hazard all for me. Wherefore go on great Queen, and may you shine as glorious in your victories, as the brightest stars in Heaven, may Pallas by your guide, and Mars the god of war fight your battles out; may Cupid give you ease, and Venus give delight; may Hymen give such nuptials as best befits your dignity; may fortune always smile, peace in your kingdom dwell[.]

And in each heart such loyal love may grow:
No disobedience may this kingdom know;
Age crown your life; and Honour close your days:
Fame's trumpet loud to blow about your praise.

She weeping said.

No sound will pierce my ear, or please my mind,
Like to those words you utter when they're kind.

But at last by his persuasions, more than by her council's advice, she consented to go, upon that condition he would take upon him the government of her kingdom until such time as she returned again, but, said she, if I die, be you heir to my crown, and ruler of my people; and may the gods keep you from all opposers[.] The people knowing her commands, and pleasure by her proclamation, fell a-murmuring, not only in that she left a stranger, but a poor slave, who was taken prisoner and sold, and a person who was of no higher birth, than a shipmaster's son, that he should govern the kingdom, and rule the people; whereupon they began to design his death, which was thought best to be put in execution when she was gone.

But he behaved himself with such an affable demeanour, accompanied with such smooth, civil and pleasing words, expressing the sweetness of his nature by his actions of clemency, distributing justice with such even weights, ordering everything with that prudence, governing with that wisdom, as begot such love in every heart, that their mouths ran over with praises, ringing out the sound with the clappers of their tongues into every ear, and by their obedience showed their duty and zeal to all his commands, or rather to his persuasions; so gently did he govern.

Thus whilst he ruled in peace at home, the armies met

abroad; and being set ready to fight, the trumpets sounded to charge, and everyone prepared to encounter his enemy; striving for the honour of reputation, which is got by the ruin of one side; so equally hath Nature distributed her gifts, that everyone would have a just proportion, did not Fortune disorder and misplace her works by her several accidents.

But the terror of the former blows was not quite extinguished in the Queen's army, nor the insulting spirits of the other army laid, but rather a new courage added to their old victory, did help them now to win that day; and with such victorious fortune, that they took the Queen a prisoner, with the destruction of the whole army.

The Prince thinking the kingdom won in having the Queen's person, made him divide his army into two parts; the one half he sent to take possession of the towns, castles, and forts; the other part he led himself to conduct the Queen, being much pleased that he had such a gift to present to the King, which present he knew his royal master would prize above the world, which made him choose to return; for had the spoils been less, he had sent them with some messengers; but being so rich, he durst trust none to guard it but himself.

The King hearing of their coming, made all the preparations of state that could be, sending the Prince a triumphant chariot, and his own robes to wear; which chariot coming as they were ready to enter the city, the Prince sets the Queen thereon, and walks on foot by the chariot side, as being mistress to the King his master. And the King being attended by all his nobles of the kingdom, met the Queen, and with great respect led her to his palace; where when she came, the King kissed her hand, and smiling, said[:]

The gods had brought her thither; for certainly, said he, the gods by their fates have decreed and destined you to be my queen; in which gifts the gods have made me like themselves, to enjoy all felicity.

She with a face clothed in a sad countenance, answered, Fortune was his goddess; and if he were like her, he might prove inconstant, and then, said she, you may change from love to dislike, if so, I may chance to have liberty, either by death, or to be sent into my own kingdom again.

If you will accept of me, said he, you shall not only have your own kingdom, but mine, wherein you shall be adored and worshipped as the only she in the world.

Answered she, I had rather have what I adore, than to be adored myself.

Then was she conducted to a strong and safe, but pleasant place, to be kept in, where the King visited her often, treated her civilly, courted her earnestly, loving her with an extraordinary passion.

The Prince in the meantime was in high favour with the King, who asked and took his counsel in everything; and sending for him one day, where when he came, he hung about his neck, as was his custom so to do, saying to him[:]

O my friend, for that was his usual name he gave him, my cruel prisoner, said he, you brought me, despises my affection, slights my addresses, condemns my suit, scorns my proffers, hates my person; what shall I do to gain her love?

Alas, said the Prince, I have had so ill success in love, that what I doted on most did hate me worst; which is the cause I have left my country, friends, and estate, lost the peace of mind, the joy of mirth, the sweets of pleasures, the comfort of life, hating myself because she doth not like nor love me; jealous I am of light, darkness, heat, cold, because they come so near as to touch her; I wish her dead, because none should enjoy her but myself; yet I cannot live without her, and loath I am to die and leave her here behind: thus hang I on a tortured life, and bear my Hell about me.

Whilst they were thus lamenting their hard fortunes in love, a messenger brought news that their forces were beaten that were sent into Amity.

How can that be, said the Prince? most of the nobles being here, and none but peasants left behind, who have no skill in wars, only to fight like beasts, to marshall forces they know not how.

But the alarms came so thick, one after another, to tell they had not only beat their forces, but were entered into their kingdom.

With that, the King in haste dispatched the Prince with a fresh supply added to those forces he brought the Queen with, so marched out to meet the enemy; for Travellia, hearing the Queen was taken prisoner, was high enraged, which choler[21] begot a masculine and courageous spirit in her; for though she could not have those affections in her for the Queen as a man, yet she admired her heroic virtues, and loved her as a kind and gracious princess to her, which obligations made her impatient of revenge: then calling all the chief of the kingdom together, thus spake unto them.

Honourable, and most noble,

You have heard the sad news of the Queen's being taken prisoner, which cannot choose but strike your hearts through your ears, and make them burn in flames of high revenge; and may those flames be never quenched until you fetch her back, and set her in her throne again; she went to keep you safe, and nothing can be more ungrateful than to let her live amongst her enemies. Nor can you here be free, whilst she is made a slave, your wives and children will be bought and sold, and you be forced to do their servile work; what goods you now possess, your enemies will enjoy: then let your hands and strength redeem your country's loss, or sacrifice your lives in services thereunto.

After she had spoke, they proclaimed her with one voice, general, raising new forces, making vows they would never forsake their Queen, but die, or be conquerors.

Then fitting themselves in order thereunto, as their general and chief governor, caused a solemn fast and procession, sacrificing to the gods for good success.

After that, she took a view of her arms and ammunition, selecting out the ablest and youngest men to fight, making the better sort commanders, that envy might not breed disobedience; the aged she chose for her counsellors, her old father being made one; the most mechanics went with the bag and baggage, as smiths, farriers, pioneers, cannoneers, sumpter men, waggoners, cooks, women, and the like. Neither did he omit to take good chirurgeons, doctors, apothecaries, and drugsters, to help the sick or wounded. And at the army's going out she caused a proclamation to be read, that all the women and children, and infirm persons which were left behind, not being fit to go, should pray incessantly to the gods for victory, and safe return; for, said he, women, and children, and the infirm, are the best advocates even to the gods themselves, being the most thriftless creatures they have made, wherefore the most apt to move compassion.

Thus settling the kingdom in a devout and orderly posture, marched on, re-taking their towns, forts, and castles lost, beating the enemy out of every place; insomuch as they did not only clear their own kingdom of their enemies, but entered into theirs; and being gone some days' journey, their scouts brought them word there was an army coming to meet them; where after a short time, the armies were in view of each other; whereupon she drew up her forces; the right and left wings she gave to be commanded by two of the valiantest and [most] experienced commanders, the rear unto another, the van she led herself, the reserve she gave her old father in charge to bring in, as he saw occasion, praying him he would not stand with it so far off, but that he might come soon enough to their aid, nor yet to stand so near as to be annoyed with their present fight. Father, said he, I give you this part to command, because I dare trust your faith, as well as your judgement, courage, and skill.

Then she commanded every captain of a company, should place himself in the midst of their second ranks, for if the chief commander, said she, in a company be killed, the spirits of the common soldiers soon die, and their nerves grow slack with fear, and all their strength will fail: unless it be to run away.

The lieutenants she ordered them to place themselves in their last ranks, to keep the soldiers from flying; for said she, shame will cause obedience to submit to authority; wherefore his eyes will be as a fort, and his breast as a bulwark to keep them in, then she gave order that every squadron should be but five ranks deep, and fifty on a breast, which number, said she, is enough to knit into a proportionable body, more makes it unwieldy, and is like a man overgrown with fat, whose bulk makes him inactive, either to assault or to defend himself, and ranks of ten deep, said she, are not only unuseful and troublesome, but so many men are lost to employment; for the hindermost ranks come seldom, or never to the charge: then in every troop of horse she placed some foot, both pikes and muskets[22], to gall and hurt their enemy's horse when they meet to encounter: for if once the horse falls, the man is down[.] After that she commanded her army to march in such a slow pace, as not to break or loosen their ranks, but commanded them to join so close, as if there were no vacuum in their troops, and so to move as one entire body or piece[.] Lastly, she commanded all the cuirassiers[23] should stand in the forefront to bear the shock, or break the ranks; thus setting the battalia[24] in order, form and figure, as the ground and places would permit to their best advantage.

The Prince ordered his battalia, as he was used to do, making it thick and less contracting it, as believing it to be the stronger: but to give a judgement, this way of setting a batallia is best, if it were only to stand still, for a defence, but not to assault; for in action those thick bodies, the half serves only as ciphers without a figure; but never helps to multiply the numeration of blows. But the armies being both ready to join, the young general thus spake to [her] soldiers;

Noble friends, brave soldiers, and wise counsellors; who knows but this our meeting may produce good and great effects, as to bring peace to the country which is molested with wars, ruin to your enemies, that hath almost ruined you; comfort to your sad friends we have left behind; liberty to your imprisoned friends; we fight for fame to after memories, honour, and profit in our living times, but if we let our enemies become our masters; they will give us restless fears, unreasonable taxes, unconscionable oaths, whereby we shall lose the peace of our minds, the conversation of our friends, the traffic with our neighbours, the plenty of our land, the form of our customs, the order of our ceremonies, the liberty of a subject, the royalty of your government, and the company and rule of our gracious, virtuous and beautiful Queen: and shall they have courage to spoil, and we none to right our wrongs? Shall they live by our hard labour, and shall we live by their hard laws? All noble spirits hate bondage, and will rather die than endure slavery. Wherefore my friends be constant to your just resolutions, circumspect in your ways, patient in your labours, heroic in your actions; for what man can remember such injuries, and let their courages be cold? Wherefore for your own sakes, your country's sake, your royal Queen's sake, go on with valiant hearts, and active strengths, and may Apollo be your friend, shooting his darts, dazzling your enemy's eyes; may Mars the god of war direct you, in your fight; may Fortune give you aid, and Pallas give you victory.

After she had thus spake, the trumpets sounded to charge, where the young general sent some flying horse to give the onset, and then to run away, which the other army seeing thought it was out of fear, and followed them as in pursuit, which haste disordered and broke all their ranks, which the Queen's army no sooner saw, but it marched in good order to meet them[.] The enemy viewing their unexpected posture, was so daunted as they neither had spirits to fight, nor power to run away, whereby there was a great number killed, and taken prisoners, which made them become absolute masters of the field.

The Prince with much difficulty retreated back about a day's march, with some few; but with the prime of his horse, where he heard of a fresh army coming to assist them; for the King fearing they were not strong enough, being forced suddenly away, caused new men to be raised to follow them. The news of this army rejoiced the Prince much, being at that time very melancholy for the great loss he received, and a disgrace, as he thought; by reason he despised the enemies to the King, and to be overcome, by those he scorned, did wrack his soul; but taking up fresh hopes with his new-come army returned back to the Queen's army again, which when they heard of a new supply, [were] much amazed and dejected, by reason they were weary and tired with their fights, and disordered with gathering up and carrying away their spoils; but the young general perceiving them to hang down their heads, thus spake.

Noble friends,

I perceive such a sadness in your faces, as if fear had taken possession of your hearts, which if it hath, except courage beats it out, it will betray your lives unto your enemies, and to be taken by a timorous thought, before your strength hath grappled with your foes, were base, and if right and truth be on your side, as sure it is, and reason rules your judgement, as I hope it doth, you have no cause to doubt: but if you fear the conduct of my youth, as wanting experience to judge or direct the best, then here are aged men who with Ulysses, and Nestor may compare; their counsel is your aid. Thus let no vain suspicion quench your hopes, but courage set your spirits on fire, and with their heat consume your enemies to ashes.

With that they all aloud did say; go on, we will die or conquer.

In the meanwhile, the Prince was encouraging his new-come army, who was struck with the news of the last battle, hearing nothing of it until they met the Prince; the sudden report like thunder shook their spirits, which to appease, the Prince thus spake.

Noble friends,

You that have humility to obey, love to unite, charity to redress, have hopes to obtain; for hope is the ground on which courage is built: let not the enemy of mistrust vanquish your faith, but perform your loyalty, through your industry, for obedient thoughts [are] not sufficient, without obedient actions[.] Wherefore take courage to fight; let not your enemies kill your spirits, weep not, nor condole at our losses, but let us regain our honours, either by victory or death[.] And they that are slothful, or cowardly in this army, may they neither enjoy the laurel, olive or cyprus, but go to the grave unregarded, or forgotten, or live in shame despised; but those that are industrious and valiant, may they sit high in honour's throne, as fame may blow their praises so loud, and far, no time can stop the sound.

Then the two armies being set in battle array, the Prince to save the infusion of blood, finding his army not full of alacrity, sent the young general a challenge, which when it came, although he knew himself unfit for a single duel, accepted it, being afraid of the dishonour of denying it: but the two armies would not consent to look on, whilst they fought, for in the encounter, both the armies joined in cruel fight.

But [Travellia] having no skill in the art and use of the sword, nor strength to assault, nor resist, was wounded, which wound bled so fast that he fainted and fell down to the ground; but the Prince, who was of a noble nature, perceiving by his shape, that he was but a stripling, ran to untie his headpiece, and viewing his face straight knew her, who grew so astonished thereat, as he had not power to stir for the present, but he stopping the wound as well as he could, brought life again, yet so faint she was, as she could not speak, neither had he power to go away, but sat by until some found him.

In the meantime, the army being left to chance, having not their general to direct them; Fortune played a part of civility, and courtship, giving victory to the ladies, so the Queen's army had the day, and some of the common soldiers, seeking for spoil, found them in this posture, he sitting by, holding her in his arms, from whence they took her, and put her in a litter, and he also in the same as a prisoner, carrying them to the body of the army; and as she went, having recovered her spirits again, thus complaining, [she] said.

I have heard of Pleasure, never could it obtain,
For what we Pleasure call, still lives in Pain:
Then Life is Pain, and Pain is only Life
Which is a Motion, Motion all is strife;
As forward, backward, up or down, or so
Sideways, or in a circle round, doth go.
Then who would live, or would not wish to die,
Since in the Grave there is no Misery?
O let me die, strive not my Life to save,
Death happy is, and Peace lies in the Grave.

The Prince told her, she preached to herself a false doctrine; for, said he;

Life is a Blessing which the Gods do give,
And nothing shows them Gods but that they live;
They the Original of Life, the Spring,
Life the beginning is of everything;
And Motion is from all Eternity,

Eternal Motions make the Gods to be.
To wish no Life, we wish no Gods, and then
No resurrection to the Souls of Men;
In Resurrection, we as Gods become
To be, – none would refuse a Martyrdom;
The very being pleaseth Nature well,
Were she to live always in pains of Hell;
Nature, nothing is more horrid to her
Than Annihilation, that quite undoes her.
Thus Gods and Nature you do wish to spoil,
Because a little pain endures a while;
Devils had rather Devils be, than nought at all,
But you like Angels that did never fall.

Thus they discoursed as they went; but he strove to conceal himself from her knowledge until such time as he thought he might make his peace with her, for fear she should run away again out of hate and dislike to him.

But the army, when they missed their young general, grew so sad, that they took no pleasure in their victory, for they were all as one dumb man, no noise was heard, all eyes were full of tears. But when they saw the litter, as supposing she was dead, they raised a cry that rent the air, and made the thicker clouds to move. Which when she heard, and saw them running to her, she shook her hand, to show them she did live.

Then sent they shouts of joy to Heaven high,
And every countenance sad looked merrily.

But when they came so near to view her face, and saw her pale and weak, they grew into such a rage, that they would have killed the Prince, hearing he wounded her: but she entreated for his life, and begged him for her prisoner; no sooner asked, but granted, who gave the charge into her father's keeping.

Then being brought into her tent, the army watched by turns whilst she was under the chirurgeons' hands for cure; nor would they take any of the spoils, but what she did divide unto them;

nor any direction, but what she gave; nor would they stir until her health permitted her to travel; but being indifferently well, gave order to march on.

But the King had raised another army in the time of her sickness, and sent it out to meet them.

Where she, although weak, went about to order and encourage her soldiers, who loved her better than their life; which affections made them fight so well, that they overcame their enemies; and before the King could raise another army, they got unto the city.

Where as soon as she came near, she gave order to her soldiers to entrench about it; then gave order that they should cast at every corner of the city a mount of earth, on which she placed her cannon to batter down the walls: then did she build forts about to place her men to shoot and cast granadoes in; and by their several assaults they battered the city, and killed many of their men by sundry and sudden assaults: at last, she resolved to storm it. But the King perceiving his weakness, and that he could not hold out long, sent to the young general, desiring a treaty, withal a cessation of arms.

In the meantime, the Queen, being weary of her imprisonment, longing for the coming of her beloved, in a melancholy humour thus spake;

O what a Hell it is to love, and not be loved again! Nay not only to love, but to love a slave, and he regards me not. Do I say, slave? No, he is none that hath no slavish passion: then he is free,

And I am only bound to Slavery;
First to my passions, then to his Tyranny:
What shall I do, you Gods above?
You punish me, and yet you make me love.
Do you delight still in a tortured mind?
Make you no sympathy in human kind?
Must all your Works consist in contradiction?
Or do we nothing enjoy but Fiction?
The Mind is nothing but Apprehension,

'Tis not a Thing, unless it hath Dimension.
But O you powerful Gods, by your Decree,
Can of Nothing a Something make to be:
Then make me Something, grant me my Delight,
Give me my lover, or destroy me quite.

Thus leaving her in a melancholy posture and humour, we return to the armies.

The cessation being near expired, the young general called a council, and thus spake to them.

Right noble and valiant heroics,

The King hath sent to treat of peace, but in my opinion there can be no honourable agreement next to the setting the Queen at liberty, but the resigning of his crown, and so his kingdom to her.

First, for raising hostility, disturbing the sweet peace, and happy condition of a kingdom that never molested them.

Then, for the dishonour, in taking the Queen prisoner, the ruin and spoil of your country, the death of your friends, and the loss of your gallant men killed in this dissension, making many widows, and fatherless children.

Besides, who can rely upon the faith of an unjust prince, who made war upon his neighbours without a just offence, but only through an ambitious attempt upon your Queen and kingdom. Have we not victory? and yet shall we return with loss? shall we despise the gifts of the gods, in making no use of what they give us? and shall the trumpet of loud fame report the Queen was taken prisoner, and resigned upon a low agreement? No; let fame divulge unto the world, her release came with the ruin of this kingdom.

After the general had spoken, one of the council, who was like Nestor for years and experience,

Our general, said he, hath spoke a speech so full of courage and honour, as shows him to be of so true an heroic spirit, that he hath left no room for policy to play a part. But states cannot subsist with valiant hands alone; unless they hold the politic head, which is the guide to great

designs; it burns more cities than granadoes do, it undermines strong towns, pulls down great works, ruins forts, sets battles, takes prisoners, makes slaves, and conquers kings and kingdoms; and that we call policy in a public state, is called discretion in a private family; and it is not, as the vulgar think it, a cheat, or mere deceit, but a wise prudence, to prevent the worst of ills, or to keep peace, or get tranquility. 'Tis true, valour is a daring spirit, but policy is the trusty friend, and covers all those faults it cannot mend with skill, it guides the bark in which man's life swims, and keeps them from the shipwreck of the world, pulls down the ambitious sails, when blown too full with pride, lest it should overturn the ship of safety, so drowned in seas of miseries: but policy will rather choose the oars of patience, and take the tides of time, than venture where the doubts are more than hopes, or hazards more than gains: then let us try to make a prudent peace, not trusting to Fortune's favour, unless she were more constant.

For in the Wars such unknown Chance may fall,
Instead of Victory, be ruined all.

I speak not this to cross my general, for I shall be as ready to obey all his commands, be it never so dangerous, as I have freely delivered my opinion.

After he had spoke, the general rose up, and said, these counsels are too solid to be contradicted by rash youth. Whereupon they all agreed to treat with the King, giving his ambassadors audience. The King's ambassadors coming into their assembly, thus spake.

You great victorious Amitenians,

My master should not need to seek for peace before it sought for him, had not the god of love proved his enemy, persuading Mars to be his foe; for those that are crossed in love, have seldom victory; for Mars doth take the part of Cupid, Venus's son. Thus our great King and master is by love undone: but since 'tis the gods that work his fate, he humbly doth submit; wherefore he sends these proffers unto you.

First, he will build your broken forts again, and raise those walls his soldiers have pulled down.

Secondly, he will repay your charges and expenses in this war, although his own is great, and his loss is more.

Thirdly, he will restore his prisoners, if you will do the like to those you have taken; but for the Queen, she is no prisoner;

For our Master is her Captive, and her Thrall,
Both to command him, and his Kingdom all.

After the Amitenians had consulted, they told the King's ambassadors, that words were not acts, wherefore they could conclude of nothing until the Queen was in her army to make her atonement for herself; and if she were no prisoner, they desired to wait on her out of the city; if not, they must use force.

Whereupon the ambassadors went back to their King to declare their answer, but to return to the captive Prince, who was more fettered in his mind than in his body, for his old father treated him civilly, and used him kindly: but perceiving him to be very melancholy, thought it might proceed from the overthrow he received; which he strove to mediate, telling him, nothing was more subject to chance than war, and that the valiantest and wisest men might fall by Fortune's hand; for, said he, she on wheels, not on firm ground did stand.

She seeks not Worth and Merit to advance,
Her Sceptre which she governed all, was Chance.
With that the Prince, he sighing said, O Fortune most unkind,
I would she were as powerless as blind.

As he was speaking, in come the young general, which when he saw, love's passion shook his manly strength, and made his visage pale; but she being of an affable and sweet disposition, wish[ed] all content of mind to every person, although she had little herself.

Noble Sir, said she, it was not for want of respect I have not visited you, but my engagements have so busily employed me, that till that cessation of arms, I have not had so much time as to examine your welfare; but I know, my father hath not omitted any service he could help you in; neither do I believe, you being commander, can be so ignorant but to know camps can afford nothing but a rude entertainment, having therein no necessary accommodations, and since my wishes cannot make it better, you will be pleased to accept of it, as it is.

Worthy Sir, answered the Prince, I am only a prisoner to your favours, but am free by your noble entertainments.

So after some discourse, telling him of the agreement which was like to be, left him, or rather carried him with her; for his soul went after her, although his person stayed behind: but to follow the ambassadors, who were got to the King, and told him the demands of the Amitenian army [were] to have their Queen before they would treat any farther. The King being very much troubled thereat, for to keep her he durst not, knowing his own weakness, and their strength; and to let her go, he could not; for his passion of love would not give him leave; neither would he call a council, knowing they would be for the departure of the Queen for their own securities; then did he wish for his friend and servant Prince; but at last resolved, went to the Queen his mistress, and taking the crown from his head, laid it at her feet.

Madam, said he, here I deliver you my crown, and with it my kingdom; and yield myself your prisoner, dispose of it, and me as you please, for it never shall be said I make conditions with her I do adore; for since my soul is yours, there is nothing I can own that is not so; and since you must, and will go from this place, let me go with you to set your triumphs out, and lead me as your slave.

Sir, answered she, I have not been so ill treated; nor am I so ungrateful to go away, and leave no thanks behind me: wherefore I will stay until there is such a peace made, as you may receive as much profit, and as little losses thereby as I. Wherefore in order thereunto, I desire that the general of my forces, and some of my council may come hither, and so confer both with myself and you.

The King gave order that the gates of the city might be set open, but the Queen sent a messenger to the army, that none of the forces should enter the city, but keep themselves where they were without: only the general and the council, and some of the chiefest commanders, to come unto her. But when they were ready to wait upon the Queen, the old man fell very sick, and sent to his son the young general, to come unto him to take his leave of him before he died, who went with a sorrowful heart, and sad countenance; and when he came close to his bed, the old man spake; Son, said he, my lease of life is expired, and death, the landlord of my body, knocks at my old and ruinated cottage, sending out my soul to seek another habitation; which soul intends to travel through the airy skies unto the mansion of the gods, where it shall pray for your success and happy days on earth[.] O Father, said Travellia, must you go, and leave me here behind.

Why will the gods so cruelly oppress,
An innocent youth to leave it in distress[.]

You were my good angel to guard me from those evils that Fortune sets about me; you were my guide, which did direct my simple youth, to just and honest ways; what will become of me when you are gone? Or who will restore me from those that seek my ruin? Said the old man, the gods, the gods, my son, they will reward your virtue; farewell, farewell, then turned his head and died.

After he had lamented and mourned over his lifeless corpse, he sent to the Queen, to give him leave to inter his father's ashes; the King hearing thereof sent to the general, inviting him to bring his father's body into the city, and there to be interred in his chief temple, which honour he accepted, whereupon all the army brought the hearse unto the gates, and then returned unto their trenches; but the chief commanders did bear it to the grave[.] The young general when he came into the temple, who was clad all in mourning, only his face was seen, which appeared like the sun when it breaks through a dark and spongy cloud: their beams[25] did shine on those watery drops that fell upon her cheeks, as banks where roses and lilies grew, there standing on a mounted pillar, spake her father's funeral speech.[26]

I come not, said she, here to flatter or belie the dead; but to speak the truth, as far as my knowledge is informed thereby; he was aged in years, not old, for those are only old whose memories and understanding are grown defective by the length of time: he was wise by experience, not led with self-opinion, he was learned in the art of navigation, and not ignorant of land-service, or command, although few that dwell on sea, and profess that art, know little more of land than the ports where they take harbour to shelter from furious storms, or to take fresh victuals in; or to deboist[27] with wine and women[.] But he was most temperate not only in moderating his passion, but appetites with reason, honour and religion; in his behaviour he was affable and free, not formal, nor constrained by vain and self conceit, his disposition gentle, sweet, and kind; he in his nature compassionated all that were in distress; he was industrious to all good effects, and had a nimble and ingenious wit, and such a superfluity of courage, as did not only banish fear in himself, but begot spirit in others; he was bred in the schools of honour, where he had learnt virtuous principles and heroic actions; he had all the ingredients that goeth to the making of an honest and gallant man; and he was not only morally honest, but most pious and devout; he offered not sacrifice to the gods for worldly prosperity, but out of pure love, and adoration to the gods; he was a pattern for all others to take example from; his soul was as the breath of gods; and his animal[28] the best of nature's extraction, but Nature makes nothing to last in one form long, for what she creates, she dissolves again.[29]

With that her tears fell so fast from her eyes, as stopped her mouth for a time; but at last she sighing said,

Although my tears are useless to him, since it is not in their power to alter the decrees of fate, nor can persuade the gods, to give perpetual life here in this world, yet natural affections, they are forced through my eyes[.]

Then bowing down her head over the corpse, which underneath was placed, said:

These as a satisfaction may assuage my grief to think my new-born tears, the issues of my love, shall be buried and lie entombed with his cold ashes, which is the only way to mingle souls, when death has parted bodies; but if that fate had the power to twist my thread of life with his, then death [had] struck me too, and so eased my grief; but since not so, his memory shall lie entombed in my heart until I die.

After he had spoke this funeral speech, he descended from the pillar, and helping to lay the corpse upon the funeral pile, and with a flaming torch, did set the fuel on fire, where after gathering up the ashes, put them in the urn, then placed it in a tomb; after he had thus executed those ceremonies belonging to the dead, he changed his mourning robes, and clothed himself fit for the court or camp again, then he and the council, and the chief commanders went unto the palace of the King, where after some discourse, [he] was brought to the Queen, who joyed more to see her Travellia than the victories they won, and after she had condoled with him for the loss of his father, she congratulated him for the good success he had in the wars, and withal told him she must set at liberty his prisoner the Prince, for she had given him back unto the King, whereupon he presently gave orders for the Prince to repair to the court, and after she heard the relations of all their several actions, and accidents; and had pleased herself with the variety of other discourses, she told them she would sit in a council, to consider what was to be done, as concerning the peace, and so dismissed them for that time, only she stayed Travellia, loving his company so well, she could not so easily part. But the King perceiving her affections, as being never pleased but when Travellia was with her, he grew so jealous, that had not honour forbid him, having past his word unto her they should all there be safe, otherwise he should not have let him live to have been his rival.

But in the meantime, the messenger had caused the Prince to repair to the court, whereat he was much troubled how to behave himself; for, said he in his thoughts, if I should make myself known unto my mistress, she will straight convey away herself either by death, or stealth; and if I go disguised, although I may make the reason known unto the King, yet the court will talk, and think it is for some ill design against the state, so bring an aspersion against my loyalty.

Thus musing a long time with himself, at last he thought it best for to take counsel of the King; and being come to him, the King with great joy embraced him, saying, O my friend, thy company is a kingdom to me. He humbly kiss[ed] his hand, and said, he thought Fortune was so much his enemy, as that she had shut him out of his royal favour: but Sir, said he, it was none of my fault I did not win; for the gods, as Jupiter, Mars, and the rest, are such lovers of the fair effeminate mortals, that they will never be against them; for wheresoever they are, victory is there also.

The King thinking he meant by it the Queen, told him how unkind[ly] she used him, and how he perceived she loved the young general even to a dotage, and withal asked his counsels therein what he should do; but he smiling, yet sighing, said,

O Sir, said he, there is no cause to fear, for those you do suspect is a woman, yet I believe the Queen knows it not. Then he told him all the story of his love, and all the several accidents thereupon, and asked his advice what he should do.

The King, who was overjoyed at his relations, discovering she was a woman, as his joy gave so many several advices, that the number confused the counsel, and confounded the choice.

But whilst they were thus talking, came a messenger to the Prince, which brought him letters from his own country by merchants that came into that country, that his wife was dead; for although they knew not where he was, yet they sent letters into several countries, in hope some might light into his hands: which when he heard, his doubts were turned into hopes. With that, the King and he embraced with joy, making no question now but Cupid was turned their friend, and that he would shoot two golden arrows into their mistresses' hearts from the forts of their affections.

The time being come when the King and Queen, and either's councillors should meet about the peace, they being all set ready to treat, the King entreated the Queen she would give him leave that the Prince might be one of his council, which, said he, without your own consent he shall not come, since he hath been your prisoner.

She told the King, he was not bound to her, since she had given him a release, and your councillors are to be chosen by yourself, and not by me.

After her answer, he sent for him; which when he came, being not disguised, but as he was himself; and Travellia looking upon his face as he was coming in amongst the society, seeing the man she most did fear, she fell into a swound; at which accident the Queen being extremely afflicted, thinking it was done by some design wrought from the jealousy of the King, broke up the juncto[30] for that time, taking all the care she could for his recovery. But Travellia being recovered out of her swound, yet was she sick in mind, though not in body, and kept her bed, as being very ill.

Whereupon the Queen's suspicion was more increased, and [she] feared some poison had been given him; and with that conceit could not endure to see the King.

The King being much troubled that the Queen was more strict to him than she was used to be, and perceiving that it was Travellia that was the cause, complained unto the Prince, and angrily merrily said, dispose of your mistress some way, for I am jealous, said he, although she is a woman.

Sir, said the Prince, I have as much reason to be jealous of the Queen as you have of my mistress, setting her masculine habit aside.

At last they did agree to discover her to the Queen. Whereupon the Prince went to the Queen, and desired by messenger to grant him half an hour's conference.

She desired to be excused.

He sent her word, it was something concerning his own affairs: whereat she gave admittance. When the Prince came to her he said,

Madam, I should not press thus rudely on your thoughts, but that I think I am part of the cause that makes them melancholy.

Sir, said she, you take upon you to know much, for it is hard to know the mind or thoughts of ourselves, much less another's.

Madam, said he, I will be so presumptuous to guess at them, if you will give me leave.

Take it, said she.

Then Madam, said he, I must tell you, you are in love; and those you love, although there is a society of all excellencies, yet cannot return such love you desire; for you have placed your affection upon a woman, who hath concealed her sex, in taking the habit of a man, and might more confirm your mistake by the actions of a soldier. I know not, said the Prince, how kind you have found her, but I have found her cruel[;] then telling the story from the first time he saw her until that present.

When the Queen had heard his relation, her colour came and went, moved by her mixed passions, anger and love; angry that she was deceived, yet still did love, as wishing she had been a man.

Then the Prince began to move unto her the suit of the King; but she was so impatient and troubled in her mind, being crossed in her love, that she would hear nothing concerning love more at that time; which he perceiving, took his leave for the present: but as soon as he was gone,

Tears from her Eyes flowed out, as if they meant
To make her there a Watery Monument;
And her oppressed Heart such sighs sent forth,
Like gusts of wind that blow from South or North.
After this furious Storm, a Calm did rise,
Her Spirits like a still, smooth Water lies.
Then laying down her gentle head to rest,
Thus to the God of Love her prayers addressed:
Thou powerful God of Love, that shoots from high,
One leaden Arrow in my breast let fly,
To quench that scorching heat thou mad'st to burn,
Unless a Woman to a Man can turn.

With that the God of Love did pity take,
Quenched out the first, and did a new Fire make;
Yet was it weak, as being made but new,
But being kindled, it much better grew.
At last, the Flame got hold upon the King,
Which did much Joy unto each Kingdom bring.

After a sweet and refreshing sleep, she rose, and went to Travellia's chamber, and told her how she was discovered; then chiding her gently for not making herself known unto her; for, said she, you have caused me many unquiet rests.

But Travellia begged her pardon, telling her, it was the cause of her misfortunes that concealed her, and not out of any evil design she had to deceive her; then desired her assistance and help to secure her[self].

Whilst they were thus talking, the King and the Prince came to see the sick person, to whom the Queen with a smiling countenance said, she was a-courting her hard-hearted lover.

The King answered, that he hoped she would take pity on him, by what she had felt herself.

The Queen told him that she was likelier to love him now, than if she had never been a lover before; for, said she, there is something pleasing in lovers' thoughts, be their fortunes never so adverse; and I believe, said she, the Prince will say as much.

Madam, said he, it is a pleasing pain, as being mixed with hopes and fears; but if our hopes do cease, all pleasure is gone, and nothing doth remain but pains of Hell.

Then, said the Queen, your mistress were in a sad condition, if she loved you, as you seem to love her, you being a married man.

No, said the Prince, I am now a widower; but I doubt, said he, that doth[31] advantage me in my mistress's affection.

But when Travellia heard he was a widower, her heart did beat like to a feverish pulse, being moved with several passions, fearing it was not so, hoping it was so, joying if it were so, grieving that she ought not to wish it so.

But the Queen asked the Prince, how that he came to know of it. Whereupon he told her.

Said she, I have promised your mistress to protect her against your outrageous assaults; but since your suit is just, and your treaty civil, I will yield her to you, upon that condition you carry her not out of my kingdom; for since I cannot marry her, and so make her my husband, I will keep her if I can, and so make her my friend.

With that, Travellia rises up in her bed, and bowed herself with a pleased countenance, giving the Queen thanks.

Said the Prince, you have given me as much as the gods could give, which is felicity.

Madam, said the King, you have given me nothing.

The Queen, with blushes, answered, that if her council would agree, she would give him herself.

The King for joy kneeled down, and kissed her hand; now I am like to the gods, they can but have their wish.

Thus passing that day in pleasing discourses, the next day they caused their councils to meet, where they concluded the marriage of the King and Queen; and that the Queen should live with their King in the Kingdom of Amours, and that her first son should be heir to the crown, and her second should be heir to the Kingdom of Amity; but in case there were no sons, or but one, then daughters should inherit.

In the meantime, the Prince, and his Princess that was to be, should be Viceroy, or rather she should rule; who was so beloved of the people, as if she had not only been a native born, but as if she had been born from the royal stock. But they thought it fit she should make herself known unto the army by word of mouth, that she was a woman, otherwise they might think she was made away by a violent death; and that the report of being a woman, was only a trick to deceive them; and from thence arise such a mutiny, as might bring a ruin to both kingdoms.

When all was agreed, they prepared for the marriages.

In the meantime, Travellia goeth to the army, attended by the Prince, where the King and Queen came soon after, that the soldiers might see they were there, as witnesses of what she told them. And being all in a circle round about her, she being upon a place raised for that purpose, thus spake.

Noble friends, and valiant soldiers,

I am come here at this present to declare I am a woman, although I am habited like a man, and perchance you may think it immodesty; but they that will judge charitably, will enquire the reason before they give their censure; for upright judges never give sentence before the party proves guilty: wherefore I believe you will not condemn me, because necessity did enforce me to conceal my sex, to protect my honour; for as the love of soul and body is inseparable, so should the love of chastity, and the effeminate sex; and who can love, and not share in danger? And since no danger ought to be avoided, nor life considered, in respect of their honours; and to guard that safe from enemies, no habit is to be denied; for it is not the outward garments that can corrupt the honest mind, for modesty may clothe the soul of a naked body, and a sword becomes a woman when it is used against the enemies of her honour; for though her strength be weak, yet she ought to show her will; and to die in the defence of honour, is to live with noble fame; therefore neither camp, nor court, nor city, nor country, nor danger, nor habit, nor any worldly felicity, must separate the love of chastity, and our sex; for as love is the sweetest, so it is the strongest of all passions; and true love proceeds from virtue, not from vice; wherefore it is to be followed by life, to be maintained till death; and if I have served my Queen honestly, condemn not my modesty.

Then bowing her head down low, first to the King and Queen, then to the army.

Whereupon the army gave a shout, and cried out, Heaven bless you, of what sex soever you be.

After she had spoke this speech, she went into her tent, and dressed herself in her effeminate robes, and came out again, standing in the same place, thus spake.

Noble Friends,

Thus with my masculine clothes I have laid by my masculine spirit; yet not so by, but I shall take it up again, if it be to serve the Queen and kingdom, to whom I owe my life for many obligations.

First, to my Queen, who bought me as a slave, yet used me as a friend; and loved me with that affection, as if nature had linked us in one line, [for] which Heaven reward her with glory and renown. Besides, her love did bestow upon me great honour, made me protector of her kingdom in her absence; and you her subjects out of loyalty obeyed all my commands, although I am young and inexperienced. And 'tis not only what your loyalty enforces, but I have found your affections of love to be such, as showed they came freely from your souls, expressing itself in grieving for my sickness, taking care for my health, joying in my company, mourning for my absence, glorying in my fame; and so much as you would lessen your own, to give it me: what shall I do to show my gratitude? Alas my life is too poor a sacrifice; had I the mansion of the gods, I would resign it for your felicity; but these are only words, not acts, to show you my thanks: yet here I do offer all that the gods or nature gave me, life, health, or beauty, peace, pleasure, or plenty; and these shall stand upon the altar of a thankful heart, ready to sacrifice to your service.

Whereupon all the army cried out, an angel, an angel, the gods had sent unto them.

Then was there a declaration read to the army of the agreement of peace: and when it was read that the Prince should be Viceroy in the Kingdom of Amity, all the soldiers, as if they had been one voice, cried out, Travellia shall be Viceregency; which was granted to pacify them. Whereupon there were great acclamations of joy.

But the Prince told his mistress, she should also govern him.

She answered, that he should govern her, and she would govern the kingdom.

Then went the King and Queen, the Prince and Travellia, the nobles and the chief commanders, to celebrate their nuptials; where on the wedding day, the Queen was adorned with a crown of diamonds, and hung about with rich jewels; yet her beauty did dim their lustre; but Travellia was only dressed in a white silk garment, which hung loosely about her: yet then[32]

Her Face did seem like to a Glory bright,
Where Gods and Goddesses did take delight;
And in her Eyes, new Worlds, you there might see
Love, flying Cupids there as Angels be;
And on her Lips Venus enthroned is,

Inviting duller Lovers there to kiss;
Winged Mercury upon her Tongue did sit,
Strewing out Flowers of Rhetoric and of Wit;
Pallas did circle in each Temple round,
Which with her Wisdom, as a Laurel crowned;
And in her Cheeks sweet Flowers for Love's Poesies,
There Fates spun Threads of Lilies and of Roses;
And every loving Smile, as if each were
A Palace for the Graces to dwell there;
And chaste Diana on her Snow white Breast
There leaned her Head, with pure Thoughts to rest;
When viewed her Neck, great Jove turned all to wonder,
In Love's soft Showers melting without Thunder;
The lesser Gods on her white Hands did lie,
Thinking each Vein to be their Azure Sky;
Her charming circling Arms made Mars to cease
All his fierce Battles, for a Love's soft Peace;
And on our World's Globe sate triumphing high,
Heaved there by Atlas up unto the Sky;
And sweet-breathed Zephyrus did blow her Name
Into the glorious Trumpet of good Fame.

After they were married, to set out their triumphs, they had masques, plays, balls, pageants, shows, processions, and the like; and when they had kept the festivals some days in the city, the Prince and Princess desired they might go and revel with the army for some days, that was without the city. The Queen being well pleased therewith, thither they went, where they had tiltings, running at the ring, fencing, wrestling, vaulting, jumping, running races of horse and foot, baiting of beasts, and many the like warlike pastimes; and such hospitality, that every common soldier was feasted; and after they were all satisfied with sports and good cheer, the Prince and Princess returned to the court again; and after they had remained there some time, the King and Queen sent them with the army into the Kingdom of Amity; and the soldiers returned, not only with all the spoils they got in the war, but the King did present all the chief commanders with presents; and the two kingdoms lived in peace and tranquility during the life of the King and Queen, and for all I can hear, do so to this day.

THE

DESCRIPTION

OF A NEW

WORLD,

CALLED

The Blazing World.

WRITTEN

By the Thrice Noble, Illustrious, and Excellent

PRINCESS,

THE

Duchess of Newcastle.

TO THE DUCHESS OF NEWCASTLE, ON HER NEW BLAZING WORLD.

Our Elder World, with all their Skill and Arts
Could but divide the World into three Parts:
Columbus then for Navigation fam'd,
Found a new World, America 'tis nam'd:
Now this new World was found, it was not made,
Only discovered, lying in Time's shade.
Then what are You, having no Chaos found
To make a World, or any such least ground?
But your creating Fancy, thought it fit
To make your World of Nothing, but pure Wit.
Your Blazing-world, beyond the Stars mounts higher,
Enlightens all with a Celestial Fire.

William Newcastle

TO THE READER

If you wonder, that I join a work of fancy to my serious philosophical contemplations;[1] think not that it is out of a disparagement to philosophy; or out of an opinion, as if this noble study were but a fiction of the mind; for though philosophers may err in searching and enquiring after the causes of natural effects, and many times embrace falshoods for truths; yet this doth not prove, that the ground of philosophy is merely fiction, but the error proceeds from the different motions of reason, which cause different opinions in different parts, and in some are more irregular than in others; for reason being dividable, because material, cannot move in all parts alike; and since there is but one truth in nature, all those that hit not this truth, do err, some more, some less; for though some may come nearer the mark than others, which makes their opinions seem more probable and rational than others; yet as long as they swerve from this only truth, they are in the wrong: nevertheless, all do ground their opinions upon reason; that is, upon rational probabilities, at least, they think they do: But *fictions* are an issue of man's fancy, framed in his own mind, according as he pleases, without regard, whether the thing he fancies, be really existent without his mind or not; so that reason searches the depth of nature, and enquires after the true causes of natural effects; but fancy creates of its own accord whatsoever it pleases, and delights in its own work. The end of reason, is truth; the end of fancy, is fiction: but mistake me not, when I distinguish *fancy* from *reason*; I mean not as if fancy were not made by the rational parts of matter; but by *reason* I understand a rational search and enquiry into the causes of natural effects; and by *fancy* a voluntary creation or production of the mind, both being effects, or rather actions of the rational parts of matter; of which, as that is a more profitable and useful study than this, so it is also more laborious and difficult, and requires sometimes the help of fancy, to recreate the mind, and withdraw it from its more serious contemplations.

And this is the reason, why I added this piece of fancy to my philosophical observations, and joined them as two worlds at the ends of their poles; both for my own sake, to divert my studious thoughts, which I employed in the contemplation thereof, and to delight the reader with variety, which is always pleasing. But lest my fancy should stray too much, I chose such a fiction as would be agreeable to the subject treated of in the former parts; it is a description of a *new world*, not such as *Lucian*'s, or the *French*-man's world in the moon;[2] but a world of my own creating, which I call the *Blazing World*: the first part whereof is *romancical*, the second philosophical, and the third is merely *fancy*, or (as I may call it) *fantastical*, which if it add any satisfaction to you, I shall account my self a happy *creatoress*; if not, I must be content to live a melancholy life in my own world; I cannot call it a poor world, if poverty be only want of gold, silver, and jewels; for there is more gold in it than all the chemists ever did, and (as I verily believe) will ever be able to make. As for the rocks of diamonds, I wish with all my soul they might be shared amongst my noble female friends, and upon that condition, I would willingly quit my part; and of the gold I should only desire so much as might suffice to repair my noble lord and husband's losses:[3] for I am not covetous, but as ambitious as ever any of my sex was, is, or can be; which makes, that though I cannot be *Henry* the Fifth, or *Charles* the Second, yet I endeavour to be *Margaret* the *First*; and although I have neither power, time nor occasion to conquer the world as *Alexander* and *Caesar* did; yet rather than not to be mistress of one, since Fortune and the Fates would give me none, I have made a world of my own: for which no body, I hope, will blame me, since it is in every one's power to do the like.

THE DESCRIPTION OF A NEW WORLD, CALLED THE BLAZING WORLD.

A merchant travelling into a foreign country, fell extremely in love with a young Lady; but being a stranger in that nation, and beneath her both in birth and wealth, he could have but little hopes of obtaining his desire; however his love growing more and more vehement upon him, even to the slighting of all difficulties, he resolved at last to steal her away; which he had the better opportunity to do, because her father's house was not far from the sea, and she often using to gather shells upon the shore, accompanied not with above two or three of her servants, it encouraged him the more to execute his design. Thus coming one time with a little light vessel, not unlike a packet-boat, manned with some few sea-men, and well victualled for fear of some accidents which might perhaps retard their journey to the place where she used to repair, he forced her away: But when he fancied himself the happiest man of the world, he proved to be the most unfortunate; for Heaven frowning at his theft, raised such a tempest, as they knew not what to do, or whither to steer their course; so that the vessel, both by its own lightness, and the violent motion of the wind, was carried as swift as an arrow out of a bow, towards the North Pole, and in a short time reached the Icy Sea, where the wind forced it amongst huge pieces of ice; but being little, and light, it did by assistance and favour of the Gods to this virtuous Lady, so turn and wind through those precipices, as if it had been guided by some experienced pilot, and skilful mariner: but alas! those few men which were in it, not knowing whither they went, nor what was to be done in so strange an adventure, and not being provided for so cold a voyage, were all frozen to death, the young Lady only, by the light of her beauty, the heat of her youth, and protection of the gods, remaining alive: neither was it a wonder that the men did freeze to death; for they were not only driven to the very end or point of the Pole of that world, but even to another Pole of another world, which joined close to it; so that the cold having a double strength at the conjunction of those two Poles, was insupportable: at last, the boat still passing on, was forced into another world, for it is impossible to round this world's globe from Pole to Pole, so as we do from East to West; because the Poles of the other world, joining to the Poles of this, do not allow any further passage to surround the world that way; but if any one arrives to either of these Poles, he is either forced to return, or to enter into another world; and lest you should scruple at it, and think, if it were thus, those that live at the Poles would either see two suns at one time, or else they would never want the sun's light for six months together, as it is commonly believed; you must know, that each of these worlds having its own sun to enlighten it, they move each one in their peculiar circles; which motion is so just and exact, that neither can hinder or obstruct the other; for they do not exceed their tropics, and although they should meet, yet we in this world cannot so well perceive them, by reason of the brightness of our sun, which being nearer to us, obstructs the splendour of the suns of the other worlds, they being too far off to be discerned by our optic perception, except we use very good telescopes, by which skilful astronomers have often observed two or three suns at once.

But to return to the wandering boat, and the distressed Lady, she seeing all the men dead, found small comfort in life; their bodies which were preserved all that while from putrefaction and stench, by the extremity of cold, began now to thaw, and corrupt; whereupon she having not strength enough to fling them over-board, was forced to remove out of her small cabin, upon the deck, to avoid that nauseous smell; and finding the boat swim between two plains of ice, as a stream that runs betwixt two shores, at last perceived land, but covered all with snow: from which came walking upon the ice str in shape like bears, only they went upright creatures coming near the boat, catched hold paws, that served them instead of hands; some them entered first; and when they came out, one after another; at last having viewed and observed all that was in the boat, they spoke to each other in a language which the Lady did not understand, and having carried her out of the boat, sunk it, together with the dead men.

The Lady now finding herself in so strange a place, and amongst such a wonderful kind of creatures, was extremely stricken with fear, and could entertain no other thoughts, but that every moment her life was to be a sacrifice to their cruelty; but those bear-like creatures, how terrible soever they appeared to her sight, yet were they so far from exercising any cruelty upon her, that rather they showed her all civility and kindness imaginable; for she being not able to go upon the ice, by reason of its slipperiness, they took her up in their rough arms, and carried her into their city, where instead of houses, they had caves under ground; and as soon as they entered the city, both males and females, young and old, flocked together to see this Lady, holding up their paws in admiration; at last having brought her into a certain large and spacious cave, which they intended for her reception, they left her to the custody of the females, who entertained her with all kindness and respect, and gave her such victuals as they were used to eat; but seeing her constitution neither agreed with the temper of that climate, nor their diet, they were resolved to carry her into another island of a warmer temper; in which were men like foxes, only walking in an upright shape, who received their neighbours the bear-men with great civility and courtship, very much admiring this beauteous Lady, and having discoursed some while together, agreed at last to make her a present to the Emperor of their world; to which end, after she had made some short stay in the same place, they brought her cross that island to a large river, whose stream ran smooth and clear, like crystal; in which were numerous boats, much like our fox-traps; in one whereof she was carried, some of the bear- and fox-men waiting on her; and as soon as they had crossed the river, they came into an island where there were men which had heads, beaks, and feathers, like wild-geese, only they went in an upright shape, like the bear-men and fox-men; their rumps they carried between their legs, their wings were of the same length with their bodies, and their tails of an indifferent size, trailing after them like a lady's garment; and after the bear- and fox-men had declared their intention and design to their neighbours, the geese- or bird-men, some of them joined to the rest, and attended the Lady through that island, till they came to another great and large river, where there was a preparation made of many boats, much like birds' nests, only of a bigger size; and having crossed that river, they arrived into another island, which was of a pleasant and mild temper, full of woods, and the inhabitants thereof were satyrs, who received both the bear-, fox- and bird-men, with all respect and civility; and after some conferences (for they all understood each other's language) some chief of the satyrs joining to them, accompanied the Lady out of that island to another river, wherein were very handsome and commodious barges; and having crossed that river, they entered into a large and spacious kingdom, the men whereof were of a grass-green complexion, who entertained them very kindly, and provided all conveniences for their further voyage: hitherto they had only crossed rivers, but now they could not avoid the open seas any longer; wherefore they made their ships and tacklings ready to sail over into the island, where the Emperor of their Blazing World (for so it was called) kept his residence; very good navigators they were; and though they had no knowledge of the lodestone, or needle, or pendulous watches, yet (which was as serviceable to them) they had subtle observations, and great practice; insomuch that they could not only tell the depth of the sea in every place, but where there were shelves of sand, rocks, and other obstructions to be avoided by skilful and experienced sea-men: besides, they were excellent augurers, which skill they counted more necessary and beneficial than the use of compasses, cards, watches, and the like; but above the rest, they had an extraordinary art, much to be taken notice of by experimental philosophers, and that was a certain engine, which would draw in a great quantity of air, and shoot forth wind with a great force; this engine in a calm, they placed behind their ships, and in a storm, before; for it served against the raging waves, like canons against an hostile army, or besieged town. It would batter and beat the waves in pieces, were they as high as steeples; and as soon as a breach was made, they forced their passage through, in spight even of the most furious wind, using two of those engines at every ship, one before, to beat off the waves, and another behind to drive it on; so that the artificial wind had the better of the natural; for it had a greater advantage of the waves than the natural of the ships; the natural being above the face of the water, could not without a down-right motion enter or press into the ships, whereas the artificial with a sideward motion did pierce into the bowels of the waves: moreover, it is to be observed, that in a great tempest they would join their ships in battle array, and when they feared wind and waves would be too strong for them, if they divided their ships, they joined as many together as the compass or advantage of the places of the liquid element would give them leave; for their ships were so ingeniously contrived, that they could fasten them together as close as a honey-comb without waste of place; and being thus united, no wind nor waves were able to separate them. The Emperor's ships were all of gold, but the merchants and skippers of leather; the golden ships were not much heavier than ours of wood, by reason they were neatly made, and required not such thickness, neither were they troubled with pitch, tar, pumps, guns, and the like, which make our wooden ships very heavy; for though they were not all of a piece, yet they were so well soddered,[4] that there was no fear of leaks, chinks, or clefts; and as for guns, there was no use of them, because they had no other enemies but the winds; but the leather ships were not altogether so sure, although much lighter; besides, they were pitched to keep out water.

Having thus prepared and ordered their navy, they went on in despite of calm or storm, and though the Lady at first fancied herself in a very sad condition, and her mind was much tormented with doubts and fears, not knowing whether this strange adventure would tend to her safety or destruction; yet she being withal of a generous spirit, and ready wit, considering what dangers she had past, and finding those sorts of men civil and diligent attendants to her, took courage, and endeavoured to learn their language; which after she had obtained so far, that partly by some words and signs she was able to apprehend their meaning, she was so far from being afraid of them, that she thought her self not only safe, but very happy in their company: by which we may see, that novelty discomposes the mind, but acquaintance settles it in peace and tranquility. At last, having passed by several rich islands and kingdoms, they went towards Paradise, which was the seat of the Emperor; and coming in sight of it, rejoiced very much; the Lady at first could perceive nothing but high rocks, which seemed to touch the skies; and although they appeared not of an equal height, yet they seemed to be all one piece, without partitions; but at last drawing nearer, she perceived a cleft, which was a part of those rocks, out of which she spied coming forth a great number of boats, which afar off showed like a company of ants, marching one after another; the boats appeared like the holes or partitions in a honey-comb, and when joined together, stood as close; the men were of several complexions, but none like any of our world; and when both the boats and ships met, they saluted and spake to each other very courteously; for there was but one language in all that world, nor no more but one Emperor, to whom they all submitted with the greatest duty and obedience, which made them live in a continued peace and happiness, not acquainted with other foreign wars, or home-bred insurrections. The Lady now being arrived at this place, was carried out of her ship into one of those boats, and conveyed through the same passage (for there was no other) into that part of the world where the Emperor did reside; which part was very pleasant, and of a mild temper: within itself it was divided by a great number of vast and large rivers, all ebbing and flowing, into several islands of unequal distance from each other, which in most parts were as pleasant, healthful, rich, and fruitful, as nature could make them; and, as I mentioned before, secure from all foreign invasions, by reason there was but one way to enter, and that like a labyrinth, so winding and turning among the rocks, that no other vessels but small boats, could pass, carrying not above three passengers at a time: on each side all along this narrow and winding river, there were several cities, some of marble, some of alabaster, some of agate, some of amber, some of coral, and some of other precious materials not known in our world; all which after the Lady had passed, she came to the imperial city, named Paradise, which appeared in form like several islands; for rivers did run betwixt every street, which together with the bridges, whereof there was a great number, were all paved; the city itself was built of gold, and their architectures were noble, stately, and magnificent, not like our modern, but like those in the Roman's time; for our modern buildings are like those houses which children use to make of cards, one storey above another, fitter for birds, than men; but theirs were more large, and broad, than high; the highest of them did not exceed two storeys, besides those rooms that were under-ground, as cellars, and other offices. The Emperor's palace stood upon an indifferent ascent from the imperial city; at the top of which ascent was a broad arch, supported by several pillars, which went round the palace, and contained four of our English miles in compass: within the arch stood the Emperor's Guard, which consisted of several sorts of men; at every half mile was a gate to enter, and every gate was of a different fashion; the first, which allowed a passage from the imperial city into the palace, had on either hand a cloister, the outward part whereof stood upon arches sustained by pillars, but the inner part was close: being entered through the gate, the palace itself appeared in its middle like the aisle of a church, a mile and a half long, and half a mile broad; the roof of it was all arched, and rested upon pillars, so artificially placed, that a stranger would lose himself therein without a guide; at the extreme sides, that is, between the outward and inward part of the cloister, were lodgings for attendants, and in the midst of the palace, the Emperor's own rooms; whose lights were placed at the top of every one, because of the heat of the sun: the Emperor's apartment for state was no more enclosed than the rest; only an imperial throne was in every apartment, of which the several adornments could not be perceived until one entered, because the pillars were so just opposite to one another, that all the adornments could not be seen at once. The first part of the palace was, as the imperial city, all of gold, and when it came to the Emperor's apartment, it was so rich with diamonds, pearls, rubies, and the like precious stones, that it surpasses my skill to enumerate them all. Amongst the rest, the imperial room of state appeared most magnificent; it was paved with green diamonds (for in that world are diamonds of all colours) so artificially, as it seemed but of one piece; the pillars were set with diamonds so close, and in such a manner, that they appeared most glorious to the sight; between every pillar was a bow or arch of a certain sort of diamonds, the like whereof our world does not afford; which being placed in every one of the arches in several rows, seemed just like so many rainbows of several different colours. The roof of the arches was of blue diamonds, and in the midst thereof was a carbuncle,[5] which represented the sun; the rising and setting sun at the East and West side of the room were made of rubies. Out of this room there was a passage into the Emperor's bed-chamber, the walls whereof were of jet, and the floor of black marble; the roof was of mother of pearl, where the moon and blazing stars were represented by white diamonds, and his bed was made of diamonds and carbuncles.

No sooner was the Lady brought before the Emperor, but he conceived her to be some goddess, and offered to worship her; which she refused, telling him, (for by that time she had pretty well learned their language) that although she came out of another world, yet was she but a mortal; at which the Emperor rejoicing, made her his wife, and gave her an absolute power to rule and govern all that world as she pleased. But her subjects, who could hardly be persuaded to believe her mortal, tendered her all the veneration and worship due to a deity.

Her accoutrement after she was made Empress, was as

followeth: on her head she wore a cap of pearl, and a half-moon of diamonds just before it; on the top of her crown came spreading over a broad carbuncle, cut in the form of the sun; her coat was of pearl, mixed with blue diamonds, and fringed with red ones; her buskins[6] and sandals were of green diamonds: in her left hand she held a buckler,[7] to signify the defence of her dominions; which buckler was made of that sort of diamond as has several different colours; and being cut and made in the form of an arch, showed like a rainbow; in her right hand she carried a spear made of a white diamond, cut like the tail of a blazing star, which signified that she was ready to assault those that proved her enemies.

None was allowed to use or wear gold but those of the imperial race, which were the only nobles of the state; nor durst anyone wear jewels but the Emperor, the Empress, and their eldest son, notwithstanding that they had an infinite quantity both of gold and precious stones in that world; for they had larger extents of gold, than our Arabian sands; their precious stones were rocks, and their diamonds of several colours; they used no coin, but all their traffic was by exchange of several commodities.

Their priests and governors were princes of the imperial blood, and made eunuchs for that purpose; and as for the ordinary sort of men in that part of the world where the Emperor resided, they were of several complexions; not white, black, tawny, olive or ash-coloured; but some appeared of an azure, some of a deep purple, some of a grass-green, some of a scarlet, some of an orange-colour, etc. Which colours and complexions, whether they were made by the bare reflection of light, without the assistance of small particles, or by the help of well-ranged and ordered atoms; or by a continual agitation of little globules; or by some pressing and reacting motion, I am not able to determine. The rest of the inhabitants of that world, were men of several different sorts, shapes, figures, dispositions, and humours, as I have already made mention heretofore; some were bear-men, some worm-men, some fish- or mear-men,[8] otherwise called syrens; some bird-men, some fly-men, some e geese-men, some spider-men, some lice-men, n, some ape-men, some jackdaw-men, some ome parrot-men, some satyrs, some giants, and hich I cannot all remember; and of these several en, each followed such a profession as was most proper for the nature of their species, which the Empress encouraged them in, especially those that had applied themselves to the study of several arts and sciences; for they were as ingenious and witty in the invention of profitable and useful arts, as we are in our world, nay, more; and to that end she erected schools, and founded several societies. The bear-men were to be her experimental philosophers, the bird-men her astronomers, the fly-, worm- and fish-men her natural philosophers, the ape-men her chemists, the satyrs her Galenic physicians, the fox-men her politicians, the spider- and lice-men her mathematicians, the jackdaw-, magpie- and parrot-men her orators and logicians, the giants her architects, etc. But before all things, she having got a sovereign power from the Emperor over all the world, desired to be informed both of the manner of their religion and government, and to that end she called the priests and statesmen, to give her an account of either. Of the statesmen she enquired, first, why they had so few laws? To which they answered, that many laws made many divisions, which most commonly did breed factions, and at last break out into open wars. Next, she asked, why they preferred the monarchical form of government before any other? They answered, that as it was natural for one body to have but one head, so it was also natural for a politic body to have but one governor; and that a commonwealth, which had many governors was like a monster with many heads: besides, said they, a monarchy is a divine form of government, and agrees most with our religion; for as there is but one God, whom we all unanimously worship and adore with one faith, so we are resolved to have but one Emperor, to whom we all submit with one obedience.

Then the Empress seeing that the several sorts of her subjects had each their churches apart, asked the priests whether they were of several religions? They answered her Majesty, that there was no more but one religion in all that world, nor no diversity of opinions in that same religion; for though there were several sorts of men, yet had they all but one opinion concerning the worship and adoration of God. The Empress asked them, whether they were Jews, Turks, or Christians? We do not know, said they, what religions those are; but we do all unanimously acknowledge, worship and adore the only, omnipotent, and eternal God, with all reverence, submission, and duty. Again, the Empress enquired, whether they had several forms of worship? They answered, no: for our devotion and worship consists only in prayers, which we frame according to our several necessities, in petitions, humiliations, thanksgiving, etc. Truly, replied the Empress, I thought you had been either Jews, or Turks, because I never perceived any women in your congregations; but what is the reason, you bar them from your religious assemblies? It is not fit, said they, that men and women should be promiscuously together in time of religious worship; for their company hinders devotion, and makes many, instead of praying to God, direct their devotion to their mistresses. But, asked the Empress, have they no congregation of their own, to perform the duties of divine worship, as well as men? No, answered they: but they stay at home, and say their prayers by themselves in their closets. Then the Empress desired to know the reason why the priests and governors of their world were made eunuchs? They answered, to keep them from marriage: for women and children most commonly make disturbance both in church and state. But, said she, women and children have no employment in church or state. 'Tis true, answered they; but although they are not admitted to public employments, yet are they so prevalent with their husbands and parents, that many times by their importunate persuasions, they cause as much, nay, more mischief secretly, than if they had the management of public affairs.

The Empress having received an information of what concerned both church and state, passed some time in viewing the imperial palace, where she admired much the skill and ingenuity of the architects, and enquired of them, first, why they built their houses no higher than two storeys from the ground? They answered her Majesty, that the lower their buildings were, the less were they subject either to the heat of the sun, to wind, tempest, decay, etc. Then she desired to know the reason, why they made them so thick? They answered, that the thicker the walls were, the warmer were they in winter, and cooler in summer, for their thickness kept out both cold and heat. Lastly, she asked, why they arched their roofs, and made so many pillars? They replied, that arches and pillars, did not only grace a building very much, and caused it to appear magnificent, but made it also firm and lasting.

The Empress was very well satisfied with their answers; and after some time, when she thought that her new founded societies of the vertuosos had made a good progress in their several employments, which she had put them upon, she caused a convocation first of the bird-men, and commanded them to give her a true relation of the two celestial bodies, *viz.* the sun and moon, which they did with all the obedience and faithfulness befitting their duty.

The sun, as much as they could observe, they related to be a firm or solid stone, of a vast bigness, of colour yellowish, and of an extraordinary splendour; but the moon, they said, was of a whitish colour; and although she looked dim in the presence of the sun, yet had she her own light, and was a shining body of her self as might be perceived by her vigorous appearance in moonshiny nights; the difference only betwixt her own and the sun's light was that the sun did strike his beams in a direct line; but the moon never respected the centre of their world in a right line, but her centre was always excentrical. The spots both in the sun and moon, as far as they were able to perceive, they affirmed to be nothing else but flaws and stains of their stony bodies. Concerning the heat of the sun, they were not of one opinion; some would have the sun hot in itself, alleging an old tradition, that it should at some time break asunder, and burn the heavens, and consume this world into hot embers, which, said they, could not be done, if the sun were not fiery of itself. Others again said, this opinion could not stand with reason; for fire being a destroyer of all things, the sun-stone after this manner would burn up all the near adjoining bodies: besides, said they, fire cannot subsist without fuel; and the sun-stone having nothing to feed on, would in a short time consume itself; wherefore they thought it more probable that the sun was not actually hot, but only by the reflection of its light; so that its heat was an effect of its light, both being immaterial: but this opinion again was laughed at by others, and rejected as ridiculous, who thought it impossible that one immaterial should produce another; and believed that both the light and heat of the sun proceeded from a swift circular motion of the ethereal globules, which by their striking upon the optic nerve, caused light, and their motion produced heat: but neither would this opinion hold; for, said some, then it would follow, that the sight of animals is the cause of light, and that, were there no eyes, there would be no light; which was against all sense and reason. Thus they argued concerning the heat and light of the sun; but which is remarkable, none did say, that the sun was a globous fluid body, and had a swift circular motion; but all agreed it was fixed and firm like a centre, and therefore they generally called it the sun-stone.

Then the Empress asked them the reason, why the sun and moon did often appear in different postures or shapes, as sometimes magnified, sometimes diminished, sometimes elevated, otherwhiles depressed, now thrown to the right, and then to the left? To which some of the bird-men answered, that it proceeded from the various degrees of heat and cold, which are found in the air, from whence did follow a differing density and rarity; and likewise from the vapours that are interposed, whereof those that ascend are higher and less dense than the ambient air, but those which descend are heavier, and more dense. But others did with more probability affirm, that it was nothing else but the various patterns of the air; for like as painters do not copy out one and the same original just alike at all times, so said they, do several parts of the air make different patterns of the luminous bodies of the sun and moon, which patterns, as several copies, the sensitive motions do figure out in the substance of our eyes.

ver the Empress liked much better than the former, d further, what opinion they had of those creatures led the motes of the sun? To which they answered, ere nothing else but streams of very small, rare and transparent particles, through which the sun was represented as through a glass; for if they were not transparent, said they, they would eclipse the light of the sun; and if not rare and of an airy substance, they would hinder flies from flying in the air, at least retard their flying motion: nevertheless, although they were thinner than the thinnest vapour, yet were they not so thin as the body of air, or else they would not be perceptible by animal sight. Then the Empress asked, whether they were living creatures? They answered, yes: because they did increase and decrease, and were nourished by the presence, and starved by the absence of the sun.

Having thus finished their discourse of the sun and moon, the Empress desired to know what stars there were besides? But they answered, that they could perceive in that world none other but blazing stars, and from thence it had the name that it was called the Blazing World; and these blazing stars, said they, were such solid, firm and shining bodies as the sun and moon, not of a globular, but of several sorts of figures, some had tails, and some other kinds of shapes.

After this, the Empress asked them, what kind of substance or creature the air was? The bird-men answered, that they could have no other perception of the air, but by their own respiration: for, said they, some bodies are only subject to touch, others only to sight, and others only to smell; but some are subject to none of our exterior senses: for nature is so full of variety, that our weak senses cannot perceive all the various sorts of her creatures; neither is there any one object perceptible by all our senses, no more than several objects are by one sense. I believe you, replied the Empress; but if you can give no account of the air, said she, you will hardly be able to inform me how wind is made; for they say that wind is nothing but motion of the air. The bird-men answered, that they observed wind to be more dense than air, and therefore subject to the sense of touch; but what properly wind was, and the manner how it was made, they could not exactly tell; some said, it was caused by the clouds falling on each other, and others, that it was produced of a hot and dry exhalation, which ascending, was driven down again by the coldness of the air that is in the middle region, and by reason of its lightness, could not go directly to the bottom, but was carried by the air up and down: some would have it a flowing water of the air; and others again a flowing air moved by the blaze of the stars.

But the Empress seeing they could not agree concerning the cause of wind, asked, whether they could tell how snow was made? To which they answered, that according to their observation, snow was made by a commixture of water, and some certain extract of the element of fire that is under the moon; a small portion of which extract being mixed with water, and beaten by air or wind, made a white froth called snow, which being after some while dissolved by the heat of the same spirit, turned to water again. This observation amazed the Empress very much; for she had hitherto believed, that snow was made by cold motions, and not by such an agitation or beating of a fiery extract upon water: nor could she be persuaded to believe it until the fish- or mear-men had delivered their observation upon the making of ice, which, they said, was not produced, as some had hitherto conceived, by the motion of the air, raking the superficies[9] of the earth, but by some strong saline vapour arising out of the seas, which condensed water into ice; and the more quantity there was of that vapour, the greater were the mountains or precipices of ice; but the reason that it did not so much freeze in the torrid zone, or under the ecliptic, as near or under the Poles, was, that this vapour in those places being drawn up by the sun beams into the middle region of the air, was only condensed into water, and fell down in showers of rain; when as, under the Poles, the heat of the sun being not so vehement, the same vapour had no force or power to rise so high, and therefore caused so much ice, by ascending and acting only upon the surface of water.

This relation confirmed partly the observation of the bird-men concerning the cause of snow; but since they had made mention that that same extract, which by its commixture with water made snow, proceeded from the element of fire, that is under the moon; the Empress asked them of what nature that elementary fire was; whether it was like ordinary fire here upon earth, or such a fire as is within the bowels of the earth, and as the famous mountains Vesuvius and Ætna do burn withal, or whether it was such a sort of fire as is found in flints, etc. They answered, that the elementary fire, which is underneath the sun, was not so solid as any of those mentioned fires; because it had no solid fuel to feed on; but yet it was much like the flame of ordinary fire, only somewhat more thin and fluid; for flame, said they, is nothing else but the airy part of a fired body.

Lastly, the Empress asked the bird-men of the nature of thunder and lightning? and whether it was not caused by roves[10] of ice falling upon each other? To which they answered, that it was not made that way, but by an encounter of cold and heat; so that an exhalation being kindled in the clouds, did dash forth lightning, and that there were so many rentings of clouds as there were sounds and cracking noises: but this opinion was contradicted by others, who affirmed that thunder was a sudden and monstrous blas, stirred up in the air, and did not always require a cloud; but the Empress not knowing what they meant by blas (for even they themselves were not able to explain the sense of this word) liked the former better; and to avoid hereafter tedious disputes, and have the truth of the phaenomenas of celestial bodies more exactly known, commanded the bear-men, which were her experimental philosophers, to observe them through such instruments as are called telescopes, which they did according to her Majesty's command; but these telescopes caused more differences and divisions amongst them, than ever they had before; for some said, they perceived that the sun stood still, and the earth did move about it, others were of opinion, that they both did move; and others said again, that the earth stood still, and the sun did move; some counted more stars than others; some discovered new stars never seen before; some fell into a great dispute with others concerning the bigness of the stars; some said the moon was another world like their terrestrial globe, and the spots therein were hills and valleys; but others would have the spots to be the terrestrial parts, and the smooth and glossy parts, the sea: at last, the Empress commanded them to go with their telescopes to the very end of the Pole that was joined to the world she came from, and try whether they could perceive any stars in it; which they did; and being returned to her Majesty, reported that they had seen three blazing-stars appear there, one after another in a short time, whereof two were bright, and one dim; but they could not agree neither in this observation; for some said it was but one star which appeared at three several times, in several places; and others would have them to be three several stars; for they thought it impossible, that those three several appearances should have been but one star, because every star did rise at a certain time, and appeared in a certain place, and did disappear in the same place: next, it is altogether improbable, said they, that one star should fly from place to place, especially at such a vast distance, without a visible motion, in so short a time, and appear in such different places, whereof two were quite opposite, and the third side-ways: lastly, if it had been but one star, said they, it would always have kept the same splendour, which it did not; for, as above mentioned, two were bright, and one was dim. After they had thus argued, the Empress began to grow angry at their telescopes, that they could give no better intelligence; for, said she, now I do plainly perceive, that your glasses are false informers, and instead of discovering the truth, delude your senses; wherefore I command you to break them, and let the bird-men trust only to their natural eyes, and examine celestial objects by the motions of their own sense and reason. The bear-men replied, that it was not the fault of their glasses, which caused such differences in their opinions, but the sensitive motions in their optic organs did not move alike, nor were their rational judgments always regular: to which the Empress answered, that if their glasses were true informers, they would rectify their irregular sense and reason; but, said she, nature has made your sense and reason more regular than art has your glasses, for they are mere deluders, and will never lead you to the knowledge of truth; wherefore I command you again to break them; for you may observe the progressive motions of celestial bodies with your natural eyes better than through artificial glasses. The bear-men being exceedingly troubled at her Majesty's dipleasure concerning their telescopes, kneeled down, and in the humblest manner petitioned that they might not be broken; for, said they, we take more delight in artificial delusions, than in natural truths. Besides, we shall want employments for our senses, and subjects for arguments; for were there nothing but truth, and no falsehood, there would be no occasion for to dispute, and by this means we should want the aim and pleasure of our endeavours in confuting and contradicting each other; neither would one man be thought wiser than another, but all would either be alike knowing and wise, or all would be fools; wherefore we most humbly beseech your Imperial Majesty to spare our glasses, which are our only delight, and as dear to us as our lives. The Empress at last consented to their request, but upon condition, that their disputes and quarrels should remain within their schools, and cause no factions or disturbances in state, or government. The bear-men, full of joy, returned their most humble thanks to the Empress; and to make her amends for the displeasure which their telescopes had occasioned, told her Majesty, that they had several other artificial optic-glasses, which they were sure would give her Majesty a great deal more satisfaction. Amongst the rest they brought forth several microscopes, by the means of which they could enlarge the shapes of little bodies, and make a louse appear as big as an elephant, and a mite as big as a whale. First of all they showed the Empress a grey drone-fly, wherein they observed that the greatest part of her face, nay, of her head, consisted of two large bunches all covered over with a multitude of small pearls or hemispheres in a trigonal order,[11] which pearls were of two degrees, smaller and bigger; the smaller degree was lowermost, and looked towards the ground; the other was upward, and looked sideward, forward and backward: they were all so smooth and polished, that they were able to represent the image of any object, the number of them was in all 14000. After the view of this strange and miraculous creature, and their several observations upon it, the Empress asked them what they judged those little hemispheres might be? They answered, that each of them was a perfect eye, by reason they perceived that each was covered with a transparent cornea, containing a liquor within them, which resembled the watery or glassy humour of the eye. To which the Empress replied, that they might be glassy pearls, and yet not eyes, and that perhaps their microscopes did not truly inform them: but they smilingly answered her Majesty, that she did not know the virtue of those microscopes; for they did never delude, but rectify and inform their senses; nay, the world, said they, would be but blind without them, as it has been in former ages before those microscopes were invented.

After this, they took a charcoal, and viewing it with one of their best microscopes, discovered in it an infinite multitude of pores, some bigger, some less; so close and thick, that they left but very little space betwixt them to be filled with a solid body; and to give her Imperial Majesty a better assurance thereof, they counted in a line of them an inch long, no less than 2700 pores; from which observation they drew this following conclusion, to wit, that this multitude of pores was the cause of the blackness of the coal; for, said they, a body that has so many pores, from each of which no light is reflected, must necessarily look black, since black is nothing else but a privation of light, or a want of reflection. But the Empress replied, that if all colours were made by reflection of light, and that black was as much a colour as any other colour; then certainly they contradicted themselves in saying, that black was made by want of reflection. However, not to interrupt your microscopical inspections, said she, let us see how vegetables appear through your glasses; whereupon they took a nettle, and by the virtue of the microscope, discovered that underneath the points of the nettle there were certain little bags or bladders containing a poisonous liquor, and when the points had made way into the interior parts of the skin, they like syringe-pipes served to convey that same liquor into them. To which observation the Empress replied, that if there were such poison in nettles, then certainly in eating of them, they would hurt us inwardly, as much as they do outwardly. But they answered, that it belonged to physicians more than to experimental philosophers, to give reasons hereof; for they only made microscopical inspections, and related the figures of the natural parts of creatures according to the presentation of their glasses.

Lastly, they showed the Empress a flea, and a louse; which creatures through the microscope appeared so terrible to her sight, that they had almost put her into a swoon; the description of all their parts would be very tedious to relate, and therefore I'll forbear it at this present. The Empress after the view of those strangely-shaped creatures, pitied much those that are molested with them, especially poor beggars, which although they have nothing to live on themselves, are yet necessitated to maintain and feed of their own flesh and blood, a company of such terrible creatures called lice, who instead of thanks, do reward them with pains, and torment them for giving them nourishment and food. But after the Empress had seen the shapes of these monstrous creatures, she desired to know whether their microscopes could hinder their biting, or at least show some means how to avoid them? To which they answered, that such arts were mechanical and below that noble study of microscopical observations. Then the Empress asked them whether they had not such sorts of glasses that could enlarge and magnify the shapes of great bodies, as well as they had done of little ones? Whereupon they took one of their best and largest microscopes, and endeavoured to view a whale through it; but alas! the shape of the whale was so big, that its circumference went beyond the magnifying quality of the glass; whether the error proceeded from the glass, or from a wrong position of the whale against the reflection of light, I cannot certainly tell. The Empress seeing the insufficiency of those magnifying-glasses, that they were not able to enlarge all sorts of objects, asked the bear-men whether they could not make glasses of a contrary nature to those they had showed her, to wit, such as instead of enlarging or magnifying the shape or figure of an object, could contract it beneath its natural proportion: which, in obedience to her Majesty's commands, they did; and viewing through one of the best of them, a huge and mighty whale appeared no bigger than a sprat; nay, through some no bigger than a vinegar-eel; and through their ordinary ones, an elephant seemed no bigger than a flea; a camel no bigger than a louse; and an ostrich no bigger than a mite. To relate all their optic observations through the several sorts of their glasses, would be a tedious work, and tire even the most patient reader, wherefore I'll pass them by; only this was very remarkable and worthy to be taken notice of, that notwithstanding their great skill, industry and ingenuity in experimental philosophy, they could yet by no means contrive such glasses, by the help of which they could spy out a vacuum, with all its dimensions, nor immaterial substances, non-beings, and mixed-beings, or such as are between something and nothing; which they were very much troubled at, hoping that yet, in time, by long study and practice, they might perhaps attain to it.

The bird- and bear-men being dismissed, the Empress called both the syrens, or fish-men, and the worm-men, to deliver their observations which they had made, both within the seas, and the earth. First she enquired of the fish-men whence the saltness of the sea did proceed? To which they answered, that there was a volatile salt in those parts of the earth, which as a bosom contain the waters of the sea, which salt being imbibed by the sea, became fixed; and this imbibing motion was that they called the ebbing and flowing of the sea; for, said they, the rising and swelling of the water, is caused by those parts of the volatile salt as are not so easily imbibed, which striving to ascend above the water, bear it up with such a motion, as man, or some other animal creature, in a violent exercise uses to take breath. This they affirmed to be the true cause both of the saltness, and the ebbing and flowing motion of the sea, and not the jogging of the earth, or the secret influence of the moon, as some others had made the world believe.

After this, the Empress enquired, whether they had observed that all animal creatures within the seas and other waters, had blood? They answered, that some had blood, more or less, but some had none; in cray-fishes and lobsters, said they, we perceive but little blood; but in crabs, oysters, cockles, etc. none at all. Then the Empress asked them in what part of their bodies that little blood did reside? They answered, in a small vein, which in lobsters went through the middle of their tails, but in cray-fishes was found in their backs: as for other sorts of fishes, some, said they, had only blood about their gills, and others in some other places of their bodies; but they had not as yet observed any whose veins did spread all over their bodies. The Empress wondering that there could be living animals without blood, to be better satisfied, desired the worm-men to inform her, whether they had observed blood in all sorts of worms? They answered, that as much as they could perceive, some had blood, and some not; a moth, said they, had no blood at all, and a louse had but like a lobster, a little vein along her back: also nits, snails, and maggots, as well as those that are generated out of cheese and fruits, as those that are produced out of flesh, had no blood. But replied the Empress, if those mentioned creatures have no blood, how is it possible they can live; for it is commonly said, that the life of an animal consists in the blood, which is the seat of the animal spirits? They answered, that blood was not a necessary propriety to the life of an animal, and that which was commonly called animal spirits, was nothing else but corporeal motions proper to the nature and figure of an animal. Then she asked both the fish- and worm-men, whether all those creatures that have blood, had a circulation of blood in their veins and arteries? But they answered, that it was impossible to give her Majesty an exact account thereof, by reason the circulation of blood was an interior motion, which their senses, neither of themselves, nor by the help of any optic instrument could perceive; but as soon as they had dissected an animal creature to find out the truth thereof, the interior corporeal motions proper to that particular figure or creature were altered. Then said the Empress, if all animal creatures have not blood, it is certain, they have neither all muscles, tendons, nerves, etc. But, said she, have you ever observed animal creatures that are neither flesh, nor fish, but of an intermediate degree between both. Truly, answered both the fish- and worm-men, we have observed several animal creatures that live both in water, and on the earth indifferently, and if any, certainly those may be said to be of such a mixed nature, that is, partly flesh, and partly fish: but how is it possible, replied the Empress, that they should live both in water, and on the earth, since those animals that live by the respiration of air, cannot live within water, and those that live in water, cannot live by the respiration of air, as experience doth sufficiently witness. They answered her Majesty, that as there were different sorts of creatures, so they had also different ways of respirations; for respiration, said they, was nothing else but a composition and division of parts, and the motions of nature being infinitely various, it was impossible that all creatures should have the like motions; wherefore it was not necessary, that all animal creatures should be bound to live either by the air, or by water only, but according as nature had ordered it convenient to their species. The Empress seemed very well satisfied with their answer, and desired to be further informed, whether all animal creatures did continue their species by a successive propagation of particulars, and whether in every species the off-spring did always resemble their generator or producer, both in their interior and exterior figures? They answered her Majesty, that some species or sorts of creatures, were kept up by a successive propagation of an offspring that was like the producer, but some were not; of the first rank, said they, are all those animals that are of different sexes, besides several others; but of the second rank are for the most part those we call insects, whose production proceeds from such causes as have no conformity or likeness with their produced effects; as for example, maggots bred out of cheese, and several others generated out of earth, water, and the like. But said the Empress, there is some likeness between maggots and cheese; for cheese has no blood, and so neither have maggots; besides, they have almost the same taste which cheese has. This proves nothing, answered they; for maggots have a visible, local, progressive motion, which cheese hath not. The Empress replied, that when all the cheese was turned into maggots, it might be said to have local, progressive motion. They answered, that when the cheese by its own figurative motions was changed into maggots, it was no more cheese. The Empress confessed that she observed nature was infinitely various in her works, and that though the species of creatures did continue, yet their particulars were subject to infinite changes. But since you have informed me, said she, of the various sorts and productions of animal creatures, I desire you to tell me what you have observed of their sensitive perceptions? Truly, answered they, your Majesty puts a very hard question to us, and we shall hardly be able to give a satisfactory answer to it; for there are many different sorts of creatures, which as they have all different perceptions, so they have also different organs, which our senses are not able to discover, only in an oyster-shell we have with admiration observed, that the common sensorium of the oyster lies just at the closing of the shells, where the pressure and reaction may be perceived by the opening and shutting of the shells every tide.

After all this, the Empress desired the worm-men to give her a true relation how frost was made upon the earth? To which they answered, that it was made much after the manner and description of the fish- and bird-men, concerning the congelation of water into ice and snow, by a commixture of saline and acid particles; which relation added a great light to the ape-men, who were the chemists, concerning their chemical principles, salt, sulphur and mercury. But, said the Empress, if it be so, it will require an infinite multitude of saline particles to produce such a great quantity of ice, frost and snow: besides, said she, when snow, ice and frost, turn again into their former principle, I would fain know what becomes of those saline particles? But neither the worm-men, nor the fish- and bird-men, could give her an answer to it.

Then the Empress enquired of them the reason, why springs were not as salt as the sea is? also, why springs did ebb and flow? To which some answered, that the ebbing and flowing of some springs was caused by hollow caverns within the earth, where the sea-water crowding through, did thrust forward, and draw backward the spring-water, according to its own way of ebbing and flowing; but others said, that it proceeded from a small proportion of saline and acid particles, which the spring-water imbibed from the earth; and although it was not so much as to be perceived by the sense of taste, yet was it enough to cause an ebbing and flowing motion. And as for the spring-water being fresh, they gave, according to their observation, this following reason: there is, said they, a certain heat within the bowels of the earth, proceeding from its swift circular motion upon its own axe, which heat distills the rarest parts of the earth into a fresh and insipid water, which water being through the pores of the earth, conveyed into a place where it may break forth without resistance or obstruction, causes springs and fountains; and these distilled waters within the earth do nourish and refresh the grosser and dryer parts thereof. This relation confirmed the Empress in the opinion concerning the motion of the earth, and the fixedness of the sun, as the bird-men had informed her; and then she asked the worm-men, whether minerals and vegetables were generated by the same heat that is within the bowels of the Earth? To which they could give her no positive answer; only, this they affirmed, that heat and cold were not the primary producing causes of either vegetables or minerals, or other sorts of creatures, but only effects; and to prove this our assertion, said they, we have observed, that by change of some sorts of corporeal motions, that which is now hot, will become cold; and what is now cold, will grow hot; but the hottest place of all, we find to be the centre of the earth: neither do we observe, that the torrid zone does contain so much gold and silver as the temperate; nor is there great store of iron and lead wheresoever there is gold; for these metals are most found in colder climates towards either of the Poles. This observation, the Empress commanded them to confer with her chemists, the ape-men, to let them know that gold was not produced by a violent, but a temperate degree of heat. She asked further, whether gold could not be made by art? They answered, that they could not certainly tell her Majesty, but if it was possible to be done, they thought tin, lead, brass, iron, and silver, to be the fittest metals for such an artificial transmutation. Then she asked them, whether art could produce iron, tin, lead, or silver? They answered, not, in their opinion. Then I perceive, replied the Empress, that your judgments are very irregular, since you believe that gold, which is so fixed a metal, that nothing has been found as yet which could occasion a dissolution of its interior figure, may be made by art, and not tin, lead, iron, copper, or silver, which yet are so far weaker, and meaner metals than gold is. But the worm-men excused themselves, that they were ignorant in that art, and that such questions belonged more properly to the ape-men, which were her Majesty's chemists.

Then the Empress asked them, whether by their sensitive perceptions they could observe the interior corporeal, figurative motions both of vegetables and minerals? They answered, that their senses could perceive them after they were produced, but not before; nevertheless, said they, although the interior, figurative motions of natural creatures are not subject to the exterior, animal, sensitive perceptions, yet by their rational perception they may judge of them, and of their productions if they be regular: whereupon the Empress commanded the bear-men to lend them some of their best microscopes; at which the bear-men smilingly answered her Majesty, that their glasses would do them but little service in the bowels of the earth, because there was no light; for, said they, our glasses do only represent exterior objects, according to the various reflections and positions of light; and wheresoever light is wanting, the glasses will do no good. To which the worm-men replied, that although they could not say much of refractions, reflections, inflections, and the like; yet were they not blind, even in the bowels of the earth; for they could see the several sorts of minerals, as also minute animals, that lived there, which minute animal creatures were not blind neither, but had some kind of sensitive perception that was as serviceable to them, as sight, taste, smell, touch, hearing, etc. was to other animal creatures: by which it is evident, that nature has been as bountiful to those creatures that live underground, or in the bowels of the earth, as to those that live upon the surface of the earth, or in the air, or in water. But howsoever, proceeded the worm-men, although there is light in the bowels of the earth, yet your microscopes will do but little good there, by reason those creatures that live under ground have not such an optic sense as those that live on the surface of the earth: wherefore, unless you had such glasses as are proper for their perception, your microscopes will not be anyways advantageous to them. The Empress seemed well pleased with this answer of the worm-men; and asked them further, whether minerals and all the other creatures within the earth, were colourless? At which question they could not forbear laughing; and when the Empress asked the reason why they laughed; we most humbly beg your Majesty's pardon, replied they; for we could not choose but laugh, when we heard of a colourless body. Why, said the Empress, colour is only an accident, which is an immaterial thing, and has no being of itself, but in another body. Those, replied they, that informed your Majesty thus, surely their rational motions were very irregular; for how is it possible, that a natural nothing can have a being in nature? If it be no substance, it cannot have a being, and if no being, it is nothing; wherefore the distinction between subsisting of itself, and subsisting in another body, is a mere nicety, and nonsense; for there is nothing in nature that can subsist of, or by itself, (I mean singly) by reason all parts of nature are composed in one body, and though they may be infinitely divided, commixed and changed in their particulars, yet in general, parts cannot be separated from parts as long as nature lasts; nay, we might as probably affirm, that infinite nature would be as soon destroyed, as that one atom could perish; and therefore your Majesty may firmly believe, that there is no body without colour, nor no colour without body; for colour, figure, place, magnitude, and body, are all but one thing, without any separation or abstraction from each other.

The Empress was so wonderfully taken with this discourse of the worm-men, that she not only pardoned the rudeness they committed in laughing at first at her question, but yielded a full assent to their opinion, which she thought the most rational that ever she had heard yet; and then proceeding in her questions, enquired further, whether they had observed any seminal principles within the earth free from all dimensions and qualities, which produced vegetables, minerals, and the like? To which they answered, that concerning the seeds of minerals, their sensitive perceptions had never observed any; but vegetables had certain seeds out of which they were produced. Then she asked, whether those seeds of vegetables lost their species; that is, were annihilated in the production of their off-spring? To which they answered, that by an annihilation, nothing could be produced, and that the seeds of vegetables were so far from being annihilated in their productions, that they did rather numerously increase and multiply; for the division of one seed, said they, does produce numbers of seeds out of itself. But replied the Empress, a particular part cannot increase of itself. 'Tis true, answered they: but they increase not barely of themselves, but by joining and commixing with other parts, which do assist them in their productions, and by way of imitation form or figure their own parts into such or such particulars. Then, I pray inform me, said the Empress, what disguise those seeds put on, and how they do conceal themselves in their transmutations? They answered, that seeds did no ways disguise or conceal, but rather divulge themselves in the multiplication of their off-spring; only they did hide and conceal themselves from their sensitive perceptions so, that their figurative and productive motions were not perceptible by animal creatures. Again, the Empress asked them, whether there were any non-beings within the earth? To which they answered, that they never heard of any such thing; and that, if her Majesty would know the truth thereof, she must ask those creatures that are called immaterial spirits, which had a great affinity with non-beings, and perhaps could give her a satisfactory answer to this question. Then she desired to be informed, what opinion they had of the beginning of forms? They told her Majesty, that they did not understand what she meant by this expression, for, said they, there is no beginning in nature, no not of particulars, by reason nature is eternal and infinite, and her particulars are subject to infinite changes and transmutations by virtue of their own corporeal, figurative self-motions; so that there's nothing new in nature, nor properly a beginning of any thing. The Empress seemed well satisfied with all those answers, and inquired further, whether there was no art used by those creatures that live within the earth? Yes, answered they: for the several parts of the earth do join and assist each other in composition or framing of such or such particulars; and many times, there are factions and divisions, which cause productions of mixed species; as for example, weeds, instead of sweet flowers and useful fruits; but gardeners and husbandmen use often to decide their quarrels, and cause them to agree; which though it shows a kindness to the differing parties, yet 'tis a great prejudice to the worms, and other animal creatures that live underground; for it most commonly causes their dissolution and ruin, at best they are driven out of their habitations. What, said the Empress, are not worms produced out of the earth? Their production in general, answered they, is like the production of all other natural creatures, proceeding from the corporeal figurative motions of nature; but as for their particular productions, they are according to the nature of their species; some are produced out of flowers, some out of roots, some out of fruits, some out of ordinary earth. Then they are very ungrateful children, replied the Empress, that they feed on their own parents which gave them life. Their life, answered they, is their own, and not their parents; for no part or creature of nature can either give or take away life, but parts do only assist and join with parts, either in the dissolution or production of other parts and creatures.

After this, and several other conferences, which the Empress held with the worm-men, she dismissed them; and having taken much satisfaction in several of their answers, encouraged them in their studies and observations. Then she made a convocation of her chemists, the ape-men, and commanded them to give her an account of the several transmutations which their art was able to produce. They begun first with a long and tedious discourse concerning the primitive ingredients of natural bodies, and how, by their art, they had found out the principles out of which they consist. But they did not all agree in their opinions; for some said, that the principles of all natural bodies were the four elements, fire, air, water, earth, out of which they were composed: others rejected this elementary commixture, and said, there were many bodies out of which none of the four elements could be extracted by any degree of fire whatsoever; and that, on the other side, there were divers bodies, whose resolution by fire reduced them into more than four different ingredients; and these affirmed, that the only principles of natural bodies were salt, sulphur, and mercury: others again declared, that none of the forementioned could be called the true principles of natural bodies, but that by their industry and pains which they had taken in the art of chemistry, they had discovered, that all natural bodies were produced but from one principle, which was water; for all vegetables, minerals and animals, said they, are nothing else, but simple water distinguished into various figures by the virtue of their seeds. But after a great many debates and contentions about this subject, the Empress being so much tired that she was not able to hear them any longer, imposed a general silence upon them, and then declared herself in this following discourse:

I am too sensible of the pains you have taken in the art of chemistry, to discover the principles of natural bodies, and wish they had been more profitably bestowed upon some other, than such experiments; for both by my own contemplation, and the observations which I have made by my rational and sensitive perception upon nature, and her works, I find, that nature is but one infinite self-moving body, which by the virtue of its self-motion, is divided into infinite parts, which parts being restless, undergo perpetual changes and transmutations by their infinite compositions and divisions. Now, if this be so, as surely, according to regular sense and reason, it appears no otherwise; it is in vain to look for primary ingredients, or constitutive principles of natural bodies, since there is no more but one universal principle of nature, to wit, self-moving matter, which is the only cause of all natural effects. Next, I desire you to consider, that fire is but a particular creature, or effect of nature, and occasions not only different effects in several bodies, but on some bodies has no power at all; witness gold, which never could be brought yet to change its interior figure by the art of fire; and if this be so, why should you be so simple as to believe that fire can show you the principles of nature? and that either the four elements, or water only, or salt, sulphur, and mercury, all which are no more but particular effects and creatures of nature, should be the primitive ingredients or principles of all natural bodies? Wherefore, I will not have you to take more pains, and waste your time in such fruitless attempts, but be wiser hereafter, and busy yourselves with such experiments as may be beneficial to the public.

The Empress having thus declared her mind to the ape-men, and given them better instructions than perhaps they expected, not knowing that her Majesty had such great and able judgment in natural philosophy, had several conferences with them concerning chemical preparations, which for brevity's sake, I'll forbear to rehearse: amongst the rest, she asked, how it came, that the imperial race appeared so young, and yet was reported to have lived so long; some of them two, some three, and some four hundred years? and whether it was by nature, or a special divine blessing? To which they answered, that there was a certain rock in the parts of that world, which contained the golden sands, which rock was hollow within, and did produce a gum that was a hundred years before it came to its full strength and perfection; this gum, said they, if it be held in a warm hand, will dissolve into an oil, the effects whereof are following: it being given every day for some certain time to an old decayed man, in the bigness of a little pea, will first make him spit for a week or more; after this, it will cause vomits of phlegm, and after that it will bring forth by vomits, humours of several colours: first of a pale yellow, then of a deep yellow, then of a green, and lastly of a black colour; and each of these humours have a several taste, some are fresh, some salt, some sour, some bitter, and so forth; neither do all these vomits make them sick, but they come out on a sudden and unawares, without any pain or trouble to the patient: and after it hath done all these mentioned effects, and cleared both the stomach and several other parts of the body, then it works upon the brain, and brings forth of the nose such kind of humours as it did out of the mouth, and much after the same manner; then it will purge by stool, then by urine, then by sweat, and lastly by bleeding at the nose, and the emeroids;[12] all which effects it will perform within the space of six weeks, or a little more; for it does not work very strongly, but gently, and by degrees: lastly, when it has done all this, it will make the body break out into a thick scab, and cause both hair, teeth and nails to come off; which scab being arrived to its full maturity, opens first along the back, and comes off all in a piece like an armour, and all this is done within the space of four months. After this the patient is wrapped into a cere-cloth, prepared of certain gums and juices, wherein he continues until the time of nine months be expired from the first beginning of the cure, which is the time of a child's formation in the womb. In the meanwhile his diet is nothing else but eagle's-eggs, and hind's-milk; and after the cere-cloth[13] is taken away, he will appear of the age of twenty, both in shape, and strength. The weaker sort of this gum is sovereign in healing of wounds, and curing of slight distempers. But this is also to be observed, that none of the imperial race does use any other drink but lime-water, or water in which lime-stone is immersed; their meat is nothing else but fowl of several sorts, their recreations are many, but chiefly hunting.

This relation amazed the Empress very much; for though in the world she came from, she had heard great reports of the philosopher's stone,[14] yet had she not heard of any that had ever found it out, which made her believe that it was but a chimera; she called also to mind, that there had been in the same world a man who had a little stone which cured all kinds of diseases outward and inward, according as it was applied; and that a famous chemist had found out a certain liquor called alkahest,[15] which by the virtue of its own fire, consumed all diseases; but she had never heard of a medicine that could renew old age, and render it beautiful, vigorous and strong: nor would she have so easily believed it, had it been a medicine prepared by art; for she knew that art, being nature's changeling, was not able to produce such a powerful effect, but being that the gum did grow naturally, she did not so much scruple at it; for she knew that nature's works are so various and wonderful, that no particular creature is able to trace her ways.

The conferences of the chemists being finished, the Empress made an assembly of her Galenical physicians,[16] her herbalists and anatomists; and first she enquired of her herbalists the particular effects of several herbs and drugs, and whence they proceeded? To which they answered, that they could, for the most part, tell her Majesty the virtues and operations of them, but the particular causes of their effects were unknown; only thus much they could say, that their operations and virtues were generally caused by their proper inherent, corporeal, figurative motions, which being infinitely various in infinite nature, did produce infinite several effects. And it is observed, said they, that herbs and drugs are as wise in their operations, as men in their words and actions; nay, wiser; and their effects are more certain than men in their opinions; for though they cannot discourse like men, yet have they sense and reason, as well as men; for the discursive faculty is but a particular effect of sense and reason in some particular creatures, to wit, men, and not a principle of nature, and argues often more folly than wisdom. The Empress asked, whether they could not by a composition and commixture of other drugs, make them work other effects than they did, used by themselves? They answered, that they could make them produce artificial effects, but not alter their inherent, proper and particular natures.

Then the Empress commanded her anatomists to dissect such kinds of creatures as are called monsters. But they answered her Majesty, that it would be but an unprofitable and useless work, and hinder their better employments; for when we dissect dead animals, said they, it is for no other end, but to observe what defects or distempers they had, that we may cure the like in living ones, so that all our care and industry concerns only the preservation of mankind; but we hope your Majesty will not preserve monsters, which are most commonly destroyed, except it be for novelty; neither will the dissection of monsters prevent the errors of nature's irregular actions; for by dissecting some, we cannot prevent the production of others; so that our pains and labours will be to no purpose, unless to satisfy the vain curiosities of inquisitive men. The Empress replied, that such dissections would be very beneficial to experimental philosophers. If experimental philosophers, answered they, do spend their time in such useless inspections, they waste it in vain, and have nothing but their labour for their pains.

Lastly, her Majesty had some conferences with the Galenic physicians about several diseases, and amongst the rest, desired to know the cause and nature of apoplexy, and the spotted plague. They answered, that a deadly apoplexy was a dead palsy of the brain, and the spotted plague was a gangrene of the vital parts, and as the gangrene of outward parts did strike inwardly; so the gangrene of inward parts, did break forth outwardly; which is the cause, said they, that as soon as the spots appear, death follows; for then it is an infallible sign, that the body is throughout infected with a gangrene, which is a spreading evil; but some gangrenes do spread more suddenly than others, and of all sorts of gangrenes, the plaguey-gangrene is the most infectious; for other gangrenes infect but the next adjoining parts of one particular body, and having killed that same creature, go no further, but cease; whenas, the gangrene of the plague, infects not only the adjoining parts of one particular creature, but also those that are distant; that is, one particular body infects another, and so breeds a universal contagion. But the Empress being very desirous to know in what manner the plague was propagated and became so contagious, asked, whether it went actually out of one body into another? To which they answered, that it was a great dispute amongst the learned of the profession, whether it came by a division and composition of parts; that is, by expiration and inspiration; or whether it was caused by imitation: some experimental philosophers, said they, will make us believe, that by the help of their microscopes, they have observed the plague to be a body of little flies like atoms, which go out of one body into another, through the sensitive passages; but the most experienced and wisest of our society, have rejected this opinion as a ridiculous fancy, and do for the most part believe, that it is caused by an imitation of parts, so that the motions of some parts which are sound, do imitate the motions of those that are infected, and that by this means, the plague becomes contagious and spreading.

The Empress having hitherto spent her time in the examination of the bird-, fish-, worm- and ape-men, etc. and received several intelligences from their several employments; at last had a mind to divert herself after her serious discourses, and therefore she sent for the spider-men, which were her mathematicians, the lice-men, which were her geometricians, and the magpie-, parrot- and jackdaw-men, which were her orators and logicians. The spider-men came first, and presented her Majesty with a table full of mathematical points, lines and figures of all sorts of squares, circles, triangles, and the like; which the Empress, notwithstanding that she had a very ready wit, and quick apprehension, could not understand; but the more she endeavoured to learn, the more was she confounded: whether they did ever square the circle, I cannot exactly tell, nor whether they could make imaginary points and lines; but this I dare say, that their points and lines were so slender, small and thin, that they seemed next to imaginary. The mathematicians were in great esteem with the Empress, as being not only the chief tutors and instructors in many arts, but some of them excellent magicians and informers of spirits, which was the reason their characters were so abstruse and intricate, that the Empress knew not what to make of them. There is so much to learn in your art, said she, that I can neither spare time from other affairs to busy myself in your profession; nor, if I could, do I think I should ever be able to understand your imaginary points, lines and figures, because they are non-beings.

Then came the lice-men, and endeavoured to measure all things to a hair's breadth, and weigh them to an atom; but their weights would seldom agree, especially in the weighing of air, which they found a task impossible to be done; at which the Empress began to be displeased, and told them, that there was neither truth nor justice in their profession; and so dissolved their society.

After this the Empress was resolved to hear the magpie-, parrot- and jackdaw-men, which were her professed orators and logicians; whereupon one of the parrot-men rose with great formality, and endeavoured to make an eloquent speech before her Majesty; but before he had half ended, his arguments and divisions being so many, that they caused a great confusion in his brain, he could not go forward, but was forced to retire backward, with the greatest disgrace both to himself, and the whole society; and although one of his brethren endeavoured to second him by another speech, yet was he as far to seek as the former. At which the Empress appeared not a little troubled, and told them, that they followed too much the rules of art, and confounded themselves with too nice formalities and distinctions; but since I know, said she, that you are a people who have naturally voluble tongues, and good memories; I desire you to consider more the subject you speak of, than your artificial periods, connexions and parts of speech, and leave the rest to your natural eloquence; which they did, and so became very eminent orators.

Lastly, her Imperial Majesty being desirous to know, what progress her logicians had made in the art of disputing, commanded them to argue upon several themes or subjects; which they did; and having made a very nice discourse of logistical terms and propositions, entered into a dispute by way of syllogistical arguments, through all the figures and modes: one began with an argument of the first mode of the first figure, thus:

Every politician is wise:
Every knave is a politician,
Therefore every knave is wise.

Another contradicted him with a syllogism of the second mode of the same figure, thus:

No politician is wise:
Every knave is a politician,
Therefore no knave is wise.

The third made an argument in the third mode of the same figure, after this manner:

Every politician is wise:
Some knaves are politicians,
Therefore some knaves are wise.

The fourth concluded with a syllogism in the fourth mode of the same figure, thus:

No politician is wise:
Some knaves are politicians,
Therefore some knaves are not wise.

After this they took another subject, and one propounded this syllogism:

Every philosopher is wise:
Every beast is wise,
Therefore every beast is a philosopher.

But another said that this argument was false, therefore he contradicted him with a syllogism of the second figure of the fourth mode, thus:

Every philosopher is wise:
Some beasts are not wise,
Therefore some beasts are not philosophers.

Thus they argued, and intended to go on, but the Empress interrupted them: I have enough, said she, of your chopped logic, and will hear no more of your syllogisms; for it disorders my reason, and puts my brain on the rack; your formal argumentations are able to spoil all natural wit; and I'll have you to consider, that art does not make reason, but reason makes art; and therefore as much as reason is above art, so much is a natural rational discourse to be preferred before an artificial: for art is, for the most part, irregular, and disorders men's understandings more than it rectifies them, and leads them into a labyrinth whence they'll never get out, and makes them dull and unfit for useful employments; especially your art of logic, which consists only in contradicting each other, in making sophisms, and obscuring truth, instead of clearing it.

But they replied [to] her Majesty, that the knowledge of nature, that is, natural philosophy, would be imperfect without the art of logic, and that there was an improbable truth which could no otherwise be found out than by the art of disputing. Truly, said the Empress, I do believe that it is with natural philosophy, as it is with all other effects of nature; for no particular knowledge can be perfect, by reason knowledge is dividable, as well as composable; nay, to speak properly, nature herself cannot boast of any perfection, but God himself; because there are so many irregular motions in nature, and 'tis but a folly to think that art should be able to regulate them, since art itself is, for the most part, irregular. But as for improbable truth, I know not what your meaning is; for truth is more than improbability; nay, there is so much difference between truth and improbability, that I cannot conceive it possible how they can be joined together. In short, said she, I do no ways approve of your profession; and though I will not dissolve your society, yet I shall never take delight in hearing you any more; wherefore confine your disputations to your schools, lest besides the commonwealth of learning, they disturb also divinity and policy, religion and laws, and by that means draw an utter ruin and destruction both upon church and state.

After the Empress had thus finished the discourses and conferences with the mentioned societies of her vertuosos, she considered by herself the manner of their religion, and finding it very defective, was troubled, that so wise and knowing a people should have no more knowledge of the divine truth; wherefore she consulted with her own thoughts, whether it was possible to convert them all to her own religion, and to that end she resolved to build churches, and make also up a congregation of women, whereof she intended to be the head herself, and to instruct them in several points of her religion. This she had no sooner begun, but the women, which generally had quick wits, subtle conceptions, clear understandings, and solid judgements, became, in a short time, very devout and zealous sisters; for the

Empress had an excellent gift of preaching, and instructing them in the articles of faith; and by that means, she converted them not only soon, but gained an extraordinary love of all her subjects throughout that world. But at last, pondering with herself the inconstant nature of mankind, and fearing that in time they would grow weary, and desert the divine truth, following their own fancies, and living according to their own desires, she began to be troubled that her labours and pains should prove of so little effect, and therefore studied all manner of ways to prevent it. Amongst the rest, she called to mind a relation which the bird-men made her once, of a mountain that did burn in flames of fire; and thereupon did immediately send for the wisest and subtlest of her worm-men, commanding them to discover the cause of the eruption of that same fire; which they did; and having dived to the very bottom of the mountain, informed her Majesty, that there was a certain sort of stone, whose nature was such, that being wetted, it would grow excessively hot, and break forth into a flaming-fire, until it became dry, and then it ceased from burning. The Empress was glad to hear this news, and forthwith desired the worm-men to bring her some of that stone, but be sure to keep it secret: she sent also for the bird-men, and asked them whether they could not get her a piece of the sun-stone? They answered, that it was impossible, unless they did spoil or lessen the light of the world: but, said they, if it please your Majesty, we can demolish one of the numerous stars of the sky, which the world will never miss.

The Empress was very well satisfied with this proposal, and having thus employed these two sorts of men, in the meanwhile builded two chapels one above another; the one she lined throughout with diamonds, both roof, walls and pillars; but the other she resolved to line with the star-stone; the fire-stone she placed upon the diamond-lining, by reason fire has no power on diamonds; and when she would have that chapel where the fire-stone was, appear all in a flame, she had by the means of artificial-pipes, water conveyed into it, which by turning the cock, did, as out of a fountain, spring over all the room, and as long as the fire-stone was wet, the chapel seemed to be all in a flaming fire.

The other chapel, which was lined with the star-stone, did only cast a splendorous and comfortable light; both the chapels stood upon pillars, just in the middle of a round cloister which was dark as night; neither was there any other light within them, but what came from the fire- and star-stone; and being everywhere open, allowed to all that were within the compass of the cloister, a free prospect into them; besides, they were so artificially contrived, that they did both move in a circle about their own centres, without intermission, contrary ways. In the chapel which was lined with the fire-stone, the Empress preached sermons of terror to the wicked, and told them of the punishments for their sins, to wit, that after this life they should be tormented in an everlasting fire. But in the other chapel lined with the star-stone, she preached sermons of comfort to those that repented of their sins, and were troubled at their own wickedness; neither did the heat of the flame in the least hinder her; for the fire-stone did not cast so great a heat but the Empress was able to endure it, by reason the water which was poured on the stone, by its own self-motion turned into a flaming fire, occasioned by the natural motions of the stone, which made the flame weaker than if it had been fed by some other kind of fuel; the other chapel where the star-stone was, although it did cast a great light, yet was it without all heat, and the Empress appeared like an angel in it; and as that chapel was an emblem of Hell, so this was an emblem of Heaven. And thus the Empress, by art, and her own ingenuity, did not only convert the Blazing World to her own religion, but kept them in a constant belief, without enforcement or blood-shed; for she knew well, that belief was a thing not to be forced or pressed upon the people, but to be instilled into their minds by gentle persuasions; and after this manner she encouraged them also in all other duties and employments, for fear, though it makes people obey, yet does it not last so long, nor is it so sure a means to keep them to their duties, as love.

Last of all, when she saw that both church and state was now in a well-ordered and settled condition, her thoughts reflected upon the world she came from; and though she had a great desire to know the condition of the same, yet could she advise no manner of way how to gain any knowledge thereof; at last, after many serious considerations, she conceived that it was impossible to be done by any other means, than by the help of immaterial spirits; wherefore she made a convocation of the most learned, witty and ingenious of all the forementioned sorts of men, and desired to know of them, whether there were any immaterial spirits in their world. First, she enquired of the worm-men, whether they had perceived some within the earth? They answered her Majesty, that they never knew of any such creatures; for whatsoever did dwell within the earth, said they, was embodied and material. Then she asked the fly-men, whether they had observed any in the air? for you having numerous eyes, said she, will be more able to perceive them, than any other creatures. To which they answered her Majesty, that although spirits, being immaterial, could not be perceived by the worm-men in the earth, yet they perceived that such creatures did lodge in the vehicles of the air. Then the Empress asked, whether they could speak to them, and whether they did understand each other? The fly-men answered, that those spirits were always clothed in some sort or other of material garments; which garments were their bodies, made for the most part, of air; and when occasion served, they could put on any other sort of substances; but yet they could not put these substances into any form or shape, as they pleased. The Empress asked the fly-men, whether it was possible that she could be acquainted, and have some conferences with them? They answered, they did verily believe she might. Hereupon the Empress commanded the fly-men to ask some of the spirits, whether they would be pleased to give her a visit? This they did; and after the spirits had presented themselves to the Empress, (in what shapes or forms, I cannot exactly tell) after some few compliments that passed between them, the Empress told the spirits that she questioned not, but they did know how she was a stranger in that world, and by what miraculous means she was arrived there; and since she had a great desire to know the condition of the world she came from, her request to the spirits was, to give her some information thereof, especially of those parts of the world where she was born, bred, and educated, as also of her particular friends and acquaintance; all which, the spirits did according to her desire; at last, after a great many conferences and particular intelligences, which the spirits gave the Empress, to her great satisfaction and content, she enquired after the most famous students, writers, and experimental philosophers in that world, which they gave her a full relation of; amongst the rest she enquired whether there were none that had found out yet the Jews' Cabbala?[17] Several have endeavoured it, answered the spirits, but those that came nearest (although themselves denied it) were one Dr Dee, and one Edward Kelly, the one representing Moses, and the other Aaron; for Kelly was to Dr Dee, as Aaron to Moses;[18] but yet they proved at last but mere cheats, and were described by one of their own country-men, a famous poet, named Ben Jonson, in a play called *The Alchemist*,[19] where he expressed Kelly by Capt. Face, and Dee by Dr Subtle, and their two wives by Doll Common, and the widow; by the Spaniard in the play, he meant the Spanish ambassador, and by Sir Epicure Mammon, a Polish lord. The Empress remembered that she had seen the play, and asked the spirits whom he meant by the name of Ananias? Some zealous brethren, answered they, in Holland, Germany, and several other places. Then she asked them, who was meant by the druggist? Truly, answered the spirits, we have forgot, it being so long since it was made and acted. What, replied the Empress, can spirits forget? Yes, said the spirits; for what is past, is only kept in memory, if it be not recorded. I did believe, said the Empress, that spirits had no need of memory, or remembrance, and could not be subject to forgetfulness. How can we, answered they, give an account of things present, if we had no memory, but especially of things past, unrecorded, if we had no remembrance? Said the Empress, by present knowledge and understanding. The spirits answered, that present knowledge and understanding was of actions or things present, not of past. But, said the Empress, you know what is to come, without memory or remembrance, and therefore you may know what is past without memory and remembrance. They answered, that their foreknowledge was only a prudent and subtle observation made by a comparing of things or actions past, with those that are present, and that remembrance was nothing else but a repetition of things or actions past.

Then the Empress asked the spirits, whether there was a threefold Cabbala? They answered, Dee and Kelly made but a two-fold Cabbala, to wit, of the Old and New Testament, but others might not only make two or three, but threescore Cabbalas, if they pleased. The Empress asked, whether it was a traditional, or merely a scriptural, or whether it was a literal, philosophical, or moral Cabbala? Some, answered they, did believe it merely traditional, others scriptural, some literal, and some metaphorical; but the truth is, said they, 'twas partly one, and partly the other; as partly a traditional, partly a scriptural, partly literal, partly metaphorical. The Empress asked further, whether the Cabbala was a work only of natural reason, or of divine inspiration? Many, said the spirits, that write Cabbalas pretend to divine inspirations, but whether it be so, or not; it does not belong to us to judge; only this we must needs confess, that it is a work which requires a good wit, and a strong faith, but not natural reason; for though natural reason is most persuasive, yet faith is the chief that is required in Cabbalists. But, said the Empress, is there not divine reason, as well as there is natural? No, answered they: for there is but a divine faith, and as for reason it is only natural; but you mortals are so puzzled about this divine faith, and natural reason, that you do not know well how to distinguish them, but confound them both, which is the cause you have so many divine philosophers who make a gallimaufry[20] both of reason and faith. Then she asked, whether pure natural philosophers were Cabbalists? They answered, no; but only your mystical or divine philosophers, such as study beyond sense and reason. She enquired further, whether there was any Cabbala in God, or whether God was full of Ideas? They answered, there could be nothing in God, nor could God be full of any thing, either forms or figures, but of himself; for God is the perfection of all things, and an unexpressible Being, beyond the conception of any creature, either natural or supernatural. Then I pray inform me, said the Empress, whether the Jews', or any other Cabbala, consist in numbers? The spirits answered, no: for numbers are odd, and different, and would make a disagreement in the Cabbala. But said she again, is it a sin then not to know or understand the Cabbala? God is so merciful, answered they, and so just, that he will never damn the ignorant, and save only those that pretend to know him and his secret counsels by their Cabbalas but he loves those that adore and worship him with fear and reverence, and with a pure heart. She asked further, which of these two Cabbalas was most approved, the natural, or theological? The theological, answered they, is mystical, and belongs only to faith; but the natural belongs to reason. Then she asked them, whether divine faith was made out of reason? No, answered they, for faith proceeds only from a divine saving grace, which is a peculiar gift of God. How comes it then, replied she, that men, even those that are of several opinions, have faith more or less? A natural belief, answered they, is not a divine faith. But, proceeded the Empress, how are you sure that God cannot be known? The several opinions you mortals have of God, answered they, are sufficient witnesses thereof. Well then, replied the Empress, leaving this inquisitive knowledge of God, I pray inform me, whether you spirits give motion to natural bodies? No, answered they; but, on the contrary, natural material bodies give spirits motion; for we spirits, being incorporeal, have no motion but from our corporeal vehicles, so that we move by the help of our bodies, and not the bodies by the help of us; for pure spirits are immovable. If this be so, replied the Empress, how comes it then that you can move so suddenly at a vast distance? They answered, that some sorts of matter were more pure, rare, and consequently more light and agile than others; and this was the reason of their quick and sudden motions: then the Empress asked them, whether they could speak without a body, or bodily organs? No, said they; nor could we have any bodily sense, but only knowledge. She asked, whether they could have knowledge without body? Not a natural, answered they, but a supernatural knowledge, which is a far better knowledge than a natural. Then she asked them, whether they had a general or universal knowledge? They answered, single or particular created spirits, have not; for not any creature, but God himself, can have an absolute and perfect knowledge of all things. The Empress asked them further, whether spirits had inward and outward parts? No, answered they; for parts only belong to bodies, not to spirits. Again, she asked them, whether their vehicles were living bodies? They are self-moving bodies, answered they, and therefore they must needs be living; for nothing can move itself, without it hath life. Then, said she, it must necessarily follow, that this living, self-moving body gives a spirit motion, and not that the spirit gives the body, as its vehicle, motion. You say very true, answered they, and we told you this before. Then the Empress asked them, of what forms of matter those vehicles were? They said they were of several different forms; some gross and dense, and others more pure, rare, and subtle. Then she enquired, whether immaterial spirits were not of a globous figure? They answered, figure and body were but one thing; for no body was without figure, nor no figure without body; and that it was as much nonsense to say, an immaterial figure, as to say an immaterial body. Again, she asked, whether spirits were not like water, or fire? No, said they, for both fire and water are material; and we are no more like fire or water, than we are like earth; nay, were it the purest and finest degree of matter, even above the heavens; for immaterial creatures cannot be likened or compared to material; but, as we said before, our vehicles being material, are of several degrees, forms and shapes.[21] But if you be not material, said the Empress, how can you be generators of all creatures? We are no more, answered they, the generators of material creatures, than they are the generators of us spirits. Then she asked, whether they did leave their vehicles? No, answered they; for we being incorporeal, cannot leave or quit them; but our vehicles do change into several forms and figures, according as occasion requires. Then the Empress desired the spirits to tell her, whether man was a little world? They answered, that if a fly or worm was a little world, then man was so too. She asked again, whether our forefathers had been as wise, as men were at present, and had understood sense and reason, as well as they did now? They answered, that in former ages they had been as wise as they are in this present, nay, wiser; for, said they, many in this age do think their forefathers have been fools, by which they prove themselves to be such. The Empress asked further, whether there was any plastic power in nature? Truly, said the spirits, plastic power is a hard word, [it] signifies no more than the power of the corporeal, figurative motions of nature. After this, the Empress desired the spirits to inform her where the Paradise was, whether it was in the midst of the world as a centre of pleasure? or whether it was the whole world, or a peculiar world by itself, as a world of life, and not of matter; or whether it was mixed, as a world of living animal creatures? They answered, that Paradise was not in the world she came from, but in that world she lived in at present; and that it was the very same place where she kept her court, and where her palace stood, in the midst of the imperial city. The Empress asked further, whether in the beginning and creation of the world, all beasts could speak? They answered, that no beasts could speak, but only those sorts of creatures which were fish-men, bear-men, worm-men, and the like, which could speak in the first age, as well as they do now. She asked again, whether they were none of those spirits that frighted Adam out of the Paradise, at least caused him not to return thither again? They answered they were not. Then she desired to be informed, whither Adam fled when he was driven out of the Paradise? Out of this world, said they, you are now Empress of, into the world you came from. If this be so, replied the Empress, then surely those Cabbalists are much out of their story, who believe the Paradise to be a world of life only, without matter; for this world, though it be most pleasant and fruitful, yet it is not a world of mere immaterial life, but a world of living, material creatures. Without question, they are, answered the spirits; for not all Cabbalas are true. Then the Empress asked, that since it is mentioned in the story of the creation of the world, that Eve was tempted by the serpent, whether the Devil was within the serpent, or whether the serpent tempted her without the Devil? They answered, that the Devil was within the serpent. But how came it then, replied she, that the serpent was cursed? They answered, because the Devil was in him: for are not those men in danger of damnation which have the Devil within them, who persuades them to believe and act wickedly? The Empress asked further, whether light and the heavens were all one. They answered, that the region which contains the lucid natural orbs, was by mortals named Heaven; but the beatifical Heaven, which is the habitation of the blessed angels and souls, was so far beyond it, that it could not be compared to any natural creature. Then the Empress asked them, whether all matter was fluid at first? They answered, that matter was always as it is; and that some parts of matter were rare, some dense, some fluid, some solid, etc. Neither was God bound to make all matter fluid at first. She asked further, whether matter was immovable in itself? We have answered you before, said they, that there is no motion but in matter; and were it not for the motion of matter, we spirits, could not move, nor give you any answer to your several questions. After this, the Empress asked the spirits, whether the universe was made within the space of six days, or whether by those six days, were meant so many decrees or commands of God? They answered her, that the world was made by the all-powerful decree and command of God; but whether there were six decrees or commands, or fewer, or more, no creature was able to tell. Then she enquired, whether there was no mystery in numbers? No other mystery, answered the spirits, but reckoning or counting, for numbers are only marks of remembrance. But what do you think of the number four, said she, which Cabbalists make such ado withal, and of the number of ten, when they say that ten is all, and that all numbers are virtually comprehended in four? We think, answered they, that Cabbalists have nothing else to do but to trouble their heads with such useless fancies; for naturally there is no such thing as prime or all in numbers; nor is there any other mystery in numbers, but what man's fancy makes; but what men call prime, or all, we do not know, because they do not agree in the number of their opinion. Then the Empress asked, whether the number of six was a symbol of matrimony, as being made up of male and female, for two into three is six. If any number can be a symbol of matrimony, answered the spirits, it is not six, but two; if two may be allowed to be a number: for the act of matrimony is made up of two joined in one. She asked again, what they said to the number of seven? whether it was not an emblem of God, because Cabbalists say, that it is neither begotten, nor begets any other number. There can be no emblem of God, answered the spirits; for if we do not know what God is, how can we make an emblem of him? Nor is there any number in God, for God is the perfection himself, but numbers are imperfect; and as for the begetting of numbers, it is done by multiplication and addition; but subtraction is as a kind of death to numbers. If there be no mystery in numbers, replied the Empress, then it is in vain to refer the creation of the world to certain numbers, as Cabbalists do. The only mystery of numbers, answered they, concerning the creation of the world is, that as numbers do multiply, so does the world. The Empress asked, how far numbers did multiply? The spirits answered, to infinite. Why, said she, infinite cannot be reckoned, nor numbered. No more, answered they, can the parts of the universe; for God's creation, being an infinite action, as proceeding from an infinite power, could not rest upon a finite number of creatures; were it never so great. But leaving the mystery of numbers, proceeded the Empress, let me now desire you to inform me, whether the suns and planets were generated by the heavens, or ethereal matter? The spirits answered, that the stars and planets were of the same matter which the heavens, the ether, and all other natural creatures did consist of; but whether they were generated by the heavens or ether, they could not tell: if they be, said they, they are not like their parents; for the sun, stars, and planets, are more splendorous than the ether, as also more solid and constant in their motions: but put the case, the stars and planets were generated by the heavens, and the ethereal matter; the question then would be, out of what these are generated or produced? If these be created out of nothing, and not generated out of something, then it is probable the sun, stars and planets are so too; nay, it is more probable of the stars and planets, than of the heavens, or the fluid ether, by reason the stars and planets seem to be further off from mortality, than the particular parts of the ether; for no doubt but the parts of the ethereal matter alter into several forms, which we do not perceive of the stars and planets. The Empress asked further, whether they could give her information of the three principles of man, according to the doctrine of the Platonists; as first of the intellect, spirit, or divine light: 2. of the soul of man herself: and 3. of the image of the soul, that is, her vital operation on the body? The spirits answered, that they did not understand these three distinctions, but that they seemed to corporeal sense and reason, as if they were three several bodies, or three several corporeal actions; however, said they, they are intricate conceptions of irregular fancies. If you do not understand them, replied the Empress, how shall human creatures do then? Many, both of your modern and ancient philosophers, answered the spirits, endeavour to go beyond sense and reason, which makes them commit absurdities; for no corporeal creature can go beyond sense and reason; no not we spirits, as long as we are in our corporeal vehicles. Then the Empress asked them, whether there were any atheists in the world? The spirits answered, that there were no more atheists then what Cabbalists make. She asked them further, whether spirits were of a globous or round figure? They answered, that figure belonged to body, but they being immaterial had no figure. She asked again, whether spirits were not like water or fire? They answered, that water and fire was material, were it the purest and most refined that ever could be; nay, were it above the heavens: but we are no more like water or fire, said they, than we are like earth; but our vehicles are of several forms, figures and degrees of substances. Then she desired to know, whether their vehicles were made of air? Yes, answered the spirits, some of our vehicles are of thin air. Then I suppose, replied the Empress, that those airy vehicles, are your corporeal summer-suits. She asked further, whether the spirits had not ascending and descending motions, as well as other creatures? They answered, that properly there was no ascension or descension in infinite nature, but only in relation to particular parts; and as for us spirits, said they, we can neither ascend nor descend without corporeal vehicles; nor can our vehicles ascend or descend, but according to their several shapes and figures, for there can be no motion without body. The Empress asked them further, whether there was not a world of spirits, as well as there is of material creatures? No, answered they; for the word world implies a quantity or multitude of corporeal creatures, but we being immaterial, can make no world of spirits. Then she desired to be informed when spirits were made? We do not know, answered they, how and when we were made, nor are we much inquisitive after it; nay, if we did, it would be no benefit, neither for us, nor for you mortals to know it. The Empress replied, that Cabbalists and divine philosophers said, men's rational souls were immaterial, and stood as much in need of corporeal vehicles, as spirits did. If this be so, answered the spirits, then you are hermaphrodites of nature; but your Cabbalists are mistaken, for they take the purest and subtlest parts of matter for immaterial spirits. Then the Empress asked, when the souls of mortals went out of their bodies, whether they went to Heaven or Hell, or whether they remained in airy vehicles? God's justice and mercy, answered they, is perfect, and not imperfect; but if you mortals will have vehicles for your souls, and a place that is between Heaven and Hell, it must be Purgatory, which is a place of purification, for which action fire is more proper than air, and so the vehicles of those souls that are in Purgatory cannot be airy, but fiery; and after this rate there can be but four places for human souls to be in, *viz.* Heaven, Hell, Purgatory, and this world; but as for vehicles, they are but fancies, not real truths. Then the Empress asked them, where Heaven and Hell was? Your saviour Christ, answered the spirits, has informed you, that there is Heaven and Hell, but he did not tell you what, nor where they are; wherefore it is too great a presumption for you mortals to enquire after it; if you do but strive to get into Heaven, it is enough, though you do not know where or what it is, for it is beyond your knowledge and understanding. I am satisfied, replied the Empress, and asked further, whether there were any figures or characters in the soul? They answered, where there was no body, there could be no figure. Then she asked them, whether spirits could be naked? and whether they were of a dark, or a light colour? As for our nakedness, it is a very odd question, answered the spirits; and we do not know what you mean by a naked spirit; for you judge of us as of corporeal creatures; and as for colour, said they, it is according to our vehicles; for colour belongs to body, and as there is no body that is colourless, so there is no colour that is bodiless. Then the Empress desired to be informed, whether all souls were made at the first creation of the world? We know no more, answered the spirits, of the origin of human souls, than we know of ourselves. She asked further, whether human bodies were not burdensome to human souls? They answered, that bodies made souls active, as giving them motion; and if action was troublesome to souls, then bodies were so too. She asked again, whether souls did choose bodies? They answered, that Platonics believed, the souls of lovers lived in the bodies of their beloved; but surely, said they, if there be a multitude of souls in a world of matter, they cannot miss bodies; for as soon as a soul is parted from one body, it enters into another; and souls having no motion of themselves, must of necessity be clothed or embodied with the next parts of matter. If this be so, replied the Empress, then I pray inform me, whether all matter be soulified? The spirits answered, they could not exactly tell that; but if it was true, that matter had no other motion but what came from a spiritual power, and that all matter was moving, then no soul could quit a body, but she must of necessity enter into another soulified body, and then there would be two immaterial substances in one body. The Empress asked, whether it was not possible that there could be two souls in one body? As for immaterial souls, answered the spirits, it is impossible; for there cannot be two immaterials in one inanimate body, by reason they want parts, and place, being bodiless; but there may be numerous material souls in one composed body, by reason every material part has a material natural soul; for nature is but one infinite self-moving, living and self-knowing body, consisting of the three degrees of inanimate, sensitive and rational matter, so intermixed together, that no part of nature, were it an atom, can be without any of these three degrees; the sensitive is the life, the rational the soul, and the inanimate part, the body of infinite nature. The Empress was very well satisfied with this answer, and asked further, whether souls did not give life to bodies? No, answered they; but spirits and divine souls have a life of their own, which is not partable, being purer than a natural life; for spirits are incorporeal, and consequently indivisible. But when the soul is in its vehicle, said the Empress, then methinks she is like the sun, and the vehicle like the moon. No, answered they, but the vehicle is like the sun, and the soul like the moon; for the soul hath motion from the body, as the moon has light from the sun. Then the Empress asked the spirits, whether it was an evil spirit that tempted Eve, and brought all the mischiefs upon mankind, or whether it was the serpent? They answered, that spirits could not commit actual evils. The Empress said they might do it by persuasions. They answered, that persuasions were actions; but the Empress not being contented with this answer, asked whether there was not a supernatural evil? The spirits answered, that there was a supernatural good, which was God; but they knew of no supernatural evil that was equal to God. Then she desired to know, whether evil spirits were reckoned amongst the beasts of the field? They answered, that many beasts of the field were harmless creatures, and very serviceable for man's use; and though some were accounted fierce and cruel, yet did they exercise their cruelty upon other creatures, for the most part, to no other end, but to get themselves food, and to satisfy their natural appetite; but certainly, said they, you men are more cruel to one another, than evil spirits are to you; and as for their habitations in desolate places, we having no communion with them, can give you no certain account thereof. But what do you think, said the Empress, of good spirits? may not they be compared to the fowls of the air? They answered, there were many cruel and ravenous fowls as well in the air, as there were fierce and cruel beasts on earth; so that the good are always mixed with the bad. She asked further, whether the fiery vehicles were a Heaven, or a Hell, or at least a Purgatory to the souls? They answered, that if the souls were immaterial, they could not burn, and then fire would do them no harm; and though Hell was believed to be an undecaying and unquenchable fire, yet Heaven was no fire. The Empress replied, that Heaven was a light. Yes, said they, but not a fiery light. Then she asked, whether the different shapes and sorts of vehicles, made the souls and other immaterial spirits, miserable, or blessed? The vehicles, answered they, make them neither better, nor worse; for though some vehicles sometimes may have power over others, yet these by turns may get some power again over them, according to the several advantages and disadvantages of particular natural parts. The Empress asked further, whether animal life came out of the spiritual world, and did return thither again? The spirits answered, they could not exactly tell; but if it were so, then certainly animal lives must leave their bodies behind them, otherwise the bodies would make the spiritual world a mixed world, that is, partly material, and partly immaterial; but the truth is, said they, spirits being immaterial, cannot properly make a world; for a world belongs to material, not to immaterial creatures. If this be so, replied the Empress, then certainly there can be no world of lives and forms without matter? No, answered the spirits, nor a world of matter without lives and forms; for natural lives and forms cannot be immaterial, no more than matter can be immovable. And therefore natural lives, forms and matter, are inseparable. Then the Empress asked, whether the first man did feed on the best sorts of the fruits of the earth, and the beasts on the worst? The spirits answered, that unless the beasts of the field were barred out of the manured fields and gardens, they would pick and choose the best fruits as well as men; and you may plainly observe it, said they, in squirrels and monkeys, how they are the best choosers of nuts and apples, and how birds do pick and feed on the most delicious fruits, and worms on the best roots, and most savoury herbs; by which you may see, that those creatures live and feed better than men do, except you will say, that artificial cookery is better and more wholesome than the natural. Again, the Empress asked, whether the first man gave names to all the several sorts of fishes in the sea, and fresh waters? No, answered the spirits, for he was an earthly, and not a watery creature, and therefore could not know the several sorts of fishes. Why, replied the Empress, he was no more an airy creature than he was a watery one, and yet he gave names to the several sorts of fowls and birds of the air. Fowls answered they, are partly airy, and partly earthly creatures, not only because they resemble beasts and men in their flesh, but because their rest and dwelling-places are on earth; for they build their nests, lay their eggs, and hatch their young, not in the air, but on the earth. Then she asked, whether the first man did give names to all the various sorts of creatures that live on the earth? Yes, answered they, to all those that were presented to him; or he had knowledge of, that is, to all the prime sorts; but not to every particular; for of mankind, said they, there were but two at first, and as they did increase, so do their names. But, said the Empress, who gave the names to the several sorts of fish? The posterity of mankind, answered they. Then she enquired, whether there were no more kinds of creatures now, than at the first creation? They answered, that there were no more nor fewer kinds of creatures than there are now; but there were, without question, more particular sorts of creatures now, than there were then. She asked again, whether all those creatures that were in Paradise, were also in Noah's Ark? They answered, that the principal kinds had been there, but not all the particulars. Then she would fain know, how it came, that both spirits and men did fall from a blessed into so miserable a state and condition they are now in. The spirits answered, by disobedience. The Empress asked, whence this disobedient sin did proceed? But the spirits desired the Empress not to ask them any such questions, because they went beyond their knowledge. Then she begged the spirits to pardon her presumption; for, said she, it is the nature of mankind to be inquisitive. Natural desire of knowledge, answered the spirits, is not blameable, so you do not go beyond what your natural reason can comprehend. Then I'll ask no more, said the Empress, for fear I should commit some error; but one thing I cannot but acquaint you withal: what is that, said the spirits? I have a great desire, answered the Empress, to make a Cabbala. What kind of Cabbala asked the spirits? The Empress answered, the Jews' Cabbala. No sooner had the Empress declared her mind, but the spirits immediately disappeared out of her sight; which startled the Empress so much, that she fell into a trance, wherein she lay for some while; at last being come to herself again, she grew very studious, and considering with herself what might be the cause of this strange disaster, conceived at first, that perhaps the spirits were tired with hearing and giving answers to her questions; but thinking by herself, that spirits could not be tired, she imagined that this was not the true cause of their disappearing, till after diverse debates with her own thoughts, she did verily believe that the spirits had committed some fault in their answers, and that for their punishment they were condemned to the lowest and darkest vehicles. This belief was so fixed in her mind, that it put her into a very melancholic humour; and then she sent both for her fly- and worm-men, and declared to them the cause of her sadness. 'Tis not so much, said she, the vanishing of those spirits that makes me melancholic, but that I should be the cause of their miserable condition, and that those harmless spirits should, for my sake, sink down into the black and dark abyss of the earth. The worm-men comforted the Empress, telling her, that the Earth was not so horrid a dwelling, as she did imagine; for, said they, not only all minerals and vegetables, but several sorts of animals can witness, that the earth is a warm, fruitful, quiet, safe and happy habitation; and though they want the light of the sun, yet are they not in dark, but there is light even within the earth, by which those creatures do see that dwell therein. This relation settled her Majesty's mind a little; but yet she being desirous to know the truth, where, and in what condition those spirits were, commanded both the fly- and worm-men to use all labour and industry to find them out, whereupon the worm-men straight descended into the earth, and the fly-men ascended into the air. After some short time, the worm-men returned, and told the Empress, that when they went into the earth, they enquired of all the creatures they met withal, whether none of them had perceived such or such spirits, until at last coming to the very centre of the earth, they were truly informed, that those spirits had stayed some time there, but at last were gone to the antipodes on the other side of the terrestrial globe, diametrically opposite to theirs. The fly-men seconded the worm-men, assuring her Majesty, that their relation was very true; for, said they, we have rounded the earth, and just when we came to the antipodes, we met those spirits in a very good condition, and acquainted them that your Majesty was very much troubled at their sudden departure, and feared they should be buried in the darkness of the earth: whereupon the spirits answered us, that they were sorry for having occasioned such sadness and trouble in your Majesty; and desired us to tell your Majesty, that they feared no darkness; for their vehicles were of such a sort of substance as cats'-eyes, glow-worms' tails, and rotten wood, carrying their light along with them; and that they were ready to do your Majesty what service they could, in making your Cabbala. At which relation the Empress was exceedingly glad, and rewarded both her fly- and worm-men bountifully.

After some time, when the spirits had refreshed themselves in their own vehicles, they sent one of their nimblest spirits, to ask the Empress, whether she would have a scribe, or whether she would write the Cabbala herself? The Empress received the proffer which they made her, with all civility; and told him, that she desired a spiritual scribe. The spirit answered, that they could dictate, but not write, except they put on a hand or arm, or else the whole body of man. The Empress replied, how can spirits arm themselves with gauntlets of flesh? As well, answered he, as man can arm himself with a gauntlet of steel. If it be so, said the Empress, then I will have a scribe. Then the spirit asked her, whether she would have the soul of a living or a dead man? Why, said the Empress, can the soul quit a living body, and wander or travel abroad? Yes, answered he, for according to Plato's doctrine, there is a conversation of souls, and the souls of lovers live in the bodies of their beloved. Then I will have, answered she, the soul of some ancient famous writer, either of Aristotle, Pythagoras, Plato, Epicurus, or the like. The spirit said, that those famous men were very learned, subtle, and ingenious writers, but they were so wedded to their own opinions, that they would never have the patience to be scribes. Then, said she, I'll have the soul of one of the most famous modern writers, as either of Galileo, Gassendus, Descartes, Helmont, Hobbes, H. More, etc.[22] The spirit answered, that they were fine ingenious writers, but yet so self-conceited, that they would scorn to be scribes to a woman. But, said he, there's a lady, the Duchess of Newcastle, which although she is not one of the most learned, eloquent, witty and ingenious, yet is she a plain and rational writer, for the principle of her writings, is sense and reason, and she will without question, be ready to do you all the service she can. This lady then, said the Empress, will I choose for my scribe, neither will the Emperor have reason to be jealous, she being one of my own sex. In truth, said the spirit, husbands have reason to be jealous of platonic lovers, for they are very dangerous, as being not only very intimate and close, but subtle and insinuating. You say well, replied the Empress; wherefore I pray send me the Duchess of Newcastle's soul; which the spirit did; and after she came to wait on the Empress, at her first arrival the Empress embraced and saluted her with a spiritual kiss; then she asked her whether she could write? Yes, answered the Duchess's soul, but not so intelligibly that any reader whatsoever may understand it, unless he be taught to know my characters; for my letters are rather like characters, than well-formed letters. Said the Empress, you were recommended to me by an honest and ingenious spirit. Surely, answered the Duchess, the spirit is ignorant of my handwriting. The truth is, said the Empress, he did not mention your handwriting; but he informed me that you writ sense and reason, and if you can but write so that any of my secretaries may learn your hand, they shall write it out fair and intelligible. The Duchess answered, that she questioned not but it might easily be learned in a short time. But, said she to the Empress, what is it that your Majesty would have written? She answered, the Jews' Cabbala. Then your only way for that is, said the Duchess, to have the soul of some famous Jew; nay, if your Majesty please, I scruple not, but you may as easily have the soul of Moses, as of any other. That cannot be, replied the Empress, for no mortal knows where Moses is. But, said the Duchess, human souls are immortal; however, if this be too difficult to be obtained, you may have the soul of one of the chief rabbis or sages of the tribe of Levi, who will truly instruct you in that mystery; whenas, otherwise, your Majesty will be apt to mistake, and a thousand to one, will commit gross errors. No, said the Empress, for I shall be instructed by spirits. Alas! said the Duchess, spirits are as ignorant as mortals in many cases; for no created spirits have a general or absolute knowledge, nor can they know the thoughts of men, much less the mysteries of the great creator, unless he be pleased to inspire into them the gift of divine knowledge. Then, I pray, said the Empress, let me have your counsel in this case. The Duchess answered, if your Majesty will be pleased to hearken to my advice, I would desire you to let that work alone, for it will be of no advantage either to you, or your people, unless you were of the Jews' religion; nay, if you were, the vulgar interpretation of the holy scripture would be more instructive, and more easily believed, than your mystical way of interpreting it; for had it been better and more advantageous for the salvation of the Jews, surely Moses would have saved after ages that labour by his own explanation, he being not only a wise, but a very honest, zealous and religious man: wherefore the best way, said she, is to believe with the generality the literal sense of the scripture, and not to make interpretations every one according to his own fancy, but to leave that work for the learned, or those that have nothing else to do; neither do I think, said she, that God will damn those that are ignorant therein, or suffer them to be lost for want of a mystical interpretation of the scripture. Then, said the Empress, I'll leave the scripture, and make a philosophical Cabbala. The Duchess told her, that sense and reason would instruct her of nature as much as could be known; and as for numbers, they were infinite, but to add nonsense to infinite, would breed a confusion, especially in human understanding. Then, replied the Empress, I'll make a moral Cabbala. The only thing, answered the Duchess, in morality, is but to fear God, and to love his neighbour, and this needs no further interpretation. But then I'll make a political Cabbala, said the Empress. The Duchess answered, that the chief and only ground in government, was but reward and punishment, and required no further Cabbala; but, said she, if your Majesty were resolved to make a Cabbala, I would advise you, rather to make a poetical or romancical Cabbala, wherein you can use metaphors, allegories, similitudes, etc. and interpret them as you please. With that the Empress thanked the Duchess, and embracing her soul, told her she would take her counsel: she made her also her favourite, and kept her sometime in that world, and by this means the Duchess came to know and give this relation of all that passed in that rich, populous, and happy world; and after some time the Empress gave her leave to return to her husband and kindred into her native world, but upon condition, that her soul should visit her now and then; which she did, and truly their meeting did produce such an intimate friendship between them, that they became platonic lovers, although they were both females.

One time, when the Duchess her soul was with the Empress, she seemed to be very sad and melancholy; at which the Empress was very much troubled, and asked her the reason of her melancholic humour? Truly said the Duchess to the Empress (for between dear friends there's no concealment, they being like several parts of one united body) my melancholy proceeds from an extreme ambition. The Empress asked, what the height of her ambition was? The Duchess answered, that neither she herself, nor no creature in the world was able to know either the height, depth or breadth of her ambition; but said she, my present desire is, that I would be a great princess. The Empress replied, so you are; for you are a princess of the fourth or fifth degree; for a duke or duchess is the highest title or honour that a subject can arrive to, as being the next to a king's title; and as for the name of a prince or princess, it belongs to all that are adopted to the crown; so that those that can add a crown to their arms, are princes, and therefore a duke is a title above a prince; for example, the Duke of Savoy, the Duke of Florence, the Duke of Lorraine, as also kings' brothers are not called by the name of princes, but dukes, this being the higher title. 'Tis true, answered the Duchess, unless it be kings' eldest sons, and they are created princes. Yes, replied the Empress, but no sovereign does make a subject equal to himself, such as kings' eldest sons partly are: and although some dukes be sovereign, yet I never heard that a prince by his title is sovereign, by reason the title of a prince is more a title of honour, than of sovereignty; for, as I said before, it belongs to all that are adopted to the crown. Well, said the Duchess, setting aside this dispute, my ambition is, that I would fain be as you are, that is, an Empress of a world, and I shall never be at quiet until I be one. I love you so well, replied the Empress, that I wish with all my soul, you had the fruition of your ambitious desire, and I shall not fail to give you my best advice how to accomplish it; the best informers are the immaterial spirits, and they'll soon tell you, whether it be possible to obtain your wish. But, said the Duchess, I have little acquaintance with them, for I never knew any before the time you sent for me. They know you, replied the Empress; for they told me of you, and were the means and instrument of your coming hither: wherefore I'll confer with them, and enquire whether there be not another world, whereof you may be Empress as well as I am of this? No sooner had the Empress said this, but some immaterial spirits came to visit her, of whom she enquired, whether there were but three worlds in all, to wit, the Blazing World where she was in, the world which she came from, and the world where the Duchess lived? The spirits answered, that there were more numerous worlds than the stars which appeared in these three mentioned worlds. Then the Empress asked, whether it was not possible, that her dearest friend the Duchess of Newcastle, might be Empress of one of them? Although there be numerous, nay, infinite worlds, answered the spirits, yet none is without government. But is none of these worlds so weak, said she, that it may be surprised or conquered? The spirits answered, that Lucian's world of lights, had been for some time in a snuff, but of late years one Helmont had got it, who since he was Emperor of it, had so strengthened the immortal parts thereof with mortal out-works, as it was for the present impregnable. Said the Empress, if there be such an infinite number of worlds, I am sure, not only my friend, the Duchess, but any other might obtain one. Yes, answered the spirits, if those worlds were uninhabited; but they are as populous as this, your Majesty governs. Why, said the Empress, it is not impossible to conquer a world.[23] No, answered the spirits, but, for the most part, conquerers seldom enjoy their conquest, for they being more feared than loved, most commonly come to an untimely end. If you will but direct me, said the Duchess to the spirits, which world is easiest to be conquered, her Majesty will assist me with means, and I will trust to fate and fortune; for I had rather die in the adventure of noble achievements, than live in obscure and sluggish security; since by the one, I may live in a glorious fame, and by the other I am buried in oblivion. The spirits answered, that the lives of fame were like other lives; for some lasted long, and some died soon. 'Tis true, said the Duchess; but yet the shortest-lived fame lasts longer than the longest life of man. But, replied the spirits, if occasion does not serve you, you must content yourself to live without such achievements that may gain you a fame: but we wonder, proceeded the spirits, that you desire to be Empress of a terrestrial world, whenas you can create your self a celestial world if you please. What, said the Empress, can any mortal be a creator? Yes, answered the spirits; for every human creature can create an immaterial world fully inhabited by immaterial creatures, and populous of immaterial subjects, such as we are, and all this within the compass of the head or scull; nay, not only so, but he may create a world of what fashion and government he will, and give the creatures thereof such motions, figures, forms, colours, perceptions, etc. as he pleases, and make whirlpools, lights, pressures and reactions, etc. as he thinks best; nay, he may make a world full of veins, muscles, and nerves, and all these to move by one jolt or stroke: also he may alter that world as often as he pleases, or change it from a natural world, to an artificial; he may make a world of ideas, a world of atoms, a world of lights, or whatsoever his fancy leads him to. And since it is in your power to create such a world, what need you to venture life, reputation and tranquility, to conquer a gross material world? For you can enjoy no more of a material world than a particular creature is able to enjoy, which is but a small part, considering the compass of such a world; and you may plainly observe it by your friend the Empress here, which although she possesses a whole world, yet enjoys she but a part thereof; neither is she so much acquainted with it, that she knows all the places, countries and dominions she governs. The truth is, a sovereign monarch has the general trouble; but the subjects enjoy all the delights and pleasures in parts; for it is impossible, that a kingdom, nay, a country should be enjoyed by one person at once, except he take the pains to travel into every part, and endure the inconveniencies of going from one place to another; wherefore, since glory, delight and pleasure lives but in other men's opinions, and can neither add tranquility to your mind, nor give ease to your body, why should you desire to be Empress of a material world, and be troubled with the cares that attend your government? whenas by creating a world within yourself, you may enjoy all both in whole and in parts, without control or opposition, and may make what world you please, and alter it when you please, and enjoy as much pleasure and delight as a world can afford you? You have converted me, said the Duchess to the spirits, from my ambitious desire; wherefore I'll take your advice, reject and despise all the worlds without me, and create a world of my own. The Empress said, if I do make such a world, then I shall be mistress of two worlds, one within, and the other without me. That your Majesty may, said the spirits; and so left these two ladies to create two worlds within themselves: who did also part from each other, until such time as they had brought their worlds to perfection. The Duchess of Newcastle was most earnest and industrious to make her world, because she had none at present; and first she resolved to frame it according to the opinion of Thales,[24] but she found herself so much troubled with demons, that they would not suffer her to take her own will, but forced her to obey their orders and commands; which she being unwilling to do, left off from making a world that way, and began to frame one according to Pythagoras's doctrine; but in the creation thereof, she was so puzzled with numbers, how to order and compose the several parts, that she having no skill in arithmetic was forced also to desist from the making of that world.[25] Then she intended to create a world according to the opinion of Plato; but she found more trouble and difficulty in that, than in the two former; for the numerous Ideas having no other motion but what was derived from her mind, whence they did flow and issue out, made it a far harder business to her, to impart motion to them, than puppet-players have in giving motion to every several puppet; in so much, that her patience was not able to endure the trouble which those ideas caused her; wherefore she annihilated also that world, and was resolved to make one according to the opinion of Epicurus; which she had no sooner begun, but the infinite atoms made such a mist, that it quite blinded the perception of her mind; neither was she able to make a vacuum as a receptacle for those atoms, or a place which they might retire into; so that partly for the want of it, and of a good order and method, the confusion of those atoms produced such strange and monstrous figures, as did more affright than delight her, and caused such a chaos in her mind, as had almost dissolved it. At last, having with much ado cleansed and cleared her mind of these dusty and misty particles, she endeavoured to create a world according to Aristotle's opinion; but remembering that her mind, as most of the learned hold it, was immaterial, and that according to Aristotle's principle, out of nothing, nothing could be made; she was forced also to desist from that work, and then she fully resolved, not to take any more patterns from the ancient philosophers, but to follow the opinions of the moderns; and to that end, she endeavoured to make a world according to Descartes' opinion; but when she had made the ethereal globules, and set them a-moving by a strong and lively imagination, her mind became so dizzy with their extraordinary swift turning round, that it almost put her into a swoon; for her thoughts, by their constant tottering, did so stagger, as if they had all been drunk: wherefore she dissolved that world, and began to make another, according to Hobbes' opinion; but when all the parts of this imaginary world came to press and drive each other, they seemed like a company of wolves that worry sheep, or like so many dogs that hunt after hares; and when she found a reaction equal to those pressures, her mind was so squeezed together, that her thoughts could neither move forward nor backward, which caused such an horrible pain in her head, that although she had dissolved that world, yet she could not, without much difficulty, settle her mind, and free it from that pain which those pressures and reactions had caused in it.

At last, when the Duchess saw that no patterns would do her any good in the framing of her world; she resolved to make a world of her own invention, and this world was composed of sensitive and rational self-moving matter; indeed, it was composed only of the rational, which is the subtlest and purest degree of matter; for as the sensitive did move and act both to the perceptions and consistency of the body, so this degree of matter at the same point of time (for though the degrees are mixed, yet the several parts may move several ways at one time) did move to the creation of the imaginary world; which world after it was made, appeared so curious and full of variety, so well ordered and wisely governed, that it cannot possibly be expressed by words, nor the delight and pleasure which the Duchess took in making this world of her own.

In the meantime the Empress was also making and dissolving several worlds in her own mind, and was so puzzled, that she could not settle in any of them; wherefore she sent for the Duchess, who being ready to wait on the Empress, carried her beloved world along with her, and invited the Empress's soul to observe the frame, order and government of it. Her Majesty was so ravished with the perception of it, that her soul desired to live in the Duchess's world; but the Duchess advised her to make such another world in her own mind; for, said she, your Majesty's mind is full of rational corporeal motions, and the rational motions of my mind shall assist you by the help of sensitive expressions, with the best instructions they are able to give you.

The Empress being thus persuaded by the Duchess to make an imaginary world of her own, followed her advice; and after she had quite finished it, and framed all kinds of creatures proper and useful for it, strengthened it with good laws, and beautified it with arts and sciences; having nothing else to do, unless she did dissolve her imaginary world, or made some alterations in the Blazing World she lived in, which yet she could hardly do, by reason it was so well ordered that it could not be mended; for it was governed without secret and deceiving policy; neither was there any ambition, factions, malicious detractions, civil dissensions, or home-bred quarrels, divisions in religion, foreign wars, etc. but all the people lived in a peaceful society, united tranquility, and religious conformity; she was desirous to see the world the Duchess came from, and observe therein the several sovereign governments, laws and customs of several nations. The Duchess used all the means she could, to divert her from that journey, telling her, that the world she came from, was very much disturbed with factions, divisions and wars; but the Empress would not be persuaded from her design; and lest the Emperor, or any of his subjects should know of her travel, and obstruct her design, she sent for some of the spirits she had formerly conversed withal, and enquired whether none of them could supply the place of her soul in her body at such a time, when she was gone to travel into another world? They answered, yes, they could; for not only one, said they, but many spirits may enter into your body, if you please. The Empress replied, she desired but one spirit to be viceroy of her body in the absence of her soul, but it must be an honest and ingenious spirit; and if it was possible, a female spirit. The spirits told her, that there was no difference of sexes amongst them; but, said they, we will choose an honest and ingenious spirit, and such a one as shall so resemble your soul, that neither the Emperor, nor any of his subjects, although the most divine, shall know whether it be your own soul, or not: which the Empress was very glad at, and after the spirits were gone, asked the Duchess, how her body was supplied in the absence of her soul? who answered Her Majesty, that her body, in the absence of her soul, was governed by her sensitive and rational corporeal motions. Thus those two female souls travelled together as lightly as two thoughts into the Duchess her native world; and which is remarkable, in a moment viewed all the parts of it, and all the actions of all the creatures therein, especially did the Empress's soul take much notice of the several actions of human creatures in all the several nations and parts of that world, and wondered that for all there were so many several nations, governments, laws, religions, opinions, etc. they should all yet so generally agree in being ambitious, proud, self-conceited, vain, prodigal, deceitful, envious, malicious, unjust, revengeful, irreligious, factious, etc. She did also admire, that not any particular state, kingdom or commonwealth, was contented with their own shares, but endeavoured to encroach upon their neighbours, and that their greatest glory was in plunder and slaughter, and yet their victories less than their expenses, and their losses more than their gains, but their being overcome in a manner their utter ruin. But that she wondered most at, was, that they should prize or value dirt more than men's lives, and vanity more than tranquility; for the Emperor of a world, said she, enjoys but a part, not the whole; so that his pleasure consists in the opinions of others. It is strange to me, answered the Duchess, that you should say thus, being yourself, an Empress of a world, and not only of a world, but of a peaceable, quiet, and obedient world. 'Tis true, replied the Empress, but although it is a peaceable and obedient world, yet the government thereof is rather a trouble, than a pleasure; for order cannot be without industry, contrivance and direction; besides, the magnificent state, that great Princes keep or ought to keep, is troublesome. Then by your Majesty's discourse, said the Duchess, I perceive that the greatest happiness in all worlds consist in moderation: no doubt of it, replied the Empress; and after these two souls had visited all the several places, congregations and assemblies both in religion and state, the several courts of judicature, and the like, in several nations, the Empress said, that of all the monarchs of the several parts of that world, she had observed the Grand Signior[26] was the greatest; for his word was a law, and his power absolute. But the Duchess prayed the Empress to pardon her that she was of another mind; for, said she, he cannot alter Mahomet's laws and religion; so that the law and church do govern the Emperor, and not the Emperor them. But, replied the Empress, he has power in some particulars; as for example, to place and displace subjects in their particular governments of church and state, and having that, he has the command both over church and state, and none dares oppose him. 'Tis true, said the Duchess; but if it pleases your Majesty, we will go into that part of the world whence I came to wait on your Majesty, and there you shall see as powerful a monarch as the Grand-Signior; for though his dominions are not of so large extent, yet they are much stronger, his laws are easy and safe, and he governs so justly and wisely, that his subjects are the happiest people of all the nations or parts of that world. This monarch, said the Empress, I have a great mind to see: then they both went, and in a short time arrived into his dominions; but coming into the metropolitan city, the Empress's soul observed many gallants go into a house, and enquired of the Duchess's soul, what house that was? She told her, it was one of the theatres where comedies and tragedies were acted. The Empress asked, whether they were real? No, said the Duchess, they are feigned. Then the Empress desired to enter into the theatre, and when she had seen the play that was acted, the Duchess asked her how she liked that recreation? I like it very well, said the Empress; but I observe, that the actors make a better show than the spectators, and the scenes a better than the actors, and the music and dancing is more pleasant and acceptable than the play itself; for I see, the scenes stand for wit, the dancing for humour, and the music is the chorus. I am sorry, replied the Duchess, to hear your Majesty say so; for if the wits of this part of the world should hear you, they would condemn you. What, said the Empress, would they condemn me for preferring a natural face before a sign-post, or a natural humour before an artificial dance, or music before a true and profitable relation? As for relation, replied the Duchess, our poets defy and condemn it into a chimney-corner, fitter for old women's tales, than theatres. Why, said the Empress, do not your poets' actions comply with their judgements? for their plays are composed of old stories, either of Greek or Roman, or some new-found world. The Duchess answered her Majesty, that it was true; that all or most of their plays were taken out of old stories, but yet they had new actions, which being joined to old stories, together with the addition of new prologues, scenes, music and dancing, made new plays.

After this, both the souls went to the court, where all the royal family was together, attended by the chief of the nobles of their dominions, which made a very magnificent show; and when the soul of the Empress viewed the King and Queen, she seemed to be in amaze, which the Duchess's soul perceiving, asked the Empress how she liked the King, the Queen, and all the royal race? She answered, that in all the monarchs she had seen in that world, she had not found so much majesty and affability mixed so exactly together, that none did overshadow or eclipse the other; and as for the Queen, she said, that virtue sat triumphant in her face, and piety was dwelling in her heart, and that all the royal family seemed to be endued with a divine splendour: but when she had heard the King discourse, she believed, that Mercury and Apollo had been his celestial instructors; and my dear lord and husband, added the Duchess, has been his earthly governor. But after some short stay in the court, the Duchess's soul grew very melancholy; the Empress asking the cause of her sadness? she told her, that she had an extreme desire to converse with the soul of her noble lord and dear husband, and that she was impatient of a longer stay. The Empress desired the Duchess to have but patience so long, until the King, the Queen, and the royal family were retired, and then she would bear her company to her lord and husband's soul, who at that time lived in the country some 112 miles off; which she did: and thus these two souls went towards those parts of the kingdom where the Duke of Newcastle was.

But one thing I forgot all this while, which is, that although thoughts are the natural language of souls, yet by reason souls cannot travel without vehicles, they use such language as the nature and propriety of their vehicles require, and the vehicles of those two souls being made of the purest and finest sort of air, and of a human shape; this purity and fineness was the cause that they could neither be seen nor heard by any human creature; whenas, had they been of some grosser sort of air, the sound of that air's language would have been as perceptible as the blowing of Zephyrus.[27]

And now to return to my former story; when the Empress's and Duchess's soul were travelling into Nottinghamshire, for that was the place where the Duke did reside; passing through the forest of Sherwood, the Empress's soul was very much delighted with it, as being a dry, plain and woody place, very pleasant to travel in both in Winter and Summer; for it is neither much dirty, nor dusty at no time: at last they arrived at Welbeck,[28] a house where the Duke dwelled, surrounded all with wood, so close and full, that the Empress took great pleasure and delight therein, and told the Duchess she never had observed more wood in so little a compass in any part of the kingdom she had passed through; the truth is, said she, there seems to be more wood on the seas, she meaning the ships, than on the land. The Duchess told her, the reason was, that there had been a long Civil War in that kingdom, in which most of the best timber-trees and principal palaces were ruined and destroyed; and my dear lord and husband, said she, has lost by it half his woods, besides many houses, land, and movable goods; so that all the loss out of his particular estate, did amount to above half a million of pounds. I wish, said the Empress, he had some of the gold that is in the Blazing World, to repair his losses. The Duchess most humbly thanked her Imperial Majesty for her kind wishes; but, said she, wishes will not repair his ruins: however, God has given my noble lord and husband great patience, by which he bears all his losses and misfortunes. At last, they entered into the Duke's house, an habitation not so magnificent, as useful; and when the Empress saw it, Has the Duke, said she, no other house but this? Yes, answered the Duchess, some five miles from this place, he has a very fine castle, called Bolsover.[29] That place then, said the Empress, I desire to see. Alas! replied the Duchess, it is but a naked house, and unclothed of all furniture. However, said the Empress, I may see the manner of its structure and building. That you may, replied the Duchess: and as they were thus discoursing, the Duke came out of the house into the court, to see his horses of manage; whom when the Duchess's soul perceived, she was so overjoyed, that her aerial vehicle became so splendorous, as if it had been enlightened by the sun; by which we may perceive, that the passions of souls or spirits can alter their bodily vehicles. Then these two ladies' spirits went close to him, but he could not perceive them; and after the Empress had observed the art of manage,[30] she was much pleased with it, and commended it as a noble pastime, and an exercise fit and proper for noble and heroic persons; but when the Duke was gone into the house again, those two souls followed him; where the Empress observing, that he went to the exercise of the sword, and was such an excellent and unparallelled master thereof, she was as much pleased with that exercise, as she was with the former: but the Duchess's soul being troubled, that her dear lord and husband used such a violent exercise before meat, for fear of overheating himself, without any consideration of the Empress's soul, left her aerial vehicle, and entered into her lord. The Empress's soul perceiving this, did the like: and then the Duke had three souls in one body; and had there been but some such souls more, the Duke would have been like the Grand Signior in his seraglio, only it would have been a platonic seraglio.[31] But the Duke's soul being wise, honest, witty, complaisant and noble, afforded such delight and pleasure to the Empress's soul by her conversation, that these two souls became enamoured of each other; which the Duchess's soul perceiving, grew jealous at first, but then considering that no adultery could be committed amongst

Platonic lovers, and that Platonism was divine, as being derived from divine Plato, cast forth of her mind that Idea of jealousy. Then the conversation of these three souls was so pleasant, that it cannot be expressed; for the Duke's soul entertained the Empress's soul with scenes, songs, music, witty discourses, pleasant recreations, and all kinds of harmless sports; so that the time passed away faster than they expected. At last, a spirit came and told the Empress, that although neither the Emperor, nor any of his subjects knew that her soul was absent; yet the Empress's soul was so sad and melancholy, for want of his own beloved soul, that all the imperial court took notice of it. Wherefore he advised the Empress's soul to return into the Blazing World, into her own body she left there; which both the Duke's and Duchess's soul was very sorry for, and wished, that if it had been possible, the Empress's soul might have stayed a longer time with them; but seeing it could not be otherwise, they pacified themselves: but before the Empress returned into the Blazing World, the Duchess desired a favour of her, to wit, that she would be pleased to make an agreement between her noble lord, and Fortune. Why, said the Empress, are they enemies? Yes, answered the Duchess, and they have been so ever since I have been his wife; nay, I have heard my lord say, that she hath crossed him in all things ever since he could remember. I am sorry for that, replied the Empress, but I cannot discourse with Fortune without the help of an immaterial spirit, and that cannot be done in this world, for I have no fly- nor bird-men here, to send into the region of the air, where for the most part, their habitations are. The Duchess said, she would entreat her lord to send an attorney or lawyer, to plead his cause. Fortune will bribe them, replied the Empress, and so the Duke may chance to be cast;[32] wherefore the best way will be for the Duke to choose a friend on his side, and let Fortune choose another, and try whether by this means it be possible to compose the difference. The Duchess said, they will never come to an agreement, unless there be a judge or umpire to decide the case. A judge, replied the Empress, is easy to be had, but to get an impartial judge, is a thing so difficult, that I doubt we shall hardly find one; for there is none to be had neither in nature, nor in Hell, but only from Heaven, and how to get such a divine and celestial judge I cannot tell: nevertheless, if you will go along with me into the Blazing World, I'll try what may be done. 'Tis my duty, said the Duchess, to wait on your Majesty, and I shall most willingly do it, for I have no other interest to consider. Then the Duchess spake to the Duke concerning the difference between him and Fortune, and how it was her desire that they might be friends. The Duke answered, that for his part, he had always with great industry, sought her friendship, but as yet he could never obtain it, for she had always been his enemy: however, said he, I'll try, and send my two friends, Prudence and Honesty, to plead my cause. Then these two friends went with the Duchess and the Empress into the Blazing World; (for it is to be observed, that they are somewhat like spirits, because they are immaterial, although their actions are corporeal:) and after their arrival there, when the Empress had refreshed herself, and rejoiced with the Emperor, she sent her fly-men for some of the spirits, and desired their assistance, to compose the difference between Fortune, and the Duke of Newcastle. But they told her Majesty, that Fortune was so inconstant, that although she would perhaps promise to hear their cause pleaded, yet it was a thousand to one, but she would never have the patience to do it: nevertheless, upon her Majesty's request, they tried their utmost, and at last prevailed with Fortune so far, that she chose Folly, and Rashness, for her friends, but they could not agree in choosing a judge; until at last, with much ado, they concluded, that Truth should hear, and decide the cause. Thus all being prepared, and the time appointed, both the Empress's and Duchess's soul went to hear them plead; and when all the immaterial company was met, Fortune standing upon a golden globe, made this following speech:

Noble Friends, *We are met here to hear a cause pleaded concerning the difference between the Duke of Newcastle, and myself, and though I am willing upon the persuasions of the ambassadors of the Empress, the immaterial spirits, to yield to it, yet it had been fit, the Duke's soul should be present also, to speak for herself; but since she is not here, I shall declare myself to his wife, and his friends, as also to my friends, especially the Empress, to whom I shall chiefly direct my speech. First, I desire, your Imperial Majesty may know, that this Duke who complains or exclaims so much against me, hath been always my enemy; for he has preferred Honesty and Prudence before me, and slighted all my favours; nay, not only thus, but he did fight against me, and preferred his innocence before my power. His friends Honesty and Prudence, said he most scornfully, are more to be regarded, than inconstant Fortune, who is only a friend to fools and knaves; for which neglect and scorn, whether I have not just reason to be his enemy, your Majesty may judge yourself.*

After Fortune had thus ended her speech, the Duchess's soul rose from her seat, and spake to the immaterial assembly in this manner:[33]

Noble Friends, *I think it fit, by your leave, to answer Lady Fortune in the behalf of my noble lord and husband, since he is not here himself; and since you have heard her complaint concerning the choice my lord made of his friends, and the neglect and disrespect he seemed to cast upon her; give me leave to answer, that, first concerning the choice of his friends, he has proved himself a wise man in it; and as for the disrespect and rudeness, her Ladyship accuses him of, I dare say, he is so much a gentleman, that I am confident he would never slight, scorn or disrespect any of the female sex in all his lifetime; but was such a servant and champion for them, that he ventured life and estate in their service; but being of an honest, as well as an honourable nature, he could not trust Fortune with that which he preferred above his life, which was his reputation, by reason Fortune did not side with those that were honest and honourable, but renounced them; and since he could not be of both sides, he chose to be of that which was agreeable both to his conscience, nature and education; for which choice Fortune did not only declare herself his open enemy, but fought with him in several battles; nay, many times, hand to hand; at last, she being a powerful princess, and as some believe, a deity, overcame him, and cast him into a banishment, where she kept him in great misery, ruined his estate, and took away from him most of his friends; nay, even when she favoured many that were against her, she still frowned on him; all which he endured with the greatest patience, and with that respect to Lady Fortune, that he did never in the least endeavour to disoblige any of her favourites, but was only sorry that he, an honest man, could find no favour in her court;*[34] *and since he did never injure any of those she favoured, he neither was an enemy to her Ladyship, but gave her always that respect and worship which belonged to her power and dignity, and is still ready at any time honestly and prudently to serve her; he only begs her Ladyship would be his friend for the future, as she hath been his enemy in times past.*

As soon as the Duchess's speech was ended, Folly and Rashness started up, and both spake so thick and fast at once, that not only the assembly, but themselves were not able to understand each other: at which Fortune was somewhat out of countenance, and commanded them either to speak singly, or be silent: but Prudence told her Ladyship, she should command them to speak wisely, as well as singly; otherwise, said she, it were best for them not to speak at all: which Fortune resented very ill, and told Prudence, she was too bold; and then commanded Folly to declare what she would have made known: but her speech was so foolish, mixed with such nonsense, that none knew what to make of it; besides, it was so tedious, that Fortune bid her to be silent, and commanded Rashness to speak for her, who began after this manner:

Great Fortune; *The Duchess of Newcastle has proved herself, according to report, a very proud and ambitious lady, in presuming to answer you her own self, in this noble assembly without your command, in a speech wherein she did not only contradict you, but preferred Honesty and Prudence before you; saying, that her lord was ready to serve you honestly and prudently; which presumption is beyond all pardon; and if you allow Honesty and Prudence to be above you, none will admire, worship or serve you; but you'll be forced to serve yourself, and will be despised, neglected and scorned by all; and from a deity, become a miserable, dirty, begging mortal in a churchyard porch, or nobleman's gate: wherefore to prevent such disasters, fling as many misfortunes and neglects on the Duke and Duchess of Newcastle, and their two friends, as your power is able to do; otherwise Prudence and Honesty will be the chief and only moral deities of mortals.*

Rashness having thus ended her speech, Prudence rose and declared herself in this manner:

Beautiful Truth, Great Fortune, and you the rest of my noble friends; *I am come a great and long journey in the behalf of my dear friend the Duke of Newcastle, not to make more wounds, but, if it be possible, to heal those that are made already. Neither do I presume to be a deity; but my only request is, that you would be pleased to accept of my offering, I being an humble and devout supplicant, and since no offering is more acceptable to the gods, than the offering of peace; in order to that, I desire to make an agreement between Fortune, and the Duke of Newcastle.*

Thus she spake, and as she was going on, up started Honesty (for she has not always so much discretion as she ought to have) and interrupted Prudence.

I came not here, said she, to hear Fortune flattered, but to hear the cause decided between Fortune and the Duke; neither came I hither to speak rhetorically and eloquently, but to propound the case plainly and truly; and I'll have you know, that the Duke, whose cause we argue, was and is my foster-son; for I Honesty bred him from his childhood, and made a perpetual friendship betwixt him and Gratitude, Charity and Generosity; and put him to school to Prudence, who taught him wisdom, and informed him in the rules of Temperance, Patience, Justice, and the like; then I put him into the University of Honour, where he learned all honourable qualities, arts, and sciences; afterward I sent him to travel through the world of actions, and made Observation his governor; and in those travels, he contracted a friendship with Experience; all which, made him fit for Heaven's blessings, and Fortune's favours: but she hating all those that have merit and desert, became his inveterate enemy, doing him all the mischief she could, until the god of Justice opposed Fortune's malice and passed him out of those ruins she had cast upon him: for this god's favourites were the Duke's champions; wherefore to be an enemy to him, were to be an enemy to the god of Justice: in short, the true cause of Fortune's malice to this Duke, is, that he would never flatter her; for I Honesty, did command him not to do it, or else he would be forced to follow all her inconstant ways, and obey all her unjust commands, which would cause a great reproach to him: but, on the other side, Prudence advised him not to despise Fortune's favours, for that would be an obstruction and hindrance to his worth and merit; and he to obey both our advice and counsels, did neither flatter nor despise her, but was always humble and respectful to her, so far as honour, honesty and conscience would permit: all which I refer to Truth's judgement, and expect her final sentence.

Fortune hearing thus Honesty's plain speech, thought it very rude, and would not hearken to Truth's judgement, but went away in a passion: at which, both the Empress and Duchess were extremely troubled, that their endeavours should have no better effect: but Honesty chid the Duchess, and said, she was to be punished for desiring so much Fortune's favours; for it appears, said she, that you mistrust the gods' blessings: at which the Duchess wept, answering Honesty, that she did neither mistrust the gods' blessings, nor rely upon Fortune's favours; but desired only that her lord might have no potent enemies. The Empress being much troubled to see her weep, told Honesty in anger, she wanted the discretion of Prudence; for though you are commendable,[35] said she, yet you are apt to commit many indiscreet actions, unless Prudence be your guide. At which reproof Prudence smiled, and Honesty was somewhat out of countenance; but they soon became very good friends: and after the Duchess's soul had stayed some time with the Empress in the Blazing World, she begged leave of her to return to her lord and husband; which the Empress granted her, upon condition she should come and visit her as often as conveniently she could, promising that she would do the same to the Duchess.

Thus the Duchess's soul, after she had taken her leave of the Empress, as also of the spirits, who with great civility, promised her, that they would endeavour in time to make a peace and agreement between Fortune and the Duke, returned with Prudence and Honesty into her own world: but when she was just upon her departure, the Empress sent to her, and desired that she might yet have some little conference with her before she went; which the Duchess most willingly granted her Majesty, and when she came to wait on her, the Empress told the Duchess, that she being her dear Platonic friend, of whose just and impartial judgement, she had always a very great esteem, could not forbear, before she went from her, to ask her advice concerning the government of the Blazing World; for, said she, although this world was very well and wisely ordered and governed at first, when I came to be Empress thereof; yet the nature of women, being much delighted with change and variety, after I had received an absolute power from the Emperor, did somewhat alter the form of government from what I found it; but now perceiving that the world is not so quiet as it was at first, I am much troubled at it; especially there are such contentions and divisions between the worm-, bear- and fly-men, the ape-men, the satyrs, the spider-men, and all others of such sorts, that I fear they'll break out into an open rebellion, and cause a great disorder and the ruin of the government; and therefore I desire your advice and assistance, how I may order it to the best advantage, that this world may be rendered peaceable, quiet and happy, as it was before. Whereupon the Duchess answered, that since she heard by her Imperial Majesty, how well and happily the world had been governed when she first came to be Empress thereof, she would advise her Majesty to introduce the same form of government again, which had been before; that is, to have but one sovereign, one religion, one law, and one language, so that all the world might be but as one united family, without divisions; nay, like God, and his blessed saints and angels: otherwise, said she, it may in time prove as unhappy, nay, as miserable a world as that is from which I came, wherein are more sovereigns than worlds, and more pretended governors than governments, more religions than gods, and more opinions in those religions than truths; more laws than rights, and more bribes than justices, more policies than necessities, and more fears than dangers, more covetousness than riches, more ambitions than merits, more services than rewards, more languages than wit, more controversy than knowledge, more reports than noble actions, and more gifts by partiality, than according to merit; all which, said she, is a great misery, nay, a curse, which your blessed Blazing World never knew, nor 'tis probable, will never know of, unless your Imperial Majesty alter the government thereof from what it was when you began to govern it: and since your Majesty complain much of the factions of the bear-, fish-, fly-, ape- and worm-men, the satyrs, spider-men, and the like, and of their perpetual disputes and quarrels, I would advise your Majesty to dissolve all their societies; for 'tis better to be without their intelligences, than to have an unquiet and disorderly government. The truth is, said she, wheresoever is learning, there is most commonly also controversy and quarrelling; for there be always some that will know more, and be wiser than others; some think their arguments come nearer to truth, and are more rational than others; some are so wedded to their own opinions, that they never yield to reason; and others, though they find their opinions not firmly grounded upon reason, yet for fear of receiving some disgrace by altering them, will nevertheless maintain them against all sense and reason, which must needs breed factions in their schools, which at last break out into open wars, and draw sometimes an utter ruin upon a state or government. The Empress told the Duchess, that she would willingly follow her advice, but she thought it would be an eternal disgrace to her, to alter her own decrees, acts and laws. To which the Duchess answered, that it was so far from a disgrace, as it would rather be for her Majesty's eternal honour, to return from a worse to a better, and would express and declare her to be more than ordinary wise and good; so wise, as to perceive her own errors, and so good, as not to persist in them, which few did; for which, said she, you will get a glorious fame in this world, and an eternal glory hereafter; and I shall pray for it so long as I live. Upon which advice, the Empress's soul embraced and kissed the Duchess's soul with an immaterial kiss, and shed immaterial tears, that she was forced to part from her, finding her not a flattering parasite, but a true friend; and, in truth, such was their Platonic friendship, as these two loving souls did often meet and rejoice in each other's conversation.

THE SECOND PART OF THE DESCRIPTION OF THE NEW BLAZING WORLD

The Empress having now ordered and settled her government to the best advantage and quiet of her Blazing World, lived and reigned most happily and blessedly, and received oftentimes visits from the immaterial spirits, who gave her intelligence of all such things as she desired to know, and they were able to inform her of: one time they told her, how the world she came from, was embroiled in a great war, and that most parts or nations thereof made war against that kingdom, which was her native country, where all her friends and relations did live, at which the Empress was extremely troubled; insomuch that the Emperor perceived her grief by her tears, and examining the cause thereof, she told him that she had received intelligence from the spirits, that that part of the world she came from, which was her native country, was like to be destroyed by numerous enemies that made war against it. The Emperor being very sensible of this ill news, especially of the trouble it caused to the Empress, endeavoured to comfort her as much as possibly he could, and told her, that she might have all the assistance which the Blazing World was able to afford. She answered, that if there were any possibility of transporting forces out of the Blazing World, into the world she came from, she would not fear so much the ruin thereof: but, said she, there being no probability of effecting any such thing, I know not how to show my readiness to serve my native country. The Emperor asked, whether those spirits that gave her intelligence of this war, could not with all their power and forces assist her against those enemies? She answered, that spirits could not arm themselves, nor make any use of artificial arms or weapons; for their vehicles were natural bodies, not artificial: besides, said she, the violent and strong actions of war, will never agree with immaterial spirits; for immaterial spirits cannot fight, nor make trenches, fortifications, and the like. But, said the Emperor, their vehicles can; especially if those vehicles be men's bodies, they may be serviceable in all the actions of war. Alas, replied the Empress, that will never do; for first, said she, it will be difficult to get so many dead bodies for their vehicles, as to make up a whole army, much more to make many armies to fight with so many several nations; nay, if this could be, yet it is not possible to get so many dead and undissolved bodies in one nation; and for transporting them out of other nations, it would be a thing of great difficulty and improbability: but put the case, said she, all these difficulties could be overcome, yet there is one obstruction or hindrance which can no ways be avoided; for although those dead and undissolved bodies did all die in one minute of time, yet before they could rendezvous, and be put into a posture of war, to make a great and formidable army, they would stink and dissolve; and when they came to a fight, they would moulder into dust and ashes, and so leave the purer immaterial spirits naked: nay, were it also possible, that those dead bodies could be preserved from stinking and dissolving, yet the souls of such bodies would not suffer immaterial spirits to rule and order them, but they would enter and govern them themselves, as being the right owners thereof, which would produce a war between those immaterial souls, and the immaterial spirits in material bodies; all which would hinder them from doing any service in the actions of war, against the enemies of my native country. You speak reason, said the Emperor, and I wish with all my soul I could advise any manner or way, that you might be able to assist it; but you having told me of your dear Platonic friend the Duchess of Newcastle, and of her good and profitable counsels, I would desire you to send for her soul, and confer with her about this business.

The Empress was very glad of this motion of the Emperor, and immediately sent for the soul of the said Duchess, which in a minute waited on Her Majesty. Then the Empress declared to her the grievance and sadness of her mind, and how much she was troubled and afflicted at the news brought her by the immaterial spirits, desiring the Duchess, if possible, to assist her with the best counsels she could, that she might show the greatness of her love and affection which she bore to her native country. Whereupon the Duchess promised Her Majesty to do what lay in her power; and since it was a business of great importance, she desired some time to consider of it; for, said she, great affairs require deep considerations; which the Empress willingly allowed her. And after the Duchess had considered some little time, she desired the Empress to send some of her syrens or mear-men, to see what passages they could find out of the Blazing World, into the world she came from; for said she, if there be a passage for a ship to come out of that world into this; then certainly there may also a ship pass through the same passage out of this world into that. Hereupon the mear-men or fish-men were sent out; who being many in number, employed all their industry, and did swim several ways; at last having found out the passage, they returned to the Empress, and told her, that as their Blazing World had but one Emperor, one government, one religion, and one language, so there was but one passage into that world, which was so little, that no vessel bigger than a packet-boat could go through; neither was that passage always open, but sometimes quite frozen up. At which relation both the Empress and Duchess seemed somewhat troubled, fearing that this would perhaps be an hindrance or obstruction to their design.

At last the Duchess desired the Empress to send for her ship-wrights, and all her architects, which were giants; who being called, the Duchess told them how some in her own world had been so ingenious, and contrived ships that could swim under water, and asked whether they could do the like? The giants answered, they had never heard of that invention; nevertheless, they would try what might be done by art, and spare no labour or industry to find it out. In the meantime, while both the Empress and Duchess were in a serious council, after many debates, the Duchess desired but a few ships to transport some of the bird-, worm- and bear-men. Alas! said the Empress, what can such sorts of men do in the other world? especially so few? They will be soon destroyed, for a musket will destroy numbers of birds at one shot. The Duchess said, I desire Your Majesty will have but a little patience, and rely upon my advice, and you shall not fail to save your own native country, and in a manner become mistress of all that world you came from. The Empress, who loved the Duchess as her own soul, did so; the giants returned soon after, and told Her Majesty, that they had found out the art which the Duchess had mentioned, to make such ships as could swim under water; which the Empress and Duchess were both very glad at, and when the ships were made ready, the Duchess told the Empress, that it was requisite that Her Majesty should go her self in body as well as in soul; but, I, said she, can only wait on Your Majesty after a spiritual manner, that is, with my soul. Your soul, said the Empress, shall live with my soul, in my body; for I shall only desire your counsel and advice. Then said the Duchess, Your Majesty must command a great number of your fish-men to wait on your ships; for you know that your ships are not made for cannons, and therefore are no ways serviceable in war; for though by the help of your engines they can drive on, and your fish-men may by the help of chains or ropes, draw them which way they will, to make them go on, or fly back, yet not so as to fight: and though your ships be of gold, and cannot be shot through, but only bruised and battered; yet the enemy will assault and enter them, and take them as prizes; wherefore your fish-men must do you service instead of cannons. But how, said the Empress, can the fish-men do me service against an enemy, without cannons and all sorts of arms? That is the reason, answered the Duchess, that I would have numbers of fish-men, for they shall destroy all your enemy's ships, before they can come near you. The Empress asked in what manner that could be? Thus, answered the Duchess: – Your Majesty must send a number of worm-men to the Burning Mountains (for you have good store of them in the Blazing World) which must get a great quantity of the fire-stone, whose property, you know, is, that it burns so long as it is wet; and the ships in the other world being all made of wood, they may by that means set them all on fire; and if you can but destroy their ships, and hinder their navigation, you will be mistress of all that world, by reason most parts thereof cannot live without navigation. Besides, said she, the fire-stone will serve you instead of light or torches; for you know, that the world you are going into, is dark at nights (especially if there be no moon-shine, or if the moon be overshadowed by clouds) and not so full of blazing-stars as this world is, which make as great a light in the absence of the sun, as the sun doth when it is present; for that world hath but little blinking stars, which make more shadows than light, and are only able to draw up vapours from the earth, but not to rarify or clarify them, or to convert them into serene air.

This advice of the Duchess was very much approved, and joyfully embraced by the Empress, who forthwith sent her worm-men to get a good quantity of the mentioned fire-stone. She also commanded numbers of fish-men to wait on her under water, and bird-men to wait on her in the air; and bear- and worm-men to wait on her in ships, according to the Duchess's advice; and indeed the bear-men were as serviceable to her as the north-star; but the bird-men would often rest themselves upon the decks of the ships; neither would the Empress, being of a sweet and noble nature, suffer that they should tire or weary themselves by long flights; for though by land they did often fly out of one country into another, yet they did rest in some woods, or on some grounds, especially at night, when it was their sleeping time: and therefore the Empress was forced to take a great many ships along with her, both for transporting those several sorts of her loyal and serviceable subjects, and to carry provisions for them: besides, she was so wearied with the petitions of several others of her subjects who desired to wait on Her Majesty, that she could not possibly deny them all; for some would rather choose to be drowned, than not tender their duty to her.

Thus after all things were made fit and ready, the Empress

began her journey, I cannot properly say, she set sail, by reason in some part, as in the passage between the two worlds (which yet was but short) the ships were drawn under water by the fish-men with golden chains, so that they had no need of sails there, nor of any other arts, but only to keep out water from entering into the ships, and to give or make so much air as would serve for breath or respiration, those land animals that were in the ships; which the giants had so artificially contrived, that they which were therein found no inconveniency at all: and after they had passed the Icy Sea, the golden ships appeared above water, and so went on until they came near the kingdom that was the Empress's native country; where the bear-men through their telescopes discovered a great number of ships which had beset all that kingdom, well rigged and manned.

The Empress before she came in sight of the enemy, sent some of her fish- and bird-men to bring her intelligence of their fleet; and hearing of their number, their station and posture, she gave order that when it was night, her bird-men should carry in their beaks[36] some of the mentioned fire-stones, with the tops thereof wetted; and the fish-men should carry them likewise, and hold them out of the water; for they were cut in the form of torches or candles, and being many thousands, made a terrible show; for it appeared as if all the air and sea had been of a flaming fire; and all that were upon the sea, or near it, did verily believe, the time of judgement, or the last day was come, which made them all fall down, and pray.

At the break of day, the Empress commanded those lights to be put out, and then the naval forces of the enemy perceived nothing but a number of ships without sails, guns, arms, and other instruments of war; which ships seemed to swim of themselves, without any help or assistance: which sight put them into a great amaze; neither could they perceive that those ships were of gold, by reason the Empress had caused them all to be coloured black, or with a dark colour; so that the natural colour of the gold could not be perceived through the artificial colour of the paint, no not by the best telescopes. All which put the enemy's fleet into such a fright at night, and to such wonder in the morning, or at day time, that they knew not what to judge or make of them; for they knew neither what ships they were, nor what party they belonged to, insomuch that they had no power to stir.

In the meanwhile, the Empress knowing the colours of her own country, sent a letter to their general, and the rest of the chief commanders, to let them know, that she was a great and powerful princess, and came to assist them against their enemies; wherefore she desired they should declare themselves, when they would have her help and assistance.

Hereupon a council was called, and the business debated; but there were so many cross and different opinions, that they could not suddenly resolve what answer to send the Empress; at which she grew angry, insomuch that she resolved to return into her Blazing World, without giving any assistance to her countrymen: but the Duchess of Newcastle entreated Her Majesty to abate her passion; for, said she, great councils are most commonly slow, because many men have several opinions: besides, every councillor striving to be the wisest, makes long speeches, and raises many doubts, which cause retardments. If I had long speeched councillors, replied the Empress, I would hang them, by reason they give more words, than advice. The Duchess answered, that Her Majesty should not be angry, but consider the differences of that and her Blazing World; for, said she, they are not both alike; but there are grosser and duller understandings in this, than in the Blazing World.

At last a messenger came out, who returned the Empress thanks for her kind proffer, but desired withal to know from whence she came, and how, and in what manner her assistance could be serviceable to them? The Empress answered, that she was not bound to tell them whence she came; but as for the manner of her assistance, I will appear, said she, to your navy in a splendorous light, surrounded with fire. The messenger asked at what time they should expect her coming? I'll be with you, answered the Empress, about one of the clock at night. With this report the messenger returned; which made both the poor councillors and sea-men much afraid; but yet they longed for the time to behold this strange sight.

The appointed hour being come, the Empress appeared with garments made of the star-stone, and was born or supported above the water, upon the fish-men's heads and backs, so that she seemed to walk upon the face of the water, and the bird- and fish-men carried the fire-stone, lighted both in the air, and above the waters.

Which sight, when her countrymen perceived at a distance, their hearts began to tremble; but coming something nearer, she left her torches, and appeared only in her garments of light, like an angel, or some deity, and all kneeled down before her, and worshipped her with all submission and reverence: but the Empress would not come nearer than at such a distance where her voice might be generally heard, by reason she would not have that of her accoutrements anything else should be perceived, but the splendour thereof; and when she was come so near that her voice could be heard and understood by all, she made this following speech:

Dear Country-men, *for so you are, although you know me not; I being a native of this kingdom, and hearing that most part of this world had resolved to make war against it, and sought to destroy it, at least to weaken its naval force and power; have made a voyage out of another world, to lend you my assistance against your enemies. I come not to make bargains with you, or to regard my own interest, more than your safety; but I intend to make you the most powerful nation of this world; and therefore I have chosen rather to quit my own tranquility, riches and pleasure, than suffer you to be ruined and destroyed. All the return I desire, is but your grateful acknowledgment, and to declare my power, love and loyalty to my native country; for although I am now a great and absolute princess and empress of a whole world, yet I acknowledge that once I was a subject of this kingdom, which is but a small part of this world; and therefore I will have you undoubtedly believe, that I shall destroy all your enemies before this following night, I mean those which trouble you by sea; and if you have any by land, assure your self I shall also give you my assistance against them, and make you triumph over all that seek your ruin and destruction.*

Upon this declaration of the Empress, when both the General, and all the commanders in their several ships had returned their humble and hearty thanks to Her Majesty for so great a favour to them, she took her leave and departed to her own ships. But, good Lord! what several opinions and judgements did this produce in the minds of her country-men; some said she was an angel; others, she was a sorceress; some believed her a goddess; others said the devil deluded them in the shape of a fine lady.

The morning after, when the navies were to fight, the Empress appeared upon the face of the waters, dressed in her imperial robes, which were all of diamonds and carbuncles; in one hand she held a buckler, made of one entire carbuncle, and in the other hand a spear of one entire diamond; on her head she had a cap of diamonds, and just upon the top of the crown, was a star made of the star-stone, mentioned heretofore, and a half-moon made of the same stone, was placed on her forehead; all her other garments were of several sorts of precious jewels; and having given her fish-men directions how to destroy the enemies of her native country, she proceeded to effect her design. The fish-men were to carry the fire-stones in cases of diamonds (for the diamonds in the Blazing World are in splendour so far beyond the diamonds of this world, as pebble-stones are to the best sort of this world's diamonds) and to uncase or uncover those fire-stones no sooner but when they were just under the enemy's ships, or close at their sides, and then to wet them, and set their ships on fire; which was no sooner done, but all the enemy's fleet was of a flaming fire; and coming to the place where the powder was, it straight blew them up; so that all the several navies of the enemies, were destroyed in a short time: which when her countrymen did see, they all cried out with one voice, that she was an angel sent from God to deliver them out of the hands of their enemies: neither would she return into the Blazing World, until she had forced all the rest of that world to submit to that same nation.

In the meantime, the General of all their naval forces sent to their sovereign to acquaint him with their miraculous delivery and conquest, and with the Empress's design of making him the most powerful monarch of all that world. After a short time, the Empress sent her self to the sovereign of that nation to know in what she could be serviceable to him; who returning her many thanks, both for her assistance against his enemies, and her kind proffer to do him further service for the good and benefit of his nations (for he was King over several kingdoms) sent her word, that although she did partly destroy his enemies by sea, yet they were so powerful, that they did hinder the trade and traffic of his dominions. To which the Empress returned this answer, that she would burn and sink all those ships that would not pay him tribute; and forthwith sent to all the neighbouring nations, who had any traffic by sea, desiring them to pay tribute to the King and sovereign of that nation where she was born; but they denied it with great scorn. Whereupon she immediately commanded her fish-men to destroy all strangers' ships that trafficked on the seas; which they did according to the Empress's command; and when the neighbouring nations and kingdoms perceived her power, they were so discomposed in their affairs and designs, that they knew not what to do: at last they sent to the Empress, and desired to treat with her, but could get no other conditions than to submit and pay tribute to the said King and sovereign of her native country, otherwise, she was resolved to ruin all their trade and traffic by burning their ships. Long was this treat, but in fine, they could obtain nothing, so that at last they were forced to submit; by which the King of the mentioned nations became absolute master of the seas, and consequently of that world; by reason, as I mentioned heretofore, the several nations of that world could not well live without traffic and commerce, by sea, as well as by land.

But after a short time, those neighbouring nations finding themselves so much enslaved, that they were hardly able to peep out of their own dominions without a chargeable tribute, they all agreed to join their forces against the King and sovereign of the said dominions; which when the Empress received notice of, she sent out her fish-men to destroy, as they had done before, the remainder of all their naval power, by which they were soon forced again to submit, except some nations which could live without foreign traffic, and some whose trade and traffic was merely by land; these would no ways be tributary to the mentioned King. The Empress sent them word, that in case they did not submit to him, she intended to fire all their towns and cities, and reduce them by force, to what they would not yield with a good will. But they rejected and scorned Her Majesty's message, which provoked her anger so much, that she resolved to send her bird- and worm-men thither, with order to begin first with their smaller towns, and set them on fire (for she was loath to make more spoil than she was forced to do) and if they remained still obstinate in their resolutions, to destroy also their greater cities. The only difficulty was, how to convey the worm-men conveniently to those places; but they desired that her Majesty would but set them upon any part of the earth of those nations, and they could travel within the earth as easily, and as nimbly as men upon the face of the earth; which the Empress did according to their desire.

But before both the bird- and worm-men began their journey, the Empress commanded the bear-men to view through their telescopes what towns and cities those were that would not submit; and having a full information thereof, she instructed the bird- and bear-men what towns they should begin withal; in the meanwhile she sent to all the princes and sovereigns of those nations, to let them know that she would give them a proof of her power, and check their obstinacies by burning some of their smaller towns; and if they continued still in their obstinate resolutions, that she would convert their smaller loss into a total ruin. She also commanded her bird-men to make their flight at night, lest they be perceived. At last when both the bird- and worm-men came to the designed places, the worm-men laid some fire-stones under the foundation of every house, and the bird-men placed some at the tops of them, so that both by rain, and by some other moisture within the earth, the stones could not fail of burning. The bird-men in the meantime having learned some few words of their language, told them, that the next time it did rain, their towns would be all on fire; at which they were amazed to hear men speak in the air; but withal they laughed when they heard them say that rain should fire their towns, knowing that the effect of water was to quench, not produce fire.

At last a rain came, and upon a sudden all their houses appeared of a flaming fire, and the more water there was poured on them, the more they did flame and burn; which struck such a fright and terror into all the neighbouring cities, nations and kingdoms, that for fear the like should happen to them, they and all the rest of the parts of that world granted the Empress's desire, and submitted to the monarch and sovereign of her native country, the King of ESFI; save one, which having seldom or never any rain, but only dews, which would soon be spent in a great fire, slighted her power: the Empress being desirous to make it stoop, as well as the rest, knew that every year it was watered by a flowing tide, which lasted some weeks; and although their houses stood high from the ground, yet they were built upon supporters which were fixed into the ground. Wherefore she commanded both her bird- and worm-men to lay some of the fire-stones at the bottom of those supporters, and when the tide came in, all their houses were of a fire, which did so rarefy the water, that the tide was soon turned into vapour, and this vapour again into air; which caused not only a destruction of their houses, but also a general barrenness over all their country that year, and forced them to submit as well as the rest of the world had done.

Thus the Empress did not only save her native country, but made it the absolute monarchy of all that world; and both the effects of her power and her beauty did kindle a great desire in all the greatest princes to see her; who hearing that she was resolved to return into her own Blazing World, they all entreated the favour, that they might wait on Her Majesty before she went. The Empress sent word, that she should be glad to grant their requests; but having no other place of reception for them, she desired that they should be pleased to come into the open seas with their ships, and make a circle of a pretty large compass, and then her own ships should meet them, and close up the circle, and she would present her self to the view of all those that came to see her: which answer was joyfully received by all the mentioned princes, who came, some sooner, and some later, each according to the distance of his country, and the length of the voyage. And being all met in the form and manner aforesaid, the Empress appeared upon the face of the water in her imperial robes; in some part of her hair she had placed some of the star-stone, near her face, which added such a lustre and glory to it, that it caused a great admiration in all that were present, who believed her to be some celestial creature, or rather an uncreated goddess, and they all had a desire to worship her; for surely, said they, no mortal creature can have such a splendid and transcendent beauty, nor can any have so great a power as she has, to walk upon the waters, and to destroy whatever she pleases, not only whole nations, but a whole world.

The Empress expressed to her own countrymen, who were also her interpreters to the rest of the princes that were present, that she would give them an entertainment at the darkest time of night; which being come, the fire-stones were lighted, which made both air and seas appear of a bright shining flame, insomuch that they put all spectators into an extreme fright, who verily believed, they should all be destroyed; which the Empress perceiving, caused all the lights of the fire-stones to be put out, and only showed herself in her garments of light: the bird-men carried her upon their backs into the air, and there she appeared as glorious as the sun. Then she was set down upon the seas again, and presently there was heard the most melodious and sweetest consort of voices, as ever was heard out of the seas, which was made by the fish-men; this consort was answered by another, made by the bird-men in the air, so that it seemed as if sea and air had spoke and answered each other by way of singing dialogues, or after the manner of those plays that are acted by singing voices.

But when it was upon break of day, the Empress ended her entertainment, and at full daylight all the princes perceived that she went into the ship wherein the prince and monarch of her native country was, the King of ESFI with whom she had several conferences; and having assured him of the readiness of her assistance whensoever he required it, telling him withal, that she wanted no intelligence, she went forth again upon the waters, and being in the midst of the circle made by those ships that were present, she desired them to draw somewhat nearer, that they might hear her speak; which being done, she declared her self in this following manner:

Great, heroic, and famous monarchs: *I came hither to assist the King of ESFI against his enemies, he being unjustly assaulted by many several nations, which would fain take away his hereditary rights and prerogatives of the narrow seas; at which unjustice Heaven was much displeased; and for the injuries he received from his enemies, rewarded him with an absolute power, so that now he is become the head-monarch of all this world; which power, though you may envy, yet you can no ways hinder him; for all those that endeavour to resist his power, shall only get loss for their labour, and no victory for their profit. Wherefore my advice to you all is, to pay him tribute justly and truly, that you may live peaceably and happily, and be rewarded with the blessings of Heaven, which I wish you from my soul.*

After the Empress had thus finished her speech to the princes of the several nations of that world, she desired that their ships might fall back, which being done, her own fleet came into the circle, without any visible assistance of sails or tide; and herself being entered into her own ship, the whole fleet sunk immediately into the bottom of the seas, and left all the spectators in a deep amazement; neither would she suffer any of her ships to come above the waters until she arrived into the Blazing World.

In time of the voyage, both the Empress's and Duchess's soul were very gay and merry, and sometimes they would converse very seriously with each other: amongst the rest of their discourses, the Duchess said, she wondered much at one thing, which was, that since Her Majesty had found out a passage out of the Blazing World into the world she came from, she did not enrich that part of the world where she was born, at least her own family, when as yet she had enough to enrich the whole world. The Empress's soul answered, that she loved her native country and her own family as well as any creature could do, and that this was the reason why she would not enrich them; for said she, not only particular families or nations, but all the world, their natures are such, that much gold, and great store of riches makes them mad, insomuch as they endeavour to destroy each other for gold, or riches' sake. The reason thereof is, said the Duchess, that they have too little gold and riches, which makes them so eager to have it. No, replied the Empress's soul, their particular covetousness is beyond all the wealth of the richest world, and the more riches they have, the more covetous they are, for their covetousness is infinite; but, said she, I would there could a passage be found out of the Blazing World into the world whence you came, and I would willingly give you as much riches as you desired. The Duchess's soul gave Her Majesty humble thanks for her great favour, and told her that she was not covetous, nor desired any more wealth than what her lord and husband had before the Civil Wars; neither, said she, should I desire it for my own, but my lord's posterity's sake. Well, said the Empress, I'll command my fish-men to use all their skill and industry to find out a passage into that world which your lord and husband is in. I do verily believe, answered the Duchess, that there will be no passage found into that world; but if there were any, I should not petition Your Majesty for gold and jewels, but only for the elixir that grows in the midst of the golden sands, for to preserve life and health; but without a passage it is impossible to carry away any of it, for whatsoever is material, cannot travel like immaterial beings such as souls and spirits are; neither do souls require any such thing that might revive them, or prolong their lives, by reason they are unalterable: for were souls like bodies, then my soul might have had the benefit of that natural elixir that grows in your Blazing World. I wish earnestly, said the Empress, that a passage might be found, and then both your lord and yourself should neither want wealth, nor long life; nay, I love you so well, that I would make you as great and powerful a monarchess as I am of the Blazing World. The Duchess's soul humbly thanked Her Majesty, and told her, that she acknowledged and esteemed her love beyond all things that are in nature.

After this discourse they had many other conferences, which for brevity's sake I'll forbear to rehearse. At last, after several questions which the Empress's soul asked the Duchess, she desired to know the reason why she did take such delight when she was joined to her body, in being singular both in accoutrements, behaviour and discourse? The Duchess's soul answered, she confessed that it was extravagant, and beyond what was usual and ordinary; but yet her ambition being such, that she would not be like others in any thing if it were possible; I endeavour, said she, to be as singular as I can; for it argues but a mean nature to imitate others; and though I do not love to be imitated if I can possibly avoid it; yet rather than imitate others, I should choose to be imitated by others; for my nature is such, that I had rather appear worse in singularity, then better in the mode. If you were not a great lady, replied the Empress, you would never pass in the world for a wise lady; for the world would say your singularities are vanities. The Duchess's soul answered, she did not at all regard the censure of this or any other age concerning vanities; but, said she, neither this present, nor any of the future ages can or will truly say that I am not virtuous and chaste; for I am confident, all that were or are acquainted with me, and all the servants which ever I had, will or can upon their oaths declare my actions no otherwise than virtuous; and certainly there's none, even of the meanest degree, which have not their spies and witnesses, much more those of the nobler sort, which seldom or never are without attendants, so that their faults (if they have any) will easily be known, and as easily divulged: wherefore happy are those natures that are honest, virtuous and noble, not only happy to themselves, but happy to their families. But, said the Empress, if you glory so much in your honesty and virtue, how comes it that you plead for dishonest and wicked persons in your writings? The Duchess answered, it was only to show her wit, not her nature.

At last the Empress arrived into the Blazing World, and coming to her imperial palace, you may sooner imagine than expect that I should express the joy which the Emperor had at her safe return; for he loved her beyond his soul; and there was no love lost, for the Empress equalled his affection with no less love to him. After the time of rejoicing with each other, the Duchess's soul begged leave to return to her noble lord; but the Emperor desired, that before she departed, she would see how he had employed his time in the Empress's absence; for he had built stables and riding-houses, and desired to have horses of manage, such as, according to the Empress's relation, the Duke of Newcastle had: the Emperor enquired of the Duchess, the form and structure of her lord and husband's stables and riding-house. The Duchess answered His Majesty, that they were but plain and ordinary; but said she; had my lord wealth, I am sure he would not spare it, in rendering his buildings as noble as could be made. Hereupon the Emperor showed the Duchess the stables he had built, which were most stately and magnificent; among the rest there was one double stable that held a hundred horses on a side, the main building was of gold, lined with several sorts of precious materials; the roof was arched with agates, the sides of the walls were lined with cornelian, the floor was paved with amber, the mangers were mother of pearl, the pillars, as also the middle aisle or walk of the stables, were of crystal; the front and gate was of turquoise, most neatly cut and carved. The riding-house was lined with sapphires, topazes, and the like; the floor was all of golden sand, so finely sifted, that it was extremely soft, and not in the least hurtful to the horses' feet, and the door and frontispiece was of emeralds, curiously carved.

After the view of these glorious and magnificent buildings, which the Duchess's soul was much delighted withal, she resolved to take her leave; but the Emperor desired her to stay yet some short time more, for they both loved her company so well, that they were unwilling to have her depart so soon: several conferences and discourses passed between them; amongst the rest the Emperor desired her advice how to set up a theatre for plays. The Duchess confessed her ignorance in this art, telling His Majesty that she knew nothing of erecting theatres or scenes, but what she had by an immaterial observation when she was with the Empress's soul in the chief city of E,[37] entering into one of their theatres, whereof the Empress could give as much account to His Majesty as herself. But both the Emperor and Empress told the Duchess, that she could give directions how to make plays. The Duchess answered, that she had as little skill to form a play after the mode, as she had to paint or make a scene for show. But you have made plays, replied the Empress: yes, answered the Duchess, I intended them for plays; but the wits of these present times condemned them as incapable of being represented or acted, because they were not made up according to the rules of art; though I dare say, that the descriptions are as good as any they have writ. The Emperor asked, whether the property of plays were not to describe the several humours, actions and fortunes of mankind? 'Tis so, answered the Duchess: why then, replied the Emperor, the natural humours, actions and fortunes of mankind, are not done by the rules of art: but said the Duchess, it is the art and method of our wits to despise all the descriptions of wit, humour, actions and fortunes that are without such artificial rules. The Empress asked, are those good plays that are made so methodically and artificially? The Duchess answered, they were good according to the judgement of the age, or mode of the nation, but not according to her judgement; for truly, said she, in my opinion, their plays will prove a nursery of whining lovers, and not an academy or school for wise, witty, noble, and well-behaved men. But I, replied the Emperor, desire such a theatre as may make wise men; and will have such descriptions as are natural, not artificial. If Your Majesty be of that opinion, said the Duchess's soul, then my plays may be acted in your Blazing World, when they cannot be acted in the Blinking World of Wit; and the next time I come to visit Your Majesty, I shall endeavour to order Your Majesty's theatre, to present such plays as my wit is capable to make. Then the Empress told the Duchess, that she loved a foolish farce added to a wise play. The Duchess answered, that no world in nature had fitter creatures for it than the Blazing World; for, said she, the louse-men, the bird-men, the spider- and fox-men, the ape-men and satyrs appear in a farce extraordinary pleasant.

Hereupon both the Emperor and Empress entreated the Duchess's soul to stay so long with them, till she had ordered her theatre, and made plays and farces fit for them;[38] for they only wanted that sort of recreation; but the Duchess's soul begged Their Majesties to give her leave to go into her native world; for she longed to be with her dear lord and husband, promising, that after a short time she would return again. Which being granted, though with much difficulty, she took her leave with all civility and respect, and so departed from Their Majesties.

After the Duchess's return into her own body, she entertained her lord (when he was pleased to hear such kind of discourses) with foreign relations: but he was never displeased to hear of the Empress's kind commendations, and of the characters she was pleased to give of him to the Emperor. Amongst other relations she told him all what had passed between the Empress, and the several monarchs of that world whither she went with the Empress; and how she had subdued them to pay tribute and homage to the monarch of that nation or kingdom to which she owed both her birth and education. She also related to her lord what magnificent stables and riding-houses the Emperor had built, and what fine horses were in the Blazing World, of several shapes and sizes, and how exact their shapes were in each sort, and of many various colours, and fine marks, as if they had been painted by art, with such coats or skins, that they had a far greater gloss and smoothness than satin; and were there but a passage out of the Blazing World into this, said she, you should not only have some of those horses, but such materials, as the Emperor has, to build your stables and riding-houses withal; and so much gold, that I should never repine at your noble and generous gifts. The Duke smilingly answered her, that he was sorry there was no passage between those two worlds; but said he, I have always found an obstruction to my good fortunes.

One time the Duchess chanced to discourse with some of her

acquaintance, of the Empress of the Blazing World, who asked her what pastimes and recreations Her Majesty did most delight in? The Duchess answered, that she spent most of her time in the study of natural causes and effects, which was her chief delight and pastime, and that she loved to discourse sometimes with the most learned persons of that world; and to please the Emperor and his nobles, who were all of the royal race, she went often abroad to take the air, but seldom in the daytime, always at night, if it might be called night; for, said she, the nights there are as light as days, by reason of the numerous blazing-stars, which are very splendorous, only their light is whiter than the sun's light; and as the sun's light is hot, so their light is cool, not so cool as our twinkling star-light, nor is their sun-light so hot as ours, but more temperate; and that part of the Blazing World where the Empress resides, is always clear, and never subject to any storms, tempests, fogs or mists, but has only refreshing dews that nourish the earth; the air of it is sweet and temperate, and, as I said before, as much light in the sun's absence, as in its presence, which makes that time we call night, more pleasant there than the day; and sometimes the Empress goes abroad by water in barges, sometimes by land in chariots, and sometimes on horseback; her royal chariots are very glorious; the body is one entire green diamond; the four small pillars that bear up the top-cover, are four white diamonds, cut in the form thereof; the top or roof of the chariot is one entire blue diamond, and at the four corners are great springs of rubies; the sea is made of cloth of gold, stuffed with amber-gris[39] beaten small; – the chariot is drawn by twelve unicorns, whose trappings are all chains of pearl; and as for her barges, they are only of gold. Her guard for state (for she needs none for security, there being no rebels or enemies) consists of giants, but they seldom wait on Their Majesties abroad, because their extraordinary height and bigness does hinder their prospect. Her entertainment when she is upon the water, is the music of the fish- and bird-men, and by land are horse- and foot-matches; for the Empress takes much delight in making race-matches with the Emperor, and the nobility; some races are between the fox- and ape-men, which sometimes the satyrs strive to outrun, and some are between the spider-men and lice-men. Also there are several flight-matches, between the several sorts of bird-men, and the several sorts of fly-men; and swimming-matches, between the several sorts of fish-men. The Emperor, Empress, and their nobles, take also great delight to have collations; for in the Blazing World, there are most delicious fruits of all sorts, and some such as in this world were never seen nor tasted; for there are most tempting sorts of fruit: after their collations are ended, they dance; and if they be upon the water, they dance upon the water, there lying so many fish-men close and thick together, as they can dance very evenly and easily upon their backs, and need not fear drowning. Their music, both vocal and instrumental, is according to their several places: upon the water it is of water instruments, as shells filled with water, and so moved by art, which is a sweet and delightful harmony; and those dances which they dance upon the water, are, for the most part such as we in this world call swimming dances, where they do not lift up their feet high: in lawns or upon plains they have wind instruments, but much better than those in our world; and when they dance in the woods they have horn instruments, which although they are a sort of wind instruments, yet they are of another fashion than the former; in their houses they have such instruments as are somewhat like our viols, violins, theorboes,[40] lutes, citherns,[41] guitars, harpsichords, and the like, but yet so far beyond them, that the difference cannot well be expressed; and as their places of dancing and their music is different, so is their manner or way of dancing. In these, and the like recreations, the Emperor, Empress, and the nobility pass their time.

THE EPILOGUE TO THE READER

By this poetical description, you may perceive, that my ambition is not only to be Empress, but Authoress of a whole world; and that the worlds I have made, both the Blazing and the other Philosophical World, mentioned in the first part of this description, are framed and composed of the most pure, that is, the rational parts of matter, which are the parts of my mind; which creation was more easily and suddenly effected, than the conquests of the two famous monarchs of the world, Alexander and Caesar: neither have I made such disturbances, and caused so many dissolutions of particulars, otherwise named deaths, as they did; for I have destroyed but some few men in a little boat, which died through the extremity of cold, and that by the hand of Justice, which was necessitated to punish their crime of stealing away a young and beauteous Lady. And in the formation of those worlds, I take more delight and glory, than ever Alexander or Caesar did in conquering this terrestrial world; and though I have made my Blazing World, a peaceable world, allowing it but one religion, one language, and one government; yet could I make another world, as full of factions, divisions, and wars, as this is of peace and tranquility; and the rational figures of my mind might express as much courage to fight, as Hector and Achilles had; and be as wise as Nestor, as eloquent as Ulysses, and as beautiful as Helen. But I esteeming peace before war, wit before policy, honesty before beauty; instead of the figures of Alexander, Caesar, Hector, Achilles, Nestor, Ulysses, Helen, etc. chose rather the figure of honest Margaret Newcastle, which now I would not change for all this terrestrial world; and if any should like the world I have made, and be willing to be my subjects, they may imagine themselves such, and they are such, I mean, in their minds, fancies or imaginations; but if they cannot endure to be subjects, they may create worlds of their own, and govern themselves as they please: but yet let them have a care, not to prove unjust usurpers, and to rob me of mine; for concerning the Philosophical World, I am Empress of it myself; and as for the Blazing World, it having an Empress already, who rules it with great wisdom and conduct, which Empress is my dear Platonic friend; I shall never prove so unjust, treacherous and unworthy to her, as to disturb her government, much less to depose her from her imperial throne, for the sake of any other; but rather choose to create another world for another friend.

NOTES

THE CONTRACT

[1] i.e. reproached me for behaving dishonourably.
[2] Obsolete form of curtsy.
[3] Ambitious rivalry.
[4] Fear *shamefastness:* bashfulness, modesty.
[5] Struggle indecorously.
[6] Cavendish's coinage, meaning spectacular, viewable.
[7] Lens by which the rays of the sun may be concentrated on an object, so as to burn if combustible; often used figuratively to suggest inflaming beauty.
[8] Perverse, difficult.
[9] Until.
[10] Phrase meaning 'a trifle'.
[11] In obsolete sense of consciousness.
[12] Harem.
[13] Ecclesiastical law, used in church courts.
[14] The unwritten law of England, administered by the King's ordinary courts; as oppposed to statute law, or canon law.
[15] The condition of being under age, minority.
[16] Cheating, deception, fraud.
[17] An estate belonging to the owner and his heirs forever.
[18] Small group of wind instrumentalists maintained at public expense; here used ironically.

ASSAULTED AND PURSUED CHASTITY

[1] See Genesis 34; Dinah's brothers, Simeon and Levi, avenged her rape in a massacre which led indirectly to the foundation of Israel.
[2] Surgeons.
[3] Knowledge of the human body.
[4] Treatises on the properties of plants.
[5] Small ship's boat.
[6] The fork or junction of the thighs.
[7] Slabs.

[8] Level, open fields.
[9] West wind.
[10] Swooning, fainting.
[11] Spartans.
[12] Africans.
[13] Emended from 'indifferent'.
[14] The text at this point bears the marginal note, 'Here ends the Kingdom of Phancy'.
[15] Parthian horsemen were famed for the rapidity and cunning of their manoeuvres.
[16] The change of pronoun in this passage, as in many others, is symptomatic of the text's instability in representing Travellia's gender.
[17] Tumours in a horse's leg caused by inflammation.
[18] Emended from 'will not hear me.'
[19] Recluse.
[20] Plans, diagrams, designs.
[21] One of the four humours of early physiology; associated with bile, temper.
[22] Spears and hand-guns.
[23] Horse soldiers wearing cuirasses, i.e. armour for the body.
[24] Order of battle, battle array.
[25] i.e. the beams of Travellia's eyes.
[26] 'spake her father's funeral speech' is added in Cavendish's hand.
[27] Debauch.
[28] Body.
[29] A marginal note printed beside this speech reads, 'the antient custom was for the nearest friend to speak their funeral speech'.
[30] Meeting.
[31] Emended from 'doth not'.
[32] A marginal note in Cavendish's hand reads 'These verses are my Lord marquis's'. William Cavendish contributed several short pieces of prose and poetry to *Nature's Pictures*.

THE DESCRIPTION OF A NEW WORLD, CALLED THE BLAZING WORLD

[1] *The Blazing World* was published together with *Observations Upon Experimental Philosophy* in both 1666 and 1668.
[2] Lucian of Samosata (AD 125?–200?), Greek satirist, author of dialogues and of an imaginary voyage (trans. 1634); Savinien Cyrano de Bergerac (1620–55), *Histoire comique contenant les états et empires de la lune* (1657).
[3] In 1649 William Cavendish, Marquis (later Duke) of Newcastle was banished from England and his estates confiscated. William's elder brother,

Charles, bought some back and the rest were restored in 1660. In her *Life* of Newcastle Margaret estimated, and inflated, his financial losses at £941,000. See Mendelson on 'the myth of the Duke's sufferings which Margaret had created' (p. 50).

[4] Sealed.

[5] Fiery precious stone, especially garnet. Christian lapidaries in the Renaissance associated the carbuncle with the light of faith, and the diamond with repentance and steadfastness (see G. F. Kunz, *The Curious Lore of Precious Stones*, 1913). For Cavendish, it is the spectacular blazing of both carbuncle and diamond which seems most important.

[6] Half-boots, associated with royalty, and the elevation of classical tragedy.

[7] Small round shield.

[8] Mermen.

[9] Outer surface.

[10] Slivers.

[11] Triangular.

[12] Haemorrhoids.

[13] Waxy membrane used in surgery and as winding sheet.

[14] A reputed substance or preparation supposed by alchemists to possess the property of changing other metals into gold or silver.

[15] 'Universal solvent' sought by alchemists; probably a pseudo-Arabic coinage by Paracelsus, pioneer of chemical medicine.

[16] Followers of Galen, celebrated physician of 2nd century AD who used vegetable rather than synthetic remedies; opposed to Paracelsian chemistry.

[17] Literally, 'tradition'; Jewish esoteric interpretation of the Old Testament, christianized by Pico della Mirandola in the Renaissance. For connections with magic see Frances Yates, *Giordano Bruno and the Hermetic Tradition* (1964).

[18] John Dee (1527–1608), influential Christian Cabbalist and Neoplatonist virtuoso, famed for his library and wide-ranging scholarship as mathematician, numerologist, astronomer, alchemist and imperialist historian, but under suspicion of heresy in his last years. Edward Kelly, alchemist and apothecary, was Dee's close associate, thought by some to have discovered the secret of transmutation. See Lyndy Abraham, *Marvell and Alchemy* (1990), ch.1, 'The Alchemical Context', and Frances Yates, *The Occult Philosophy in the Elizabethan Age* (1979). Cavendish compares Dee to Moses, who was 'often interchangeable with Hermes Trismegistus as the founder of the art of alchemy' (Abraham, p. 174), and Kelly to Aaron, elder brother of Moses, who made a golden calf to be worshipped (Ex29:1–7).

[19] *The Alchemist* was first acted in London at the Globe Theatre, 1610 and published in 1612; it was revived at the Restoration. In Act 2, Scene I Jonson satirizes the claim that Moses was an alchemist. Newcastle was a patron of Jonson.

[20] Heterogeneous mixture, medley.

[21] 'Then she enquired...forms and shapes?' omitted from 1668.

[22] Galileo Galilei (1564–1642), Italian astronomer, defender of Copernican system, author of *Dialogue Concerning the Two Chief World Systems* (1632); Pierre Gassendi (1592–1655), French philosopher who developed a theory of matter within a mechanistic framework (for a comparison with Cavendish's natural philosophy see Sarasohn, p. 306 n.49); Renée Descartes (1596–1650), French mathematician and philosopher, author of the *Discours sur la Méthode* (1637), a crucial figure in the 'scientific revolution' of the seventeenth century; Jan Baptista Van Helmont (1577–1644), renowned Flemish chemist, author of 'Alkahest'; Thomas Hobbes (1588–1679), English mechanistic philosopher and political scientist who had a long association with the Cavendish family, author of *De Cive* (1642), *The Elements of Law* (1650) and *Leviathan* (1651); Henry More (1614–87), one of the anti-materialist Cambridge Platonists, argued for the importance of reason in apprehending the immanence of God in the creation, author of *The Immortality of the Soul* (1659). In her *Philosophical Letters* (1664) Cavendish had entered into dialogue with the previous four. Hobbes, Gassendi and Descartes were all in Paris in the 1640s, along with the Newcastles and Sir Charles Cavendish.

[23] 'not possible', 1668.

[24] One of the Seven Sages who, according to Aristotle, believed that the world originates from and returns to water.

[25] None of Pythagoras's writings survive, but his theories of mathematical relations and number symbolism were widely known in the Renaissance. See S. K. Heninger, *Touches of Sweet Harmony: Pythagorean Cosmology and Renaissance Poetics* (1974).

[26] Sultan of Turkey.

[27] West wind.

[28] Newcastle's main residence in Nottinghamshire before and after the Restoration; see Ben Jonson's masque, *The King's Entertainment at Welbeck* (1640).

[29] This castle in Nottinghamshire was Newcastle's favourite property. Confiscated by Parliament, it was bought back and saved from demolition by Newcastle's brother, Charles, who soon after died and was buried there (25 February, 1654). In October 1662 Newcastle angered his adult children by willing Bolsover Castle and manor, along with other properties and money, to Margaret. In fact, he outlived her. See Margaret's poem, 'A Dialogue between a Bountifull Knight, and a Castle ruin'd in War' (*Poems, and Fancies*, 1653, pp. 89–90), and Jonson's masque *Love's Welcome at Bolsover* (1640).

[30] Ménage, the trained movements of horses. Newcastle was a famous horseman whose writings on this courtly discipline include *A New and Extraordinary Method to Dress Horses* (1667).

[31] Harem.

[32] (Figuratively) overthrown or defeated.

[33] This speech before the immaterial assembly is the favourable fictional rewriting of Cavendish's unsuccessful appearance before the parliamentary Committee for Compounding in London in 1651, where she met with a

hostile reception and remained silent (see Grant, 108–9). In this episode her fictional counterpart supplies the missing defence, but is also unsuccessful.

[34] Fortune's court is here an allegorized version of the Restoration court of Charles II, at which Newcastle was similarly passed over in favour of the next generation of courtiers.

[35] 'commended', 1668.

[36] 'on their backs', 1666, emended to 1668, 'in their beaks'.

[37] England. The Empress's native country, EFSI, is another version of England.

[38] *foolish farce, a farce extraordinary pleasant, plays and farces:* both printed texts have 'verse' in each case. I have adopted the marginal authorial emendations of the Bodleian library copy of 1668.

[39] Perfumed waxy substance.

[40] Large double-necked lutes, popular in the seventeenth century.

[41] Guitar strung with wire, played with a plectrum, related to the zither.